THE
INVITATION

THE
INVITATION

Rachel Abbott

GRAND CENTRAL
PUBLISHING

NEW YORK   BOSTON

Grand Central Publishing
Hachette Book Group
1290 Avenue of the Americas, New York, NY 10104
grandcentralpublishing.com
twitter.com/grandcentralpub

Originally published by Bookouture in 2020. An imprint of Storyfire Ltd. Carmelite House, 50 Victoria Embankment,London EC4Y 0DZ

First Grand Central Publishing Edition: September 2020

Grand Central Publishing is a division of Hachette Book Group, Inc. The Grand Central Publishing name and logo is a trademark of Hachette Book Group, Inc.

The publisher is not responsible for websites (or their content) that are not owned by the publisher.

The Hachette Speakers Bureau provides a wide range of authors for speaking events. To find out more, go to www.hachettespeakersbureau.com or call (866) 376-6591.

Library of Congress Control Number: 2020938837

ISBN: 978-1-5387-1941-1 (trade paperback)

Printed in the United States of America

LSC-C

10 9 8 7 6 5 4 3 2 1

PROLOGUE

I reach for the door handle with shaking fingers, wishing I'd said no—that I'd refused to play the game that is planned for tonight. Maybe I'm not as brave as I would like to think. I clutch the black envelope in my other hand, holding it close to my body as if somehow the words on the card inside might burn their way through its satin-smooth parchment for all to see.

As I step into the corridor, other doors open and I struggle not to gasp at the sight of Isabel in her silver sheath and Chandra in her long turquoise silk skirt. I feel dizzy with memories. But I suppose that is the point of the game.

No one speaks and without a shared smile between us we trail down the elegant stairway. I glance at Matt, my husband of three years, and I don't know if I recognize him anymore. His face is set, his mouth a straight line, and his own black envelope is peeking out of his jacket pocket. He sees me looking and reaches up to push it firmly out of sight.

How different from the night a year ago when we had spilled from our rooms, excited about both the evening ahead and the wedding the following day.

I've tried to ask Matt what he thinks tonight's game is all about, but he refuses to discuss it. Apparently, it's what Lucas wants—and what Lucas wants, Lucas gets. At least as far as my husband is concerned. Not that I know what Matt is thinking anymore.

Most unhappy couples, I suspect, are unable to identify the moment their relationship begins to disintegrate; when closeness turns to distance and banter becomes thinly disguised contempt. I, on the other hand, can pinpoint exactly when my marriage began to crumble.

Our life together had seemed effortless up to that point, as if we were swimming side by side in a calm river. But then the surface of the water changed. We hit the rapids and we were wrenched apart. Now we can see each other in the distance, but we seem unable or unwilling to steer ourselves back into still waters together.

It's one year to the day, almost to the hour, since we began to hurtle in opposite directions, and now it feels as if there is nothing to cling to, no rescue in sight.

Yet we have never discussed it, because to acknowledge it we would have to refer to the event that tore us apart.

And we would have to talk about Alex.

PART ONE

CHAPTER 1

One year ago

I pull the car over to the side of the road, wheels on the grass verge, and turn to Matt.

"Okay, you can stop twitching. I'll let you drive the last stretch."

He gives me a look of mock surprise. "Twitching?"

I laugh as I open the door and jump out. Matt hates my driving. According to him, I drive too fast and brake too hard. He's probably right. I consider driving to be one of life's necessities—like doing the washing-up or buying toothpaste—but it's a long way to Cornwall and Matt had been at the wheel for two and a half hours when I took over.

I grab a bottle of water and a white envelope from the back seat as Matt walks round the front of the car to join me, and we both lean on a metal field gate and gaze out over the countryside, listening to the sound of cows munching on grass, passing the water between us.

"Excited?" I ask him.

"Yes, I think so." That's a typical Matt response—cautious, measured.

I pull a thick white card from the envelope. Matt has told me the date and the venue, but I've never bothered to look at the invitation until now.

Nina Bélanger
AND
Lucas Jarrett
REQUEST THE PLEASURE OF THE COMPANY OF
Matt and Jemma Hudson
AT THEIR MARRIAGE
POLSKIRRIN, CORNWALL
17 JULY 2018
4:00 P.M.

"Polskirrin's where we're staying too, isn't it? Has he hired a country house or something?"

Matt stares straight ahead. "No. It's his home."

I had forgotten that he'd told me Lucas is well off. I've never met my husband's friends and he hasn't seen them for ages, although he's in touch with Lucas fairly regularly. We didn't invite them to our wedding two years ago. We kept it small because my mum was ill, and life has been hectic ever since with demanding jobs and a new home.

"Where did Lucas meet Nina? Do you know?"

"Paris, I believe. He was there on foundation business."

"Foundation?"

"Yes, the Jarrett Foundation."

I spin round to Matt. "You are joking, aren't you? He's not part of Blair Jarrett's family?"

Matt grins. "He *is* Blair's family—his son, in fact."

"Oh—my—God! Why didn't you tell me? Shit, Matt—he must be absolutely loaded."

"I didn't *not* tell you. It never came up. You knew I had a friend called Lucas and that I spent a lot of time at his house in my teens. I didn't think it necessary to give you details of his bank balance or his family tree."

Classic Matt. He wouldn't have thought it either relevant or interesting that Lucas was the son of a man who had made a fortune writing some early search-engine algorithm or other and had gone on to form a charitable foundation with the proceeds.

"Tell me again how you got to know him?"

Matt turns towards me. "I told you when the invitation arrived—his dad played golf with mine."

"Matt! That's not an explanation. I'm sure your dad had lots of friends with sons. Be more specific, will you?"

He leans towards me and kisses me so gently that it tickles my lips. I'm not so easily distracted though. Matt is always economical with information, but this time I'm not giving up, and I give him a fierce glare.

Matt chuckles. "Okay, you win. Our fathers both decided when we were about fourteen that we should learn to play golf. My dad wanted me to master at least one sport, and I'd been a total disappointment at all the others, so golf was something of a last resort. Lucas and I, together with our dads, went out as a foursome for about three weekends. Obviously I was rubbish. It wasn't helped by the fact that I was short for my age, and Lucas was already a giant at nearly six feet. We must have looked ridiculous. Lucas could see how miserable it was making me, so he suggested to his father that instead of playing golf, the two of us should spend the weekends hanging out at his place. They had a pool, and when the weather was bad we played snooker."

"That was very thoughtful for a teenage boy," I say, resting my head on his shoulder. I know he didn't have the most comfortable time growing up, failing to live up to his father's sporting expectations and wondering if he was ever going to achieve any height above five feet—which, of course, he did. Eventually.

"It's typical of Lucas. He's always been sensitive to other people's feelings. Anyway, we spent the whole of that first spring together. Then we were joined by Nick, and finally Andrew. I'm sure they'll both be ushers at the wedding too."

Matt's tone of voice has changed. "You don't sound too happy about the fact that two became four."

He sighs. "It's not that. They're okay. They're good fun, and I'm sure you'll like them. I had a bit of a time keeping up with them, if I'm honest. They were both nearly as tall as Lucas, and I suppose I sometimes felt like the runt of the litter."

I wrap my arm around his neck and pull him close again. "But not anymore, Mr. Esteemed Plastic Surgeon."

I lean back and look at him, at his near-perfect features. He looks as if he's modeled his face with his own scalpel: straight nose, even lips, and eyes that are absolutely symmetrical. I sometimes wonder why he chose me, with my slightly over-wide top lip and high eyebrows, which I think make me look perpetually startled. But he swears he wouldn't change a thing.

"Why don't you still see them now?"

"You know how it is—we're all busy, and we don't live near each other. I call and email Lucas, and get to see him if he's in London, but mostly he's either down here or somewhere remote on foundation business. Since his father died, he's taken the reins. Andrew's off sailing the world whenever he gets a chance, and although Nick's a banker in the city, he lives in St. Albans." He gives me one last squeeze. "Come on, let's get back in the car. We've only got about half an hour to go, and it's too bloody hot out here."

He's right. The weather is astonishing for England. It feels like we're in southern Italy.

We climb back into the car, Matt in his preferred position behind the wheel. I'm having a minor panic about whether my wedding outfit is good enough, but I don't mention it. I hadn't realized what fancy company we were going to be keeping.

"Tell me more, Matt. What do I need to know about these guys before we get there? How did Lucas meet them?"

He shakes his head in mock despair. "You'll be able to ask them yourself very soon, Jem. The only thing I will say is that money doesn't make anyone special, so don't let it define your perception of them. It's their least important attribute."

I nod slowly; I know he's right. But whatever he says, the little kernel of excitement that had been growing inside me as we drew closer to our destination has now lodged itself in my throat.

The last ten minutes of the journey are driven in silence, Matt leaning forward unnaturally in his seat, like a child arriving at the seaside for the first time. Or maybe it's because the lanes are narrow with high hedges on either side, and he has no idea what's coming round the corner.

He turns his head every now and again to look at me and smile reassuringly, as if he can read my thoughts. I've just about convinced myself that I'm being silly, and that it doesn't matter a toss whether I have the right clothes or not—it's not about me anyway—when we turn a corner.

"Oh, my Lord!" I whisper.

The lane has reached a crest and is about to plunge down towards the coast, and ahead is a panoramic view of the sea. Perched on a headland above the crashing waves is our destination. Polskirrin: the home of Lucas Jarrett.

Even Matt is speechless. He carries on but slows the car to a crawl. He clears his throat. "It's rather beautiful, isn't it?"

I laugh at his attempt at nonchalance. Polskirrin is stunning. I suppose you would call it a manor house. It's built of mellow stone and at a guess is a couple of hundred years old.

A long gravel drive cuts through wide lawns, sweeping from double wrought-iron gates to a formal garden immediately in front of the property. A fountain is playing in a brick-edged oblong pond that somehow I know will be full of golden fish, and beyond the house between the garden and the sea is woodland. I'm certain there will be a path through it to the shore, and I can't wait to feel cool seawater lapping around my ankles.

Even from a distance of around a quarter of a mile, we can see that someone has stepped out of the front door. We must have been spotted.

"Oh well," Matt says. "No backing out now, darling." He turns to grin at me, his eyes sparkling.

The gates open as if by magic, and Matt steers the car down the drive to where a man with dark hair stands waiting. I glance at my husband, who's beaming from ear to ear, and I know that this must be Lucas. He's dressed in navy-blue shorts and a plain white T-shirt, smiling a welcome.

Matt is out of the car in a flash, striding towards him, and it's only then that I realize how tall Lucas is. My husband is around five feet ten inches, but his friend is a good head taller. Matt reaches up to grasp Lucas on the shoulder, extending his other arm for an enthusiastic handshake. I can't hear what they're saying, but I give them a moment before I grab my sun hat off the back seat and walk across to join them.

"Lucas, this is Jemma—well, Jemima really, but we call her Jemma. She's my wife, but then you knew that." Matt is talking quickly, saying too much, now holding out his hand as if to draw me into the circle.

"Welcome, Jemma. It's good to meet you." Lucas bends towards me for the obligatory kiss on both cheeks and lifts his head back to smile. It's only then that I notice his eyes. They are a light amber color, almost like a lion's—warm and friendly now, but I can't help wondering if, like a lion's, they burn brightly and are all-seeing in the dark.

CHAPTER 2

Nina Bélanger wiped her hands hastily on a tea towel as she watched a man and a woman get out of a car and walk towards Lucas. She should go out to say hello, but she felt strangely nervous. Maybe they would wonder why their friend was marrying this little woman from a small town in central France when he could take his pick from the endless stream of glamorous women who vied for his attention at charity events. She sometimes wondered herself.

She remembered the day they'd met. Lucas had been invited to a conference in Paris as the keynote speaker. She had been employed by the organizers to make sure the presenters were looked after, and hundreds of people had turned out to listen to him. Everything went wrong: the lighting failed, his microphone didn't work—it was a disaster. Nina had been in a blind panic. The electrics weren't her responsibility, but the keynote speaker—Lucas Jarrett—was. She felt she had failed him.

Lucas had carried it off with aplomb, moving to the front of the stage and raising his voice so the audience could hear him. He walked off to resounding applause, only to find Nina stomping around in a rage, swearing at the electricians. When she realized Lucas was there, she'd felt her cheeks burning as she turned to apologize to him, but he had laughed.

"It didn't matter at all. These things happen," he'd said. "If you want to make it up to me though, you could have dinner with me tonight?"

How could she refuse?

Nina hadn't dared to hope that he would want to see her again after he left Paris, but he had promised to return, and he had. Now she was about to marry him.

She watched as the new arrivals walked towards the house and realized they had to be Matt and Jemma. They looked happy, smiling at each other frequently as Lucas spoke first to one and then the other. Would she and Lucas be that happy? Only time would tell.

When she agreed to move here six months ago Nina hadn't realized how often she would be left alone in this huge house while Lucas traveled the world seeking out those in greatest need of funding from the Jarrett Foundation. She didn't have the heart to tell him that, beautiful as it was, she didn't feel that Polskirrin welcomed her. She knew how it would sound to him. He would think it was because of Alex.

Nina sighed. She wanted to make their wedding amazing and had worked tirelessly on every minute detail, but before the big day she had to entertain and feed six house guests—people she had never met. Lucas wanted his three oldest friends to be his ushers and had asked if it would be too much trouble to have them stay at the house. She'd said it would be fine. Of course it would! But not for the first time she wished her own family were here. There were so many of them though, and with two sets of aging grandparents who weren't up to the journey they had decided to hold a second ceremony in France later in the month. Her mother seemed determined to outdo the British wedding, and Nina smiled at the thought of her flapping around, issuing orders.

She turned away from the window and back to the job at hand. Lunch. If there was one thing she could do with confidence, it was cook, and the kitchen would be her refuge—her place of safety—should she need it.

CHAPTER 3

Smiling my thanks to the boy who has been dragged in from weeding the herb garden to carry our bags upstairs, I sit down on the edge of the bed and look around.

What a lovely room. Double French windows are slightly ajar and a thin white curtain is billowing in a gentle breeze. I can smell apricots and notice a bowlful on an antique chest of drawers, the fruit perfectly ripe with a soft blush on their skins. I feel the mattress with my hands and bounce slightly to test it. I have no doubt we will sleep well between the crisp sheets.

I turn to grin at Matt, who has already started to unpack, neatly folding clothes into drawers or placing them on padded hangers in the wardrobe. He is the organizer, and I am the dreamer. I should help, but I take a moment to soak up the atmosphere. There is something captivating about old houses; I can't help but wonder how many other people have slept within these four walls, and what their lives might have been like.

Walking to the windows, I pull back the curtain to discover a small balcony with its own stone staircase leading down to a wide tiled terrace. I can hear voices and laughter below as the other guests gather for pre-lunch drinks, and although Lucas told us that lunch can wait until we're ready—no one will mind as long as the wine is flowing—it would be rude of us to stay up here for much longer.

I need to get changed, but I am mesmerized by the view. The house is built on a rise above the sea, and the view of the ocean is spectacular, the water a deep, rich blue. Despite the hot, still day, waves are crashing onto the shore and I wonder if there might have been a storm out at sea during the night.

I've only been on the balcony for a few moments when I hear a light step behind me. Matt wraps his arms around my waist, nuzzling my neck and making me shiver, but as I turn towards him I feel his body tense and twist back to follow his gaze. He's staring at someone walking across the terrace—a young woman. Her head is down, her features hidden by straight black hair hanging like curtains on either side of her face. Although dressed in loose gray linen trousers and an even looser tunic in the same fabric, it's easy to see how thin she is as she hurries along.

She seems to sense our eyes on her, because suddenly she lifts her head to look towards us and her step falters. It's over so quickly that I wonder if I've imagined it.

"Who's that?" I ask Matt, still stroking the arm that holds me firmly.

For a moment he doesn't answer.

"Matt?"

"That's Lucas's sister." His voice is quieter, softer, and I turn my head to look at him.

"I didn't know he had a sister. She seems…" I don't know what to say. *Disturbed* is the word that springs to mind from the tension in her thin body and the way she moves, but that seems too harsh. *Unhappy* might be more appropriate.

"Yes," Matt says without waiting for me to finish my sentence. "She is."

"Tell me about her."

Matt's arms drop from my waist and I feel him turn away.

"Not now, Jemma. We need to get ready for lunch." He is disappearing into the room.

"Well, at least tell me her name."

"Alex. She's called Alex."

I don't know why the sight of Lucas's sister has unnerved Matt so much. All he will say is that it's a long story and there's no time.

"Surely you expected her to be here?" I ask. "It *is* her brother's wedding after all."

"I suppose so, but I thought—hoped—that she would be better by now. That she would have recovered."

I want to ask him what she needed to recover from, but he's anxious about holding up lunch. No doubt I'll be meeting her soon anyway.

I have a thing about people who seem to be struggling. When I see a troubled soul, my inclination is to try to help them. But I also know when not to push my husband, and he turns to me now with his best attempt at a happy smile.

"Let's go and meet the others." He holds out his hand and I take it, hoping the excitement he was feeling earlier will return.

We make our way down the outside staircase and follow the sound of laughter to the south side of the house, where I see a large table in the shade of a pergola covered in climbing roses.

Lucas turns towards us.

"Jemma, Matt, come and say hello to everyone."

A woman sitting at the far side of the table raises a languid hand in greeting. As she moves into the light to smile hello, I can see that her hair is a rich mahogany, expertly waved and tucked behind one ear. She is wearing a short silk sheath in bright emerald green, which looks amazing against her long, tanned legs. I force myself not to look down at the shorts that I thought appropriate for an al fresco lunch and lean over to shake her hand.

"Hi. I'm Isabel." She turns towards Matt. "And how are you, Matt? Still making the world a more beautiful place?"

Matt flushes. It's not clear if she's alluding to his work or his looks. Either way it sounds like a compliment, but he gives her an uncertain smile. I've no idea where she fits in. Matt never mentioned her, but she clearly knows my husband.

A man with spiky dark blond hair, wearing a loud Hawaiian shirt, steps towards us. I would have described him as tall had he not been standing next to Lucas.

"Matt!" he says, clapping Matt on the back. "Great to see you! God, it's been a while." He turns to me and leans forward for the kissing ritual, which I always find a little uncomfortable, coming as I do from a family who love a lot, but don't kiss a lot. "Jemma. I'm Nick. Delighted to meet you, and as Lucas has nominated me head barman, let me get you both a drink."

"Chandra!" Lucas says suddenly. "I'm sorry—I nearly missed you back there." He raises his arm to indicate a woman sitting in the deepest shade. I can't really see her until she pushes herself out of her chair and walks towards us, her long cream skirt clinging to her thighs, hands clasped in front of her. I can see she is of Asian descent, with gentle brown eyes and a generous mouth.

"Hello, Jemma, Matt. I am pleased to meet you."

Her hands are still folded together, and it seems inappropriate to reach out to her, so I just give her a wide smile.

"Good to meet you too, Chandra."

She returns my smile and turns back to her corner in the shade. It's clear Matt hasn't met her before either and I wonder if she's a friend of Nina's.

"Come and have a seat." Lucas points us to two chairs and is about to sit down next to me when he glances towards the entrance to the terrace. "Here she is!"

I see a petite woman with short dark hair and huge deep-brown eyes coming towards us. Her white linen skirt has a brightly colored silk scarf threaded through where the belt should be, and she's wearing a straw fedora to keep the sun off her face. It is all done with such style that somehow she makes the rest of us seem either over- or underdressed.

"Nina, let me introduce you to everyone." Lucas puts an arm around her shoulders. Her head reaches about halfway up his chest.

The bride-to-be smiles up at him before moving away to kiss each of us in turn on both cheeks.

"Welcome to you all. I know how much Lucas has been looking forward to seeing you, and I hope you enjoy your stay. Can I apologize if I seem a bit distracted?" She gives a little laugh. "As you can imagine, it's going to be rather busy here for the next day or so."

"What can we do to help?" I ask, and she makes a tutting sound and shakes her head.

"Nothing; nothing at all. We have extra staff—Lucas insisted. You just enjoy. I will come back soon with lunch. I like to cook."

She speaks perfect English, and her French accent just adds to her charm. Lucas watches her as she walks away and turns back to the table with a look of pride in his eyes.

"Now, where the hell is Andrew?" he says, glancing over his shoulder. "Nina's going to bring lunch out as soon as we're all here." When he has spun through 360 degrees, he shrugs. "Oh well, we all know what he's like. He'll turn up eventually. Drink up. We'll have another while we wait."

I have a feeling it's going to be a few days of overindulgence. Nick seems to have taken the instruction to drink up to heart and is jumping up every few minutes to top up glasses.

He sits himself down next to me and turns to face me.

"Well, Jemma, I'm delighted to finally meet you. I've heard all about you from Lucas."

"Really?" I had no idea Lucas knew anything about me, apart from the fact that I'm Matt's wife.

"Of course. I gather that Matt's been singing your praises. You're a speech therapist, aren't you?"

We chat for a few minutes about my job, Nick nodding as I tell him about my fascination with all forms of human communication, but in particular speech and the use of language. I know I have a habit of droning on for hours about my chosen profession, which I find infinitely fascinating, but he probably finds it as interesting as I find banking.

"How do you know Lucas?" I ask, seeking to change the subject.

"I went to school with him. We were weekly boarders—Lucas because his dad was a single parent and had to be away occasionally during the week, me because my parents couldn't stand me."

I give a small, involuntary gasp.

He laughs with rather more enthusiasm than his comment warrants. "Only joking. My dad went to boarding school and said it would impose some discipline and help me curb my wayward tendencies. I didn't want to go at all; they assured me I would love it."

"Who was right?" I ask.

He gives me a lopsided smile. "Complex question—a bit too deep for lunchtime conversation and I'm not sure I know, to be honest. Anyway, I met Lucas, and with his help I was out of my parents' hair for the weekends as well as during the week. Everyone was a winner!" I get the feeling that the laughter and smiles hide more than a little pain. "That's when I met Matt. We hung around together at Lucas's for at least the next four years, especially during the school holidays. Got up to all sorts—not that I expect Matt will admit to some of our darker deeds."

He wiggles his eyebrows, and the moment of tension passes. I'm pleased at the thought that Matt may have got up to some harmless mischief as a teenager. Sometimes he takes life too seriously.

Andrew still hasn't appeared by the time we've downed the second of our drinks and started on the third, and it isn't until that moment that I realize no one has mentioned Alex.

I'm about to ask when there's a small cheer from Lucas and Nick, and I swivel round in my chair. A man dressed in orange and white swimming shorts is emerging from a path through the trees, rubbing his shoulder-length wavy hair with a towel.

Drops of water cling to the dark hairs on his broad chest and flat stomach, catching the sunlight, and he looks slightly bemused by the attention.

"What? Oh shit. I'm late for lunch, aren't I? Sorry, guys." He walks into the shade and pulls out a chair, oblivious, it seems, to his wet shorts. It is only then that he seems to notice me, and then Matt.

"Hi, you must be Matt's wife. I'm Andrew." He stands up and walks round the table to lean in and give me a kiss, carefully keeping his dripping body away from mine. "Matt, how are you doing?" He grins at Matt and sits back down, grabbing a bottle of beer from a huge pewter bowl filled with ice.

Lucas pushes himself up from the table.

"Right, I'll go and grab Nina, who'll still be perfecting our lunch. One of the joys of marrying a French woman and having an Italian housekeeper is that they're both obsessed with food. Keep the wine flowing, Nick. I won't be long." He turns and disappears round the corner.

This time I don't stop to think.

"Is Alex not joining us?" I ask.

There is a moment of silence, and I feel as if I've said something wholly inappropriate. Finally, Andrew comes to my rescue.

"You'll probably meet her this evening, Jemma. I think she likes to keep to herself during the day."

I'm about to respond when I sense Matt looking at me. He shakes his head slightly, and I say nothing. Alex is clearly a topic not to be discussed.

CHAPTER 4

Lunch is a noisy affair with Nick taking center stage. He doesn't completely dominate the conversation, but when anyone else is talking he perches eagerly on the edge of his seat, waiting for the next opportunity to jump in with one of his stories.

"What about that time we were building the tree house and Matt couldn't get up there?" Nick leaps up from his chair and lifts his hands above his head, stretching as if to imitate Matt hanging on to a branch.

Everyone laughs, including Matt, but I can see he doesn't enjoy being reminded. Isabel leans across and plants a loud kiss on his cheek. I've still not worked out where she fits in, because I'm sure Matt said he hadn't met any of his friends' partners.

"As you seem intent on taking the piss out of everyone, Nick," Lucas says, a benign smile on his face, "why not tell us about that time you invited the hottest girl in school to a party. God knows what you put in the text you sent her, but guess who turned up instead?"

"Her father!" Isabel and Andrew chorus in unison, banging their hands on the table in a drum roll.

Nick punches Andrew lightly on the arm. "I was trying to keep her to myself before you stepped in and stole her from under my nose. God knows how many women Matt and I lost to you, evil Lothario that you were."

"Rubbish. I just knew how to treat a girl, and if it hadn't been for Lucas intervening that night, you'd be dead," Andrew adds, grinning from ear to ear.

It seems that Lucas has a habit of coming to the rescue. I'm enjoying listening to their banter, leaning back in my chair and wondering for a moment if life can get any better than this—warm sunshine, the distant roar of the sea, sharing laughter with a group of friends, and eating delicious food. Nina fusses around us, making sure we all try some of everything and never have an empty plate for more than a minute, until Lucas reaches out a hand and touches her lightly on the arm.

"Everyone's fine, darling. Relax."

She looks as if she's about to object but then breathes out, smiles, and sits back.

I haven't been able to work out the other pairings. Is laid-back, easygoing Andrew, who is still dressed in his wet shorts, here with sleek, sophisticated Isabel? Or has he brought serene, quiet Chandra to the wedding? Isabel seems most closely matched to Nick; they both like to attract attention. She's very tactile, especially with Matt. Every now and then she puts her hand possessively on his shoulder. The first time she did it he looked at me and raised his eyebrows, as if to say, "What can I do?" I just grinned back at him to show I was amused.

Finally everyone admits defeat on the food and we drift back to our rooms to recover from the alcohol, no doubt so that we can start again in a few hours' time.

Hand in hand, Matt and I saunter up the outside staircase to our small balcony. I know we will make love, and I've been feeling the thrill of anticipation for the last half hour. But first I need to clear my mind of questions.

"Who is Isabel, and how do you know her so well? Is she the one who's come with Andrew?"

"I knew you'd do this. Jemma—can't you ask me later?" Matt says, fiddling with the button on my shorts. I laugh and grab his hands to stop him. Temporarily.

"No, because I don't want to think about anything but you, and I've still got two questions. That's all."

Matt gives me an exasperated look. "Okay, Chandra's with Andrew. That's one question."

"So Nick is with Isabel." I can see that. Despite the wild shirt and excessive waving around of his arms, I suspect there's a sleek, sophisticated side to him. "But you knew her already?"

Matt throws his head back and laughs. "I've known her as long as I've known Nick. They're not a couple—they're twins. Isabel followed us around all the time when we were younger. She was a pain in the neck, to be honest—largely because she was besotted beyond belief with Lucas."

"I thought she seemed rather keen on you."

"Hah! Not a chance. It's all for show. Watch more carefully. She looks at Lucas every time she touches me, as if she's hoping he's jealous."

"Really?"

"Shut up, Jemma, and come here."

I reach towards him and start to lift his T-shirt over his head.

"Final question. I'm sorry if I put my foot in it when I asked about Alex, but why do you think she didn't join us for lunch? And why did everyone go quiet when I asked about her?"

Matt lowers his arms and pulls his T-shirt down. "Jem, I know you like to save everyone and you can't stand to see anyone hurting, but please don't ask questions about Alex. Something happened when she wasn't much more than a kid—something awful—but no one knows exactly what, except maybe Lucas. She was deeply traumatized, so we don't talk about it. I don't even like to think about it." Matt takes two steps away from me.

"I'm sorry, darling, but I'm feeling a bit hot. I'm going to have a quick shower."

I don't know what I've said or done, but I do know that expression on my husband's face. He's shut down. This is something he is not going to talk about.

CHAPTER 5

Our first day at Polskirrin has passed in a blur of sun, sleep, food, and too much alcohol, and now, as I lie on our bed, trying to raise the energy to take my make-up off and get undressed, I curse myself for failing to stick to my pledge to control my wine consumption. Matt's still downstairs, drinking and chatting, so God knows what state he's going to be in by the time he comes to bed. I groan and roll over to face the fresh air coming through the open door to our balcony.

We ate dinner on the terrace tonight as it's so warm, and I was relieved when Lucas said it was to be informal so we could help ourselves to food. I chose to sit next to Chandra. I had noticed at lunch that she was eating different food from the rest of us, and it seems kimchi is her staple diet. How she resists the glorious offerings from Nina's kitchen, I don't know, but I like her calm manner and her thoughtfulness, and as she doesn't drink I thought she would be a good influence. Andrew was in charge of the rosé though, and every time I turned my head I saw the bottle hovering as he topped me up with lovely blush-pink wine.

The ninth chair remained empty until Nina asked the house-keeper, in halting Italian with plenty of sign language, to bring out the food. At the last moment, just as we were all about to pick up our knives and forks, the wraith-like figure of a young woman, whose face was again practically hidden by her hair, slid into place between Lucas and Matt. I saw my husband lean towards her and cover one of her hands with his. I think I heard him say my name but there were no introductions, so I waited to catch her eye and smiled hello. Alex smiled back. She has a sweet face beneath all that hair, and the size of her wrists confirmed my guess that she is very thin.

I found it interesting that everyone included her naturally without making any big deal of her arrival.

"Alex, pass the black pepper, please?" Nick shouted from the far end of the table.

"Do you want some more salad, Alex?" Nina asked.

To everyone except me it was apparently perfectly normal that she should appear without comment or introduction, and should sit silently at the table while others spoke to her and around her as if they expected nothing of her. Perhaps they didn't.

Lucas was particularly attentive, and I could see his eyebrows draw together as he looked at her. Matt was making sure she was offered every dish, although she took little food.

Isabel's attitude to the men was even more competitive than it had been at lunch, but now that I know she's Nick's twin and spent a lot of time with them as they were growing up, perhaps it makes sense. No doubt she had learned to fight her own corner. She told brief anecdotes about each of them—with the exception of Lucas, who was perhaps exempt because he was the host. When it was Matt's turn to be teased, she turned towards me.

"Matt always had to have the flashiest of everything, Jemma— and I bet that's not changed, has it?"

I declined to answer and gave a rather weak smile, but it didn't stop her.

"Not that he ever knew what to do with any of his precious gizmos. He had the best games console but didn't know how to play, and the best mobile phone—the first BlackBerry I'd ever seen, in fact. But he hadn't got a clue how it worked. He just used to leave it lying around for show, didn't you, Matt?" She blew him a kiss.

Matt flushed slightly but seemed to take it all in good spirit.

"I remember that!" Nick called, ever eager to be part of the conversation. "It was a present from your dad, wasn't it? Finally proud of you for getting into the right university, even if you were never going to be a Cambridge Blue."

"Well, at least his dad was proud of him for something, which is more than we can say for our caring pops, isn't it?" There was hint of bitterness in Isabel's tone, and Nick gave her a black look.

"Listen," I said, trying to lighten the atmosphere. "Matt might be useless with technology—and don't look at me like that, Matt, because it's true—but he's brilliant with a scalpel, so I think he can be forgiven, don't you?"

"Absolutely, and I think we could all tell a few stories about you if we wanted to, Isabel," Andrew said mildly.

She laughed, and the tension eased. "What about you, Andrew? Are you still obsessed with boats? Apart from girls, it's all you ever talked about when you were a teenager."

"True, and it very possibly still is. Anything to be out on the water—or in it."

Lucas, who was on my other side, leaned towards me.

"Andrew had more girlfriends than the rest of us put together, and we never knew who he was going to turn up to parties with, or whether he'd come at all. Invariably he'd forgotten and gone off sailing somewhere."

If he looked then like he does now, with the same easy relaxed attitude, I can see how he had attracted the girls.

"How did you meet him?" I asked Lucas.

"Ah, that's quite a story. My dad enrolled me in a sailing school in the holidays. Andrew was helping out, already a skilled sailor. I was tall and gangly and hadn't quite learned how to dodge the boom. First trip out, it hit me hard on the head and knocked me into the water. Andrew fished me out."

I wanted to ask more, but we were interrupted by Chandra making one of her rare forays into conversation.

"Andrew has shown me the home you were brought up in, Lucas," she said. Somehow, she made it sound like an institution rather than the grand house in the middle of the Hampshire countryside that I'd seen in a documentary about Blair Jarrett. "Why did you decide to leave to come here, to Cornwall?"

Everyone went quiet. Alex dropped her head low, and Lucas gave her a worried glance. For an uneasy moment, no one spoke.

"When my father died it seemed to make sense to move away." Lucas turned back to me as if to continue where we'd left off.

"Maybe his death left a spiritual imbalance there. Perhaps you felt it." Chandra hadn't given up.

Lucas gave an uncomfortable laugh. "I don't think I'm that sensitive, Chandra. I don't have your ability to appreciate anything metaphysical."

"Hey, guys," Nick said cheerily after a couple of very long seconds. "We've got a wedding to look forward to, so let's focus all our energies on *good* things, shall we?" He jumped to his feet. "Let's have an impromptu toast—the first of many. To Nina and Lucas!"

Everyone raised their glasses and the level of chatter went on as before, but I saw Lucas reach a hand to Alex and wrap his fingers gently around her wrist.

Chandra lowered her head and carried on eating. I saw Andrew look at her with concern, but she didn't seem upset by the mild rebuke. It appeared that everyone, with the exception of Chandra and me, knew something about that house. And no one wanted to talk about it.

I've not had a chance to ask Matt why it was such a touchy subject, and I'm not going to wait up for him. I force myself off the bed and into the bathroom. All I want to do right now is rest my head on a cool pillow and sleep.

CHAPTER 6

Polskirrin has always felt like my safe place. There are no memories here—only the ones locked in my mind that I am unwilling or unable to examine. I rarely leave the grounds and never alone. Only with Lucas, when he's here. Nina tries to tempt me with trips, but I politely refuse. The only way I can live in peace is by surrounding myself with beauty, and just a glimpse of the raw reality of life outside the boundaries of Polskirrin is enough to plunge me into a dark place. I make myself useful, helping Lucas with the foundation, and I'm good at it. I have a purpose.

Today, however, it has been unsettling to see my brother's friends here. I watched them from the wood, wondering if I would recognize them. I thought time would have changed them, but they are just adult versions of their fourteen-year-old selves.

I was nine when Lucas first took them under his wing, and they seemed so grown-up to me. But after years of spending weekends and school holidays with them, I had their measure. Nick: always desperate to impress Lucas, to be the witty one; Andrew: the most self-contained, but never feeling totally at home because of his impoverished background; Matt: in awe of the others, reserved, insecure, the one I had most looked forward to seeing again. And Isabel. The less said about Isabel, the better.

I hadn't expected the sight of them, the sound of their voices, to have such an impact, but they have opened wounds held together with flimsy Band-Aids for years. I've been told over and over—by psychiatrists, counselors, and any other experts that Lucas could find—that I have to face what happened to me; I have to go back there in my mind and accept it. Only then will I truly recover.

But I haven't been able to. I have blocked it—every single agonizing moment.

Until now.

Seeing them, hearing them, talking to them tonight at dinner, took me back and led me to another time. Suddenly, beyond my control, the images have burst through in technicolor, and they're hurting—tearing me apart.

It's as if I'm floating above the world, looking down, and I can see us at Lucas's dad's house, playing in the pool, eating barbecued sausages. Then I'm in the summerhouse, laughing at their antics, hiding when they threaten to throw me in the cool water. The summerhouse was always my hiding place. Everyone knew that.

As I watch myself happily peeping out through the door, pretending they don't know where I am, the edges of the images grow dark, as if a thick fog is creeping in from each corner. The sunlight has gone, and it's night. I can't breathe. How did I get here?

Then the picture changes. I'm at home, in my bedroom, and it's just before Christmas—I know because down the street I can see a house lit with a multitude of cheerful lights and a blow-up Santa dancing on the roof in the wind. But there are no lights in our house. Santa won't be paying us a visit.

Sleet-like rain is driving hard against my window and I pray it will get louder to block out the shouting and obscenities coming from downstairs. I know there is only one person down there, so the anger is aimed at the world in general and everyone in it. Especially me.

I hear a shout, ordering me to get downstairs, but I stay where I am, looking out of the bedroom window into the dark, wet night, aching with unhappiness and longing to see my brother. And that is the moment I decide that whatever the weather, I have to leave. I can't stay a moment longer.

It is the worst decision of my life.

I push the images from my mind. I don't want to see what happens next. I'm not ready, so instead I look up at the stars. The light has gone now; another day is over. Despite everything, I've made it through. But with the memories come questions—some from all those years ago, others from tonight. I have no answers though.

I quickly strip to my underwear and walk towards the black sea, the reflection of a waning moon shimmering on its surface. I feel the water cold on my feet, my ankles, my shins, my knees. The earlier choppy water has calmed now, and it feels silky-smooth on my skin. As soon as it reaches my thighs, I plunge into its cool depths and with strong strokes swim towards the mouth of the bay. So many times I have thought I should just keep on going until Polskirrin is nothing more than a dot on a distant headland and I am out of energy, out of breath, waiting for the surface to part so I can sink beneath the waves, tumbling down and down as I let the ocean claim me.

But not tonight. I roll onto my back and float, weightless, looking up at the stars, emptying my mind by staring at a single star in the sky, knowing it is light years away, trillions of miles, and I focus on my own insignificance.

CHAPTER 7

I wake this morning to the clang of metal on metal and push my head under the pillow. My mouth is dry, my stomach unsettled, as if copious quantities of wine are still sloshing around in there.

The banging and crashing continues; preparations for tomorrow's wedding are under way. They must be erecting the gazebo for the reception on the terrace right outside our window.

I turn to Matt, but the bed is empty. The bathroom door stands open, and I can see he's not in there either. Maybe he's gone for a walk. I'd like to go back to sleep and wake up when the nausea has passed, but I know that's not possible.

Tomorrow is the wedding, and if I'm going to enjoy it I need to feel good. So I must try to be sensible tonight. Apparently there are plans for a lavish pre-wedding dinner, but that doesn't mean I have to drink too much. I know that part of the reason I overindulged yesterday is because there was a distance between Matt and me. It seems I upset him when I asked about Alex. I didn't hear him come back last night, and the only reason I know he was here at all is because the pillow now bears the imprint of his head.

I groan as I lift myself out of bed. Maybe I should put on a swimsuit and try to find the cove that everyone was raving about last night. The sea is bound to liven me up a little.

As I root around in the drawers, the door opens.

"Morning, darling."

I lift my head to give my husband a pained smile. He pulls a similar face. "Heavy night, wasn't it? Are you going for a swim?"

"I think so. Do you want to come?"

Matt shakes his head and points at his shorts, which I can now see are wet. "I've already been. It's lovely though. You'll feel better." He heads to the bathroom but stops in the doorway. "I'm sorry I was so late last night. We were catching up on all that's been happening since we last saw each other and I lost track."

"I don't mind. I was dead to the world in about ten seconds flat. Were you reminiscing about your younger days? I was a bit worried when Chandra started talking about a spiritual imbalance at Lucas's old home. Everyone went very quiet."

Matt's mouth tightens. "Andrew needs to tell her to keep her thoughts to herself. We don't need anything dragged back up. We don't talk about what happened there. None of us. So if she asks you any questions, don't tell her anything."

He shuts the door and I stare at the dark wood for a few moments. I have no idea what he thinks I might say to Chandra or anyone else, because the truth is I have nothing at all to tell.

I grab a towel and head for the balcony and the stairs to the terrace. Looking down, I see that the area is flooded with workmen, and metal poles are lying at angles everywhere as they construct the huge open-sided gazebo. I don't want to get in the way, so I turn back into the room and head to the main staircase.

Everywhere is deadly quiet and I wonder if everyone else is still in bed. Maybe those with rooms at the front of the house won't be disturbed by the workmen and can sleep off their hangovers.

I make my way gingerly down the stairs, hoping I can find my way out of the house and to the path to the sea. It's a big house, and several doors lead from the square entrance hall, so I head towards the back, through a large, elegant sitting room furnished with cream sofas and Chinese rugs. A door leads to a small snug, and at the far end I spot a patch of sunlight streaming through an open doorway.

As I get closer I can hear the murmur of voices coming from outside. There is something in their tone that suggests the speakers don't want to be overheard, so I pause, wondering what to do. I can see Chandra and Alex sitting at a table close to the door, away from the cacophony on the terrace. Both are clutching large cups between their hands as if they need the warmth, their heads close together. They appear to be deep in conversation. I don't want to eavesdrop, but I'm not sure if I should interrupt by walking past. There is an intensity about both of them. Then I hear Chandra's voice.

"Hatred will only increase your suffering and unhappiness, Alex. You must let it go. It's you that's getting hurt, not the person you hate. You must untie the knot inside you."

She is handing something across the table to Alex. I can't see exactly what it is, but then the light catches it. It looks like a bracelet made from a shiny black material.

"I have a gift for you. I believe it will help," Chandra says. "It's a mala. In my religion, we use it to count our mantras or our breaths when meditating, but I am giving it to you because I believe it will help give you the strength and determination to overcome all obstacles in your way. It's made of black onyx, which transforms negative energy."

Alex's voice is low and I struggle to catch her words.

"I know you mean well, Chandra, but I don't think it will help. For years I've managed to block the fear, the pain, the sheer horror of it all from my mind. But now—seeing everyone here—thoughts, memories, fragments of moments I thought long forgotten are hurtling towards me, and I can't catch them all. I can't make sense of them."

"You should ask yourself why those people did such bad things to you. They must be haunted by demons of their own to be able to inflict such pain on another."

Alex puts her cup down and drops her head, long strands of dark hair falling around her face.

"The police never found out who it was, so I don't have anywhere to direct my hatred. It's floating around me all the time with nowhere to land. But something was said last night ... maybe someone here knows more than I thought."

Chandra reaches across and puts her hand over Alex's. "Is it really worth pursuing? You can't change what happened, but you can change how you let it affect the rest of your life."

Alex slips the bracelet on. "I need to know, Chandra," she says, twisting the bracelet round and round on her wrist. "One way or another, I have to find out if my suspicions are right."

I back away slowly, certain that neither Chandra nor Alex has seen me standing in the shadows. I'll find another way out of the house.

CHAPTER 8

I head back towards the main hall, slip out through the front door, and wander over to the formal pond to sit on its raised brick edge. It's so peaceful here; even the sound of the waves crashing onto the shore below is muted. I watch the golden fish gliding through the shallow water and dangle my fingers below its cool surface.

The tranquility is shattered by the deep hum of an expensive-sounding engine starting, and a long, low car comes around the side of the house. Two people are inside: one is Lucas, and as the car turns slightly I see the other is Nina.

For a moment, I wonder where they're going, but it's none of my business so I shrug and pick up the towel that I seem to have been carrying for hours.

The path to the beach is easy to find and I follow the enticing sound of the waves. I love the feel of breakers as they wash over me, knocking me to the ground, only for me to stagger to my feet ready to dive through the next one. It will be cold, but it's just what I need.

The path starts with a gentle gradient, but after a few meters it steepens as it cuts deeper into the banks on either side, and the bramble hedges are covered in creeping ivy. Ahead is a wooden gate, broken away from one hinge, hanging at a strange angle, and beyond are stone steps which plunge down towards the cove. The steps are slick with dew, the sun unable to penetrate the bushes that choke the gully, and suddenly I feel uncomfortable, as if someone is watching me. I glance over my shoulder but can't see anyone beyond the bend in the path.

I'm being ridiculous. These are all friends. Why should I be worried about someone behind me?

Then I hear a pebble tumble down the path.

"Hello," I shout. But there's no reply.

I shiver and hurry through the gloomy corridor, down the steps—taking care not to slip on the slimy surface—until finally I emerge to a sight which takes my breath away. The sea is a rich, deep aquamarine, the breakers pure white, crashing up onto a tiny beach of pale pebbles. On either side of the cove are huge, smooth black rocks stretching far out into the bay, and above them green fields and the South West Coastal Path.

About a hundred meters to my left is a boathouse with a long jetty running straight into the deep water of the sea. Above the jetty is a balcony with a glass and stainless-steel railing. A floor-to-ceiling sliding window leads into what must be an apartment. The window is slightly open, and fine white curtains are moving in the sea breeze. Someone must live there.

I have forgotten my earlier fear, certain now that I'm out in the open no one can hurt me. I glance over my shoulder, back towards the path, and see a pair of legs making their way down the steep incline of the cutting. It seems I'm not going to have the beach to myself.

When Andrew's head appears below the overhanging branches, I can see he's wearing earplugs attached to the phone in his hand. He smiles and waves as he walks towards me, lifting a hand to pull them out.

"Hi, Jemma. How are you feeling this morning?"

"Pretty rubbish, but nothing a nice cold swim won't fix. You must be okay though if you can stand to listen to music." I shudder at the thought.

"Oh, it's not music. I'm trying to learn Spanish. It's for when I get my boat."

I vaguely remember everyone discussing Andrew's boat at one point last night.

"Oh yes. Isabel mentioned something about that, didn't she?"

"Isabel mentioned a lot of stuff. She's a bit of a mischief-maker, so don't take any of her comments to heart. It's a good job we don't choose to talk about *her* murky past."

Before I can ask more, he throws a towel on the beach, drops his phone onto it, and turns to me with a grin.

"Okay—come on then. No hanging around thinking about it. I'm warning you, the sea's cold, so for me there's only one way to get in."

With that he runs to the far end of the beach, leaps onto the rocks, and jumps from one to the next until he's reached the furthest point. Then, with an exuberant shout, he executes a spectacular dive, breaking the surface of the sea with hardly a splash.

My heart is in my mouth as I look out into the bay, raising my hand to block the sun from my eyes as I scan the water. *Where is he?*

I can't help but worry about rocks below the surface. What if he hit one when he dived?

Suddenly, to my relief, he rears up out of the ocean like Triton. There is something magnificent about those strong shoulders and that long hair, and I force myself to look away.

As I glance around the cove, my gaze lands on the boathouse and I can just make out a figure dressed in loose black clothes standing on the balcony.

It's Alex, and she's watching us. She turns when she sees me looking at her and goes back through the sliding window.

CHAPTER 9

The fortress I built to protect myself from the memories of that time is under attack. Sights, smells, and sounds advance, circle, and bombard me with brutal images of those days, and I can no longer fight them. I know that to be truly healed I have to let them come and I must examine every moment, face each reality. Only then can I lock it all away in the dark reaches of my mind, never to be explored again. But I've resisted for so long and it's agonizing.

I swam much farther than usual last night and for far longer. I wanted to tire myself so I would sleep, and it worked for a while. But I woke in the early hours feeling restless. I have no work to do for Lucas today—he has declared this week a holiday for all of us—but without it I feel lost. There is nothing for me to focus on to block my tormented thoughts. I tried to follow my normal daily routine; Ivana, Lucas's housekeeper, brought me some delicious pastries, anxious as always to fatten me up, and I believed for a while that if I stuck to my rituals everything would settle and the ball of panic in my chest would subside. But it didn't work.

I tried to read, but I couldn't concentrate so I stepped onto the balcony thinking the sea might soothe me. Andrew was showing off his diving skills to Matt's wife. He never could resist the temptation to impress the women, but however attractive he is, I could see last night how much Jemma loves her husband. Matt was always special to me, even though a tiny part of me blamed him for what happened.

I go back into the apartment and close the door, unwilling to witness their simple pleasure in the sea, and busy myself making coffee.

Snippets of the conversation at dinner last night still cloud my thoughts. Am I reading too much into what was said? It wasn't clear—little more than a cold breath of air on the back of my neck—but I need to know if I'm distorting the significance of a few words spoken in jest.

The last of my defenses crumble as I force myself to go back there, to expose what happened twelve years ago, to remember every detail. I was just a fourteen-year-old girl, wishing she was in another place, another life. I pull up a stool to the kitchen counter and close my eyes.

I am in my bedroom, gazing out from my window at a view distorted by the sleet slithering down the glass. The yelling from downstairs has stopped, and I dare to hope that might be the end of it. But then I hear feet thundering up the stairs and the door to my room crashes open.

"Don't you dare ignore me, you little bitch! I need you to go to the shops. I'm out of vodka." With that, the door slams closed and I am alone again, shaking—more with horror and disgust than fear. This is my life.

I know that if I give in to the demands I will have to pay for the drink with what I have in my own pocket—barely enough, and I will have to walk to school next week—but the alternative has never seemed to be an option. Until now. This time I will leave the house, as instructed, but not for vodka. This time—finally—I won't be coming back. I grab my rucksack from under the bed and randomly stuff clothes inside.

I don't want anyone to know where I've gone, so I leave a note to say I'm going to stay with a friend. I'm not specific, but it doesn't matter. No one is likely to look for me.

I sneak down the stairs, expecting a door to burst open with a scream demanding that I get a move on. Or maybe I will be rewarded for taking my time by a hard slap across the face.

I make it to the bottom step. Only a few meters now to the front door. As I creep through the hall, I spot a mobile phone. It must be stolen. My own was stolen from my room and sold for cash, so I take it, even though the battery is nearly dead and there is no sign of a charger.

Glancing over my shoulder to keep an eye on the door to the living room, I quietly turn the latch and, without a sound, step out into the cold night. The wind drives the freezing rain into my face, tiny icy daggers piercing my skin. I am soaked, shivering, but I know where I'm going. To the one place that I will be able to seek refuge. The one place that I will be safe.

CHAPTER 10

I'm beginning to get the measure of my fellow guests after another day spent lazing around chatting, eating, and drinking, although I've stuck to fizzy water all day.

Lucas seems like a charming and affable man, but I wonder if he realizes how much power he exerts over his friends. Does he notice how often Nick seeks his approval, glancing his way after he tells one of his stories? Matt certainly does—his eyes narrow as he watches Nick's display of boisterous joviality.

Isabel is especially attentive to Matt. I saw her bend to whisper in his ear as she walked past him on her way for a cigarette, resting her manicured hand on his shoulder. He swiveled his head to look at her and I couldn't see his expression. But he knew I noticed and gave me a brief smile. Of all of them, she's the one I am warming to the least.

Nick only lost his air of bonhomie briefly, and strangely it was Lucas he appeared to be angry with. I was talking to Chandra, but it was quite hard work and there were moments of silence while I thought of something else to say. Lucas was to my right and Nick came and crouched down between our chairs to speak to him.

"What did you think of the email I sent? Interesting?" He bounced slightly on bent knees.

"I don't think I've seen it, I'm afraid."

Nick sat back abruptly onto his heels. "What do you mean? It was sent to your private account."

"Very probably, Nick, but Alex deals with all my mail—electronic or otherwise. She's my PA, and she filters everything."

"*Shit!* It was sensitive stuff, Lucas—meant for your eyes only because you're a mate. It's not something that should get into the wrong hands." His words were little more than a sibilant hiss.

Lucas's voice was quiet but cold. "Alex is as honest as the day is long. If there was anything in any email that shouldn't be there, she would know what to do with it." He got to his feet and leaned across the table, grabbing a bottle from the cooler. "More wine, anyone?"

Nick stood up slowly and returned to his chair, but there was a reserve about him that I hadn't seen before. He attempted to revert to his usual sparky behavior, but it didn't quite work.

Whatever it is about Lucas that makes everyone leap around in a thinly disguised frenzy trying to attract his attention, I can't see it. Surely it's not solely because of his wealth? That's certainly not true of Matt; he didn't even tell me that Lucas is Blair Jarrett's son. Maybe his authority is historical: he's the boy who had the power to include or exclude the others from his circle.

Andrew seems amused by it all. Bare-chested, he tips back his chair, a half-smile on his lips, saying little.

Chandra watches silently and rather unnervingly, gazing at Andrew when he's not looking her way. I can see how much she adores him. They seem such an unlikely couple—Andrew the Adonis, with his toned body and easy manner, and Chandra, the spiritual confidante with her quiet intensity.

By mid-afternoon everyone had drifted off to do their own thing—in my case to sit in the shade and read. Matt vanished on some mission of his own. I presume he went for a walk, but he didn't say anything or ask me to join him. He simply disappeared, which is so unlike him.

I haven't seen Alex again since that glimpse of her down at the cove this morning. I'm told she lives in the apartment over the boathouse and I feel a twinge of envy. What an amazing place that must be to live, with the sea painting a different picture through her window every day.

I make my way back up to our room to shower and give myself plenty of time to get ready for this evening. The room is too hot, so I walk over to open the French windows. Matt keeps asking me to keep them closed and switch on the air conditioning, but I prefer fresh air and the sound of the sea. I walk out onto the balcony, but the glorious view is almost totally obscured by the undulating white roof of the gazebo.

I gaze over to my right, where I can just make out the path to the beach. I see Matt emerge from the trees, marching towards the house, his arms swinging furiously. I'm about to wave when I realize someone is behind him. She follows him into the open and stops, puts her hands on her hips, and shouts something. Then she laughs.

Matt doesn't turn but puts his head down and strides away from her.

Isabel watches his back as he heads towards the house, but she doesn't move from the spot.

For reasons I can't explain, I don't want Matt to know that I saw him. We've never had secrets before—at least as far as I know—and I want to see if he will tell me what was going on with Isabel.

By the time he makes it to the room, I'm lying on the bed with my eyes closed. He marches in and pushes the door closed a little too heavily. I open my eyes to look at his flushed cheeks.

"Hi, darling. I missed you this afternoon."

"Yes. Sorry. I thought a walk would be good for me. The coastal path runs above the beach. It goes for miles. I just kept walking and then realized that it was a long way back."

"Was there anyone on the beach?"

Matt has his back to me, getting out some clothes for the evening.

"I don't think anyone ever goes to that beach other than people from this house. It's a long walk to the nearest town or car park."

Clever Matt. He didn't lie to me, but he avoided the truth.

"I was the only woman still around so I thought I would leave the men to it and escape up here. Nina was busy getting ready for tomorrow, Chandra was meditating, and I've no idea where Isabel was."

That offers him another chance to say something, but he just pulls clean underwear out and slams the drawer shut.

"We need to think about getting ready."

CHAPTER 11

In spite of Matt's mood and the fact that he hasn't told me what he was talking to Isabel about, I am excited about this evening. Whatever ails my husband, I'm sure it will blow over and we'll have a good time.

I've taken time over my hair, waving it gently so it bounces when I move. I pull my dress from its hanger and slip it on, pleased with the deep-pink, silk organza full-length shift that I have chosen.

By the time I'm ready, Matt has dressed in a pale gray linen suit and a lilac shirt with a thin white stripe. I walk over to him and wrap my arms round his waist.

"I'm not going to kiss you, because I don't want to get lipstick on you, but you look very handsome," I tell him with a smile.

He smiles back, but it's forced. "That dress looks wonderful. You look great." It's as if he knows something is required and has dredged up a few words from somewhere.

I lift my hands to each side of his face and rub my thumbs gently against the outer corners of his eyes as if to ease the strain there. I know there's no point asking him what's worrying him. He'll say, "Nothing," and make his best attempt at a reassuring smile.

I have no time to say anything though, because at that moment we hear the gong that Lucas told us he would sound to summon us for dinner. We're eating early because Nina wants to make sure everything is cleared, ready for the following day. I give Matt a bright smile as we open the door. Another door opens, and Andrew and Chandra step into the corridor at the same time as us.

Andrew looks at me, and my eyes meet his. "We're all looking gorgeous tonight, aren't we?" His words include everyone, but I feel as if he's just talking to me. Chandra watches but says nothing.

Farther down the corridor two more doors open, and Isabel and Nick appear at the same moment, as if they have timed their entrance onto the landing. Isabel looks stunning in a silver sheath, her dark hair falling over one shoulder, and Nick, who has been lounging around for the last two days in multicolored shorts and shirts, now looks every bit the high-flyer in an immaculate cream linen suit with a white open-necked shirt.

We all take a moment to compliment each other on our outfits. Nick makes a flippant remark about how it's good to see that none of us has made any special effort tonight, and everyone laughs.

I push concerns about Matt's mood to the back of my mind as we head down to dinner. Based on the delicious smells wafting towards us, it's going to be a treat. I find myself coming down last, walking beside Andrew, my arm brushing against his.

Dinner is being held indoors, in the long dining room, and I stop on the threshold, enchanted by the sight in front of me. The dark oak table has an arrangement of white and vibrant-green flowers running down the center—low enough so as not to impede conversation between people sitting opposite each other—and the antique chests at the sides of the room are decorated with a multitude of candles, which fill the room with their soft flickering light.

The table is set for nine people, and I'm glad Alex is joining us. I feel as if I should have made more of an effort with her, but I've barely seen her. A memory of that morning's conversation comes back to me. Alex thinks someone here knows more than they ought to about what happened to her. I wonder what she meant.

Every setting has a place card, and as I scan the names I am disappointed to see that Alex will be seated at the opposite end of the table, next to Matt. I watch his face as he reads the names and he frowns when he sees Isabel is on his left. She is smiling, but that's maybe because she has Lucas on her other side.

Only the bridal couple and Alex have yet to make an appearance, and it isn't long before Lucas and Nina walk arm in arm into the room, and we all give a little cheer and clap our hands. Lucas looks down at his wife-to-be and smiles.

"Everything looks beautiful, Nina. And you look incredible."

He's not lying. Nina's elegance is undeniable. Tonight she is wearing a black silk crêpe dress with a floral panel running down the front. With her short black hair and dark eyes, she looks amazing.

But there is no sign of Alex.

CHAPTER 12

Nina looked around the room, at the flowers she had worked so hard to perfect, the flickering candlelight, and finally the guests, standing smiling behind their chairs, waiting for her and Lucas to take their seats at opposite ends of the table. She felt a shudder of relief. She had wanted this night to be special—a night to remember—and it seemed everyone was in the mood to celebrate. Tonight was more than a pre-wedding dinner though. It had a far greater significance than anyone knew, but she and Lucas had agreed to keep their secret from everyone, including Alex.

As they were about to sit down, Lucas spoke. "Where's Alex sitting, Nina?"

"I've put her next to me," Nina said. She could hear the slight note of defiance in her tone and hoped it wasn't going to mar the closeness between them tonight.

He looked at her for a long moment and then nodded. "Fine. Let's all sit down. I'm sure she'll be along shortly."

No sooner had they all taken their seats than the door from the terrace opened and Alex slid in, closing it silently behind her. She moved so quietly, but somehow it drew more attention to her. Lucas seemed to know she was there even though she was behind him, and he turned to look at her over his shoulder, indicating with his head that she was to sit at the other end of the table, between Nina and Matt.

As always, Alex was wearing long, baggy clothes—tonight in navy blue—with her hair hanging loose on either side of her pale face. Nina hoped she would try to enjoy the evening. Lucas's friends seemed to treat her with casual detachment—always pleasant but without being oversolicitous, and Nina wished she could be the same. She understood how damaged Alex was, and she was never anything other than polite and grateful for everything that was done for her, but Nina seemed to find herself oscillating between fussing around the girl and feeling frustrated at her dependence on Lucas. Sometimes she wanted to shake her—to tell her that she had so much of her life left to live; that she needed to accept the help that Lucas was eager to pay for and move forward with her life; that the only person suffering from her withdrawal from the world was Alex herself. But how could Nina possibly understand how the girl was feeling? It was impossible to truly comprehend the damage not only to Alex's mind and body, but also to her soul.

She seemed to feel comfortable with Matt though, and Nina was glad she had put them together. She watched as he turned to her and spoke quietly, and then he touched her hand gently, a frown lining his brow as if anxious about her response. Alex lifted her head to smile at him and then nodded.

For a moment Nina wondered if she had misheard Matt's question. She was sure he had asked Alex if he was forgiven. She had no idea what he might have done because according to Lucas none of them, including Matt, had seen Alex for twelve years, and Matt had barely talked to her since he'd arrived the day before—at least as far as Nina knew. But Alex seemed content, and she let her concern slide away.

Nina took a moment to think about these strangers who had entered her life just the day before: Nick, who played the fool but had a responsible job in banking; Andrew, who skippered boats wherever and whenever he could, living hand to mouth according to Lucas; Matt, the plastic surgeon, making quite a name for himself apparently. Despite her initial apprehension, she was pleased that they had all agreed to come. It meant a lot to Lucas.

The conversation was flowing, as was the wine, but Nina noticed that Matt rarely turned to his left where Isabel was sitting. Not that it seemed to be bothering her; she had Lucas all to herself as Jemma was chatting to Andrew.

Now Nina watched as Matt lowered his head once more towards Alex, who was speaking quietly. He was frowning, and then his head jerked back slightly and he gave her a puzzled look. She nodded slowly. Whatever she had just told him, it was a surprise to Matt—and not a good one.

CHAPTER 13

"It was someone here, Matt. I know it was." I whisper the words, and he looks shocked, as if he doesn't believe me. But someone heard me. Someone knows I'm right. I can feel it in the room. And now that feeling is closing in on me like a black shadow, about to envelop me, encircle me, suffocate me.

I still haven't been able to face remembering that moment—the moment I always think of as the instant my life was over—but if I'm to understand what happened and what secrets Lucas's friends hold, I must try.

I tell myself I'm an observer, watching but not participating, experiencing the thoughts but not the pain as I look down on the child that I still was, walking out of the door of my home into the cold, wet night. But it isn't working. I can't isolate what I see from how I feel, and I find myself there—back on the dark country road, heading away from the orange glare of the street lights on the estate.

I am so young, so vulnerable. But I feel invincible, as if I have a secret power because I have somewhere to go, somewhere I know I will be cared for and treated with kindness. I am naïve and believe that the only place where wickedness lives is within the four walls of my own home. And I've escaped!

My moment of euphoria quickly fades. I've been walking for more than an hour, and it seems so much farther in the cold dark night than it does by day. But when I arrive I know I will be welcomed, and that's enough to keep me going.

As I hurry along the country lanes, head down against the pinpricks of sleet that sting my cheeks, I jump every time I hear a car engine and dodge into the bushes, convinced someone is going to leap out of their car and grab me. But the fear slips away as an imposing entrance comes into view. I've made it; I'm safe at last.

I push open the gate, glad to be off the road, and start to get my breath back. But as I turn the corner of the drive, to my horror I see that the house is in darkness. Not a light is showing, and I feel a deep thud in my chest. It never occurred to me that no one would be home.

I make my way to the front door and, in case I'm wrong, press the bell. I hear an echoing ring that speaks to me of emptiness. The whole place is deserted.

I wander round the back, hoping to hear loud music coming from the study—the sounds of ZZ Top and Aerosmith that always make me smile. But deep down I know I am alone. There will be no beating throb of seventies and eighties rock. I knew Lucas wouldn't be here, but where is Blair?

I crouch on the terrace, sobbing, praying for the twin beams of a car's headlights to split the dark night as they come round the bend. But I know it isn't going to happen, and I'm getting colder and wetter with every minute that passes.

Then I remember the summerhouse. My hideaway. How could I have forgotten the place that witnessed so much raw emotion the summer before?

I know where the key is hidden—where it always is, under the third stone to the right of the door. Inside I find some throws to cover myself and lie down. I will wait for however long it takes.

I'm safe here.

As soon as that thought comes to me, another follows, but I can't pin it down. It's a sense of unease, as if darkness is speeding towards *me, waiting to wrap me in its malevolent blanket, but I brush the feeling aside.*

I breathe deeply, relaxing my limbs. Someone will come, I'm sure of it.

And eventually someone does come. Three of them. To the summer-house.

But not to rescue me. To take me.

CHAPTER 14

Dinner has been a triumph for Nina. The food was spectacular, and on the face of it everyone has enjoyed the evening up to now. But there are undercurrents that I don't quite understand. Perhaps it's just pre-wedding tension reaching out its tentacles to draw us all in.

I was glad that Matt spent time speaking to Alex. There was a moment when she lifted her head and I saw that her eyes are a wonderful shade of green. As she tucked her long dark hair behind one ear I noticed a bright, square-cut diamond earring glittering in the candlelight. Then she seemed to think better of exposing so much of herself and pulled her hair back down to cover most of her face. It's sad that someone so lovely feels she has to hide herself away. After that she fell silent, and not even Matt seemed able to draw her back from wherever she had gone in her mind.

As the meal ends, Lucas suggests we all move outside for post-dinner drinks. We make it as far as the terrace, flopping onto the sofas as if the meal has exhausted us. The light is fading, and it's that delicious time in the evening when everything seems quiet, as if the world is preparing for night. Our voices drop, laughter becomes muted, our bodies are replete. Only Nina has stayed inside, saying she'll join us when she's happy everything is tidy for tomorrow. She has refused all offers of help.

I look at Matt, about to give him a lazy smile that he will recognize as an early signal that I want him to make love to me later. But he's sitting straight in his chair, eyes staring but not focused, as if he's trying to work something out.

"Let's have some music," Nick says, placing a wireless speaker on the coffee table and pressing a few buttons on his phone. "Who remembers this?"

Lucas throws his head back and groans as the voice of Nelly Furtado singing "Maneater" demolishes the sense of peace. "Christ, Nick—*really?*"

"Don't you remember that last summer at your place? We played it all the time. Now, who's going to dance?" He looks hopefully round the assembled group, but he gets no takers.

Isabel lights a cigarette and leans back, a half-smile on her face as if she too is remembering that summer, and blows a cloud of smoke into the air above her. No one seems to feel the need to speak. Chandra sits quietly, her hands folded in her lap, a slight look of bemusement on her face. Alex is hunched, head bowed, at the end of a sofa, her slender body pushed up as close to the arm as she can get. I sense how much she doesn't want to be here. And yet she stays.

Nick gets more enthusiastic with each song from his playlist, but there are repeated cries of "Next" from either Lucas or Andrew as the speaker blasts out music their eighteen-year-old selves delighted in but they now scorn. Matt says nothing, a fixed smile on his lips.

"Give your phone to me, Nick, and stop being a twat," Isabel says after about ten minutes of her brother's choices being rejected. She reaches across the coffee table, beckoning with her fingers.

"Miserable buggers," he mutters with a chuckle as he hands over the phone.

Isabel scrolls through the playlist and raises her eyes to look around the group, a faint smile playing round her lips. "Here we go. Bring back memories, anyone?"

As soon as I hear the two notes, repeated over and over, I know what this is. Isabel pushes herself to her feet, her eyes on Lucas. "Dance with me," she says as Snow Patrol begin to sing "Chasing Cars."

Matt knows how much I love this song, and I want to look at him, to share the moment, but my eyes are drawn to Isabel and then to Lucas. For a man so relaxed, so comfortable in his own skin, he seems uneasy. He doesn't want to do this, but he doesn't know how to say no. Isabel is a guest, she is asking something of him, but for some reason the thought of dancing with her repels him. Isabel sees it too, and there's an awkward moment when I sense her fear of rejection.

"Leave the bridegroom alone, Isabel," Andrew says, rising from the sofa. "He needs to reserve his moves for his wife tomorrow. Come on, you can make do with me."

Isabel stares at Lucas for a moment longer, then slips into Andrew's open arms, wrapping her own too tightly around him, hiding her face in the crook of his neck. Over her head, I see Andrew wink at Chandra as he guides Isabel slowly across the terrace.

"Come on, Jemma," Nick says, leaping up and reaching out a hand to me. "As your husband doesn't seem up for it, you can dance with me."

Matt takes a swig of whatever concoction Nick has put in his glass and gives a distracted shrug. He's here, but he's not with us, and so when Nick grabs my hand and pulls me towards him, I move into his arms, listening as he sings quietly in my ear. He moves well and makes me laugh as he steps back and twirls me under our joined hands, then back again.

As the track finishes, he bows over my hand like a medieval courtier and thanks me for the pleasure.

We all return to our seats, but now everyone seems restless, and no sooner have we sat down than Andrew's phone rings. He looks at the screen and excuses himself, disappearing round the side of the house, and I see him turn down towards the orchard, where there's apparently a better signal.

It's as if his departure breaks up the party, because shortly after he leaves Alex goes too, quietly saying a few words to Matt as she stands up. He looks at her and nods. She doesn't head towards the path to the beach, towards her home, but follows Andrew round the side of the house. But Nick stands up to get a drink at that moment, and I can't see if she too turns towards the orchard.

"She's getting an early night then?" I say to Lucas, nodding in the direction that Alex took and wondering if tonight she's sleeping in the main house, ready for the next day. "It seems like a good idea—I might take a page out of her book."

"Alex won't be going to bed yet. She waits until it's dark and the beach is deserted and then she swims. She's like a fish, but she prefers to swim at night. It worries me, but she's an adult and I can't persuade her of the dangers, I'm afraid."

"Is she not scared she might swim into a protruding rock or something, if it's dark?"

Lucas smiles and looks out into the night. "Not at all. Those green eyes of hers are all-seeing. She has better than twenty-twenty vision, you know—I think it was tested at twenty-twelve." He pushes back his chair. "You'll have to excuse me for a moment, Jemma. I'm going to check that Nina's okay. She should have been out here by now, enjoying the rest of the evening with us."

He leans forward and gives me a peck on the cheek, then stands, glass in hand, and makes his way towards the dining-room door.

I think about Alex swimming at night, gazing up at the stars, and then a vision of Andrew diving off the rocks that morning pushes itself uninvited into my head. It looked so dangerous, although he told me later that according to Lucas it's safe to dive when the tide is high.

The mood has quietened since the dancing finished, and it seems Nick has given up on his playlist. There's now some mellow jazz playing quietly, and Isabel lights up another cigarette, but there is a sense that the evening is over, and with a murmured goodnight Chandra takes herself off towards the formal garden at the front of the house. Apparently she likes to sit by the little fountain there. She says the sound is peaceful and it settles her.

It's still not late, but I decide to go to bed too. I want some time alone with my husband, so I walk over to where Matt is sitting and crouch down to speak softly into his ear, hoping no one will hear over the noise Nick is making as he attempts to persuade Isabel to try one of his more obscure liqueur combinations.

"Do you fancy an early night, Matt?"

I see my husband glance over to the sofa opposite, where Isabel is sitting. She smirks and I realize she heard me. Matt half turns towards me.

"I'll be up soon. I'll just finish this drink." He holds up a glass that is almost empty. One mouthful is all it would take.

Now is not the time to question him, but suddenly I realize I will be glad when this is all over and we can go home—back to some sense of normality.

As I walk past the door to the dining room, I hear Nina's voice. She's angry, I can tell that, but she's speaking French so I don't catch what she's saying, and I scurry towards the stone stairway to our balcony. When I get to our room I decide to have a quick shower to cool down.

Feeling a bit fresher, I lie down to wait for Matt, expecting to hear his tread outside on the balcony any moment. But there's nothing. *Where is he?*

I push myself off the bed and wander out into the night through the French windows. Perhaps he's on his way, or maybe he's still chatting to his friends. But only Nick and Isabel were with him when I left, and I can't hear either voices or music.

At first I can see nothing other than the vast white top of the gazebo, but beyond that on the far side of the terrace I catch a glimpse of Nina walking down some steps into what I discovered earlier is a Japanese garden, where water ripples over stones into a koi pond with a tiny bridge leading from one area of beautiful planting to another.

No one else seems to be around. I sigh, and I'm about to turn back into the room when I glance towards the path to the cove. The ground-level lights illuminate both the path and the silhouette of someone heading to the beach. I imagine for a moment that it might be Alex, but the figure walks like a man. I turn back into the room, and somewhere in the distance I hear what sounds like the buzzer at the front gate, now closed for the night. It's not that late, but surely too late to be delivering more paraphernalia for tomorrow?

I lie down and feel myself drifting off, but I don't want to sleep until Matt's here. I don't know why—it's irrational—but I need to know he's safe.

I'm jolted out of my semi-sleep by a voice floating up from below. I don't know who it is, but I'm sure it's not Matt. I quietly walk out onto the balcony again. The voice is coming from under the gazebo, muffled by the thick PVC. It's a man's voice, but then a woman responds. She is speaking with an accent, but it's not Nina, so perhaps it is Ivana—the housekeeper. Then I hear footsteps as one of them—the man, I'm sure—strides away. I stare up at the sky. There's no moon yet, but the stars are bright. It's a beautiful night.

I glance over towards the path to the beach, the boathouse, and Alex's apartment. Is that where Matt was earlier today? Was he talking to Alex? Is that where he is now?

I stare at where the path disappears into the trees. I can't decide whether I want to see my husband emerging from them or not.

CHAPTER 15

Nina hadn't meant to fall asleep in the hammock. She hadn't meant to argue with Lucas either—not tonight. But when he came into the kitchen after dinner, his first question was about Alex.

"What was Alex saying to Matt? He looked shocked. Did you hear?"

And Nina had lost her temper. What did it matter what Alex had said? Tonight wasn't about her. She felt that she should have been Lucas's sole focus of attention for once, but when she voiced her irritation, he had looked bemused.

In the end she had stomped off, the argument unresolved, and to make matters worse, in honor of some stupid tradition, Lucas would be sleeping in the spare room tonight. She would have no chance to make it up with him before tomorrow. Nina didn't know why she had agreed to the ridiculous suggestion, given that—unbeknown to anyone else—they had sneaked off into town that morning and got married at the register office in Penzance. Tomorrow would be a symbolic ceremony only—the big show for all their guests—and now she was angry at herself for letting the tension get to her. Tonight shouldn't have been like this.

The house felt stifling so Nina had gone to the Japanese garden for some fresh air and to try to find a little peace. But the hammock seemed so inviting, and within moments the tension had seeped out of her and she'd dozed off.

She woke to the sound of someone crying. The noise was coming from the far end of the wood, close to the path to the beach.

She swung her legs out of the hammock and moved quietly between the trees, but she couldn't see anything in the darkness. The sounds became louder and she began to make out some words, bursting unrestrained between fierce sobs.

"No, please, I can't do that! Please, please don't make me do that. Please, Lucas."

Lucas.

The voice sounded desperate, and Nina wasn't sure what to do. She didn't want Lucas to think she was spying on him, but she couldn't ignore it.

She could just make out the white of her husband's shirt now, his arms out, holding someone by the shoulders, but she couldn't see who it was.

"I'm begging you, Lucas. Please, please don't make me do that."

To Nina's horror she saw Lucas give the woman a short, sharp shake and she heard his voice, low and fierce.

"For God's sake, Alex, calm down. You're hysterical, and you need to keep your voice down. I have to think. You could be wrong, you know."

"I'm not wrong! I know I'm not. Christ, I thought you would understand. But you don't care, and why should you? I've been a burden for too long."

Nina didn't hear his response, but his tone remained low and fierce.

There was more sobbing, and then he seemed to spin Alex round and almost frogmarch her to the top of the path.

"Come with me, and don't bloody argue. Just do as I say."

The lights on the path were off, and after a few seconds she could see nothing but their shadows, Lucas gripping Alex's arm.

CHAPTER 16

I knew something was wrong. I've been feeling it since they all arrived, that same sensation—just as I had all those years ago—that a darkness was coming, that something was about to happen, something over which I would have no control. I know that feeling; I recognize it. And now I know I'm right.

I didn't know where the threat was coming from though. I still don't know; it was nothing more than a whisper in the breeze, as if the words "I'm coming for you" were tickling my ear as they brushed past.

I looked at each of them tonight—Lucas's friends, who I always believed tolerated me, even if they thought I was a nuisance. I know that one of them needs to silence me, but who?

Whatever Lucas says, no matter how wrong he believes I am, I can't spend another day like this, waiting, knowing that if I don't act, something will happen. I have to take control.

I'm out of options.

CHAPTER 17

It's the scream that wakes me. It pierces the air and silences the early-morning twittering of birds, but I'm not sure if it's real or whether it's the last lingering note of a bad dream, so I lie still for a moment, listening to see if the cry comes again.

I must have fallen asleep last night waiting for Matt. I got out of bed one more time, thinking I might go down and see if I could find him, but I was almost afraid of what I might discover. I wandered back out onto the balcony, hoping I would hear laughter to tell me that Matt was drinking with his friends, but the night was silent. As I glanced over the roof of the gazebo, I saw someone heading down the path. Not the same person as earlier, I'm sure. Not as tall. Could it be Matt? The figure disappeared round a bend, and I watched to see if he or she would come back, but then suddenly the lights went out. I wondered if perhaps it was Alex, and I presumed it meant everyone was safely in their beds. Everyone, it would seem, except Matt.

I don't remember him coming back to the room. I seemed to be floating in and out of oblivion, my dreams filled with bright images of candles, flowers, black rocks; the fragrance of apricots, cigarette smoke, whiskey; the sounds of music, anger, a car engine, pounding waves, and I was unable to distinguish between those that were real and those that were memories replaying themselves vividly in my semi-conscious mind. It was only when I felt the heat from Matt's body on my back and realized he was in bed next to me that I floated into a dreamless sleep.

He is snoring softly beside me now and has clearly heard nothing. The scream must have been in my dream. I don't want to wake him, so I lie looking at him, his face in sleep smooth and so perfect in my eyes. I lift my arm and I'm about to rest my hand on his flat stomach when the air is rent in two once again, and this time there is no doubt in my mind that it's the real thing. I leap out of bed, fling open the door, and rush to the edge of the balcony, leaning out as far as I can over the stone parapet. I can just see the far end of the path to the beach, and as the morning is shattered by a third scream, I see the wide figure of the housekeeper lumbering through the opening in the trees.

"*Aiuto, aiuto!*" she shouts.

My knowledge of Italian is sketchy, but I'm fairly sure it means *help*. I turn and race down the staircase, stumbling at the bottom over huge cables, pushing past stacks of chairs delivered by the caterers the evening before. Swerving around blue plastic boxes of glasses and crockery, I run barefoot over the stone-flagged terrace and onto the lawn beyond.

I haven't stopped to get dressed or put shoes on, and wearing nothing but a pair of pajama shorts and a tank top I hurry across the newly watered grass towards the path.

Where *is* everyone? I can't understand why they haven't all been driven from their beds by the screams.

At the far end of the lawn I step gingerly onto the gravel path, the small sharp stones cutting into my feet. The housekeeper is shouting in Italian, but I have no idea what she's saying and I shake my head, so she just points towards the cove.

I plow down the slope, through the tunnel of overgrown ivy, down the steps, and as I reach the cove I hear a sound that I will never forget. It is the howl of an injured animal—deep and low, sounding as if it starts in the guts, then travels up through the body to burst unchecked from the mouth. A sound I know is human.

I can make out just one word.

Alex.

Ahead of me is a tableau that seems frozen in time. Lucas is kneeling on the pebbles, the water lapping over his thighs, his head back as he releases the last notes of his roar of pain.

Beside him, facedown in the shallow water, is the body of a young woman, her long hair creating a swirling black halo around her head as it floats on the gentle waves.

Alex.

CHAPTER 18

Stephanie King was running, tearing along the path at the back of the three-story block of flats. The breath was burning in her throat, and she could feel her shirt sticking to her. She could see the little toerag she was chasing up ahead, but he was getting away. And where the hell was Jason, her young probationer? He should have been able to keep up.

"Shit!" She panted, bending down, hands clasping her legs just above the knees. Her short spell in CID a few months ago must have made her soft. "Where the bloody hell were you, Jason?" she asked as he appeared, out of breath, at her side.

"Sorry, Sarge, I'm not feeling that great. I think it was that kebab I had last night."

"Not again! What is it with you? Why the hell do you keep eating kebabs if they make you sick?"

She looked at his face and had to admit that he looked a bit green. But before she could say anything more, she heard a crackle from her radio.

"King," she said, pausing to listen. "Okay, I've got it. We'll be there in about fifteen minutes."

Replacing her radio and taking one last gulp of air, she turned back towards her car. They had been driving past the flats when she'd seen the kid trying to break in. They would have caught him if Jason hadn't decided to shout, "Police! Stop right there," which of course the kid had totally ignored as he ran off.

"Where are we off to, Sarge? Only I could do with a cup of coffee."

"Tough. We've had a report that a young woman's been drowned in Polskirrin Cove."

"Can we stop off somewhere on the way? A couple of minutes won't make any difference, will it?"

"No, we can't. The deceased woman's brother is supposed to be getting married at Polskirrin today, and the least we can do is deal with it quickly, don't you think?"

"What, you mean so they can still get married?"

Stephanie blew out through pursed lips. "No, I didn't mean that. But how the hell do I know what they'll do? We need to get there so they can do whatever they need to do—cancel it or carry on."

"Jesus," muttered Jason.

He looked fed up, and Stephanie felt guilty for a moment. She always seemed to get frustrated with him. He wasn't such a bad lad; he just needed to take the job seriously, and the regular kebab problems—a euphemism for too much alcohol if she had ever heard one—just had to stop.

She knew why she was being hard on him. Her nerves were jangling. She was due to hear that day whether her application to join CID on a permanent basis had been successful, and it mattered more than she could say. Her recent stint out of uniform had taught her that, more than anything, she wanted to be a detective.

Her tension wasn't only down to the pending news. To make things worse, Detective Inspector Angus Brodie was due back from a three-month assignment in Leeds that day. She could handle either of these two events with a degree of decorum, but together they were killing her. She just hoped he wouldn't turn up at the scene of the drowning. She wanted to be prepared when she saw him: full make-up, every hair in place. Not sweaty after running after a little thief with her hair stuck to her head.

She and Gus had been a couple once—rock solid, she had thought. But it had all gone sadly wrong. Since then, despite everything Gus said, she had been too stubborn to let him back into her life. Truth be known, she was terrified of having her heart broken again.

Gus had suggested she took the time he was away to make a decision. If absence really did make the heart grow fonder, perhaps it would be worth trying again. But if out of sight meant out of mind, they would have their answer.

She knew which way it was with her. Her only doubt was whether she would be brave enough to tell him that she'd tossed and turned every night, longing to feel the length of his body next to hers.

For now, she had to think of someone else's misfortune. The death of someone you love was always a tragedy, but for it to occur on your wedding day had to be twice as devastating.

CHAPTER 19

As Stephanie turned into the driveway of Lucas Jarrett's house she could practically feel Jason's jaw dropping, and even she was having to work quite hard to be nonchalant in the face of the drama going on in the grounds. There were vehicles of every size and description, people milling around lifting endless boxes out of vans parked randomly on the drive, the grass—anywhere, in fact, where there was an inch of space.

"Christ, they really are going ahead with the wedding, then?"

"Looks like it. Maybe nobody's told the organizers what's happened."

Stephanie looked for somewhere to pull up, but the parking area was full and two big lorries blocked access to the back of the house. From one of them a steady stream of catering staff was unloading crate after crate of food, the green fronds of herbs spilling over the sides of some, others stuffed with huge pieces of what looked like whole fillets of beef. The doors of the second lorry were opened briefly before there was a shout and they were slammed shut—but not before Stephanie had seen inside. Cases of wine were piled on top of each other—at least a hundred of them—and shelves were packed with bottles of spirits, held secure in special mesh holders. As she stepped out of her car, she could hear the steady hum of the lorry's refrigeration unit.

Men and women were climbing ladders at the front of the house, arranging garlands of white peonies, and she saw boxes overflowing with roses of every hue being carted round the back of the house.

A man with shoulder-length hair in striped shorts walked towards them, his face pale beneath his tan.

"I'm Andrew Marshall, a guest staying here for the wedding and a friend of Lucas Jarrett."

"Sergeant Stephanie King. I understand a body has been found in Polskirrin Cove. Can you show us the way please, sir? I expect some of our colleagues will be joining us shortly."

"I can point you to the path, but Lucas has said he doesn't want any of us to see her. He's told us all to keep away."

Stephanie looked at the man, who seemed bemused by this thought.

"I think that's understandable, don't you, Mr. Marshall?"

Andrew lifted his shoulders slightly. "We all know Alex. We could have helped him take her out of the water. He won't even let his wife go to him."

"Best if no one else touches her. What's happening about the wedding, do you know?" Stephanie asked.

"I can't imagine Lucas will want to go ahead. I can't speak for Nina. She might have a different view."

"Okay, well, we can talk about that later, but for now point me to the path, please."

Andrew walked Stephanie and Jason to the back of the house, dodging waiters pushing trolleys bearing boxes of glasses and men carrying ladders with coils of wire slung over their shoulders. This would be a hell of an event to cancel.

He led them towards a narrow path, at the top of which stood a group of people, their faces wearing the blank stares of those in shock. A small woman with short black hair was shouting at a taller, blond woman, her voice brittle with unshed tears.

"It has nothing to do with you, Jemma. He's my husband. Let me go to him."

"I'm so sorry, Nina, but he asked me to make sure that no one, and he was very specific that it included you, should see his sister this way. Only the police and the paramedics can go down."

Stephanie winced. She assumed Nina was the bride to be, in spite of her use of the word "husband."

"Paramedics? *Merde!* You're a doctor, Matt. Can't you do something?"

A man of average height with excessively white teeth lifted a hand to rub his short brown hair.

"They may need the paramedics to confirm life extinct, Nina. We know they can't help her."

Stephanie took a step towards them.

"I'm sorry to interrupt you, but I'm Sergeant King. We need to get down to the cove, so if we could pass, please? We may not need the paramedics. This officer"—she pointed at Jason—"will come back up to let you know once we're certain of the facts."

The small French woman folded her arms. "You mean once you're certain she's dead? I'm coming with you."

The blond woman who seemed to be keeping guard appeared to be about to argue when the doctor with the white teeth put out his hand.

"You've done your best, Jem. Let them sort it out between themselves."

As Stephanie passed she heard one of the other men call out, "Nina, do you want me to speak to the wedding crew?"

Nina, who was two steps ahead of Stephanie, must have heard, but she didn't turn round.

Stephanie walked down the path, her eyes skimming the ground on either side. She wasn't looking for anything specific, but she had learned to be on the lookout for anything that seemed out of place. Passing through a rickety gate, they followed stone steps down beneath shrubby growth that blocked out the sky and finally emerged into the sunlight to view the scene ahead of them.

Polskirrin Cove wasn't easily accessible from anywhere but the house, but she had looked down on it many times when walking the coastal path, something she had done almost daily in the months after she and Gus split up.

She only had seconds to take in the picture though, because a man who must have been close to two meters tall leaped up from where he was kneeling on the shingle, next to the facedown figure of what appeared to be a young woman, and started to run towards them.

"Nina, go back. *Go back!*" he shouted as he ran.

The woman called Nina stopped in her tracks and Stephanie turned towards her.

"I think it's best if you don't come any farther," she said. "We need to be certain this isn't a crime scene, and we can't have you anywhere near the body, I'm afraid."

Nina took a step back and lifted her hand to her mouth. "Crime scene?"

"We have to establish what happened here. Until then I can't let you near her. I'm sorry."

The crunch of pebbles under running feet alerted Stephanie to the fact that Lucas Jarrett had reached them.

"I told Jemma to keep you away," he yelled. "Go *away*, Nina! Go back to the house!"

He reached for her arm as if to spin her round, but she shook his hand off.

"I wanted to be here for you, Lucas. I thought you might need me."

Oh boy, Stephanie thought. She didn't know who she felt more sympathy for—the man who had found his sister dead in the sea, or the woman who had been about to marry him and just discovered that he didn't want her with him in his darkest hour.

"Listen," Stephanie said, "this is a difficult time for everyone. Nina, I can't let you get any closer, but I do need to go down to the shoreline now. I would prefer my constable, Jason, to be helping me to check the scene, but if you insist on staying he will have to remain with you. I know you only want to help, but honestly the best thing you could do is go back to the house and sit down with your friends. It's a huge shock, especially today."

Nina seemed defeated and hung her head, not looking at Lucas. She glanced to one side and gasped. "Her clothes," she whispered and stepped towards a bundle of navy-blue fabric.

Stephanie reached out a hand. "Please leave them. Are they Alex's?"

Nina nodded, not taking her eyes from the pile of clothing.

Lucas was staring at her, eyes blazing. "Go, Nina. Just go."

Nina lifted her head and looked at her husband, her chin raised as if about to argue. Stephanie decided to intervene.

"Jason, will you take Nina back to the house, please, and come back here as quickly as you can?"

Nina turned her head, dignity restored. "I don't need an escort, thank you. I'm perfectly capable." She swung on her heel and tramped back to where the path disappeared into the undergrowth.

Stephanie turned back to Lucas.

"Mr. Jarrett, I'm so sorry for your loss. Are you certain this is your sister?"

Lucas was staring after Nina, and it took him a second to register Stephanie's words. When he turned towards her, his eyes were bleak.

"Yes."

"I need to go down there to see her. If you prefer, you can stay here."

Lucas shook his head. "No, I'll come."

Instructing Jason to stop anyone else from coming onto the beach, Stephanie trudged over the loose pebbles towards the body.

The young woman, wearing only black knickers, a white bra, and a black bracelet, lay facedown, dark hair splayed around her head. Stephanie had no doubt she was dead but checked the pulse in her neck anyway. Her body was stone cold.

"She's dead," Lucas said unnecessarily.

"I'm so sorry, Mr. Jarrett, but I had to check. Was she like this when you found her?"

He nodded. "She was in the sea, floating facedown, but the tide was going out and I didn't want it to take her with it. I waded out and lifted her head, just to be sure there was nothing I could do." He bit back a sob. "But there wasn't, so I held her by the hand until the waves ebbed and lowered her onto the shore. I didn't want to pull her out. I didn't know if I should or not. She must have hit the rocks on the far side, I think, as she was washed ashore. The skin on her cheek is scratched."

Stephanie lifted the woman's hair slightly and could see some damage to her face. She let it drop again quickly.

"You did the right thing. Her name's Alex, is that right? Alex Jarrett?"

"Yes, Alexandra, but her surname's Lawrence. Different fathers—both dead, as is our mother. I'm all she's got." Lucas stared at the back of his sister's head. "She always went for a late-night swim. Every night from May to October. I didn't like it. She knew that."

Stephanie turned and gave a tiny shake of the head to Jason, hoping he understood to tell the paramedics they wouldn't be needed. As she did so, she thought of the walk down from the house, along the narrow path between the bushes, and shuddered. Not much scared her physically—although emotionally was an entirely different matter—but you had to be brave to attempt that walk in the pitch dark.

"Did she always come down here on her own?"

"She lived here." Lucas nodded to the boathouse.

Stephanie was about to ask him more when she heard the clatter of pebbles behind her and twisted her head.

"Good morning, Sergeant King."

The broad figure of Angus Brodie was heading towards her. She should have been prepared for this moment, but she wasn't, so she lowered her head back over the body of Alex Lawrence to hide the flush in her cheeks.

CHAPTER 20

Gus held his hand out to Lucas, who stood up and took a step towards him.

"Mr. Jarrett, I'm Detective Inspector Angus Brodie. My condolences for your loss. It's never easy to deal with the death of someone close to you, and finding her yourself must have been a dreadful experience. DI Wilcox is on his way. I'm here as an observer, sir, until we can establish exactly what happened."

Stephanie understood the subtext. If this was an accident or suicide, it would be her local DI's case. But if it turned out to be murder, it would be Gus who would take the lead for the Major Crimes team.

She stood up and moved across to join them, knowing there was nothing she could do for the woman at the edge of the water and keen to keep the scene as clear as possible.

"I'm sure you understand that we need to bring in a small team to take photographs and collect any items that might be relevant to your sister's death. You might prefer to be somewhere else while that's going on."

Lucas looked slightly bewildered. "Photographs?"

"Until we know what happened here, we just need to be sure we have all the facts." Gus glanced behind him. A short man in his mid-fifties with a wide girth and a red face was negotiating the pebbly beach cautiously and heading towards them. "DI Wilcox, this is Lucas Jarrett, the deceased's brother."

Stuart Wilcox nodded at Stephanie and shook Lucas's hand, repeating the condolences that Gus had offered.

"Do you have any idea what might have happened, sir?" he asked.

"She must have passed out or hit her head on a rock in the dark, or something. Maybe she got a cramp—I don't know. She swam every night. I *told* her it was dangerous to swim alone. The sea's a cruel beast, and it's never completely calm around here." Lucas was shaking his head, looking at the beach as if talking to himself.

"We need to leave your sister with these people for now," Stuart said, indicating the Crime Scene Investigation team making their way towards them. "They'll take good care of her until the coroner's office has made arrangements to move her to the mortuary. We need you to move away please, sir."

"Can't I stay here? I can talk to you, but I don't want to leave her. Not until…"

"Let's move over there, shall we?" Gus indicated the black rocks that rose up at the side of the cove, and steered Lucas as far away as he could, knowing that Alex's body would have to be turned over.

"Can you tell me what happened this morning—how you came to find her?" Gus asked.

Lucas shook his head again. "I didn't find her. It was Ivana, our housekeeper. She comes down early every morning to bring Alex some fresh bread, croissants—whatever she's made for everyone else. She's very fond of my sister and says she needs fattening up."

Stephanie resisted the temptation to glance over her shoulder to take another look at the body on the beach.

"She saw Alex floating on the water and ran—as best she could—back to the house. She was screaming. I was about to come down here myself to say good morning to my sister, so when I heard her scream I just started to run." Lucas bit back a sob. "It was her hair.

I knew who it was straight away. I hoped she was just floating, watching a fish under the surface or something. I waded into the water, but as soon as I touched her I knew she was dead. I pulled her a little closer to the shore—the tide had just turned and was on its way out. If I hadn't come just then she'd have been washed out to sea. We might never have known what happened to her. Anyway, I held her, like I told the sergeant, until the sea had ebbed and then I lowered her onto the beach. I didn't want to pull her out—not when I knew she was dead."

"You did the right thing, I'm sure, Mr. Jarrett."

Over Gus's shoulder, Stephanie saw Stuart Wilcox step away from the body and signal her to join him. She excused herself, leaving Gus to look after the grieving brother.

"What do we know, Steph?"

"Not much yet. I haven't been here long. Lucas Jarrett is the deceased's half-brother, and today is supposed to be his wedding day."

"So I gathered from the hive of activity up at the house. How awful for him—and for his future wife. Looks like it was supposed to be a hell of an occasion too. Has he given us a positive ID?"

"Yes, sir. She is Alexandra Lawrence, and he's her next of kin."

"Okay, good. No need to drag anyone down to the mortuary then. He'll have to sign a written statement confirming that. Can I leave that with you?"

Stephanie nodded. "Of course. The bride is in a bit of a state. She wanted to comfort Jarrett, but he wouldn't let her near him or Alex, and her wedding is collapsing round her ears."

"Poor woman. A tragedy any day of the week, but today..."

"Well, hopefully she'll get some support. There are a number of people staying with them for the wedding—friends, I think."

Stuart nodded and pointed up the beach. "Are those Alexandra's clothes?"

"According to Nina, yes—and it makes sense as she only has her underwear on."

"Okay." He glanced over to where the path opened onto the beach. "Oh good—here comes Molly Treadwell. Let's see what she has to say on the subject."

Molly was a pathologist and Stephanie enjoyed her occasional dry wit, even in the face of death. She trudged across the beach in her oversized Tyvek suit, her gray hair falling out of a poor attempt at a bun.

"Looks like you've brought the A-team out today, Stuart" she panted, nodding towards Gus, who was standing about fifty meters away. "Always a sight for sore eyes is young Angus. You thinking we've got a crime?" She crouched down by Alex's head. "Ah, the poor lass."

"We don't know if it's an accident or not yet, Molly," Stuart said. "But better to be safe than sorry. Gus is here to observe until we know more. He's keeping the brother talking for now."

As Molly started her examination, Stuart spoke to Stephanie.

"I've had a quick look, and her face has suffered a few cuts on the rocks, so I'd like to get the brother well away before we turn her fully. Can you and Gus talk to him? After today, this might well be your job anyway." He gave her a grin, and Stephanie couldn't help wondering if he already knew the result of her CID application.

She nodded her agreement and walked back across the beach towards Gus, unable to resist looking at him as he stood speaking to Lucas Jarrett, drinking in the sight of his broad body and short springy hair. She was glad he had kept the close-cropped beard too. It suited him.

As she drew close, she switched her gaze to the bereaved brother.

"Mr. Jarrett, DI Wilcox has asked if DI Brodie and I could ask you some questions. We need to move a bit farther away from the investigating team, to make sure we don't get in their way. Is that okay?"

Lucas was staring at the ground and didn't speak. Gus clearly took that as assent and held out a hand to indicate that they should walk towards the boathouse.

"You said your sister swims late at night, Mr. Jarrett, but do you know what time that might have been?" Gus asked as they walked.

"She only went in after dark. She liked it that way, and at this time of year it doesn't get dark until late. She was up at the house having dinner, but she left before ten so it would have been some time after that, though probably before midnight."

"And did she always swim alone?"

Lucas nodded. "Always."

"Sergeant King tells me that your housekeeper came down to bring her some breakfast. Does your sister not have breakfast at home?"

Stephanie saw the confusion on Lucas's face. "Excuse me, sir," she said. "Alex lived up there—above the boathouse."

Gus raised his eyes to the large glass windows overlooking the beach, and Stephanie wondered if Alex had left the apartment, run straight down, and stripped to her underwear, confident there was no one to see her.

"Mr. Jarrett, we will have to go inside your sister's home. Would you like Sergeant King to take you back up to the house?"

"No. If you're going in, I'm coming with you," he said with a hint of defiance.

Stephanie was never shocked or surprised by how people behaved after the death of someone close. Responses varied from total collapse to absolute fury, and she had a feeling that Lucas Jarrett was angry—perhaps with his sister for letting this happen.

"We'll need the key, sir. You are welcome to go inside, and you may be helpful in pointing out some details, but you won't be allowed to touch anything until we're certain how your sister died. I'm sure you understand."

Lucas lifted his head abruptly and looked about to say something, but then clearly thought better of it. He dropped his head again and murmured, "Could I have a few minutes on my own, please?"

"Of course. We'll be just over here."

Gus signaled Stephanie to walk with him as Lucas sat down on a rock, his forearms resting on his knees, his head bent.

"Poor bugger," Gus said quietly. He moved his eyes to Stephanie's and gave her a look of such intensity she found she was holding her breath. "Good to see you, Steph."

He was asking her a question, and she knew it. All he needed from her was a smile; no words would be necessary. But this wasn't the time or the place. When she told him how she felt, she wanted to be able to feel his reaction, to respond to him.

"You too," she said, her face expressionless.

His eyes narrowed slightly as if not sure what to make of her response; then he glanced up at the boathouse.

"If she lived up there, why would she come down dressed and then swim in her underwear?" Gus asked.

"What, you mean she should have put a swimsuit on? Why? If I was here on my own, I wouldn't have bothered."

"No, I know that." She saw the shine in his eyes and looked away. She knew he would be remembering the many times they had driven to a secluded beach late at night to swim. And there had been no underwear involved. "There's no towel though. And the sea's bloody cold. It just seems an odd way of doing things."

"Each to their own, I suppose. Maybe it's what she always did."

Gus nodded and turned back towards the water.

"It sounds like the tide was on its way in when she went into the water. Which is why she was washed up here rather than down the coast."

"That makes sense. It's on its way out now again, but it only just turned."

They both looked at the sea, which seemed too calm and benevolent to have taken this young woman's life.

"I'm sure Jarrett will want to stay here until his sister's body has been moved, and then we'll have to see if Stuart wants me involved or not. I gather you're going to hear today if you've been accepted as a detective?"

Stephanie was annoyed, but not surprised, that everyone seemed to be aware of this.

"We'll just have to see," she said without enthusiasm.

"Typical Steph," Gus said, keeping his back to Lucas so he couldn't see his smile. "Never show your excitement or fear to the world." He tilted his head towards the body, which was still being examined. "What's your gut telling you about this?"

She knew what he was asking. It could have been nothing more than an unfortunate accident—a significant percentage of people who drown are good swimmers, and there had been a party the night before. Maybe Alex had had a lot to drink.

Tragic as that was, it wasn't the only option they had to consider though. They couldn't rule out anything, even murder.

CHAPTER 21

Finally they were ready to remove the body. Stuart and Gus were keen to take a look around Alex's apartment but had agreed to wait while Lucas accompanied his sister up the steep path to the house. Stephanie said she would go with him.

"He needs to tell his wife-to-be what's happening, and I guess there are some decisions to be made," Stephanie said, imagining for a moment the horror of the next few hours before the grieving could begin.

The team traipsing up the path made a sorry sight, with Alex now shrouded in a black body bag. Molly had said the post-mortem would be conducted later that day, Stuart in attendance. That was one task that Stephanie didn't envy.

The group who had gathered at the top of the path earlier were still there—three men, the woman with the blond hair who had been asked to keep people away, and a tall, striking woman with long dark hair. Sitting on a bench a short distance from the group was another woman, who looked to be of Asian origin. Her eyes were closed as if she was deep in thought. There was no sign of the bride.

They all stood back, lowering their heads in respect as the procession passed. The dark-haired woman reached out as Lucas passed, as if she believed her touch would convey sympathy, but her hand fell short. Birds were singing inappropriately in the trees, and there was no doubt it would have been a perfect day for a wedding.

Stephanie took a few steps past the group, then stopped and waited while the body was transferred to the vehicle. As the doors were gently closed, Lucas dropped his head and stood silently as his sister was driven away. Stephanie heard a smothered groan behind her, and a woman's voice spoke softly.

"Matt, I'm so sorry, darling. I know you were fond of her."

"You don't, Jemma. You don't know anything at all."

The voice was flat, at odds with the groan, and she heard footsteps as the man whom she understood to be a doctor pushed past. She turned her head towards the group, and it seemed as if the blond woman was about to follow her husband, but the man with the long hair and the striped shorts—Andrew, if she remembered correctly—spoke gently.

"I'd give him a moment, Jemma, if I were you."

The woman's eyebrows drew together, clearly perplexed by her husband's grief, and the other man moved to her side.

"We all felt bad for Alex, but Matt more than anyone. He was the closest to her, and he tried to help her, you know, all those years ago. But she wouldn't let him."

"Jemma, is it?" Stephanie asked.

The woman nodded. "Jemima Hudson, but everyone calls me Jemma. I suppose you're going to want to talk to me about what I saw, aren't you?"

"We are, yes. DI Wilcox and DI Brodie are down at the beach right now, but one of them will definitely want to have a word with you, to ask you about this morning." She looked at the other guests. "In fact, we'll probably want a word with all of you. So if you could please stay close by for the next few hours, that would be great."

"We're not going anywhere, unless Lucas and Nina ask us to leave. And who could blame them?" Andrew said.

Stephanie turned towards a huge open-sided gazebo where a team was still working on the wedding preparations, placing tall vases tumbling with vibrant roses in every shade from crimson to yellow in the center of each of a dozen or more circular tables. A couple of the staff cast puzzled glances at each other as if they didn't know whether or not to carry on. It seemed no one had yet made a decision.

The black van carrying Alex finally disappeared from view, and Stephanie waited until Lucas walked back towards her. Ignoring his friends, he headed towards the path, back down to his sister's home.

A man with dark blond hair wearing a loud Hawaiian shirt spoke. "Lucas, is there anything we can do, mate?"

Lucas held up his right hand, palm flat as if warding off any contact, and continued past them, his eyes moving neither right nor left as he set off towards the beach.

Stephanie glanced once more at each of the members of the group before she followed.

Gus and Stuart were talking to the crime-scene manager, but when they saw Lucas and Stephanie emerge from the path, they walked towards them.

"Are you sure you want to come in with us, Mr. Jarrett?" Stuart asked.

"Of course," he answered without breaking his stride. With slumped shoulders, he picked his way over the larger pebbles towards the boathouse and pushed the door. It wasn't locked.

The police officers snapped on disposable gloves. They weren't expecting this to be a crime scene, but they couldn't afford to take any chances.

Following Lucas into his sister's apartment, Stephanie looked around. It was neat, tidy, and compact. Decorated in pale blues and greens with bleached wooden floorboards, it felt restful. She pointed to a mobile phone on a small white-painted desk.

"Your sister's?"

Lucas nodded. "Yes. She barely used it though."

"And no one's been in here since you found her?" Stuart asked. "No."

"I'm sorry to have to keep asking you questions, Mr. Jarrett, but apart from the housekeeper who saw your sister in the water, has anyone else been close to her this morning?"

"Jemma came when she heard me shout, but I didn't let her get near Alex. I didn't want anyone to see her that way. She deserves some privacy."

"Did Jemma know your sister well?"

"Barely at all. I only met Jemma myself a day or so ago. She's here with her husband—one of my ushers. I've known him since I was a teenager."

Gus moved across the room to look out at the bay. The patio door was open and Stephanie had noticed steps down from the balcony to the beach. Maybe that was the way Alex had gone out each night.

Next to the telephone on the desk was a laptop, and Stephanie could see that the lid wasn't fully closed. It couldn't have shut down properly, because a weird green glow was seeping out from the edges.

"Sir," she said, indicating the laptop to Stuart.

"May I?" he asked Lucas, indicating the lid.

"Of course."

As the lid was raised, the screen became brighter, displaying the first frame of a video, the Play arrow in the center. It had clearly been shot at night because lamps illuminated the space, casting the face on the screen in deep shadow and revealing nothing other than a hint of white teeth, glints of light reflecting from tear-filled eyes and from wet patches on her cheeks. Stephanie knew who this was. The long dark hair that had been spread like a wreath around the head of the girl on the beach was hanging limply on either side of her shrouded face.

She turned to Lucas, whose gaze was locked on the screen, his face gaunt.

"Alex?" Stephanie asked.

He nodded.

"You don't have to watch this, Mr. Jarrett," Stuart said.

This had to be a message, and it suggested only one thing to Stephanie. She could sense Lucas's fear, but he shook his head.

"I'm staying."

Stephanie reached forward with a gloved hand to click the Play icon.

There was a sniff and a cough, as if Alex needed to clear her throat before she began to speak. She lifted a hand to wipe away her tears.

"Hello, Lucas. I'm sorry you're going to find this message on the morning of your wedding when you come down as you always do to check that I'm okay. But the truth is, I'm not. Okay, I mean."

The voice was breaking, the young woman clearly trying to control herself and find the right words.

"I'm struggling, you see—far more than I ever wanted you to know. I've tried and tried, but this week—with everyone here—it's brought the past back to me in ways I could never have imagined." Her voice rose as if she was struggling to get the words out without screaming. She took a few deep breaths, blowing out through her mouth. "I don't think I can handle it. The memories are flooding back, and they're unbearable. I've fought so hard to beat the depression that's haunted me for all these years, because God knows I don't want to go back into that dark dungeon of despair, but I can feel myself falling."

She lifted a hand as if to push back her hair, and then thought better of it and reached for a tissue to blow her nose. Something glimmered in the light falling over her shoulder, and Stephanie was sure it was a bracelet. She remembered noticing it on Alex's wrist as her body lay in the shallow water.

She continued after a brief pause.

"For so long you've put me first. I often find you looking at me to make sure I'm okay when you should be looking at Nina. She'll soon be your wife, and she deserves better."

There was a loud sob, almost a wail, and she dropped her head, the words difficult to hear, spoken quickly as if she couldn't bear what she was saying.

"You're amazing, but I can't be here any longer, not even for your wedding. So please, please apologize to Nina. She has tried to be so kind to me, and I know I've not made it easy. I find it hard to trust, you see. Right now I feel that all I want to do is escape the world—to swim out into the sea and never return; to swim and swim until my energy has gone, and then slowly let the water take me. I know I can't face tomorrow, but my heart will be with you, even though I won't be. I'm so sorry, Lucas."

The screen went blank.

Stephanie heard the sound of running feet. Lucas had gone.

CHAPTER 22

The detectives didn't follow Lucas—there was no point and he deserved some time alone. Stephanie still had to take his statement to make sure they had all the facts, including the confirmation of the deceased's identity, but for now they could check over the apartment while Lucas was out of the way.

She had been given the job of looking through the bedroom, and after five minutes Gus popped his head round the door. "Anything?"

"No. Nothing stands out. That message was tragic, Gus. I wonder how she got to be like that?"

"I don't know, but I've had a look on her phone, which isn't locked, and it tells a sad tale for someone so young." Gus lifted one hand and rubbed the back of his neck, a habit he had when he was stressed. Stephanie longed to walk across to him and put her own hand there. "There are a few shots from the veranda here when the sea's rough, and a couple of a seal swimming out in the bay, but no pictures of people, friends, family—just one or two of Lucas, and not a single one of herself."

"Did you look at her social-media accounts?" Stephanie asked.

"She doesn't appear to have any. It looks like this is going to be Stuart's case now—or yours, maybe, after today. So I'm going to leave you to it. He'll get the techs to check further, but I couldn't find anything in her Internet history that gives a clue as to who she is or what mattered to her."

As they left the apartment Gus touched her arm. "You've gone very quiet. Are you okay?"

Stephanie didn't turn towards him. She looked instead at the sea, watching the waves—calm as they caressed the shore.

"I'm fine. Just thinking about the sadness of a life lost, that's all."

"I know. I hate suicides. Give me a good murder any day, because it gives me something to get angry about—something to fight for. This just makes me feel helpless."

It was at moments like this that Stephanie wondered why she had ever let this man go, and she turned to give him a somber smile.

"I'd better get back up to the house," she said. "See what Jason's up to."

He fixed his eyes on her face. "Before you go, can I come round to see you tonight? I thought maybe we could celebrate your move to CID."

Stephanie knew he wanted more than that. He wanted to know if she was prepared to give their relationship another go.

"We could very well be commiserating—there's no guarantee I'll get it."

Gus laughed. "You're priceless. I know you're trying to convince yourself you're not going to get it so you can say 'Told you so' if it's true. Have some faith in yourself—believe in the best."

"And if the worst happens?"

Stephanie knew they were no longer talking about the job.

"To travel hopefully is a better thing than to arrive. I can't remember who said it, but can't we travel hopefully together, Steph?"

She knew who had said it, but this wasn't the moment to be smart. And Gus was right.

"If you're coming, you'd better bring wine."

The light in Gus's eyes told her everything she wanted to know.

CHAPTER 23

Nina paced the bedroom, trying to dislodge the huge ball of anguish in her chest that was threatening to choke her.

What had happened? Why was Alex dead?

She lifted both hands and pushed them hard against the sides of her head as she marched back and forth, as if to stop her thoughts from colliding, crashing into each other.

She had tried her hardest with Alex, she really had. But the girl had barriers that she'd been unable to break down. She had wanted to get close to her, but when Lucas was away on one of his many trips for the foundation, Alex had rarely shown her face at the house.

"Give her time," Lucas had said. "She's a private person—she's scared of trusting people. But she likes you, Nina. She thinks you're perfect for me."

Lucas had smiled as he said it, but Nina had never been able to rid herself of the belief that Alex thought she was in the way and wanted her brother all to herself.

She had never been told the full story of what had happened when Alex was fourteen. All she knew was that she had been abducted. Nina couldn't imagine how traumatic that must have been. But since that day Lucas had considered Alex his responsibility.

And now this. Alex was dead. Today, of all days.

Nina let out a deep growl of pain. She shouldn't even be *thinking* about the fact that this was her wedding day. Lucas was distraught, but why wouldn't he let her help him, comfort him?

Nina felt tears trickling down her cheeks, dripping off her chin, and with an angry motion she brushed them away with the back of her hand.

Obviously the wedding had to be canceled. There was no other choice, but she had so looked forward to seeing the love and pride in her husband's eyes at all she had achieved, and a sob caught in her throat. It had been a monumental task to organize something so perfect, so exquisite, and she had done it for him. For them both.

She could only imagine how Lucas must be feeling, especially after his argument with Alex the night before. In Nina's head, she could still hear her voice, her hysteria, her fear. And all she could see was Lucas shaking his sister, marching her off down the path, telling her to be quiet. She had never heard him raise his voice to her before.

Nina had intended to ask Lucas what the argument had been about, but he would be so distressed by the fact that she had died right after they had quarreled. So she vowed then that he must never know what she had seen and heard. If he wanted to tell her, she would help him to see that one argument didn't negate all the years of love that he had given his sister.

Finally, she heard footsteps trudging slowly up the stairs. She turned towards the door, watching, waiting.

Lucas's face was white, his eyes red-rimmed. She wanted to go to him, but he was holding himself rigid and she sensed he didn't want to be touched.

She said nothing, waiting for him.

"I've done something, Nina. Something unforgivable."

Lucas dropped to his knees, lifted his hands to cover his face, and wept.

PART TWO

CHAPTER 24

One Year Later

My heart is thudding as I drive along the lanes from the village towards Lucas's house praying I don't meet anything coming the other way. A vision of the same journey exactly one year ago springs unwanted into my mind. We'd been so excited, and I'd been looking forward to meeting Matt's friends, although I was slightly daunted by Lucas's wealth. The one thing I was certain of, though, was our love for each other. And that made us invincible.

Now Matt and I are back, but this time everything is so different. The couple who used to laugh together, to share each other's hopes and dreams, are a distant memory. I'm driving because Matt only just missed a cyclist he seemed not to have noticed, and now he's engrossed in something apparently fascinating on his phone. He clearly took last year's jibes about his lack of technical expertise to heart and now has a top-of-the-range iPhone that's rarely out of his hand. I'm sure he's not paying attention to what's on the screen though. It's a ruse to stop me from talking to him, and it's worked. We haven't spoken more than two words since leaving home.

I feel compelled to break the silence.

"Matt, do you think just for a moment you could put your phone down and talk to me? You know I'm uncomfortable about coming back here after what happened last time. And why do you think Lucas has chosen this week—this date specifically—for a reunion? It's an odd thing to do."

"He said he wants to celebrate his wedding anniversary. What's weird about that?" Matt says, still fiddling with his phone as he talks. The only thing I can imagine he's doing is adding up how many charging hours he's losing by being here instead of working. He never used to do that. It's something else that's changed—this obsession with money and working every hour that God sends. But I can feel the tension in his body, and I know he's not happy to be here either.

"What's weird is that there never *was* a wedding. So if they're married now, the anniversary would be on a different date altogether. Look, can I just pull over like we did last time, so we can talk?"

Matt glances at me with a look that suggests it's a ridiculous idea. "We'll be late."

I sigh with frustration. Matt was never a great talker, but now he has withdrawn almost completely into himself and his barriers seem impenetrable.

For a while I thought the change was due to grief at Alex's death. I hadn't realized how fond he had been of her until Andrew told me last year. The two of us were sitting at the gates of Polskirrin, tasked with turning away the army of guests due to arrive for what should have been the wedding of the year.

"Matt was always kind to Alex," he said. "Much kinder than either me or Nick, and I think she had a bit of a crush on him when she was in her early teens."

I've tried to understand, to give him time, but instead of gradually returning to the old Matt, each day he grows quieter, more remote. Now the silences are charged with an emotion I don't understand. Sometimes I find him looking at me, his eyes sad. But when my eyes meet his, he looks away and takes another sip of the whiskey he has taken to drinking.

I have always felt that Polskirrin was in some way the catalyst for all that is now wrong with my marriage, although I'm not ready to admit defeat, not quite yet. Surely there's something to resurrect? Until today I almost believed that to be true, but as we approach Polskirrin, the stark contrast between then and now hits me full on. I have to accept that Matt has fallen out of love with me, and I don't know if it's possible to rekindle a fire that has died.

My eyes burn at the thought, and I blink away hot tears, forcing my mind away from my husband and whatever ails him—or maybe us.

I want to say something about Alex, about how desperately sad it is that she killed herself on the eve of her brother's wedding—something I'm still struggling to understand. From what little I've read about the mind of suicide victims, I imagine that to Alex it seemed like the only way to eliminate the pain and torment that life appeared to offer her.

It will be strange to be at Polskirrin without her, even though we only saw her at dinner and caught brief glimpses of her during the day. The specter of her was always with us though, as if everyone was thinking about her but no one wanted to mention her name. In a strange way, she was more present than if she had been sitting in the sunshine with us, chatting, an active part of the group. I'm ashamed to say I have felt angry with her sometimes, because it feels that as she swam out to sea, she took my marriage with her.

There is little chance to say anything more as Polskirrin comes into view. This time we don't stop to stare. We drive in silence towards the gates, and when I risk a sideways glance, Matt's eyes are narrowed as if he is steeling himself for what's ahead. When he sees me looking at him, his gaze falls back to his phone.

It's not until we reach the entrance that I recall the full scale of Lucas's home. Not just the house, but the outbuildings, the gardens. I pull the car up at the double gates that had opened as if by magic when we arrived last time, welcoming us. Today they are closed, as if forbidding us to enter. I feel an almost irresistible urge to turn round and go home, certain that once we drive through and the gates close behind us, we will be trapped.

My eyes go to the wrought-iron fence that surrounds the grounds. Six feet high and decorative, it feels like a prison perimeter, its sharp finials waiting to rip the flesh of anyone who tries to climb over.

I lower my window to press the buzzer. I've stopped too far away though, so I have to open the door and get out. The heat is oppressive, as hot as it was last year, but this time it seems heavier.

There is no welcome greeting over the intercom—just a click and a buzz as the gates slowly glide open. Such is my state of mind that even this seems sinister—two inanimate objects moving without apparent human intervention.

"Get a grip," I mumble under my breath as I get back in the car.

"What?" Matt says rudely.

"Nothing." We approach the house. "Look, there's Lucas."

The tall figure of Lucas Jarrett steps out of the front door. I park, and he walks towards the car. Finally, Matt pushes his phone back into the pocket of his chinos.

As I open the car door the heat hits me again.

"It's roasting out there," I say to Matt.

"You'll just have to go for a swim to cool off."

I swivel round to stare at him, but he is climbing out of the car, raising an arm to Lucas. I was about to say that among all of my concerns about coming back here, I had never given a thought to the idea of swimming in the exact spot where Alex died. I'm not sure I'll be able to do that. But he's gone.

As Matt strides across the gravel to shake Lucas's hand and clasp him on the shoulder, I step out of the car. Hiding behind a large pair of sunglasses, I stand for a moment in the shade of a tree, giving my husband and his friend a moment before I finally make my way to where Lucas is waiting.

"Jemma." He leans towards me for the obligatory kiss on each cheek. "You're looking well."

It's good of Lucas to say so, but I know it isn't true. I've gained weight, had my hair cut into a style that doesn't suit me, and I have dark circles under my eyes, currently hidden by the sunglasses.

It's only been three months since I saw him. I'd been asked to go to Alex's inquest because, other than Lucas and the housekeeper, I was the only one to see her body before the police arrived. Despite the fact that it wasn't obligatory for anyone else to attend, I was surprised Nina wasn't there. Lucas told me he'd asked her not to come because it was too devastating; neither Nina nor anyone else should have to sit through it if they didn't need to.

Matt had taken Lucas at his word, and even though I would have appreciated his company and was sure Lucas would have too, he refused to come, citing pressure of work.

Fortunately, not everyone had felt the same, and I was pleased when Andrew slipped into the seat beside me.

"I thought I'd lend a bit of moral support," he'd whispered, leaning across me to give Lucas's arm a squeeze. But Lucas had no more than glanced his way, and who could blame him? What a dreadful day it must have been for him. He'd appeared tightly wound, his movements jerky, those pale amber eyes burning fiercely, his hands clamped into fists.

The coroner had outlined the facts, including Alex's history of depression and the content of the video, and I could only imagine Lucas's pain as the verdict of suicide was given.

Today he seems different again, and nothing like the affable Lucas I met a year ago. There is a hard glitter to his eyes, and as he smiles, his jaw is set. There's an intensity to him that I am certain wasn't there before, but it's hardly surprising.

"How have you been, Lucas?" I ask with genuine concern.

"I'm fine. I don't think I ever thanked you properly for coming to the inquest, Jemma. It was a long way for you to travel, and I barely spoke to you. I'm sorry about that. Now, come on in out of the sun. Nina's looking forward to seeing you both. Let me take one of your cases."

The men walk ahead, each carrying a bag, Matt's free hand reaching up to rest on Lucas's shoulder. Their voices become a low hum as they make their way up the three steps to the open front door.

I stop and look around. Now that the men are inside it is quiet, with only the sounds of the countryside breaking through the silence—birdsong, a distant tractor and the murmur of the sea. It is a slice of heaven, and I wish with all my heart that it hadn't also been the scene of such a tragedy.

CHAPTER 25

Nina sat on the bed, her head bowed. She hadn't wanted Lucas to invite everyone here again, but he'd brushed her objections aside. "It's something I have to do, Nina. And I need you to help me."

She had done as he'd asked. She rarely refused him anything if it was within her power to give. She wanted so much for him to be happy, for the tension in his body to ease, but as the weeks passed, the strain around his eyes intensified and there was a tautness to him that scared her. It felt as if at the least thing he might snap in two, and she did what she could to soothe him.

If the days were bad, the nights were worse. Lucas tossed and turned, sometimes moaning in his sleep, and while she understood his sorrow, this felt like so much more. Nina hated herself for it, but she couldn't help wondering if what he was feeling was guilt.

She often thought back to that morning when Alex's body had been found. She remembered the look of dismay on her husband's face when he'd told her he had done something unforgivable, and although she'd asked him what he meant, he had brushed the question aside, saying he was simply out of his mind with grief.

She had struggled to believe him, but there was nothing she could do except watch as he drove himself with work, traveling far more often than before. And when he was at home he took himself off, day after day, walking the coastal path or sitting down on the beach, alone.

She was certain that Lucas blamed himself and had resolved that he must never know she'd seen him arguing with Alex just before she killed herself. If that meant she had to lie to him, so be it.

"That night, Nina, the night Alex died. Where were you?" Lucas had asked on the day their guests left and they were finally alone.

"You know where I was. I told you I wanted an early night to be ready for the next day, so after I'd finished clearing up, I went to bed."

Lucas had stared at her for longer than she was comfortable with, then turned and walked out of the room. He had never mentioned it since.

Maybe that had been her chance. If she'd told him what she had seen, she could have comforted him, helped him to understand that he mustn't blame himself. But she had missed her opportunity.

Nina sighed and stood up. Everyone would be arriving, settling into their rooms. She wondered what they were thinking, what they might be expecting the next few days to bring.

Whatever their expectations, she knew they would be wrong.

CHAPTER 26

There is no boy to carry our bags upstairs this time, and Lucas hefts the larger of the two through the house and up the outside staircase—the easiest route, apparently. He leaves us at the French windows and says he'll see us downstairs on the terrace when we're ready.

"Cocktails at six," he says.

I remember being thrilled with this room last year, the beautiful antique furniture, the doors leading on to our very own balcony, and the sweet smell of apricots. They are there again—the apricots—in exactly the same spot, with an identical fragrance. I feel I have been transported back in time.

I wish we hadn't been given the same room. The sense of familiarity only serves to highlight the difference between then and now. Matt sits on the bed and pulls off his shoes, suddenly talkative.

"I'm glad they've given us this room again; it's the best one in the house, apart from Lucas and Nina's, you know. Anyway, Lucas says we're the first to arrive, so I'm going for a swim before the others get here. Andrew and Chandra should be arriving in about an hour. I wonder if she's still as batty?"

I like Chandra. She means no one any harm, as far as I can tell. Then I remember Andrew, how comfortable I had felt with him and how I had enjoyed the time I spent with him the evening after the inquest. I had booked into a hotel and we had eaten dinner together. I had only just prevented myself from sharing my worries about Matt and my marriage with him. But it was as if he sensed my unhappiness because afterwards, as I walked with him from the hotel to his car, he gave me a hug.

"Take care of yourself, Jemma. You were brilliant today, and I know how difficult it must have been."

I clung to him for a moment or two longer than I should have, feeling the warmth from his broad chest and allowing the tension to seep from my body.

I push the memory from my mind. "In what way is Chandra batty?" I ask Matt, thinking he was never this uncharitable in the past.

"Come on, Jemma. She's a bit intense, isn't she? I don't know what Andrew's doing. Well, that's not quite true—I know exactly what he's doing. But she's not his type at all."

Matt looks at me with a frown. He's expecting me to say something in Andrew's or Chandra's defense, but I can't see the point. Matt seems at odds with the world right now. After a moment, he stands up to unfasten his trousers.

"Whatever. Do you know where my shorts are? I'll unpack properly later."

I open the suitcase and rummage around until I find Matt's swimming shorts, wondering if I'm the only one who has an issue with going in the sea at the cove.

Matt is now standing naked in the middle of the room, and I feel a pang for all that is lost. I wonder what would happen if I were to reach out to him, but I'm too scared to try. We rarely make love now, and when we do there's a new intensity to it, but none of the intimacy. It leaves me aching with sadness and regret.

Walking into the bathroom, I decide to relax in a cool bath. I will try to let my mind drift, to calm myself before I face the others. I empty half a bottle of foaming gel into the water, and as the perfume fills the room, my eyes flood with tears. I sink low under the bubbles and surrender to the sobs that are never far below the surface.

Matt came back from his swim ages ago, but I pretended to be asleep. With little regard for me, he banged about the room, unpacking his suitcase, opening and closing drawers, and selecting something appropriate to wear for the evening. I sometimes think he's trying to make me hate him.

As soon as he goes, I creep out onto our balcony to see if I can catch a glimpse of the others. I can see the terrace, but a wide gray cantilevered sun umbrella is hiding the area where people are sitting.

It sounds as if the men have assembled ahead of the six o'clock deadline, and I can hear Lucas's deep voice telling some story or other. Matt laughs, but the pitch is wrong. He's uncomfortable being here, and I can sense it in his every action.

I leave it another twenty minutes before getting ready, selecting a peach-colored linen dress and a thin silver necklace. Finally, it's time to go down—I can't put it off any longer. Once again, I step onto the balcony. I pause at the sight of another figure coming out of a door at the back of the house carrying a couple of bottles. He is wearing shorts and a Hawaiian shirt, and even from above I recognize the short, spiky hair of Nick Wallace. Nick and Lucas are like a photograph and its negative—Lucas so dark, with his designer stubble and pale amber eyes with their new intense stare, Nick clean-shaven, with fair hair and dark blue eyes. He never seems to sit still.

I hear Andrew call out a friendly greeting and realize Isabel must have joined the men. I didn't warm to her last year, although I don't know if that's just because she was so familiar with Matt and gave him meaningful glances that I didn't understand, or because I saw them arguing.

I take a deep breath and make my way downstairs. It seems I have timed my entrance well, because as I arrive Nina and the housekeeper—a different one, I notice—come out from the kitchen, each bearing a tray of delicious-looking canapés.

As the artfully arranged morsels are placed on the table, Andrew looks up.

"Jemma!" he says, jumping up from his chair and striding round the table to give me a kiss. I feel myself blushing and sit down, fiddling with my napkin.

Nick raises his hand in greeting. "Excuse me if I don't get up, Jemma. I started earlier and I'm already two martinis down, so until I've had some of these small delights"—he lifts a *crostino* strewn with slivers of roasted pepper—"I'm staying put. But it's good to see you, and I'll save my kisses for later." He puts the whole piece of toasted bread into his mouth and winks.

"Let me get you a drink," Lucas says.

I smile my thanks.

When I finally glance at my husband, he isn't looking at me; he's looking at Isabel, and it's a look that seems to burn its way across the space between them.

I turn my head away.

CHAPTER 27

The next couple of hours before dinner are uncomfortable. Everyone appears to be in good spirits, but there is a sense of superficiality to it all, as if being jolly is a prerequisite of the event. The laughter seems forced, the bodies taut. And nobody—not one person—has mentioned Alex. I feel that barrier needs to be broken so we can all acknowledge that something truly dreadful happened here. Maybe then we could relax.

I think about Alex, how she covered her body with loose clothes, her dark hair hiding her face, and her silence. I'll never forget how she looked on the beach, her arms flung wide, her body so white and that same dark hair spread around her head like a halo on the pebbles, Lucas kneeling by her side. It's a memory I want to drive from my mind.

I am brought back to the present by Lucas tapping his glass with a knife.

"I'd like to say a few words." He smiles as he looks around the assembled group, but his eyes are flint hard. "I appreciate you all coming here again. It's been a difficult year. I know you all understand why, but you've been too polite to mention the tragedy that occurred last time you were here. I also realize you don't know why I've chosen to invite you all back on this day. But what I haven't told you is that Nina and I are married, and this really is our anniversary."

There are a few murmurs around the table, as if people think it important to acknowledge what Lucas has said without knowing what might be an appropriate response. I glance at Nina, whose smile is at odds with the frown lines between her brows.

"We have no license for weddings here, so we were married at the register office the day before the planned big event. That means tomorrow won't only be the anniversary of Alex's death but a chance to celebrate the first year of our marriage, rather than tarnish the whole day with unhappiness, which seems unfair to Nina."

I remember seeing Lucas and Nina leaving the house that morning, and realize that's where they must have been going. Everyone raises their glasses in silent acknowledgment of Lucas's words, uncertain whether we should be congratulating them or not, but I am relieved that the elephant in the room has now at least been acknowledged.

Out of the corner of my eye, I see Nick casting a worried glance at Isabel, who is smiling, teeth showing, but her eyes are flat, lifeless.

Lucas continues: "And to make sure that tomorrow evening remains a celebration rather than a wake, I've arranged a party game. I'm not going to tell you any more yet—I'll give you all the details at lunch. You'll each have a role to play, and Nina has prepared costumes for everyone."

He glances towards his wife, who nods and starts to speak, her words lacking inflection as if she's practiced what she must say. "I think all your costumes should fit, although, Jemma, you might need a sneak preview of yours because I think we may have to alter it slightly. For the rest of you, the costumes will really help you get into character, so please, we hope you will all join in and make it a fun evening."

I look down at the table knowing my face will be flushed with embarrassment. Nina must have based the size of my outfit on how I looked a year ago, and now it isn't going to fit.

"Don't worry, Jemma. I think it might be a little too long, that's all."

I give Nina a smile of thanks. I don't know her well, but she seems to have a kind heart.

It seems that is all we're going to learn for now, and Lucas leans back in his chair as everyone feigns excitement at the idea of a party game. Matt is still trying to be jolly, but he's laughing too long, too loud, at Nick's stories and grinning as if he's trying to convince us that he's all fun and bonhomie.

I switch off, wondering how tomorrow will be and whether I'll be able to pretend to be cheerful for the sake of the anniversary when I know that all I'll feel is the spirit of Alex, watching us.

"Jemma, are you with us?"

Matt is speaking to me, smiling, but I recognize the edge in his voice. I glance around and realize that everyone is standing up and making their way across the terrace to where a circular table has been laid for dinner. I hear snatches of light-hearted conversation, but to my ears it sounds hollow, and I wonder what kind of game Lucas is going to have us playing that will drive out the phantom of Alex.

I pick at the delicious food placed before me. It looks and smells wonderful, but I don't feel much like eating. My face aches with the effort of smiling, pretending that Matt and I are just the same people we were a year ago. I'm laughing in all the right places, I think—not because I'm listening to the conversation, but whenever there is a burst of merriment I join in.

There is one point when I refuse to laugh. I am picking at a plate of *pappardelle al tartufo* when Isabel leans across the table towards me with a smile.

"Not eating, Jemma? Don't tell me you're on a diet." She gives a light laugh.

I realized last year that Isabel is one of those women who thinks it amusing to make jokes at the expense of others. I've never learned the art of responding appropriately to bitchy remarks, but Andrew comes to my rescue.

"I certainly hope not. You look lovely tonight, Jemma."

I turn towards him and see him give Isabel a fierce stare. Her eyes dart from Andrew to me and back again, and the side of her mouth twists up in a parody of a smile. But she says nothing more and turns to talk to Lucas.

"Thank you," I say quietly.

"What for? It's true; I think you look great—and don't for God's sake try to emulate Isabel. She lives on her nerves—I guess that's because she never knows where the next buck is coming from."

"What do you mean?" I'd never asked what Isabel does for a living and she has never talked about it.

"She's a dealer, a trader—in just about anything. She buys things for next to nothing if she thinks she can sell them on at a profit, mainly online. Lots of people are doing it, but most have some integrity. Isabel is happy to fleece people if she thinks she can get away with it. The problem is, they never come back twice, and I have no idea what she's living on. Fresh air, it would seem. Or Nick's charity."

"Gosh, that must be intense though—taking a risk on what you buy."

"Making money is what drives her," Andrew said. "She's been a dealer of one sort or another for a long time, but Nick made her knock the dodgy stuff on the head a long time ago, or at least that's what he thinks. I'm not so sure. He's undoubtedly more worried about his own reputation than hers—the opinion of others matters a lot to Nick, and he's always been terrified that Lucas will find out."

"How do you know, if Lucas doesn't?"

Andrew laughs. "We live in different worlds, Jemma."

I'm sure he's right, but somehow knowing about Isabel's past makes me even more uncomfortable around her. Does Matt know?

As everyone finishes eating and the brandy is brought out, I escape to our room on the pretext that I'm tired after the journey. It's a feeble excuse after a few hours in a very comfortable car, but it isn't the journey that has worn me out. It's the edginess of those around the table that is making my head ache. Am I the only one who can feel it?

I'm not sleepy, so I step onto the balcony and look out into the dark night. I lean my elbows on the warm stone and listen. The late-night drinkers have moved to the terrace at the side of the house now, and I catch an occasional burst of laughter. I can hear the waves washing over the pebbles on the beach below, and in my mind I see Alex, stripped to her underwear, wading into the sea for her swim.

It feels so much like the eve of the wedding a year ago. There is no moon, and apart from the puddles of brightness surrounding the low-level lighting along the paths, the night is black. I remember standing here, wondering if Matt was ever going to come to bed. I couldn't help noticing the way he'd looked at Isabel, and it made me uncomfortable then. It's worse now. There is something about it, as if he is mesmerized by her long mahogany hair and sharp blue eyes. But his expression holds no warmth.

As I drink in the atmosphere of the night, the lights on the path to the beach suddenly go out, leaving a black void in their wake, and a memory of that other night strikes me hard. I was standing on this very spot, wondering if I should go and look for Matt, but something stopped me—a fear of what I might find, perhaps.

I had assumed everyone except Matt had gone to bed, but there was a moment when I saw someone head down the path. Then the lights went out, just as they had a moment ago. What if it was Alex? What if she had been contemplating suicide, and if I'd just gone down to talk to her I might have been able to help? It's a ridiculous notion, of course. I didn't know she was so troubled, and what could I have done?

My thoughts are dragged back to the present as I hear a few quiet calls of goodnight. I go back into the bedroom and slip under the sheets. I don't know whether to pretend to be asleep or not as I wait to hear Matt's tread on the stairs.

A few moments later all is silent. But there is no sign of Matt.

CHAPTER 28

The stone steps from my bedroom feel warm under my bare feet, and I find myself trying to move silently. Is it because I want to remain undetected? I know this is a mistake, but I have to find out where Matt is. I can't imagine him sitting out here alone, so who is he with? I can't stop thinking about Isabel.

Clutching a pair of flip-flops in one hand, I tiptoe onto the terrace. I'm halfway across when I have the feeling I'm being watched. I stop and spin round, but I can't see anyone.

I creep along the edge of the paving towards the south terrace. The detritus of their drinking remains on the table—half-empty bottles, dirty glasses, the chairs in disarray.

But no Matt.

My heart is thumping as I turn and step onto the grass that borders the terrace. I never did find the time to properly explore the Japanese garden that I had seen Nina disappearing towards on the night Alex died. It's secluded down there—almost hidden from the lawn and terrace above—and surrounded by woodland. The perfect spot for someone to hide. Is that where Matt is?

I walk soundlessly towards the steps. I can hear nothing. No one is talking, but that doesn't mean no one is there.

Down here, away from the house, the only light is from the small solar-powered cubes illuminating the edge of the lawn where it falls sharply down to the woods and garden below, lining the path into the Japanese garden. I glance back at our balcony. I'm sure if Matt had returned he would have come out to look for me, but there is no silhouette against the light from the open window.

I stop when I reach the gravel-covered steps and slip my flip-flops on. I can hear the rubber of the soles as they slap against the bottoms of my feet, and it makes me wary. If Matt is here, he'll know I'm coming. Perhaps he won't be alone.

The path zigzags down through overhanging trees that intensify the blackness above me. I turn the final corner. There is nothing. Nobody.

It's a bigger area than I thought, with narrow paths winding between rocks and perfectly shaped shrubs, which I can just see in the low-level lighting. A pond is reached via a tiny humpbacked bridge over a narrow stream, and on the other side is a small pagoda. The night beyond this small oasis is impenetrable; away from the light pollution of towns and cities that I'm used to, it's startling to experience the true black of night, and if anyone is in the woods, I won't be able to see them.

I continue slowly down the path towards the pond. The only sound is the tinkling of water running over the stones in the stream. I lower myself onto a stone seat. I don't know what I'm doing here, what I was hoping or perhaps dreading to discover, but I take some deep breaths and try to relax.

There is no clear moment when I begin to feel afraid. It creeps up on me, and my body reacts before I acknowledge my fear. The short hairs on my arms stand on end, and I don't know why. Then I hear a sound—a rustling—as if someone is walking through the dry grass of the wood right behind me. It stops for a few seconds and then starts again—louder this time.

There's someone there, but the woods are shrouded in darkness.

I can't breathe. I don't know which way to turn, which direction the sound is coming from.

For a moment there is nothing, then the sound comes again, and I don't know whether to stand up and run or stay where I am. If I'm silent, perhaps whoever is there won't see me. I don't know why I'm afraid. Surely there's nobody here to be frightened of?

I want to run, but I don't know which way to go. I look towards the far end of the pond, but I can see nothing. I stand up, ready to dash back to the house, but then I see a single unsteady light coming down the steps towards me.

I hear a voice.

"Jemma! I thought I saw you heading down here. I found some wine that the lazy buggers left out on the table after dinner. Red okay? The white's a bit warm."

It's Andrew, and I breathe out slowly.

"That's fine. Thank you. Just what I need."

He switches off the light on his phone and puts the glasses on an ornamental stone table. He fills one and passes it to me, then sits down.

"Are you okay?" he says, giving me a worried look. He can probably feel my heart hammering from where he's sitting.

"I'm fine. I feel a bit exposed sitting here. Anyone could be watching."

Andrew laughs. "Why on earth would anybody be lurking around spying on you?"

I feel myself flush and focus on my glass. Andrew gets up and goes into the small pagoda, calling to me from the entrance.

"Let's decamp to this place. There's a comfy-looking sofa and a couple of storm candles. I'll light them so we can actually see each other."

I had liked Andrew when I first met him. He's relaxed and isn't in awe of Lucas, as the others appear to be. There's something reassuring about the strength of his body, and for a moment I imagine his arms holding me tight, as they had done that night after the inquest.

I take a large gulp of wine as he sits down next to me, just a flickering candle lighting the space.

"So what brought you down here at this time of night?"

I don't feel quite ready to answer that.

"I could ask you the same thing," I reply.

"Oh, I've got an excellent excuse," he says. "I came down to do a bit of thinking, away from the rest of them. I didn't want to have to listen to the bollocks they have a tendency to talk. Oh, sorry. Except Matt of course."

I smile. "Of course. Heaven forbid that Matt could be accused of talking bollocks."

Andrew is quiet. I can feel him watching me, so I switch my attention to the wine I'm swirling in my glass.

"Tell me to shut up if you want, but given what you said—or didn't say—when I last saw you, and based on Matt's rather distant behavior tonight, would I be right in thinking he's being a bit of an arse right now?" he asks, touching my hand gently to still it while he pours more wine.

I don't respond, still staring at the contents of my glass. He says nothing more, giving me space, so in the end I give in to the pressure of the silence.

"I'm not entirely sure *who* is being the arse, if I'm honest. I don't know if it's him or me. I just seem to irritate him, and I don't know why or how to put it right."

"Well, he doesn't know how lucky he is. You're beautiful, you know, and you seem to be the only one who doesn't realize it. If he does anything to hurt you, he's *definitely* an arse, although not quite on the same scale as Nick, of course. That goes without saying."

He grins at me and I laugh. It feels good to have someone else say the words.

"If that's what you say about your friends…" I say, raising my eyebrows.

"We don't have to think our friends are perfect to still enjoy their company. Thank God we're not all identical and permanently well behaved. How tedious would that be?" His smile drops. "And you must have noticed that we don't spend time together without Lucas?"

I nod. I had asked Matt about this, but he'd fobbed me off.

"You see, Jemma, in his youth Lucas liked to collect people—the poor in my case, and the needy in the case of the other two—three if you include Isabel. We all fell under his spell, and we couldn't have rejected each other because that would have meant rejecting Lucas. So we rubbed along."

We're quiet for a while, and then the words burst out of me, unbidden.

"Do you think Matt's having an affair with Isabel?"

Andrew reaches over and grasps my wrist gently. "Jemma, Isabel doesn't do relationships. She is, and always has been, a schemer. If she's playing with him, it's because either she, or possibly Nick, wants something from him. But she's honestly no long-term threat, and I am fairly certain Matt hasn't seen her since they were here last year."

"How can you possibly know that?"

"I can't, but I know them both, and Isabel would have let it slip by now, even if only to create chaos. So just take it from me."

"I'm not sure it matters anyway," I say, my voice low. "A year ago, the thought would have made me ache with unhappiness, but now it's just the idea of the mess that would inevitably follow."

I hear a slight rustle from the undergrowth and for a moment I think someone is there again, listening.

"Anyway, enough of me and Matt. Let's talk about you and Chandra. I think she's lovely."

Andrew lets go of my wrist and runs his fingers through his long wavy hair. The space on my skin where his fingers were feels their absence.

"She *is* lovely—you're right about that. She's kind and thought-ful, and I suspect she deserves better than me. We're not exactly an obvious match."

"That doesn't matter if you love each other. Are you having doubts about marrying her, if that's not too personal a question?"

"Given that I've just called your husband an arse at least twice, I think you have the right to ask." He smiles but then looks away and says nothing for a moment. "The truth is that I allowed myself to be drawn into something, and now I'm in too deep with no obvious way out."

He leans back and puts his hands behind his head, gazing at the roof of the pagoda.

"What do you mean?" I ask. "There's always a way out, you know."

"You'd think so, wouldn't you? But not without hurting someone—Chandra, in this case—and I can't bring myself to do that."

Andrew falls silent. I sip my wine and give him some time. Finally, he sits up and holds his arms out, palms upwards.

"Do you know what, can we forget I started this? Let's just say that I've done something I'm not proud of. Now, can we talk about something else? Preferably something that doesn't include bloody relationships."

I'm not going to push him. I can see he's uncomfortable, so I change the subject.

"Okay, tell me why you think Lucas has really invited us all here. It all seems very odd, and I don't know why we all agreed to come."

I feel his body relax now that we have moved on to a safer topic.

"Lucas has a habit of making people do what he wants. He has this innate self-belief, and it's almost mesmerizing. To refuse him anything somehow seems wildly inappropriate."

Andrew is sitting so close that I can feel the heat from his body burning through my thin linen top, and I don't want this evening to end. I know he's looking at me, waiting for me to turn my face towards his. I want to, but I mustn't. This isn't the way things must go, however much I long for someone to make me feel desirable.

To fill the lengthening silence, I raise a subject that I know will throw cold water on the heated atmosphere.

"Can we talk about Alex? Is that okay?"

He shakes his head sadly. "That poor kid. She had such a bad time of it."

"I don't know anything about her, and Matt won't say a word. Will you tell me what happened to her?"

"Only Lucas knows the full story. The rest of us mainly know what was in the papers. She was fourteen, but only just. Lucas was off traveling the world and had arrived in New Zealand in time for Christmas, so Blair had gone out to join him. Alex ran away from home and went to Blair's house. He had always been kind to her because she was Lucas's sister, and also I guess he knew what a nightmare her mother—his ex-wife—was. But when Alex got there, there was no one home. She was taken—abducted—and it was five days before her mother even thought to tell anyone. Alex was in a bad way when she was found. I know she was hospitalized, but no one has ever said what happened to her. The bright, sparky kid we all knew had gone."

That poor child. For a moment, I imagine the terror she must have felt. What a horrific experience.

"Did they ever catch the person who took her?"

"Sadly, no. In the end, the police assumed she was followed that night. No one knew she'd gone to Blair's house—she hadn't planned it or anything—but I wish I'd known how she was feeling last year."

"Me too. I remembered tonight as I looked down from our balcony that I'd seen someone at the top of the path down to the beach that night. I suppose it must have been Alex, but how she found her way I don't know because the lights went out moments after she stepped onto the path. I guess they must be on a timer."

"What time was that? Do you remember?" Andrew asked.

"Funnily enough, I do. I was wondering where Matt had got to, and I looked at my watch. It was twenty to eleven."

Andrew is silent.

"What is it?" I ask.

"Nothing really. It's just that when people set timers they usually go for the nearest hour, half hour, or possibly quarter of an hour. If you were setting a timer to switch off lights on a path, why would you choose something as arbitrary as twenty minutes to the hour?"

"I don't think anyone switched them off manually. There was no one anywhere near the control box. It's on the edge of the terrace, isn't it?"

"Yes, that's true. But it's not the only switch. There's another one. Lucas told me where to find it. He knows I sometimes get back late if I've taken the boat out."

I looked at him expectantly. "Where is it?"

"On the wall of the boathouse. Below Alex's apartment."

CHAPTER 29

I wake early, despite the late night. I didn't sleep well, my mind spinning with memories of the Japanese garden and thoughts about what Lucas has planned for today.

Matt's indifference to me was never more apparent than when I got back to our room. He was sitting up in bed reading.

"Where've you been?" he asked with a cursory glance over the top of his book.

"Just chatting."

He looked for a moment as if he was about to ask me who I'd been chatting to but shrugged as if he wasn't really that interested. Now he's sleeping, snoring gently, lying on his back. I turn my head to look at his face.

"Where have you gone, Matt?" I whisper quietly.

I pull the covers back, trying not to wake him, and make my way into the bathroom. I can't stop thinking about last night and how much I wanted to lean into Andrew and feel his arms around me. I'd felt that the slightest shift in my body towards his would have been enough, and neither of us would have been able to stop.

But that's not who I am. It would have been a mistake to take advantage of the moment. It would have distorted the truth.

Much as I wish we had never come back to Polskirrin, I've decided I need to make an effort for Lucas and Nina. It seems they're trying to make it a special occasion, and I need to play my part, strange as I find the whole idea. I quickly dress in shorts and a brightly patterned top and make my way downstairs.

The only other person on the terrace is Chandra, and I feel a pang of remorse. I have no right to be fantasizing about her husband-to-be. She welcomes me with a smile.

"Good morning, Jemma. Did you sleep well?"

I nod and reach for a croissant. "How about you?"

"I did when Andrew finally came to bed. I guess they were all up chatting for half the night."

I look at the table as if mesmerized by the array of food on display.

"What do you think this game is that Lucas wants us all to play tonight?" I ask, eager to change the subject.

"I've no idea. He's gone off in the car with Nina. He asked if we could all be here for lunch at one o'clock. He'll give us our parts then."

I look at Chandra and see she's frowning. "What's up, Chandra? Is something bothering you?"

"It seems strange to me that Lucas wants to play some sort of game this evening. Grief is a natural emotion and should be met with a positive attitude, but it's as if Lucas and Nina are trying to be jolly to cover their pain rather than dealing with it. People need to accept that to suffer is the nature of life."

I can't think of an appropriate answer, so I give her a warm smile.

"Well, I suppose we need to be ready for anything and at least make the effort to join in, if it's what they want. If you'll excuse me, I'm going to wander down to the Japanese garden, out of the sun. I'll see you later."

I don't know why I want to go back there, but maybe it's to recapture a little of the night before.

Relieved that no one else has had the same idea, I put my book down on a bench and wander to the edge of the wood, wondering where it ends. Given that it slopes steeply down, it must lead to the far end of the beach.

I glance to my right and notice something I haven't seen before. Deep in the wood, a hammock has been hung between two trees, and it seems the perfect place to spend the morning. I go back to pick up my book and walk across to the hammock, kicking my shoes off.

"*Ouch!*"

Something is digging into the sole of my foot and I reach down. It's an earring, the post standing upright. I pick it up, swing my legs up into the hammock, leaning forward to rub my foot and peer at the culprit.

It's a diamond set in silver or maybe platinum, and I try to think if anyone was wearing earrings like it the night before—Isabel, Nina, Chandra? But I can't remember, and it could have been here for weeks.

I think back to the night before and my concern that someone was in the woods watching, listening. Nothing had happened between Andrew and me, but then I remember what we were talking about, and I feel a shiver of unease.

I wasn't able to relax in the hammock. I tried but kept imagining what a person lurking in the woods might have heard about my marriage and the night Alex died, so in the end I gave up and took myself off into the pagoda to sit on a reclining chair.

I must have dozed off, and I wake with a start. I know I was dreaming—something happened that terrified me—but the more I try to capture the fragments of the dream, the faster they float away.

I push myself upright and rub my eyes. I need something to bring me back down to earth. Coffee.

As I head towards the house I hear the low hum of a car engine. I stop for a moment as a vague memory hits me. Was this the sound I thought I heard during the night on the eve of Lucas and Nina's wedding, or was it part of a dream?

The memory ebbs away as quickly as it came, and I smile at Lucas and Nina as they climb out of their car. Nina gives me a little wave.

"Jemma, have you got five minutes so we can decide what to do about your outfit for tonight?"

I walk towards them. "Of course. Do you mind if I make myself a cup of coffee first? Do you want one?"

Nina declines, and we walk together into the kitchen, where the new housekeeper—Adrianna—is preparing lunch. Another Italian woman, and once again I don't know how to speak to her.

"What happened to your other housekeeper, Nina? She was a jolly soul."

"Ivana? She left the same day as you. She didn't want to stay after what happened." Nina has her back to me and I can't see her face, but her shoulders tense. "Come on, let's take your coffee up with us."

I follow Nina upstairs into what appears to be a spare bedroom, where there is a huge wardrobe. Nina opens the door and rifles through some dress bags.

"Oh, by the way, Nina, I found an earring this morning." I fish in the pocket of my shorts. "Here."

Nina lifts her eyes to mine. "Where did you find it?"

"In the wood. I thought maybe it was yours. Shall I leave it with you?"

She stares at it for a long moment before she reaches out her hand. "Yes, thanks. I wondered where that had got to." She pulls open a drawer and drops the earring inside. "Now, let's sort out this dress for you."

Nina unzips one of the bags.

My breath catches in my throat. I stare, transfixed. *This can't be right*. Slowly I turn to look at Nina. She isn't looking at me; she's looking at the long, deep-pink, silk organza dress.

"It's just like the one I wore last time we were here," I whisper.

"Similar, yes. You looked so beautiful in it that Lucas thought it would be great to give you something a bit like it to wear tonight."

But it's not similar. It's not a bit like it. It's exactly the same—identical in every detail.

I can feel the tension in her body as she holds the dress towards me as if willing me to make light of the fact that the fabric, the color, and the cut of the dress are an exact match to the one I wore at their pre-wedding dinner.

Surely they can't want this? Won't it bring back memories of that night? Won't it make the evening unbearable for them?

I try to gauge Nina's expression, but if there's something hiding behind the bright smile, I don't know what it is. I clear my throat.

"Is it okay for me to wear this? It's beautiful, but I don't want to do anything that will remind you or Lucas of that night."

"Oh, don't worry about that," Nina says. "Just slip it on, and we'll see if anything needs to be altered."

Feeling slightly self-conscious, I peel off my shorts and top and pull the dress over my head. It's a bit tight.

"I don't think we should let it out," Nina says, standing back and looking at me through narrowed eyes. "It's flattering where it skims your hips. It's a little long though, so I'll take it up an inch. I'll ask Adrianna to put it in your room when it's done."

I feel dazed, but Nina has become brisk and business-like. She lays the dress on the bed and returns to the wardrobe, turning to talk to me over her shoulder.

"Do you want to take Matt's outfit with you?"

Matt isn't going to like being told what to wear, but as it's Lucas I've little doubt he will do as he's asked. Nina unzips one of the suit carriers and pulls out a hanger. I can feel her watching me, assessing my reaction.

I am speechless. The pale gray linen suit and the shirt take my breath away. On the eve of the wedding Matt wore a lilac shirt with a thin white stripe. The shirt that Nina is now showing me is the same in every detail, as is the suit.

Despite the heat in the room, I feel tiny icy prickles along my arms. What are Nina and Lucas playing at?

CHAPTER 30

With Matt's outfit in a suit bag over my arm, I make my way back to our room, my head spinning. Matt is on his way down the stairs in his swimming shorts, obviously on his way to the cove.

"Matt, can you come back to the bedroom for a moment, please?"

"I'm just about to go swimming. Will it keep?"

"I don't think so."

He gives a theatrical sigh, but at least he follows me.

"What's up?" he asks, leaning into the open door.

"Can you just come in and close the door?"

He tilts his head to one side as if he's going to question me again, but he must see something in my eyes because he does as I ask.

"What is it, Jemma?"

I unzip the bag and pull out the hanger. "This is your outfit for tonight."

Matt's eyebrows go up, and I think that maybe he understands my concern.

"Wow. That's very smart of Nina. It's exactly my sort of thing. Didn't I have a shirt like this at one time?"

He doesn't remember.

"You did, yes. It's the shirt you wore for their wedding eve celebration a year ago."

He gives me a wide smile. "Well, fancy Nina remembering that. How kind of her."

I can't believe my ears.

"It's not kind, Matt. It's bloody weird. The dress they've had made for me is a replica of the one I wore that night too, and I'm sure it's not just us two who've got identical outfits. I didn't see all the others, but when Nina was trying to find yours she opened a bag and I got a glimpse of a turquoise silk skirt just like the one Chandra wore."

Matt frowns. "So what are you thinking? I don't get what you're concerned about."

"Jesus, Matt! It's creepy." I sit down heavily on the bed. "What are we going to do? I don't want to wear it. I don't want to be reminded of that night or what followed, and I can't imagine why you would either. We'll all be there, looking the same, but there'll be one person missing—the phantom at the feast. I'm not doing it. I'm going to wear the white dress I brought for the occasion."

Matt looks horrified. "You can't do that! Lucas has asked us to go along with this, and so we will. Don't be difficult, Jemma. Just let him do whatever it is he's planning. Maybe it's his way of dealing with it."

I look at Matt's face and think about what Andrew said last night. People always do what Lucas asks. But maybe I'm not as deeply under his spell as my husband clearly is.

"Why should we do something we're not comfortable with? Why do we have to do what Lucas says? It feels all wrong to me."

Matt starts pacing up and down the room, ignoring my questions. In the end, he selects an unusual weapon in his armory: anger.

He bangs the flat of his hand on a chest of drawers. "Why do you have to make things so fucking difficult, Jemma? Why do you have to suggest it's something sinister? Not everyone's motives are suspicious, you know."

His anger has no impact on me but I'm not giving up.

"Why are we here at all, Matt? Surely we're not commemorating Alex's death with a party?"

Matt turns his back on me and storms out, leaving me with the distinct impression that his anger is fake—an act to cover something he doesn't want me to know.

CHAPTER 31

Whatever is going on, it seems I'm the only one who's concerned. As we congregate on the terrace for lunch, I look around at the smiling faces. Everyone seems more relaxed today, but maybe they don't know about the costumes yet.

Isabel laughs at something Matt says to Nick and slaps him playfully on the leg. His lips tighten momentarily at her touch, and I turn away.

I can feel Andrew watching me. I don't want him to see the confusion behind my eyes, so I stare blindly around as if taking in the scenery. Chandra is quiet, as she often is, and Nina seems tense. I wonder how things have been for them this year. Terrible, I imagine.

The air is hot and still today, with barely a breath of breeze. The glass on the table in front of me has been filled to the brim with cold white wine by Nick, who seems once again to have taken on the role of volunteer barman, and condensation is running down the outside. I take a large gulp as Lucas comes out of the house and approaches us, clutching a wooden box in his hands.

Everybody falls silent as he places it in the center of the table and sits down. He casts his eyes over each of his guests in turn, holding everyone's gaze for a couple of seconds before moving on. After a long pause, Lucas begins to speak.

"As I mentioned to you yesterday, I'm grateful that you all agreed to come, and to make tonight memorable I've prepared a party game." Lucas points to the wooden box, which looks a little like an old-fashioned cigarette box. "In here are a number of envelopes—one for each of you. Inside is a profile of the role you'll be playing tonight, but please don't open them yet—not until after lunch. When we've eaten, I'd like each of you to find a private place to read your character description. True to this type of game, each of you has been given a secret which may or may not be revealed during the evening, depending on how well you play the game. But to make the party a success you mustn't tell anyone—not even your partner—what that secret is."

As I watch Lucas's face, I don't like what I'm seeing. There's a hard edge to him, and although he's smiling, there's a bitter twist to his mouth.

"To avoid unnecessary confusion, you will each use your own name for your character. Let's stick to reality. Learn your parts well, bring your envelopes with you tonight—and let's make the evening a success."

Suddenly it seems I may not be the only one who's uncomfortable. Nick has omitted to fill Lucas's glass, and Isabel is staring blankly at a spot in the center of the table. I will Matt to look at me so I can tell what he's thinking, but he doesn't. He has a slightly inane grin on his face that tells me nothing. I need to see his eyes.

But no one questions Lucas.

He pulls the box towards him and opens it, taking out eight black envelopes, each with a name on the front, beautifully written in silver ink. He hands them out to the now silent table, placing one in front of himself and one in front of Nina. She reaches for hers, and I see her fingers tremble a little. How much does she know of her husband's plan?

Nina clears her throat. "As you know, I've prepared costumes for each of you. You'll find everything you need in your rooms before dinner." She looks at no one as she speaks.

I desperately want to open my envelope now, and I'm sure I'm not alone. I prop it against my water glass, but I can't take my eyes off it so I pick it up and stuff it into the pocket of my shorts, where it's hidden from view. Everyone starts to talk at once, as if compelled to cover the momentary hiatus, and there is a distinct sense of frenzy around the table, the laughter sharp, brittle.

Everyone seems to be trying to be jovial, the wariness of a few moments ago hidden under the pretense that this is perfectly normal. Only Chandra is quiet as she helps herself to some of the salad that Adrianna brought out to accompany her kimchi. When I lift my eyes to look around the table, I find Lucas is staring at me as if he can see right into my thoughts. I don't even attempt a smile and look straight back at him. After a few seconds, one corner of his mouth lifts, and he gives me an almost imperceptible nod, as if I have passed some test I hadn't been aware I was taking.

Lunch seems to take forever, and just when I think it's over, Adrianna appears again, this time with a dish of strawberry semifreddo. It's sitting in a puddle of raspberry coulis, which to me looks exactly like a pool of blood.

CHAPTER 32

By the time everyone has finished their coffee it's well into the afternoon, usually my favorite time of day on holiday, when I can put my feet up and laze under a sunshade with the gentle sounds of the countryside lulling me to sleep. Today I just want to get away from everyone.

Finally, our host pushes back his chair and stands up.

"I can see you're all looking suitably dozy and probably want to find yourself a bed, lounger, or hammock, so I won't detain you. Take your envelopes, and in the words of Shakespeare or Sherlock, 'The game's afoot.'"

Lucas raises his glass as if in a toast, and it's not entirely clear if he's expecting us to chant the phrase back to him. Nick tries his best, always eager to please, and both Matt and Andrew half-heartedly raise their glasses. Isabel gulps down the rest of her wine.

Matt doesn't seem inclined to budge from his chair, so I wander round to the front of the house, which is still in the shade. To the left of the drive, away from the main house, is a small cottage that I have never explored, and I notice the door is standing ajar. Lucas told us to open our envelopes in private, so, casting a quick glance over my shoulder, I hurry towards the building and step through the open door.

I stand still, hit by the silence of the single long room, open to the rafters. The walls are whitewashed stone, the windows small and high. No one can see in, and the only view is of the sky. The floor is flagged, and the furniture consists of nothing more than a few low tables bearing fat white candles in glass vases. A pile of yoga mats and blocks tells me how this room must be used, and a slight mustiness in the air suggests someone has recently burned a spicy candle.

I push the door closed behind me, then unroll a mat and lower myself to the ground, feeling the calmness of the room easing some of my stress. I know I'm putting off the moment when I have to open the envelope, and I have no idea why. It's just a character description, after all, and I'm secretly hoping that Lucas has assigned me the role of some eccentric old lady, although the dress suggests otherwise. In fact, I don't like to think what the dress suggests.

"Oh, get a grip, Jemma," I mutter to myself, pulling the envelope out of my pocket.

I slip my thumb under the flap and rip it open. Inside is a single sheet of paper, folded.

Do not share these details with anybody—including your partner—until this evening. At that point it's up to you how much you are prepared to disclose and how much to hide.

Character name
Jemma Hudson

Character description
Jemma is a 32-year-old speech therapist who enjoys her job.

She is married to Matt, her husband of three years.

The marriage is in crisis and Jemma doesn't understand why, although she doesn't want it to be over. At least, not yet. Maybe the game will help her understand what has gone wrong.

She is attracted to Andrew, who she met a year ago and again three months ago.

No one knows for certain how far this attraction has gone.

Perhaps the truth—or a version of it—will be revealed tonight.

Who will Matt believe? The man who rescued him from an overambitious father nearly twenty years ago, or the woman he has known for just over four years, from whom he has been distancing himself?

Despite his professional success, Matt is emotionally insecure.

Jemma knows he would consider her attraction to Andrew a betrayal and that regardless of the truth, whatever that is, he would struggle to trust her again.

But what about Matt's secrets? What is he hiding? Why has he changed so much in the past year, and why has his previously happy marriage to Jemma fallen apart?

Jemma's role in the game tonight is to find out what Matt has been keeping from her. This might be her only chance.

Play the game, Jemma. You may not like it, but I think you—
out of everybody—will understand it.
Until this evening.

I feel sick. What does Lucas think he's playing at? These are not random characters. We're playing ourselves—or at least I am.

I read it again. And again. I put the sheet of paper down on the mat between my crossed legs and wrap my arms around my waist.

What sort of a sadistic game is this?

He's right about Matt though. However much I might deny that I've been unfaithful, he would doubt me, especially with the way things have been between us.

My eyes fill with tears and I rock gently backwards and forwards as if to comfort myself. The sense of peace I felt when I came into this room has evaporated, and I want to curl up in a tight ball. What does he mean about Matt's secrets? Lucas seems to know so much more than I do, and right now I'm not sure I want to find out.

I can't sit here, panicking about what might happen. I need to speak to Matt—tell him I'm not prepared to bow to Lucas's command, so I brush the tears from my cheeks and push myself to my feet.

As I turn towards the door it swings slowly inwards. Backlit against the sky beyond is the bowed figure of Nina. Her head is down and I can hear her sobbing. I walk quickly towards her.

"Nina, whatever's the matter?"

I reach out and put my arm around her shoulders and she lifts her eyes to mine.

"It's Lucas. I can't believe what he's done. Why would he do this to me?"

I want to tell her that I can't believe what he's doing either—to me, or to any of us. But surely it's no surprise to Nina, who provided the costumes? She notices my puzzled frown.

She pushes me away and paces across the room, then spins on her heel towards me. The tears are still flowing, but anger has taken over.

"Oh, I knew he was planning a game—he told me what he needed me to do, although he never explained why. He said I would find out, and it would be more fun if I didn't know. But I've read my character description. I'm in the game too, Jemma. I don't know why he would hurt me like this."

"I thought we were all in the game, Lucas included."

"We are, but not like this. He says my secret is going to be revealed tonight, and I don't know what he means—what he thinks I've done."

I feel a prickle run up my spine.

"I'm sure Lucas wouldn't upset you intentionally. Come on, Nina. Let's go and find him so we can straighten this out."

Nina shakes her head. "He's gone out. He said people would have questions, and he didn't want to answer them until tonight."

What is he doing? Whatever he has planned, this is no ordinary game; it's not meant to be fun. He's expecting something to happen. He's forcing secrets into the open, making us dance to his tune for some motive of his own. But what is it?

CHAPTER 33

I do my best to calm Nina, but she alternates between anger and tears, and I can't persuade her to tell me any more about the game, so I walk her back to the house and to the bottom of the stairs to their room.

"Are you going to be okay?"

Nina's whole body is rigid, and I'm not surprised by her answer. "No. I had hoped that tonight would put paid to Lucas's obsession, but perhaps I'm wrong."

"Obsession?"

She turns away from me and starts to walk upstairs. "You'll see. I've said enough."

I want to go after her, to ask her what she means, but I'm sure she won't tell me.

As I walk away, I can feel my character description rustling in my pocket. I don't know what to do with it, but I can't risk Matt finding it. I want to burn it, but I have an awful suspicion that Lucas would know.

My first impulse is to rush to find Matt, to ask him what was in his envelope, but he'll ask me what mine says, and I'm certain he will be more inclined to believe what Lucas has written than the truth.

I don't know where to go. As I approach the door to the rear terrace, I hear people talking. I don't want to see anyone, so I dodge back inside. I try the side door, but then I glimpse Andrew coming up from the beach, water dripping from his shorts. I pull my eyes away from his tanned body and turn to make my way to the front of the house to escape into the open air. If I skirt the edge of the property I should be able to find my way into the Japanese garden through the trees.

Fortunately there is no one there, so I slip into the pagoda, out of the sun, and lower myself onto a soft floor cushion, propping my back against the wall. I need to try to get my thoughts in order, but I'm not sure where to start—with Lucas, Matt, Nina, or with the message in my character description.

I'm so lost in thought that it takes me a moment to realize someone is standing in the doorway, and it's probably the last person I want to talk to.

"Are you hiding, Jemma?" Isabel asks, folding her arms and leaning against the door jamb.

"Yes."

"Well, that's tough, I'm afraid. I want to talk to you." She kicks another cushion across the floor and flops down onto it, stretching her long, bronzed legs in front of her. "What's he up to, Jemma?"

"Who?" I know who she means, but she has to be the one to say it.

"Lucas, of course. Why's he being such a dick?"

I hide my surprise. I thought Lucas could do no wrong in her eyes.

"Look, we've got to stop him. Whatever the game is, it's just not funny. Can't you say something to him?"

"*Me?* Why do you think he would listen to my opinion?"

"Because there are only two people here who have no history with him and don't feel beholden to him in some way—who aren't under his spell. The rest of us have spent years kowtowing to him, believing he knows best, and of the two, you're the better option because you're not all hippy-dippy like Chandra."

I'm not sure if that's a compliment or not, but it doesn't really matter. "Lucas has gone out and he's not due back until dinner. He doesn't want to be asked any questions."

"I bet he doesn't. Bastard. I don't know how he can do this to any of us, but especially not to me."

I'm about to ask her why, but I'm sure that's what she wants so I focus my attention on a small insect bite on my knee, rubbing it gently with my thumb. As expected, Isabel carries on without any prompting.

"We were in love when we were eighteen, you know. We saw each other on the quiet because he didn't want the other guys to know. I thought it would never end." The faraway look in her eyes suddenly turns hard. "Then Blair found out, and of course he didn't approve, so he sent Lucas off on his round-the-world trip to get him away from me. It was Alex who told him."

Her tone is flat, unemotional. But her face tells a different story.

"She thought she owned Lucas and couldn't stand the thought of sharing him. I'm surprised Nina managed to get him to the altar—but Alex nearly put paid to that, didn't she? I bet she didn't know they were already married."

It's such an uncharitable thought that once again I don't comment, and Isabel carries on, regardless of my silence.

"Of course, when the incident that we're not supposed to talk about happened, Lucas came rushing back from the other side of the world to look after his sister. He didn't have time for me anymore."

I wonder if Lucas realizes that he broke her heart, and that—by the sound of things—she's still damaged. Finally, I speak.

"Why did you come this week—or even last year—if you feel the way you do?"

Isabel gives a weak laugh. "Because I wanted to see if he and Nina are as rock solid as he claims. And anyway, we always run when he calls—I thought you'd have realized that by now."

I have, but until today it always seemed that they simply valued his friendship. He is perhaps a natural leader, but with his game he's taking advantage of their deference. And how do Isabel's feelings for Lucas tie in with my suspicions about her and Matt? Is her behavior really just a ruse to try to make Lucas jealous?

It's as if she reads my mind.

"What about you and Matt? We can all see that things aren't the way they were."

"Sorry, Isabel. That's no one's business but ours."

"I've known Matt since we were about fourteen years old, Jemma. He has no secrets from me, you know."

I can feel my blood pressure mounting. "What's that supposed to mean?"

She shakes her head slowly. "I think you should ask your husband. But you jump to conclusions too easily. Things are rarely what they seem."

I've had enough of Isabel's innuendoes, so I push myself up off the floor.

"I don't know what to say to you, Isabel. I don't know what game you're playing any more than I know what game Lucas is playing. Why can't you all be bloody straightforward?"

"Where's the fun in that?"

There's a twist in her smile, and I can see the reminder about Lucas and his game has knocked her.

"I'll see you later," I say, the last vestiges of politeness coming to my rescue.

Rather than head back to the house I decide to go through the wood to where I imagine the trees stretch to the far end of the beach. Maybe I need to be watching the sea and thinking of the permanence of life.

There's no path but I follow the steep slope downwards, the sound of the sea in my ears. I'm relieved not to have met anyone as I make my way round the back of the boathouse and down to the shore. It's the first time I've been here since the morning I saw Alex's body spread-eagled on the pebbles. I stare at the space now, willing her to reappear so I can rush to her aid and rescue her.

The high black rocks that border the narrow cove look inviting, and I walk to the far end and perch on the edge of a smooth dry slab, the spot from which Andrew dived the year before. Gazing out to sea, I think of Alex swimming out there, the water cool on her flesh but the effort of swimming keeping her blood flowing. How must it have felt at the moment she ran out of energy and knew that the sea was about to take her?

I find it hard to imagine why she couldn't have saved herself. As a child, the first thing my mum taught me was how to float on my back. "If ever you're stuck and run out of energy, you can just turn over and float until you get your strength back," she told me. So why couldn't Alex have done that? How was she able to just let go and sink down into the depths of the ocean?

I think back to her conversation with Chandra and can't quite equate the girl who seemed determined to find out what had happened to her with the girl who, a few hours later, decided to take her own life.

My gaze travels across to the apartment above the boathouse, now closed up, the white curtains hanging limply at the window.

I stare harder. The curtain to the right moved. I know it did. Someone must be in there.

I'm not sure what to do. I look again, and all is still.

Slowly I climb down from the rock and, without taking my eyes from the window, I make my way across the beach. Nothing stirs. I walk up the ramp to the huge double doors that lead into the boathouse and quietly climb the steps at the side of the building towards the door of the apartment.

I rattle the handle, but it's locked.

I walk round the back and lift my hand to peer in through the window. I can't see anything other than vague shapes through the voile curtains. It is still, quiet, apparently deserted.

I go to the window at the side. I can just make out a bed, but there's no one on it. Despite that, I'm certain someone is in there; I can feel it.

A sudden coldness rushes through me as I feel the touch of a hand on my shoulder.

CHAPTER 34

"What are you doing here, Jemma?" Lucas asks.

"I thought I saw something."

"What?"

"I was sure a curtain moved. I thought someone must have broken in. I was checking."

Lucas stares at me, his eyes cold, and I can almost feel the strain of the threads that are holding him together. "There's no one there. It's locked, as it has been for a year now. No one is allowed in, so please go back to the house, and I'll see you tonight."

I should tell him right now that I'm not going to play his game, whatever it is, but I don't. I can barely speak. Lucas is so tall, and with the sun behind him and his face in shadow, I feel my heart begin to thump, telling me to run. Only his lion eyes glow, and all I want to do is get away from him—away from here.

I run all the way back to the house and burst into the bedroom out of breath. Matt is lying on the bed, his hands behind his head, staring into thin air. He lowers his eyes to look at me, and I see a flash of concern. But it's instantly hidden by his mask of indifference and without asking why I am panting, he speaks.

"Before you say anything, don't ask. I'm not going to tell you what's in my character description. End of story." He's trying to sound belligerent, but there's a tremor in his voice. Whatever was in his envelope, he didn't like it.

"I wasn't going to ask you," I answer, my breathing slowing. "But I'm not going to the dinner tonight, Matt. I don't like being played with, and I think whatever Lucas is doing, it's totally inappropriate. I want to leave."

Matt pulls himself upright on the bed, and his mouth drops open. He shakes his head fiercely.

"You *have* to come tonight. It's not optional, Jemma. You've got to be there."

"Why? Why do I have to do what Lucas says? I don't give a flying fuck what he thinks. It's one thing trying to help him deal with his grief; it's another jumping through bloody hoops for him."

"Oh no." He starts to get off the bed, and for one moment I think he's going to walk over and shake me, but he stops and sits back down again. He looks defeated, and his voice drops. "You're doing this, Jemma. You're going to do as he asks. We're guests in his house—getting a free holiday."

I can't resist a derisive hoot, but Matt continues. "We're eating his food, drinking his wine, so if Lucas wants to play a game and has devised some character outlines—"

"They're *threats*, Matt. They're not character outlines."

Matt's eyes are looking away, to one side. "Maybe he's threatened you, but that doesn't mean he's threatened everyone else. What the hell has he got on you, if I might ask?"

"I thought you didn't want to talk about it? What about you? For you to bow to his every whim, there must be something?"

All of a sudden the anger and frustration drain out of me and I collapse onto the end of the bed as if my legs won't hold me up any longer, my back to my husband.

"What are we doing, Matt? What's going on? Why can't we talk?"

I twist my head to look at him over my shoulder. Once again his eyes slide away from mine, but not before I see how much he's hurting. For a moment I feel a surge of hope, but then he speaks.

"We're going tonight. Both of us. We're not leaving, so please—for once—don't make a stand just because you can."

I don't know what he means. Is that what he thinks I'm like? Is he right?

I wait to see if he'll say more, but he lies back down, his hands behind his head, and closes his eyes. I know he doesn't want me to see what he's thinking.

CHAPTER 35

Detective Sergeant Stephanie King reached out to switch off her desk light just as the phone on her desk started to ring.

"Bugger," she muttered. Tomorrow was her day off, a day she was hoping to spend with Gus. They had some serious talking to do, and she'd been planning to get away on time for once so she could shop for some food, maybe soften the edges of what might be a fraught conversation.

With a sigh, she picked up the handset.

"Sarge, it's Jason. I'm sorry to bother you. I know you're off tomorrow, and I could pass this on to someone else, but given where it is I thought you might want to know about it."

"Jason, what are you talking about?" she said in the tone of mild irritation she seemed to reserve for her ex-probationer.

"Well, as you were involved in the case a year ago, it seemed best to see if you wanted to handle it."

"Handle *what?*" she asked, unable to mask her exasperation. She heard a deep breath from the other end of the phone, as if he thought she was being deliberately dense.

"About ten months ago a young Romanian woman was reported missing. Her mother doesn't speak English, so she got an interpreter and everything, and she said her daughter had come here but she hadn't been able to contact her for a while. We did the usual risk assessment, but she wasn't ill or on any medication, didn't seem to be particularly at risk, and she moved about from hostel to hostel and so on—you know the story—so we had no reason to fear for her safety."

"But that's changed?"

"Yes—well, maybe. That's why I'm calling you. It concerns Polskirrin."

CHAPTER 36

Against my better judgment I've decided to play the game tonight because maybe it will take someone who is one step removed from these friends and their shared past to stop this from getting out of hand.

The lives of all these people are so tightly bound. They pretend to be close, but there's more to it. There is jealousy, contempt, disappointment—a whole host of feelings weaving their tendrils around us all. There is something dangerous in the air, and I can't ignore it.

As I slip into the beautiful dress that Nina has now altered, I feel strangely pleased that at least my hair has changed since last year. Any small difference seems like a victory. Matt is already dressed, slumped into a chair in the corner of the room, watching me.

My hands tremble as I try to apply a thin layer of lip gloss just as the gong sounds, the signal for us all to make our way down to the dining room. I turn to look at Matt, and he meets my eyes for the first time since lunch.

I read one thing in his expression. Matt is scared too.

The look lasts no more than three seconds. Then he leaps up from the chair, pasting a smile on his face.

"Come on. At least we know the food's going to be good. Don't forget your envelope."

I don't respond to his false joviality and step into the corridor just as the door opposite opens and Isabel appears, dressed in an identical silver sheath to the one she wore last year. Her fingers are fluttering where she's clutching a small evening bag. Close behind is Nick, and from farther along the corridor I see Andrew and Chandra walking towards us.

No one speaks, but Andrew glances my way and lowers his eyebrows. I give him what I hope is an imperceptible shake of the head, hoping he will realize I know no more than he does. Chandra's head is bowed. She isn't looking at anyone, and I know she must be as confused as I am.

As we approach the dining room, the scents from the kitchen waft towards us, but I already know what we'll be eating and the thought makes me nauseous.

Isabel is first into the dining room, and I hear her gasp. As I follow I see why. The same candles burn in the same candle holders, the flowers down the center of the table every bit as stunning as they were a year ago. I feel a lurch in my stomach.

I'm about to turn and run for my room when the door to the kitchen opens and Nina walks in. Her face is blotchy from crying and her eyes bloodshot. I walk over and touch her arm.

"Are you okay?"

Her eyes flood with tears again, and she shakes her head. Before I have the chance to offer some words of encouragement, Adrianna moves quietly into the room and nods to Nina.

In a shaky voice, our distraught hostess makes her announcement: "Ladies and gentlemen, would you all please take your seats for dinner?"

Nobody speaks, although one or two people make a show of checking the place cards even though by now they must realize they don't need to. It's only as I pull out my chair that I realize that not only is there an empty space at the head of the table where Lucas was sitting, but in the gap between Matt and Nina another place has been laid.

For Alex.

CHAPTER 37

The uneasy silence is broken by the sound of brisk footsteps approaching along the corridor, the antique floorboards resonating with a heavy tread. Lucas walks in, a tight smile on his face, the wooden box in his hands again.

"Welcome, friends. I am so glad you all agreed to join me this evening."

He walks across to the table, places the box in front of him but remains standing.

"Before we begin, I'd like to propose a toast." He lifts his glass and people push back their chairs to stand. "To my wife, and our first year of marriage."

Lucas looks at Nina and raises his glass a little higher, but he can't quite meet her tearful eyes. He must know what he's doing to her, and it seems to be hurting him too. So why?

He straightens his back to loom above us. Close as I am, I have to crane my neck to see his face.

"Before we start our first course, I have more envelopes to hand out."

Lucas directs a smile at each of us in turn, and it feels once again as if his eyes settle on me for a little longer than the others. But I meet his gaze full on and refuse to look away. I will not allow myself to be intimidated.

"This morning I gave you your character descriptions. Each of you will have discovered secrets about the character you are playing this evening. It's up to you how many of those facts you reveal, and to whom. But there is one rule: you must not lie. You can refuse to answer, but if you offer information, it must be the truth. For each lie that I detect I'll reveal one of your character secrets."

He opens the box and pulls out more black envelopes with silver writing on them.

"There's another envelope for each of you. In these you will find your objectives—the questions you need to ask other people and the information you need to uncover. Questions can be asked between courses, when you can move around and chat to others, but keep your eyes and ears open while we eat. Someone may inadvertently give something away."

Lucas deals out the envelopes as if they are cards at a casino, and I feel my breaths become shorter, shallower. Everybody stares silently at Lucas. Only Nick seems to find the words, his false joviality hitting a jarring note.

"What's the game, Lucas?"

"I thought by now that would be obvious, Nick. We're going to enjoy that good old dinner-party favorite—we're playing the murder game."

CHAPTER 38

The stillness around the table seems all the more stark in comparison to the bustle that can be heard coming from the kitchen, with the banging of pans, an occasional burst of laughter from Adrianna, and the soft voice of the girl helping her. In the dining room, no one either speaks or moves. Lucas is still standing, but his eyes have taken on a glazed look, and he seems to be staring at a point on the wall above Nina's head at the far end of the table.

I wonder who will speak first, because it's not going to be me. I feel a sense of outrage at what Lucas is doing, but I'm not ready to question him. I expect Nick will say something. He usually does.

To my surprise, it's Chandra's gentle voice that breaks the silence.

"Lucas, everyone in this room understands how devastating the events of last year were for you. The shock and horror must have been immense. But I, for one, find it troubling that you would introduce a party game that involves a death—even a fictitious one—on the anniversary of such a tragedy. Grief can poison you. It gets too dark, too heavy if you don't let it go. Maybe it's time to begin the process of acceptance."

Lucas's eyes swing to Chandra, and I lean forward to look at her, sitting on the other side of Andrew. Her expression is calm, but I see her tongue flick out to wet her lips.

To my surprise, Lucas laughs.

"Do you always accept the hand that you're dealt, Chandra? Or do you sometimes manipulate a situation to get the result you want?"

Chandra is unable to hold his gaze, and I'm pleased when Andrew leaps to his fiancée's defense.

"Leave her alone, Lucas. Chandra has never harmed anyone, and we all know she's the most honest person you could ever wish to meet."

"Really?" Lucas says. "Maybe your character secret will be the first I reveal, Chandra. What do you think?"

"Lucas. Come on, mate. What's all this about?" Nick's voice is conciliatory, as always trying to appease Lucas.

"It's a game, I told you. Why are you all looking so bewildered? Why all this fuss? Have none of you ever been to a murder-mystery party before?"

Isabel reaches forward and stretches a hand towards Lucas.

"I'm in, Lucas," she says. She looks around the table. "Listen, guys, Lucas is our friend, and if this is what he wants to do tonight, let's go along with him. It's just a bit of fun."

That is the complete opposite of what she said to me earlier, and I wonder why she's decided to play the role of his supporter. What has Lucas threatened her with?

I glance at Matt. The strain around my husband's eyes is evident to me. He doesn't want to be doing this, but for some reason he feels compelled to.

"Shall I explain how to play?" Isabel asks. Without waiting for Lucas to reply, her words tumbling over each other, she starts to speak. "What usually happens—but do stop me if I'm wrong, Lucas—is that everyone has a role to play. We got those earlier. We have to discover each other's secrets, track down evidence, alibis, and so on. At the start, you don't know if you're the murderer. You get that information later in the game, so for now you have to assume you're not. But one of you must already know you're the designated victim, and at some time during the evening you'll be murdered. Then you sit out the game and watch as people try to discover who killed you."

Nick and Matt are both trying their best to pretend they're excited about the game. Andrew is leaning back in his chair, which gives me an opportunity to look at Chandra. Her cheeks are flushed, and I can see she's stroking a bracelet on her arm similar to the one she gave Alex. Nina's eyes have not left her husband's face.

Finally, Isabel finishes talking. She looks at Lucas for his approval. He still hasn't sat down and is gripping the back of his chair with both hands. His knuckles are white.

"You're right in all but one detail, Isabel. Tonight, none of you will be the victim."

"Sorry, Lucas," Isabel says. "We need a body for a murder party."

I wonder at that moment if Isabel is being intentionally obtuse. Surely she has realized by now what this is all about.

"I'm not doing this," I say, pushing my chair back and screwing up the napkin that has been sitting on my lap, flinging it on the table. I feel Andrew's eyes on me, but it's my husband who speaks.

"Sit down, Jemma," he says quietly. "We have to go along with Lucas. It's his house. His rules."

Whatever I feel about Matt, I have never doubted his intelligence. Either I have been wrong for all these years or Lucas's control over him is much greater than I imagined.

I turn to face Lucas and take a step towards him. He isn't going to make me cower or defer to him.

"It's not a game though, is it? Nobody needs to be assigned the role of the victim because you've already got one, haven't you, Lucas?"

He stares at me, his face expressionless. I turn to look at the faces around the table—some, like Andrew's, full of the knowledge of what I am about to say, others a little less certain.

"Your victim is Alex, isn't it? You think she was murdered."

CHAPTER 39

The air outside the double glass doors of the dining room is still and warm. The perfume of the jasmine climbing up the pillars of the pergola makes me feel slightly queasy.

I couldn't have stayed in that claustrophobic room for another moment, and there was a stunned silence as I marched outside. But now, through the open doors behind me, I can hear the hum of conversation, the level rising in volume and tension as voices begin cutting across each other, and it seems pandemonium is about to break out. I can't hear what anyone is saying, and I don't want to know.

My heart is thumping, my skin tingling. Lucas thinks Alex was murdered, but it's more than that. Now I understand the threats, the character descriptions, and I can only think that his grief has driven him to this madness. I swallow the saliva that has flooded my mouth. Why hasn't he told the police? What about the suicide video she left?

Before I can decide what to do next, I hear a footstep behind me as someone steps out from the dining room.

"Bravely done, Jemma."

I don't turn. I've always thought there is something mesmer-izing, hypnotic almost, about Lucas's eyes, and I'd rather not meet them right now.

"If you genuinely believe Alex was killed, you have my sympathy. But what a way to reveal your suspicions! Those people are supposed to be your friends. The way you set up the game, the clothes, the identical food—it's sick."

I can sense his eyes on the back of my head, but I still don't turn.

"It's interesting how you refer to 'those people' as my friends. Don't you count yourself among them?"

I make a sound that is supposed to be a contemptuous laugh but comes out as almost a sob. "You're a bunch of guys who've known each other for nearly twenty years. And Isabel was more or less one of you. I never knew that you two were once in love though; Matt didn't tell me that. I don't know your past or understand your secrets—I'm an outsider."

"Did she tell you that?" Lucas asks, his voice little more than a whisper.

"Did who tell me what?"

"Isabel. Did she tell you that I was in love with her?"

"Yes, she did."

I finally turn towards him, wanting him to see my anger.

"Did she say why we broke up?" he asked.

I seem to have stirred up something here, but I have no interest at all in Lucas's love life, past or present.

"For God's sake, what does it matter? The fact is that I don't know anything. I barely even know what happened to Alex when she was fourteen—the events that led to what we all believed was her suicide. So no, I'm not your friend. I feel like a satellite, orbiting but never being invited to land." I fold my arms tightly across my chest. "How could you threaten to tell Matt those lies about me and Andrew? What's to be gained by that?"

"Because I need you to stay. If you leave, Matt might choose to go with you. I know things aren't good between the two of you, but he loves you."

"He's got a bloody funny way of showing it," I say, a scoff in my voice that I hope hides the pain.

"That may be true, but he's insecure and he doesn't think he's worthy of your love, so he'd believe me about Andrew."

"Then you're a bigger bastard than I thought you were."

"I know you don't like this, Jemma, and I'm sorry. I have to make everyone play the game, but I hope, when the truth comes out, all but one person will forgive me."

The horror is growing in me. I've been trying to ignore my suspicions, but he's just confirmed the worst of them.

He thinks one of us killed Alex.

CHAPTER 40

Nina had quietly followed Lucas out of the dining room, her head spinning at the thought that he had been harboring these feelings all this time, and she hadn't known. Why hadn't he told her?

She could hear Jemma trying her best to make him see reason.

"You're wrong, Lucas," she said. "You have to be. Even if she was killed, it could have been anyone: one of the team building the gazebo, a waiter, a total stranger."

Nina watched as Lucas reached out a hand and pulled Jemma closer, lowering his head to hers until they were close enough to kiss.

"I'm sorry, Jemma, but I know without a shadow of a doubt that one of the people here, sitting in *my* house, at *my* table, killed my sister. And I'm going to find out which of you it was."

Nina lifted her hand to cover her mouth and stop herself crying out. Since the morning of Alex's death—the day Lucas told her he had done something unforgivable—she had believed he was consumed with guilt for arguing with his sister. Until the inquest he had been restless, unsettled, anxious, but she had thought once it was over he might begin to heal. Instead he became obsessed with organizing this event, almost frenzied in his dedication to making sure everything was perfect.

Lucas had asked Nina to make costumes so everyone was dressed the same, and she knew he wanted the room to look identical, the food to taste as it had a year ago. Of course she'd asked him why, but all he would say was that he was planning a game, and could she please not ask questions. He had seemed so focused, so fierce in his determination that she hadn't wanted to argue; their marriage was too fragile.

She had started to believe that Lucas was looking to lay the blame for Alex's death at someone else's door—that he hoped by reliving that night he would uncover something cruel or hurtful that had been said, enough to drive a young woman as vulnerable as Alex over the edge. Then she'd read her own character description and realized he didn't trust her any more than he trusted his friends.

But in all of her horror Nina had never thought for a moment that Lucas believed his sister had been murdered, and from everything he'd said to Jemma it seemed clear that he included her, his *wife,* in his list of suspects. The thought that he would even consider this a possibility suddenly transformed the churning feeling in her stomach to a hot ball of anger. How could he?

"Lucas, I want to speak to you," she said, trying to keep her voice level.

"Not now, Nina," he said quietly. "I'm talking to Jemma."

Jemma held her hands up, palms forward. "No, Lucas. We're done. Speak to your wife. She needs you."

With that Jemma turned and walked away—not back into the dining room but around the corner towards the north terrace.

"Nina, I don't have time. I need to get back to our guests."

"Don't you dare try to fob me off, Lucas Jarrett." She could hear the quiver in her voice and hoped he didn't misinterpret it as fear. "How could you *possibly* think it acceptable to question me? What gives you the right? And if you've had this doubt about me all this time, why in God's name didn't you say something? *T'es un bâtard!*"

Lucas looked down at her, his mouth a tight line. "You lied to me. You shouldn't have done that."

"What do you mean? When did I lie to you?"

"You lied about where you were the night Alex died. You said you were in your room, but you weren't." He put a finger under her chin to lift her face, but she angrily pushed it away. "I came looking for you that night. You weren't in our bedroom, were you?"

Before she could say a word to stop him, to explain, he walked past her and back into the dining room.

Nina stared after his disappearing back. For a year he had believed she'd lied to him because she had something to hide. And she did. She was hiding her knowledge of what *he* had done.

As fast as it had come, the anger bled from her body to be replaced with sadness. She sagged and grabbed the back of a garden chair for support. What could he possibly think she had done? Was he just angry that she had lied, or did he suspect her of something worse?

Her throat constricted and she swallowed hard. Enough tears. She needed to help him now, make him understand what she had done and why.

She wanted nothing more than to go to bed and bury herself under the covers. But she wouldn't do that. She would return to the dining room and offer Lucas whatever support he needed.

CHAPTER 41

It feels good to get away from everyone. Round here on the north side of the house the shadows are longer, the air cooler.

I can only think Lucas has gone mad in his grief. Alex had rarely left the grounds of Polskirrin and didn't appear to have any life beyond here, so it was madness to think she had been murdered. And why would she have made a video, explaining her death? Lucas hadn't said a word about his suspicions at the inquest. So why now?

There are too many questions, and I have no answers.

I realize I'm still clutching the second envelope in my right hand. I can't decide whether to find a bin or read it. Will there be more threats? Will he have more to reveal about me—about Matt? I know I will have to look at the contents of the envelope.

I can see it's a list of instructions. I head towards an antique wall lamp so that I can read better in the failing light.

Objectives for stage one of the party

Character name
Jemma Hudson

You must try to remember what you heard and saw on this night one year ago. We were sitting in the same places, wearing the same clothes, eating the same food. Think about the conversations, the details, and make notes on the pads in front of you.

Consider the possible motives of each and every person.

Remember who did what, who was speaking to whom. What did you hear that night, or at any point, that seemed out of place, that might provide a motive?

You were sitting next to Andrew Marshall. What did you talk about? Ask him tonight where he was, what he was doing, who he saw, and let's see if his version is the truth or a pack of lies.

Note the lies.

The game doesn't end tonight. Tomorrow each of you will reveal what you saw, what you heard.

Only in this way will we expose the killer among us.

I pull a chair into the dark shadows cast by the wall and sit down heavily. There's a burning sensation at the back of my throat, and I have to accept that Lucas is deadly serious. We really are all suspects.

What will he do if he discovers one of us *did* kill Alex?

I suddenly feel afraid, sitting here, out of sight of my husband and the other guests. Do I know something that could make me a threat to the killer?

I shake myself. Lucas has to be wrong. If he was certain, he would have called the police.

I hear voices and realize the others have now come out onto the terrace. Lucas's voice rises above the rest as he tells them I will be joining them later. I don't know what gave him that impression.

And yet I know he's right.

The sound of footsteps heading my way makes my heart race, and I feel a moment of relief when Andrew appears round the corner. Then the reality hits me: I hardly know this man. I want to get up and move towards the light, but he is between me and the terrace. He must sense my discomfort because he comes no closer.

"I've been looking for you. Are you okay?"

"No. Are you? Can any of us be okay, given what Lucas is doing? You do know he thinks it's one of us—that his game is to try to catch someone out?"

"I guessed that, and it's appalling. But that's Lucas for you. He's always had his own agenda, even when we were kids."

"What do you mean?"

Andrew blows out a long, slow breath. "It's difficult to say. He was kind and thoughtful on many levels, but I sometimes felt he was watching us—as if we were his own personal experiment. So we all tried a little harder at everything, just to make sure the invitations to his home weren't rescinded."

"God, that sounds brutal."

Andrew shakes his head. "We just wanted to please him, and because of that we did things we wouldn't normally have done. He made us braver, if you like, so he probably did us all a favor—made us better versions of ourselves."

"Well, whatever hold he has over the rest of you, I'm perfectly happy to defy him, and I don't care if he rescinds any and all future invitations. I've told him I'm not playing. And I can't believe you'll go along with him."

Andrew looks at me silently and then drops his head.

"Oh no, Andrew. You don't believe all of this, do you? That Alex was murdered?"

"It's not that simple, Jemma."

"Of course it bloody well is! We don't have to dance to Lucas Jarrett's tune, or at least I don't."

"Yeah, well, some of us might have no choice." There is a note of bitterness in Andrew's voice that I haven't heard before. "Anyway, everyone's heading back inside, so let's go and eat, if you can get any food down your throat. I'm not sure I can."

I don't know if it's because it seems like the path of least resistance, but when Andrew holds out his hand, I take it and let him pull me to my feet.

CHAPTER 42

Nina looked up as Jemma and Andrew walked back into the dining room. Jemma had an air of defiance about her, and Nina was certain she would try to disrupt the proceedings. She was the only one who didn't feel obliged to do Lucas's bidding. Nina knew why the others did: deferring to Lucas was ingrained. She had thought Andrew was different though. He had more self-assurance, and if anyone was going to balk at Lucas's plans, he was the most likely. But then maybe he had the most to lose. Lucas provided him with a seemingly endless list of potential clients from his extensive contacts with the rich and famous, each of them eager to hire a yacht with an experienced skipper. One word from Lucas could destroy Andrew's livelihood.

Nina watched as plates of food that she would normally have been proud to offer were set before each guest. Unlike last year there was no clatter of cutlery. No one picked up a fork, although glasses were being emptied with startling regularity.

Lucas was looking at each person in turn. Most avoided his gaze, but Jemma was the first to speak.

"What are you expecting us to do? I was talking to Andrew most of the night about my job. How is that going to help you?"

Lucas drummed his fingers on the table, his voice tight. "Your instructions are explicit, are they not? You each have a notepad. Use it. Is there anyone here that doesn't understand?"

Nina wanted to jump up and run from the room. It was unbearable having to witness his intensity, because whatever was going on in his head, she could see it was pushing him to the edge. "When we've finished eating, we'll move to the terrace, and in turn you will each follow the paths you took that night. Then we'll see who has a gap in their story. Is that clear enough, Jemma?"

"But it will prove nothing!" Jemma's voice had risen. "Even if someone here can't account for where they were, it doesn't mean they killed Alex. What about motive? And why haven't you called the police?" She paused for just a second, but Lucas didn't deign to answer. "Okay, well explain why Alex left that video then, saying she was going to kill herself. I was at the inquest, Lucas, and you didn't say a bloody word when they pronounced the verdict of suicide. Why not?"

"I have my reasons," he said.

With one last glare at Jemma he pushed back his chair, not blinking as it clattered to the floor behind him, and stood, hands on hips. "You may object to what I'm asking you to do. You may think it's unfair, embarrassing, and unreasonable of me. To the innocent I apologize unreservedly in advance. I will, I promise, make it up to you. But I ask you this: is there anyone in this room who can stand up and say they don't care how or why Alex died?"

He paused, his eyes moving from Jemma to Andrew as if he saw them as the greatest threat to his plans. "If you really couldn't give a damn about my sister, then fine. Get up and leave. But if it matters to you that a young woman—one you all knew—was killed here one year ago tonight by someone at this table, you will indulge me and play the bloody game!"

Lucas's last words were shouted. The atmosphere in the room was intense, but no one spoke.

The silence was shattered by the sound of the buzzer at the gate.

Was this another of Lucas's tricks? One look at her husband's face told Nina it wasn't. He was clearly furious at the interruption.

She stood up. "I'll see who it is," she said, glad of an excuse to escape the room.

CHAPTER 43

Detective Sergeant Stephanie King parked her car next to an antique lamppost. It wasn't completely dark yet, but the lamp was already on, and she was glad of it as she stepped out into the silence of the grounds of Polskirrin. Beautiful as Lucas Jarrett's home was, there was something forbidding about it. No lights shone from the windows, and they merely reflected back the darkening sky. But she could see a dim, flickering glow from a room on the far right. It looked like candlelight. She really hoped she wasn't interrupting a vigil because she was fully aware of the significance of the date.

As she approached the front door it opened, and the slight figure of Nina—the woman who was to have married Lucas Jarrett a year ago tomorrow—was standing on the threshold, backlit by a lamp. It was only as Stephanie got closer that she could see the woman had been crying. She had known coming here tonight was a bad idea, but it felt marginally better than leaving it until tomorrow, when someone other than Stephanie would have picked up the case. On balance, it had seemed to make more sense if she came rather than a stranger. At least she knew the history.

"Good evening," Stephanie said. "I'm so sorry to interrupt you this late, but we have an inquiry you might be able to help with. I don't know if you remember me. I was here last year. Detective Sergeant Stephanie King."

Nina's puffy eyes opened a little wider. "Detective?"

"Yes, I've moved to CID. Bearing in mind this might be a sensitive time, I volunteered to be the officer to come and have a chat with you. I hope that's okay, Miss..."

"Mrs.," Nina answered. "I'm Mrs. Jarrett. Lucas and I are married. Come through. Lucas doesn't know you're here—he's with our guests."

"You've got company? I'm so sorry. I don't want to disturb you, but perhaps your husband can pop out to have a word with me. I need to speak to you both."

Just then a door opened, and Stephanie caught a glimpse of candlelight and a table decorated with white and green flowers. A woman walked out into the hall. She bowed her head slightly when she saw Stephanie and Nina.

"I apologize for disturbing you, Nina. I didn't mean to intrude. I've told Lucas I don't want to play the game. I'm going to my room."

Nina threw a nervous glance at Stephanie, then back at the woman.

"I'm sorry, but weren't you here last year for the...celebration?" Stephanie asked, feeling it was perhaps a little inappropriate to mention weddings.

"Yes. I'm Chandra Tran."

"Then I'm afraid I need to talk to you too. Is anyone else here from that time?"

There was an uncomfortable moment of silence before Nina spoke. "Yes. We have the same guests tonight as last year."

Stephanie tried to keep her face neutral. Were they all here for some sort of belated wake? What was it that Chandra Tran had said about a game?

"In that case could I speak to everyone together, please? It won't take long."

Chandra turned back towards the dining room, Stephanie and Nina close behind. As Chandra pushed the door open, Stephanie was struck by the lack of noise—with all those people she would have expected to hear a buzz of conversation or at least the clatter of cutlery against plates.

She followed Nina into the room and tried to take in the whole scene without staring. It was a strange sight. The guests were dressed in their finery as if this was a celebration of some sort, but no one was smiling.

In front of each of them on the table was a notepad and pen. From where she was standing, the pages of those closest to her appeared to be blank.

"Lucas, this is Detective Sergeant King. You may remember her."

It was hard to decipher the expression on Lucas's face, but Stephanie knew that her interruption was unwelcome, and Lucas threw an accusing glance at his wife.

"Mr. Jarrett, I apologize for disturbing you this late, but an inquiry has just come in to us that might relate to Polskirrin."

"So your business is unrelated to my sister's suicide?"

His tone held a note of surprise, and it felt to Stephanie that the tension in the room had eased a notch.

"I'm here because ten months ago we had a report of a missing young woman—Lidia Dalca. She's Romanian, and this time last year she had only recently arrived in the country, looking for work. I'm afraid she's disappeared."

"I'm sorry to hear that, but if it was ten months ago, why are you only checking it out now?"

"We did look into it as far as we could. But new information has just come to light. Lidia's family have paid for an English-speaking cousin to come to Cornwall to see if they can find out what happened to her, and it appears her mother last spoke to her a year ago tonight. Lidia told her she was heading to a house where she'd heard there was to be a big wedding the following day. She was planning to ask if there was any work for her. It was quite late in the evening, but due to the date we wondered if perhaps she had come here, to Polskirrin."

Lucas frowned. "You probably realized when you were here last that there were a substantial number of people milling around, some working well into the night, but I have no idea what any of them were called. Why wasn't she reported missing for two months?"

"It seems Lidia had a row with her mother, who told her it was too late to be traveling down lonely roads in a place she didn't know. She thought it might be dangerous."

"It sounds like her mother may have been right."

Lucas gave her what was supposed to pass for a rueful smile, but she could see it was an effort.

"When her mum didn't hear anything for a few days, she thought her daughter was sulking, but when she called her she got no response. Of course, we checked out her mobile, but it had a prepaid SIM, and now it seems to be out of use."

"I'm sorry, Sergeant, but as you can see, we're in the middle of dinner. Given the amount of time that's already passed, is this something we could pick up tomorrow, do you think?"

Despite his thin veneer of politeness, Lucas Jarrett clearly wanted her gone. But she wasn't to be deterred.

"I won't keep you long, but I wonder if any of you remember someone turning up here—did any of you see her, speak to her? This is the best photo we have, but we're waiting for a more recent one." She held out her phone so they could pass it round, aware the quality wasn't great. It appeared to be a selfie taken from low down, and the girl's chin was out of proportion to the rest of her face. "Lidia is twenty-two, slim, average height, speaks very little English—or at least she did then. According to her mother, if she was looking for work she'd have had her hair up, in a bun similar to the one in the picture."

Stephanie looked at the faces turned towards her, but they weren't engaging. There was something else going on—something no one was saying—she could feel it. They were silent, as if united in their desire for her to leave, and yet they didn't seem connected to each other. No one was looking at anyone else: some were looking at the flowers, or at the wall above the head of the person opposite them, or the wine in their glass. With the exception of Chandra Tran and the woman Stephanie remembered as Jemma Hudson, they gave the photo little more than a cursory glance.

"Do any of you remember seeing someone that matches this description? I know it must be difficult now, tonight of all nights, but I have to ask."

As she was speaking, Stephanie's eyes fell to the empty chair just in front of her. A place card was resting on a silver charger. *Alex.*

She lifted her gaze to Lucas, who gave her a level stare. Stephanie had no idea what she had walked into, but she wished now that she had sent someone else.

CHAPTER 44

The detective has gone now, having taken our names, some of which were given with a degree of reluctance. I suppose no one likes to think of their details being stored on a police computer, however innocent they might be.

I remember the police officer. She struck me then, as she did just now, as a woman you would want to have on your side—great as a friend but a formidable adversary. She left her card propped up on the mantelpiece and asked us all to think about anything we might have heard or seen that night. If only she knew that it was our sole topic of conversation. I feel as if the card is staring at me, telling me to pick it up and use it.

I wanted to tell her what's happening here, what Lucas suspects and what he is subjecting us all to. If he decides that one of us *did* kill Alex, what revenge will he exact on that person, even though he may be wrong? And while we all decide if he's right, who else among us is in danger?

No one has spoken since Sergeant King left. The food is sitting on plates in front of us, and we are picking at it as if for some reason we need to be polite. We don't.

Lucas's lips are tightly clenched. The detective has disrupted his game, broken the thread that was barely holding it together, and now he needs to get it back on track.

Chandra gets up from the table again and heads towards the door.

"Andrew, please tell your fiancée to stay. I need you all to play this my way."

Andrew slowly pushes back his chair, stands up, and goes to Chandra. For one awful moment I think he's going to do as Lucas asks, but I'm wrong. He reaches out an arm and rests it on Chandra's shoulders. His cheeks are flushed, and I can see he's barely controlling his anger.

"Fuck you, Lucas. I'm not Chandra's keeper. *She* can do as she likes."

Lucas gives him a lopsided smile. "Really? Chandra, I need to find out who spoke to or saw Alex after dinner. If you leave, one of the pieces of the puzzle will be missing, and the wrong person might be accused. Is that what you want?" He pauses for a moment, his eyes flicking between Chandra and Andrew. "Maybe the time has come to reveal the first of our characters' secrets. What do you say, Andrew? Shall we start with you?"

Chandra looks up at Andrew and she bites her bottom lip. "I'll stay, if you'd like me to."

I watch as he drops his head. "Thank you," he finally says. Lucas has won again.

Chandra walks quietly back to her seat, and I lean across to give her arm a gentle squeeze before Andrew fills the space between us.

Lucas leans his forearms on the table. "I hope you are now all with me, and that everyone in the room—bar one person, of course—is as committed to finding Alex's killer as I am. You have your instructions."

With that, he sits back.

I watch as Matt turns to Isabel. I wish I could hear what he's saying, but he's speaking quietly, almost hissing. His fingers are curling, claw-like, then straightening—in, out, in, out. Isabel is smirking; there's no other word for it. But her cheeks are flushed as if the effort of maintaining her poise is costing her dearly.

I don't know where Matt was that night, but I'm not prepared to tell Lucas how late it was when he came back. Not until I've spoken to him myself.

Only then does it occur to me that if each person in the room chooses to hide one piece of information that might incriminate the person they love the most, Lucas will never achieve his aims.

"Make notes, please," Lucas says, interrupting my thoughts. "We'll need them when we regroup tomorrow."

I turn to Andrew. "What are we going to do?" I ask. "I don't want to do this—to question you or anyone else."

"Jemma, I don't believe for a single moment you have anything to hide, and neither do I. So why don't we just play along?"

I feel a twinge of guilt. I *am* hiding something; I'm hiding the fact that my husband was out there, and he hasn't accounted for where he was.

To cover my confusion, I am the first to ask a question.

"Where were you? Who did you see?"

The earlier flush has gone from Andrew's skin, leaving him looking sallow beneath his tan.

"We were all on the terrace apart from Nina. If you remember, a few of us were dancing, but the music changed and we all sat down. Then I received a phone call, so I headed off to the orchard, where the signal is better. I didn't see Alex, and when I'd finished my call I returned to the house and went to bed. Chandra was already there."

I remembered Alex leaving just after Andrew. Had she followed him to the orchard?

"I'm also apparently supposed to check for motive, so I suppose I should ask if there was anything in that call that you wouldn't want anyone else to hear? That would be worth killing for?"

Andrew reaches for his wine glass, staring at the dark liquid as he swirls it round. "Of course not."

A young waitress with strawberry-blond hair and bright red lipstick comes into the room to clear the barely touched plates of food, and for a moment I wonder what she must make of all this, to see this delicious meal taken away, no doubt to be tossed out.

The girl removes a plate of wafer-thin slices of bresaola with tiny pieces of orange, celery, and Parmesan cheese, a dish I had devoured with relish last year. But the blood-red meat made my stomach turn tonight.

To my surprise Chandra leans forward so she can look at me across Andrew.

"I heard what Andrew just said, Jemma. He's being kind to me. I know who he was talking to. It was my father, and it was about the terms of our marriage. I knew what my father was offering him, and I'm glad Andrew accepted. I suspect that's the secret Lucas is threatening to reveal."

She gives Andrew a sweet smile, but he looks horrified. Whatever the terms were, I'm sure he wasn't aware that Chandra knew, although clearly Lucas did.

To my surprise, Chandra hasn't finished.

"And Andrew is also trying to protect me by saying I was in the room when he got back. I wasn't. I say this now, in case anything I saw might prove important when other people have had a chance to speak."

Andrew flashes me a guilty look, but I don't blame him. I'm prepared to cover for Matt, so I can quite understand why he didn't tell me Chandra wasn't in the room.

Just as I'm about to tell Andrew exactly where I was, Nick speaks up for the first time. "Lucas, I don't think *anyone* here believes Alex was murdered. We're trying to help, mate, but we're all a bit lost."

Lucas rests his amber eyes on Nick.

"Nick, you have a sister. If you believed that someone—one of us—had killed her, what would you do?"

Nick looks as if he's about to make an inappropriate joke at his sister's expense, but he stops himself in time and stays silent.

I can't keep quiet any longer. "I presume Nick would do what any sensible person would do—he would tell the police. We just had a detective here less than half an hour ago, and you said nothing. Why the hell not?"

I know that I'm thwarting Lucas's plans, and I'm certain he's wishing he hadn't invited me, because surely I can't be a suspect. I had never met Alex before that weekend.

"Can you please tell us why you're so convinced that someone killed her?" I persist.

When his eyes meet mine, they dazzle me with the intensity of his feelings. He's angry, but I don't think I'm the source of his rage.

"I can't tell you what I know—that would give the killer an advantage. I need one more piece of the puzzle." Lucas lifts his chin, and I can see his chest moving in and out as he tries to control his breathing. "Alex told me the afternoon she died that she was certain someone here was harboring a dangerous secret. Maybe about what happened to her when she was younger. She was determined to expose it."

Everyone is still, frozen to the spot, unwilling to move in case it draws attention to them. But I don't care. I haven't finished.

"Why leave a suicide message then?"

"There's more than one way to interpret her message. But I tell you this: she didn't want to die. She wanted revenge."

"Then why wait a year? Why didn't you do something straight away?"

"I've not been waiting; I've been preparing. For this. For tonight."

CHAPTER 45

Stephanie drove home from Polskirrin in a state of confusion. What the hell had been going on there? It was one thing getting together to remember someone they had lost, but a year ago she hadn't had the impression that any of them were particularly close to Alexandra Lawrence, with the obvious exception of her brother. They had understandably been stunned by her death, but there were few signs of genuine grief. And yet tonight some of the guests had the black wide-eyed stare of a person in shock.

No one had shown any interest in the missing girl, Lidia Dalca, although at one point Jemma Hudson had looked as if she might be about to say something. But she had clearly changed her mind.

Lucas Jarrett was probably right—there were far too many people rushing about at the time of the thwarted wedding for him to have noticed one girl, but according to her mother it had been quite late when Lidia arrived, so surely he wouldn't have forgotten that. Unless, of course, she never got beyond the gates. Maybe the housekeeper answered the buzzer and told the girl to go away. That was perfectly feasible.

What was going on in that room? Stephanie had seen open notepads in front of each guest, and more to the point she had seen a heading on one of the pages: "The Murder Game." Why the hell would you play a dinner-party murder mystery game on the anniversary of your sister's death? Wasn't that a bit ghoulish?

Stephanie sighed as she pulled the car into her drive. She wished it had been anywhere but Polskirrin, a place that held such a mixture of memories for her because it was there, on the beach, that a year ago tomorrow she had seen Gus for the first time in months.

She remembered feeling sad that a young girl had been unhappy enough to take her own life, knowing how it felt to believe life had little to offer, recalling how devastated she had been by the events of the previous year: her split from Gus, the baby she had lost. But through it all she had known she would survive. And then suddenly Gus was there, standing beside her, asking if he could come round that evening, and she had known that he wanted her. She would never forget the sensation of warmth spreading through her body, the tears that threatened, the relief that she didn't have to pretend anymore.

Gus had never pretended. He had told her months before that he wanted them to get back together, but she had been too scared to admit how she felt. Losing him the first time had been so excruciating that she hadn't been sure she wanted to risk it again. But on the night of Alexandra Lawrence's death, Gus had held her as they talked about their confusion, their pain, and most of all their love for each other, and she knew then that she never wanted to let him go.

Tomorrow would be the anniversary of them getting back together, and now everything had changed. Despite them working miles apart—Gus as part of the Major Crimes team based in Newquay and Stephanie as a detective in Penzance—they had managed to make things work—sort of—with lots of driving and too few whole days and nights together. But it was about to get a whole lot worse, and she wasn't sure if she could deal with it.

As she stepped out of the car she saw lights on in the kitchen. Gus was home. Pleased as she was to see him, she almost dreaded going through the door in case he had news. News she didn't want to hear.

"Hey," she said, dumping her bag on the floor in the hall, looking everywhere but into his eyes.

"Relax, Steph," he said. "Nothing to report, as yet. Come here."

She walked towards him and wrapped her arms around his waist, burying her head in his neck and breathing in the scent of his skin. "I'm glad you're home."

"Me too," he answered, his voice muffled by her hair. "Have you eaten?"

"No, but we can make a quick macaroni and cheese if you're hungry." She slowly released herself and went into the kitchen.

She pulled open the door of the fridge to hide her face while she tried to compose herself. No news yet. They could at least have what was left of today, and hopefully tomorrow. She took a deep breath.

"You'll never guess where I've just been. Polskirrin. To the house, not the beach. What a coincidence."

Gus gave her a puzzled glance.

"You know, where we dealt with that suicide a year ago."

He shook his head and smiled. "Do you honestly think I would have forgotten? I just wondered what had dragged you back out there."

"It was all down to Jason."

Gus groaned.

"Oh, come on, Gus. He's turned into not too bad a policeman, you know. Now that I'm CID and don't have to deal with him on a daily basis, we get on a bit better. Anyway, he was working on the desk earlier today when a woman came in to inquire about a Romanian girl who'd been reported missing ten months ago. She didn't seem to be at risk, so it was assumed she'd moved on. It now appears that she was last heard from on her way to look for work on the eve of the Jarretts' wedding. We think she may have gone to Polskirrin, so I went to check it out."

Gus looked up from where he was pouring wine into two glasses. "And?"

"No one remembers seeing her, so it's a bit of a dead end. But there was something odd. Lucas Jarrett had a house full of guests, all decked out in their finery with glorious smells coming from the kitchen. It was like a party—but a strange time to have one, don't you think?"

"Well, I don't suppose I would consider it appropriate on the anniversary of my sister's death, no. But as my old grandad used to say, 'There's nowt so queer as folk.' Maybe it was some kind of commemoration, now the inquest's finally out of the way."

"Yes, possibly. But it's even odder than that, because the people there were the same guests—you know, the ones staying with them last year—and they looked vaguely terrified, or at the very least bewildered by something."

Gus pushed a glass of wine towards her. "Don't go making something out of this. You might have interrupted them moments after they'd been talking about how she died, or what she was like as a child. Anything at all."

"So why did Chandra Tran—the Asian woman who was there last year—say they were playing a game? They had pads of paper in front of them, and I saw one of them had 'The Murder Game' written at the top of the page."

Gus sat on a stool at the kitchen island and rested his forearms on the counter. "Okay, I'll grant you that's a bit odd."

"Not only that, but there was an extra place at the table, and the place card had *Alex* on it."

His eyes opened wide. "Jesus, that *is* freaky. I've heard of people laying a place for a lost loved one before, but a place card's a bit bizarre. I can't see how it's related to your missing girl though. If all you have is that she arrived at the gates of what might have been Polskirrin and nobody remembers seeing her, it's going to be hard to find an excuse to question them again."

"You're right, but I had this horrible feeling—you know, like it was one of those hard-to-believe TV programs where a group of people all get together on the same night each year to kill someone. Lidia might have been their victim. So who's next?"

Gus dropped his forehead onto his hands and groaned. "Bloody hell, Stephanie. Even for you, that's a stretch."

"Okay, maybe it's a bit extreme, but we've got one dead girl and one missing—both at Polskirrin. I don't like it."

He lifted his head and gave her a lopsided smile, as if to acknowledge that she had a point. "So what are you going to do?"

"I don't know. I might try to track down the housekeeper they had at the time. She left immediately after Alex died, but maybe she saw Lidia—either let her in or turned her away. At least we'd know one way or the other."

Stephanie took a sip of her wine. Something didn't feel right about what was going on at Polskirrin, but she needed more to go on before she could legitimately ask any more questions. And at least it took her mind off the thought that one day very soon she was going to lose Gus.

CHAPTER 46

More food has been brought out from the kitchen by the house-keeper and the girl helping her, although no one seems interested in it. Even Lucas is pushing it around with his fork, and Nina is staring at her plate.

I can't stand the silence, and eventually I feel I have no option but to speak.

"I have two things I'd like to say, Lucas." I see Matt raise a shocked face, but I ignore him. "First, you're insisting that Alex was murdered, and yet you haven't told us how you think she died, given that she clearly drowned and there were no marks on her. Second, you think her death may be related to what happened to her twelve—no, it's thirteen years ago now. But as far as I can tell, no one knows what really *did* happen to her, other than the fact—bad enough in itself—that she was abducted. You want us to be honest with you. Why can't you be straight with us?"

Lucas puts the palms of his hands flat on the table and pushes himself to his feet, leaning forward to loom over the rest of us.

"Fair comment, Jemma. I know exactly how Alex died, but I need to keep that information to myself for now, until I'm certain who the killer is. To give too much away would provide an opportunity for the truth to be concealed. But I *will* tell you about Alex."

Lucas moves to the side of the room where I can see he has a laptop set up. He clicks a few keys, and the TV on the wall springs to life. I twist round to get a better view, my back to the others. I wish I could watch them and the screen at the same time.

"In recent years Alex wasn't a fan of having her photo taken," Lucas begins, "although I did manage to grab one or two last summer when she was still with us. But first you need to see Alex as a child—how some of you might remember her."

There's a bitter edge to his voice, as if this should be significant to one or more of the people in the room, but he says no more, hitting the space bar. The screen is filled with the image of a young girl. I hear a breath sharply drawn in, quickly stifled by a hand.

"Alex, on her thirteenth birthday." Lucas's voice isn't entirely steady, and I understand why.

She looks little more than a child, with her long dark hair in a ponytail, white teeth that still look slightly too large for her head and those beautiful green eyes that I remember. There are still the remnants of a layer of puppy fat on her cheeks, and her smile is wide. She was beautiful.

"What one or two of you don't know is that her mother—*my* mother too, sadly—was a drunk. Alex's father died when she was five, and she lived with this awful woman who did nothing but make demands on her. My father, who'd had the sense to leave our mother several years before Alex was born, gave Alex some pocket money even though he had no ties to her. He did this because she was my sister, and he felt sorry for her. But my mother took every penny to buy vodka."

I look at Alex's face, expecting to see signs of her sad life. But all I can see is the resilience of youth and possibly happiness at being with her brother.

"A little over a year later, just after her fourteenth birthday, she ran away from home, planning to seek refuge in my father's house. I was away in New Zealand, but she didn't know that Dad had decided to join me for Christmas. The house was deserted, and she was cold and wet, so she hid in the summerhouse. It had always been her hiding place. And that was where they found her—no one knows how—cold, wet, tired. And they took her."

Lucas clicks the keyboard again. A photo of an unrecognizable girl is displayed on the screen. This time there is no attempt to disguise the intakes of breath from those behind me.

"This photo of Alex was taken two months after she was rescued—only fifteen months after the previous one I showed you. She never knew I had it, but I needed it to remind me of how much I hate whoever did this to her."

The girl on the screen is thin. The plump cheeks have been replaced with hollows, and the skin surrounding her eyes is black. Her eyes appear dead, her hair limp.

"I only learned exactly what had happened to her in the months before she died. She had told the police but wouldn't tell me because it would have hurt me too much, she said."

Lucas's voice breaks on the words, and for the first time in twenty-four hours I feel real sympathy for him.

"Alex was tied, gagged, had a sack pulled over her head, and was bundled into a van and taken to an old army camp on Salisbury Plain, where she was subjected to a horrific series of rapes." Lucas turns from the screen and reaches for his glass, taking a gulp of wine, which he seems to have difficulty swallowing. His eyes are no longer on the picture of Alex but are raking the room as if in search of a reaction. "She was raped not only by the men who took her, but by others who paid for the pleasure. She heard her captors arguing about how much to charge the bastard who got to go first. She was barely fourteen years old—a prize worth money, it seems."

I feel physically sick and my eyes fill with tears. I hear a sob from behind me—Nina, I think. We all know that girls of this age are raped, that the circumstances are always shocking, the act loathsome. But never before has it felt so close. Her pretty little face shows the impact of every single man who brutalized her.

I risk a look over my shoulder at Matt. His eyes are burning with tears.

"Alex was held for five days, naked, the sack tied over her head so she couldn't see her captors. In the end, my disgrace of a mother finally realized her daughter had been missing for days, and her disappearance was all over the news. Dad and I flew back from New Zealand, of course, but by the time we returned she had been found. Someone had called from a phone box to say where she was, but not before they had washed down her body with hydrogen peroxide to remove all traces of their DNA. She had the scars for years until they finally faded. The men were never caught. Alex came to live with us after that, and Dad became her legal guardian when our mother died a year later."

Lucas clicks the screen again. "Finally, this is Alex last year, about a month before she died. I managed to catch a quick shot of her when she didn't know I was there."

For the first time I see Alex's adult face full on. Last year I had never been able to get a clear look at her features; her hair always covered most of her cheeks. But now it's swept back, and I notice a slightly hooked nose that suits her angular cheekbones. It's a captivating face. Her expression is solemn, and I can see the sadness there.

It feels as if no one in the room is breathing. All I can think of is that young girl, trying to escape from a drunken mother, believing she was going to a place of safety and arriving to find that she was totally alone. I can feel her panic, her pain, even without what happened afterwards.

Lucas has left Alex's photo on the screen and is looking around the room again. When he breaks the silence, his quiet voice feels like an intrusion.

"Now do you understand how my sister suffered? Now do you understand why I want to find out how she died?" He bangs the flat of his hand on the table. "She said there was something about the night she was abducted that hadn't made sense to her, and when we were all gathered here for the wedding she heard something that made her wonder if there was an explanation for how it had happened. She asked herself the same question the police had asked over and over again. Why would three people randomly turn up in my father's garden where she was hiding? And she thought she might have found the answer."

"Surely if the police asked that question, they must have reached some conclusion," Nick says, his voice more tentative then I've heard it before.

"The police decided she must have been followed. That was the best they could offer."

"Perfectly plausible, I would have thought. Look, mate, just sit down and let me get you another drink."

Clearly alcohol was Nick's answer to every problem, but Lucas wasn't to be sidetracked.

He leaned two fists on the table. "I've been planning this for a long time, Nick, so please don't try to distract me. As it seems no one has any interest in food, can I suggest we move to the terrace, as we did last year? I'd like you to do exactly what you did that night—except the dancing. We can skip that. And please make notes of who you saw, at what time, and where they were or where they were going. Tomorrow the game will continue, and we'll see where our stories differ. Does anyone have any questions?"

I don't. Except I would love to ask if I could just go to my room.

"Shall we?" Lucas puts out an arm, inviting us all to go ahead of him to the terrace.

Everyone shuffles out through the door, heads down. No one could fail to have been moved by Alex's story, and it feels more appropriate for us each to go our separate ways to think about the child and how she suffered. But Lucas is having none of that, and everyone tries to do as he asks and take the same seats. Nina hasn't joined us, but last year she had remained inside to clean up. I remember the dancing, the music, and Nick trying to make it into a party. But then it was over.

It's now that brief period of the evening when twilight makes the shadows longer, blacker, more threatening than night. I feel safe while we are all here, but in a minute Andrew will leave, then Lucas. And I'll have to make my way back to our room, along the back terrace, up the private staircase, which is hidden from view. I won't know where Lucas is and Andrew will be out there somewhere too. Is he a threat? I'm suddenly terrified at the thought of the walk in the dark to our room and the hours I might be there alone before Matt comes to bed.

People are doing as Lucas asked, and as Chandra starts to move from the terrace towards the front of the house I realize that however appalled I was by the identical outfits we were asked to wear this evening, it all makes sense now. It's as if I'm seeing things through last year's eyes, and I remember crouching down by Matt to suggest an early night.

I look at him now, and I'm not sure what to do, but it's time for me to leave. I walk over to where he's sitting, and for a moment he looks almost scared, as if I'm going to say something that will embarrass him, so I bend down and speak to him quietly.

"I remember that just before she left, Alex spoke to you. What did she say, Matt?"

He turns his head quickly. "I don't remember her speaking to me, Jemma. For God's sake, don't make a thing of it now, okay?"

"I don't believe you've forgotten. However, just like last time, I'm going to bed. This time I won't wait up for you."

I didn't need to say that, but I want him to realize that I remember he didn't come straight to bed as he had promised. In fact, I never heard him come back at all.

CHAPTER 47

As I turn the corner to the wide, empty terrace, I stop in my tracks and look around. I can't see anyone, but there is a dark archway beneath the outside staircase and I don't know if anyone is standing there in the shadows. The door to the dining room stands open, a gaping black void now the candles are all out. Is someone hiding, waiting for me to walk past? There are no sounds of Nina and Lucas arguing as there were last year.

The distance from the corner to the staircase is no more than twenty meters, but it feels like a mile, and I slip my shoes off, walking on the warm flagstones in my bare feet so I can hear footsteps if anyone else is near.

I reach the bottom step and glance up. The light over our French windows is on, and I sigh with relief as I run up the stairs, only stopping at the top as I realize that all this time the door has been unlocked. Someone could have been in. They could be in there now.

I push open the door and stand well back, but the room is empty and I can finally breathe again. I check the bathroom, the wardrobe, even under the bed, but there is no one there. I open the drawers. Are they as we left them? Has someone been in here, examining our things? I don't know; I can't tell.

The room seems claustrophobic so I creep back out onto the balcony. I am jittery, unsettled, and I can't help wondering if Lucas is right. Does one of us hold a vital piece of the puzzle?

An icy shiver runs up my spine. I think of Alex's face, of how the poor child suffered so badly at the hands of those monsters, and how even on the day she died she was scared of someone—one of us.

I'm not sure if I'm safe out here, looking down on the empty terrace below. If anyone comes up the steps, I will hear them, see them. But if they come through the bedroom, I won't know they're behind me. I cast an anxious glance over my shoulder. The room is empty, the door closed. I wish there was a lock.

I gaze out over the trees towards the sea. In the failing light, the water seems menacing, hypnotic, as if it's waiting—perhaps to seize another body tonight. There isn't a breath of air, no rustle of leaves to offer background accompaniment to the rhythmic whoosh of the waves washing over the pebbles. And no sounds of voices or laughter either. Where is everyone?

Something is niggling at the back of my mind, trying to force the anxiety to one side, but I can't grasp the thought. It's to do with the photo of Alex that Lucas took last year, but it won't come to me.

I feel so restless. I get ready for bed, climb on top of the covers, and push myself up against the headboard so I can see both entrances to the room, ready to scream if the door opens and it's anyone other than Matt.

As I stare at the door to the corridor, I realize there is something different about the room. I don't know what it is. I look towards the bathroom. The door is closed. The wardrobe door is slightly ajar, but I might have left it that way; according to Matt, I often do. I look at the chest of drawers, the bowl of apricots sitting untouched on the top. A small bookstand contains a selection of paperbacks, just like before, but there's a gap. One of them has been removed.

I glance at my bedside table. The missing book is there, but I know I didn't take it from the bookstand. It's romantic fiction and not the kind of book I would choose to read right now, with things as they are in my life.

I pick it up. Who moved it? I know Matt wouldn't have put it there.

There is something sticking out, like a bookmark, and I open the pages. It's a black-and-white photograph of a young girl, and I know immediately who she is as she stands in the doorway of a wooden building of some sort. Could this be the summerhouse that Lucas mentioned? She's not posing for the photograph, and it's clear it was taken without her knowledge.

I peer more closely at the face. I would never have recognized her had Lucas not shown us those photographs earlier, but now I'm sure it's Alex. The corners of her mouth are turned down, and I can see she's crying, leaning against the door frame as if she needs to be held up. Then I look more closely. Someone is standing behind her, head bowed, in the gloomy interior of the building. Dark as the image is, in my mind there is no doubt who it is: Matt.

What had he done to upset Alex? And why has the picture been left here now?

I turn it over. On the back is one word.

Motive?

I'm desperate to talk to Matt, but I don't know where he is and I'm not prepared to go and look for him. I don't know what this means, but someone is trying to implicate Matt in Alex's death. And whoever it is, they've been in our room.

I pace back and forth, trying to convince myself that this is just someone out to make trouble. I try to focus instead on the night Alex died. If we answer Lucas's questions, we can get out of here, away from this toxic atmosphere.

Forcing the photograph from my mind, I wedge a chair against the door to the landing. It's not strong enough to keep anyone out, but the clatter it would make as it falls over will be enough to alert me to their presence, and I need to relive each moment.

The order of events won't come straight in my head. I saw someone heading down to the beach soon after I came upstairs. There was someone later too, and I felt sure it was Alex. Or maybe I just assumed. Then, moments later, the lights went out.

I remember something else. I'm sure at one point I heard the intercom buzzer, echoing in the house. Someone was at the gate. Could it have been the Romanian girl the detective was inquiring about?

Gradually impressions of that night flood back. I remember now. I could hear talking from below the white roof of the gazebo. Two people—a man, and a woman with a foreign accent. I presumed it was one of the staff—the Italian housekeeper, maybe. But Ivana was a plump woman in her late fifties. Her voice would have been different, deeper, slower. This voice was light, animated.

Could it have been the missing Romanian girl?

If it was, where did she go? Who was she speaking to? And why did no one admit it to the detective?

Whatever their motives, I'm not prepared to ignore what I heard. I need to contact the detective and tell her, even if I'm wrong, and for that I need her phone number, which is downstairs in the dining room. But the thought of wandering about in this vast house alone is disconcerting.

I shake myself. Surely I'm no threat to anyone. I barely know these people, so even if there is a killer here, he has nothing to fear from me.

I decide for no logical reason that being inside the house feels safer than outside, and I grab my phone to take a photo of the card so I can leave it where it is. No one needs to know I'm planning to speak to the police.

I move the chair out of the way and open the door slowly. There's no one in the corridor, and all the doors are shut. I tiptoe through the dark, silent house, terrified of meeting someone, anyone, not knowing if they can be trusted.

The door to the dining room is closed, so I push it open cautiously, hoping no one is there.

The candles have been extinguished, the smell of wax rich in the air, and only a faint glow is coming from the TV screen, which Lucas has left on. Something moves, and my heart leaps into my mouth. A girl is standing by the wall, staring at the photo of Alex on the screen. I gasp before I can stop myself, and she spins round, as scared as I am. I see it's the young blond waitress. She stares at me for a second and then bolts for the door, running from me as if I plan to hurt her. Maybe Lucas has infected her with his theories too. The poor girl had no doubt just finished clearing up, thinking everyone had gone to bed, and then I came sliding stealthily round the door. I must have terrified her.

I look at the photo of Alex again, and I realize that whatever I think of Lucas's mad way of going about things, I now desperately want to know what happened last year. If Alex killed herself, why? If she didn't do it, who did?

I have no more time to think about it; I need to find the detective's card. She propped it up on the mantelpiece, so I walk over, but I can't see it. I don't want to switch a light on and advertise the fact that I'm here, so I use the light on my phone.

I search the mantelpiece, the shelves of the dresser, and even the dining table, but the detective's card is nowhere to be found. Someone has taken it.

CHAPTER 48

Nina waited in their bedroom. She had no intention of following Lucas's instructions. She hadn't seen or heard anyone that night as she left the house to go down to the Japanese garden except Lucas and Alex, so there was no reason for her to go anywhere tonight.

She lifted her arms and massaged her tired cheeks with the heels of her hands, wishing Lucas would come. The revelations about Alex's abduction and rape had been devastating, and Nina felt every atom of her husband's pain. Maybe it excused his behavior, but she wasn't prepared to let him believe for another moment that she had intentionally lied to him.

She perched on the edge of the bed and tucked her hands under her thighs, waiting for the moment he walked through the door.

Nina suddenly remembered the earring that Jemma had found in the wood and jumped up. Lucas mustn't find it—it would be too much for him. She had known immediately that it was Alex's. She was wearing them at dinner the night she died, and maybe one had fallen out when she and Lucas were arguing.

Opening the drawer, she took it out. Apart from being a little dirty, it had survived well in the open air for all this time, and after a gentle rub with a tissue it was as good as new. Maybe too good, too perfect, to have lain there for all that time? Perhaps it wasn't Alex's, just something similar.

Nina felt her stomach churn. There was one explanation that she had to force herself to consider. The first year of her marriage had been anything but good, and Lucas had been away for much of the time—far longer than the previous year. When he was home he was never unkind, but he wouldn't let her get close to him, and she had to ask herself if there could be another reason for his distance. The earrings had been a present from Lucas to Alex, and they were precious to him. What if, after her death, he had given them to someone else—someone who mattered to him more than Nina did, and who was here now, in their home?

She thrust the earring back in the drawer and slammed it shut. She was making too much of this. She had probably been right the first time, and it had just been lying there for a year. She mustn't assume the worst. But now she didn't know whether to mention it to Lucas or not.

The minutes dragged. Lucas had to be watching the others, seeing what they did, where they went. So she walked over to the window. Their room faced east, and she could see nothing. No one was on the wide terrace below, and there were no sounds.

Suddenly she saw a flash of light-colored clothing as someone ran out of the back of the house from the dining room. Who was it? The figure passed under one of the lamps on the back of the house, and Nina recognized her. It was Essi, the girl Lucas had employed to help Adrianna with the cleaning while their guests were staying. Despite a momentary burst of indignation at Lucas's high-handed decision, Nina hadn't interfered with the arrangements other than to insist that the girl kept out of the kitchen when she was cooking. And she had.

Nina jumped as she heard the click of the door catch and spun round. Lucas was back. He pushed open the door and stopped dead, his lips tight. She could feel the heat of his anger, and her heart skipped.

"You shouldn't be here, Nina; you should be wherever you were on this night a year ago."

Nina wanted to scream at him for his lack of trust. But then she remembered his face tonight when he'd talked about Alex, and her fury subsided under a thick blanket of compassion.

"Come in, Lucas, and close the door. I need to talk to you. I need to tell you why I lied."

He seemed about to argue, but finally he took a step forward and closed the door, leaning back against it with his arms folded, waiting for her to explain herself. Once more she tamped down her outrage.

"After Alex died, before you had even asked where I was that night, you told me you had done something bad—something 'unforgivable.'" She looked at her husband's face. Only his eyes told her this wasn't a conversation he wanted to have. "I know what that something was, Lucas. That's why I never spoke to you about that night."

For a moment Lucas was still. Then in two strides he reached her, his hands heavy on her shoulders.

"You know nothing. Do you understand me? *Nothing.*"

Nina raised her chin defiantly. "I know you argued with Alex. She was crying, begging you to do something, although I don't know what. You shook her, Lucas. I couldn't believe you would do that, but you shook her. Then you spun her round and marched her down the path. You think you're the reason she killed herself, don't you?" Nina could hear her voice rising, and she tried to get it under control. "You blame yourself, and you can't live with that, so you have to push the blame onto someone else!"

To her surprise Lucas's shoulders dropped. The tension melted from his body, and he pulled her towards him.

"God, if only it were that simple." He held her quietly for a moment. "I need to ask you, Nina, is that all you saw? Did you follow us?"

She pulled her head back and looked up at him. "Of course I didn't. I came straight back here, but you slept in the other room, as we agreed. So the first chance I had to tell you was when you said you'd done something terrible. Of course I couldn't tell you then that I'd seen you. You were carrying a big enough burden of guilt without knowing that I'd witnessed your argument."

To Nina's surprise, Lucas let out a breath that caught in his throat. "Lovely, wonderful Nina. I'm so very sorry that I didn't trust you. I don't deserve you, and now I'm going to bring you nothing but unhappiness. I never intended it to be like this."

He pulled her even closer and she buried her face in his chest. She didn't know what he meant about bringing her unhappiness. Did it mean she was right? Was there someone else? Nina didn't want to think about that. She could smell the clean heat of her husband's skin though the thin linen shirt and wanted to undo the buttons to taste him.

As she lifted her hand towards the top button, Lucas spoke again. "It will all be over soon. I just hope you will forgive me."

Her hand stopped and came to rest on his collarbone. "What do you mean?"

"Please, whatever you do, don't tell another soul what you saw. It will ruin everything, and I have to know which of my friends is a murderer. The game must continue."

Nina kept her head lowered to hide her shock. She had believed this whole ridiculous charade would be over, and Lucas would admit it was his own guilt that was driving him.

Why, then, was he berating himself if it wasn't for his argument with Alex? And what was it that Lucas had done that was so terrible?

CHAPTER 49

After a restless night's sleep, when I wake up I still haven't decided what to do about the police. I know I need to say something, but I don't feel I can ask who has taken the detective's card because then Lucas will know I want to call her. I don't know who to trust, and I can't even be sure about Matt.

He came back to the room at about midnight, much earlier than the same night a year ago. I was sitting up in bed, watching the doors, and he looked slightly alarmed to see I was awake.

"Don't start, Jemma," he said, holding his hand up before I'd had a chance to speak. "I know you've probably got plenty to say about tonight, but I can't cope with a discussion. It's all too disturbing."

With that, he strode off towards the bathroom, but I leaped out of bed and blocked his way.

"Look at this," I said, thrusting the photograph under his nose. There was no point going for a subtle approach.

He looked into my eyes, then back down at the picture as if he wasn't sure whether to take it or not.

"Just bloody look at it, Matt. And turn it over."

Finally, he took the photo from my hand, and his eyes fell to Alex's face. He flipped it over and read the word on the back. The only light was from my bedside lamp, but I swear he lost all color from his cheeks. For a moment he didn't speak; then he threw the picture onto the bed.

"It's just someone out to make trouble."

"Lucas, you mean?"

"I don't know. Maybe. He's pushing all the right buttons, and you're reacting exactly as he might have predicted. He's trying to get under your skin—make you doubt me so you'll reveal everything you know. I've no idea what story you think this picture tells, but Alex was a young teenager, given to adolescent fits of tears. I don't remember that particular occasion. I was probably trying to make her feel better about something. So let it rest, will you?"

"No, I won't let it rest. Why does someone think you might have had a motive to kill her? Why won't you tell me where you were and what you were doing on this night last year, Matt? Why all the secrecy?"

"*Jesus!* Alex is the last person I would have killed. And I went for a walk—so leave it. I'm not saying another word."

With that he pushed past me and disappeared into the bathroom. I waited, drumming my fingers on my knees as I sat propped up in bed. But when he came out I could see small white discs in his ears and realized he'd put his Sleepbuds in and wouldn't hear a thing I said.

I wanted to shake him, rip them out, and force him to talk to me. But I could tell from the set of his mouth that I would get no more from him. If I'd pushed it, we would have ended up having a shouting match from which nothing would be gained.

He's sleeping now, so I've decided to get up. I creep around, getting dressed, dreading the moment when I have to force him to tell me the truth.

I make my way to the kitchen, hoping to find Nina. I need to ask for the Wi-Fi password so I can go online and track down the phone number for the detective, but the housekeeper is alone in the kitchen, and she can't help. From what I understand of her limited English, I think she's telling me the Wi-Fi isn't working at the moment. I glance at my phone. No signal. Sighing with frustration, I push it back into my pocket.

The housekeeper kindly makes me a cup of coffee and I take it outside to the front of the house and sit on the brick wall that edges the formal pond. I don't want to talk to anyone, but I'm out of luck as I see Andrew heading towards me.

"Are you okay?" he asks, lowering himself onto the wall next to me. "Last night was pretty intense, wasn't it?"

"Awful."

"Do you think any of us learned anything?"

"I learned what happened to Alex when she wasn't much more than a kid, which was shocking. I could see how Lucas felt about her." I take a sip of my coffee and hesitate before asking the next question. But the words burst from my mouth. "Do you think he's right—that she was killed? We were at the inquest, Andrew, and there didn't seem to be any doubt that it was suicide, so maybe it's the only way he can live with her death—by imagining someone is to blame. The trouble is, I have this uneasy feeling that if we all told the truth, things would emerge that would prove *something*, although I have no idea what."

Andrew looks a little shocked, but it seems I'm not the only one thinking that way. "Chandra thinks she knows something, and she's insisting that I don't lie for her again. I don't think Lucas has the power to hurt her with his threats though. She's tougher than she looks."

I can believe that. Chandra will stand by her principles, and I wish I was as strong.

"There's one thing you need to know," I say, wondering if it's a mistake to tell him. "In my character description Lucas threatens to tell Matt that you and I are having an affair."

"The *bastard*! Why would he do that?"

"Because he has to manipulate us—all of us—so we'll bow to his command. And you know Matt; it won't matter if it's true or not."

"It might be easier if it were anyone other than me," Andrew says.

"What do you mean?"

Andrew lifts his eyes to the sky, avoiding looking at me directly. "I had a bit of a reputation for stealing all the best girls, sometimes girls my friends were keen on. It was my childish way of proving that despite not having their affluent backgrounds, I was every bit as good as they were. I'm not proud of it, but Matt will think the worst."

I know he's right.

"Well, if he's manipulating me by using Matt's vulnerability, God knows what he's got on everyone else."

"Oh, I'll tell you what he thinks he's got on me—something else I'm not proud of." He gives a self-deprecating laugh. "Chandra's dad is absolutely loaded—he's a Korean online games billionaire. She doesn't talk about it if she can help it. Her mother is Hindu from Nepal, and as her parents have lived apart since she was very young, Chandra's spent her life vacillating between different religions, different cultures. All she wants now is to settle on one life, in one country, with one man. When she decided I was the one for her—God knows why—her dad offered to buy me a yacht in exchange for agreeing to marry her. He asked me never to tell her, and Lucas threatened to reveal our secret."

"That was kind of him."

Andrew grunts. "Well, it hasn't worked, because she told me last night that she's known all along. Christ, I feel so appalled at myself even as I say the words. You must be disgusted."

I glance at the deep frown between his eyebrows, and understand now what he meant about getting in too deep.

"I'm not the one you should worry about, am I? And anyway, how the hell did Lucas know?"

"Because I bloody well told him. In confidence. What infuriates me the most is that I would have played his stupid game anyway, without any threats, because I care about him."

I dangle my fingers in the cool water while I think what to say.

"How is Chandra coping with all this?"

"She's more than coping. She's amazing. She's taking the whole thing in her stride. But she would really like to talk to you, if you're up for it."

"Of course. Why wouldn't I be?"

"I'll go and get her." He leans towards me and kisses me on the cheek, then jumps up, glancing towards the house. Chandra is standing quietly in the doorway as if waiting for a signal. When she sees us both looking her way, she walks across.

"I'll leave you to it," Andrew says and heads for the terrace.

"How are you this morning, Jemma?" Chandra asks, taking a seat beside me.

"I would say I'm fine, but I'd be lying. Confused, worried, a bit scared. Any and all of those. What about you?"

"I'm okay. Has Andrew told you about his conversation with my father?" Without waiting for my reply, she carries on talking. "Many cultures—including my mother's—have marriages that rely on the dowry of the wife, and I never had a problem with Andrew being offered something for taking me. My father can afford it, and I think Andrew is a good man. We'll make good babies."

She gives me one of her gentle smiles, but despite the calm cadences of Chandra's voice, I still feel agitated.

"I'm glad Lucas didn't manage to cause a rift between you," I say. "And I think you're right about Andrew."

"He likes you, and I think he makes you feel good about yourself. You need that right now because Matt can't see your bright inner light. He is blinded by his own confusion. He has some problems, you know. They are related to Alex but not entirely."

I lift my eyes to stare at her. "What do you know, Chandra? What has he done?"

She reaches a hand out to mine, and I notice she's wearing a bracelet with an inward-facing stone. Something tugs at my memory.

"Nothing. I know only that he is tormented by something, and that Alex mattered to him."

I'm only half listening. "Chandra, you gave Alex a bracelet, didn't you?"

She meets my eyes. "Yes, to keep her safe. How do you know that?"

"I'm sorry. I heard you talking that morning and didn't want to disturb you, but I saw you hand it to her."

"I am only sorry it didn't work."

I close my eyes and concentrate. For some reason it seems important, but I don't know why.

"I know why you are thinking about it," she says softly.

I have no time to ask what she means because a shadow suddenly falls across us. Lucas is standing right beside me, and something in his eyes tells me he heard everything we said.

CHAPTER 50

Lucas has asked Chandra and me to join him in the dining room, so I do as he asks and Chandra silently follows. The table is groaning under platters of fruit, pastries, and a selection of hot food in covered dishes. It feels like something out of a costume drama and totally unnecessary. Everyone seems subdued and no one is eating.

Matt is down too, and I can see the strain in his eyes.

"Good morning," Lucas says, his face solemn. "I trust you all did some thinking last night and are prepared to share your thoughts. The game must continue. Who would like to start?"

Andrew is leaning against the wall, idly ripping a croissant to shreds. "I tell you what, Lucas, why don't we start with you and Nina? You seem to think we've all got something to hide, but why don't we hear from you two first?"

Lucas stares at his old friend.

"We'll get to me. None of us is exempt."

Nick rests his elbows on the table. He looks tired this morning, the habitual bonhomie absent. "Mate, do we have to do this? I can't remember much. I think I was taking advantage of your generosity and swigging back Armagnac on the terrace. I don't remember—honestly."

For a moment, I have a quick flash of recall. I saw someone heading down the path to the beach. Maybe it was Nick.

Lucas ignores him. "We all know that Andrew was on the phone, but where were you, Chandra? And don't look at me like that, Jemma. I'm not suggesting Chandra was involved, but unless we know what everyone saw, we're not going to know who's lying."

I shake my head, still unsure whether I should be going along with this. But I know why I'm still here—I want to know what Matt is going to say.

"I was meditating," Chandra says. That's all she offers, and Lucas doesn't push her, although I have a feeling it's a temporary reprieve.

Lucas turns to Matt, and my husband looks at me briefly before he speaks.

"I went for a walk."

"Where to?"

"I walked along the coastal path a way."

"Alone?"

Matt drops his eyes. "No, I was with Isabel."

One corner of Lucas's mouth turns up in a derisive smile, but I'm distracted by Chandra. She's looking puzzled. She doesn't believe him, but like me she's saying nothing.

"Isabel?" Lucas asks.

"Like Matt says. Walking."

He stares at Isabel for a moment before turning to me.

"Jemma?"

"I was in my room."

I want to say that I was waiting for my husband, but I don't want anyone's sympathy. I should tell Lucas that I think I saw Nick going down the path to the beach, that I heard voices, saw Nina. I want to say all these things, but still I say nothing. I feel as if my truths will in some way expose Matt's lies.

Lucas looks from Matt to Isabel and then back to me.

"At least one of you is lying. Maybe it's time for me to expose a character secret or two. We'll start with you, Matt."

Matt is staring at Lucas, and I can see a pulse beating in his neck.

"You first, Lucas," says Andrew, who has clearly not given up on his mission. "Let's hear what you have to say about where you were before you begin ruining the lives of your friends."

Lucas gives him a cold stare, but Andrew is unmoved.

"Fine. I was busy outside for about thirty minutes, making sure everything was locked up, particularly the drink delivered earlier that day. Nina was in her room. I know this because I went to say goodnight to her."

He's lying. I saw her going into the Japanese garden and suddenly I see red.

"What the hell is the point of us being truthful, Lucas, if you tell blatant lies? Nina *wasn't* in her room, and I strongly suspect that you weren't either. This is a bloody farce if you, of all people, are not prepared to admit where you were. Call the police, for God's sake, if you believe you're right, or I'll do it for you."

I march out of the house and onto the terrace. I'm going to my room to pack my things and leave.

The urge to escape is strong, but as I reach the bottom of the staircase to our balcony I realize that before I go anywhere I need to speak to Matt. We have been avoiding the truth for so long it's become second nature to ignore the problems between us, and it can't continue. I sit down on the bottom step, not sure whether to go back. Lucas will be furious with me now, and I don't want to meet his anger head-on.

As the adrenaline drains from my system I feel a tremor run through my body and I drop my head. I can't hide out here forever though, so after a few minutes I stand up to go in search of Matt. As I walk across the terrace towards the open dining-room door, I hear talking but no raised voices. I glance in and see that Lucas and Nina have both gone. Matt looks up, and I signal with my head that I want him to come and talk to me.

There is a bench on the lawn far enough from the house for us not to be heard but close enough for him to see where I am when he comes out, which I'm sure he will. He knows he can't ignore me forever.

After two or three minutes, just as I'm beginning to think I may have misjudged him, I hear footsteps on the flagged terrace, the heavy tread changing to little more than a whisper of sound as he moves onto the grass.

"Here you go. I've brought you a cappuccino." He hands me a cup, and I can't help looking up at him with surprise.

"Thank you." I take the cup from him and he sits on my left.

"This is uncomfortable, isn't it?" he asks.

I don't know if he's referring to things between the two of us, or the whole set-up.

"It's awful, but I'm more concerned about you and me. I don't know where to start, Matt. When we arrived her a year ago, we were happy. And yet in just twelve months we've fallen apart. There's a gap a mile wide between us, and I don't know why, or what I can do to fix things."

Matt is silent. We're not looking at each other, and I can see out of the corner of my eye that he's doing the same as me—switching his gaze from his coffee cup to the view of the seemingly endless miles of ocean straight in front of us.

"Do you want to fix things?" he asks quietly.

The truth is, I no longer know. It's been so hard for the past year, and every attempt I've made has been rebuffed. I can't keep trying and getting nowhere.

"Can you tell me why it started, do you think? Did I do something? Maybe if I understood what went wrong, at least from your perspective, I might be able to see where we're heading. I feel certain it was something that happened while we were here, but I've no idea what. I know there's something between you and Isabel, and I need you to tell me. Be honest with me. Are you in love with her, or even just having an affair with her?"

Matt lets out a bark of harsh laughter, and there's a tinge of relief in it, as if he's glad I've got the wrong end of the stick. "God, no. How could you even think that?"

"How could I *not*? You were with her that night, and you didn't come back until the early hours of the morning. You must have been with her for about four hours, so what am I supposed to think?"

Matt is staring at me. His pupils are dilated, his emotions on a knife edge. *What has he done?*

"What kept you from me that night? If only you would tell me the truth, Matt, all of it, then we might be able to salvage something."

"I'll tell you this much. I despise Isabel. She tried hard to ruin Lucas's life all those years ago, and if it hadn't been for Alex, she might well have got away with it."

"What do you mean? What happened?"

Matt turns to look over his shoulder, clearly worried that he might be overheard.

"You've seen the way she is with him. She's obsessed and always has been. Lucas was kind to her. He was the kindest boy I'd ever met and made time for everyone, but he kept his distance from Isabel as much as he could. Until his nineteenth birthday party. It's the only time I ever saw him drunk. The rest of us used to get hammered regularly. Why is it that as a teenager you think there's something really great about getting plastered? Anyway, Lucas was the sensible one, and I seriously don't know what happened that night. The rest of us were too pissed to notice."

Matt takes a sip of his coffee and grimaces. It must be stone cold by now.

"Apparently, and I was too far gone to see this, Isabel managed to lure him down to the summerhouse. We only have her word for what happened next, but she says they had sex. Lucas was too much of a gentleman to confirm or deny it—either that or he couldn't remember, and then she hung on to him like a clam, touching him all the time, acting as if they were boyfriend and girlfriend."

"Did he like her?"

"*No!* But I think he liked Nick back then—not so sure now—and despite recent evidence to the contrary, Lucas has always been an honorable guy. Anyway, after about a month of trying to avoid her, he finally plucked up the courage to dump her."

There is something slightly wrong in all of this. "If he was so honorable, how come he told you all this? It's quite cruel to share that kind of stuff."

"He didn't tell me; Alex did. She couldn't stand Isabel."

"Why the hell did Lucas invite Isabel to the wedding last year, then?"

Matt sighs. "He didn't. He invited Nick with a plus one. He didn't know she was coming until she got here. Again, Alex told me that."

I want to ask him more about Alex—when he had these conversations with her—but he hasn't finished the Lucas and Isabel story yet.

"About two weeks after he dumped her, Isabel turned up claiming she was pregnant. She swore Lucas was the father, and he believed her. Blair told him he would provide for mother and child, and she could have anything she wanted. Except Lucas, who he didn't want to see saddled with a madwoman—his words apparently. He'd already been there himself with Lucas and Alex's mum, and he wouldn't have wished that on his son. But Isabel said she would prefer to be penniless, if only she could have Lucas."

I can picture it all. There's nothing original about the story, and for a moment I wonder how many times this stunt has been pulled. I know Isabel doesn't have any children, so I can guess what's coming next.

"Alex was the one who brought it all to an end. She found Isabel in her room one day. As Alex walked in, Isabel was rooting around in one of her drawers and she spun round and hid something behind her back. Alex was quite tough back then—living with her mother would have done that. She walked over and fought with Isabel to find out what it was. It was a tampon. She wasn't and never had been pregnant."

"What did Isabel expect to happen? Surely she knew she couldn't keep up the pretense?"

"Of course. But she claimed she'd lost the baby and sobbed about how devastated she was. Lucas chose to believe her. But Blair never did, and so he packed Lucas off on an extended gap year. Then all that shit happened to Alex, and when he got home Lucas had nothing to do with anyone—just looked out for his sister and spent all the time he could with her. By then he was certain that his drinks at the party had been spiked. He swore he'd been drinking Coke for most of the evening, and yet he was totally hammered. Isabel, no doubt. It was the only way she was going to get him."

I say nothing, but I have a sneaking suspicion he's wrong about the drinks. If I had to put money on it, I would guess that Isabel persuaded her twin to do her dirty work.

Matt has just told me more than ever before. But this is about other people and their relationships. I can't see how it could have affected ours, nor does it help me understand his relationship with Isabel now. It's a start, but I need more.

I offer to go and get him another cup of coffee to give him a bit of breathing space, in the hope that when I return I can persuade him to tell me more.

"Don't go anywhere, Matt. We've only scratched the surface here."

I squeeze his arm gently and he turns sad eyes to mine, as if getting beneath the skin of this problem is going to be more than he—or maybe I—will be able to bear. I stand up and leave him in the sunshine.

*

The dining room is quiet, and only the young waitress I scared last night when I came down into the dining room is in the kitchen.

"I was hoping to get another couple of cappuccinos. Can you tell me how to work the machine, please?" It's a fancy Italian model, and I don't feel competent to fiddle with it.

"Of course," she says, turning her gray eyes to mine and smiling politely. "I will make the coffee but show you too."

As she describes which buttons to press in a strong accent which I am certain is Scandinavian, I feel I should apologize for scaring her last night. But she seems shy, so instead I smile, thank her for her help, and step back outside, only to discover Chandra is now sitting next to Matt on the bench. The stone of the terrace feels warm under my bare feet and I approach without a sound. I'm about to speak, to ask Chandra if I can fetch something for her, when I hear her say to Matt, "I didn't say anything because I didn't want to stir up any more problems, but I know you weren't with Isabel. I heard you on the terrace when I was going to the cottage to meditate. You were talking to Alex, weren't you?"

It's as if some sixth sense makes Matt turn his head slightly, and he sees me standing there, coffee cups in my hands.

Chandra turns too and gives me a gentle smile. "I think if we are ever going to silence Lucas, we are all going to have to tell the truth, don't you, Jemma? I know there was something you wanted to say when we were in the dining room earlier. I saw you tense. Why don't we all say what really happened, and then Lucas might accept that Alex took her own life?"

I don't know what to say to that, but it's as if none of it matters. I need to know why Matt hasn't told anyone that he was talking to Alex that night.

"Matt, is Chandra right? Were you with Alex?"

Matt shakes his head, but he won't look at either of us. "It was something and nothing. I'd forgotten all about it."

I put the coffee cup down on a small table with too much force, and the hot liquid spills.

"Oh, come on, Matt. If you were talking to Alex, you might have been the last person to see her alive. Of course you hadn't forgotten, so why for God's sake can't you just tell us what happened—what you were talking about?"

It's as if he's been struck dumb. He's searching for something to say, and Chandra speaks softly. "You possibly can't remember, but I think you were asking Alex if she had ever told anybody something—some secret or other?"

For the first time, I think there might be slightly more to Chandra. She asked that as if with total innocence, and yet it's a huge question.

Matt swallows and turns towards her. "I don't think so. I can't think what that might have been."

"I heard you—both of you. It might help Jemma to understand your current confusion if you were honest with her, and maybe with all of us."

I can't take my eyes off Matt's face, and when he raises his eyes to mine I can see he's scared. Really scared.

"Chandra, can you leave us to have a chat, please?" I ask.

I see sympathy in the other woman's eyes as she gets slowly to her feet and dips her head slightly. I find myself wanting to shake her, and it shocks me. I'm not given to violence, and I realize how this whole game of Lucas's is damaging everyone around him. I sit down in her vacated space.

"Matt, we have to talk about this, but more than anything I want to get away from here. Now, not in two days' time. I'm beginning to think that Lucas isn't as mad as we think. There are so many undercurrents, so many lies. If he's right and someone here is a killer, any one of us could be in danger just by knowing too much."

Matt licks his lips as if his mouth is too dry to speak. "We can't leave, Jemma—at least I can't. You go, but please don't ask me to go with you."

"Well, tell me about Alex then. Why didn't you say you were with her? What secret did you want her to keep, and why let me believe you were with Isabel for all that time?"

Matt says nothing, and I jump to my feet, glaring down at him. "This is ridiculous. I'm out of here, and if you won't take me, I'll get a bloody taxi!"

I turn back towards the house. Nick and Isabel have come out into the sunshine, and I can't stand looking at either of them right now: Nick in his garish shirt, still trying to pretend this is a party, although even I can see the strain around his eyes; Isabel with that permanent half-smile and the knowing looks she casts at everyone—I don't trust her an inch.

I leave Matt staring into thin air as I stomp back towards our room. He's not going to help me, but I'm sure Stephanie King will.

CHAPTER 51

Stephanie had been full of good intentions when she and Gus had gone to bed the night before. She'd planned for them to celebrate their one-year anniversary with a long lie-in followed by a breakfast of fresh fruit, scrambled eggs, and smoked salmon, and maybe—if they were still hungry—an almond croissant. But try as she might, she couldn't ignore the fear that she might be about to lose him again, and she didn't want to let her anxiety ruin the day.

After Gus had very satisfactorily reminded her of the joys of waking up next to him—a rarity in their hectic lives—she did her best to relax and lie still in his arms, but he could feel her tension.

"Steph, we don't know what's going to happen yet. Let's wait until we have all the facts before we start to panic."

She nestled closer to him, her head on his chest where he couldn't see the worry lines between her eyebrows. He was right, and anyway, unless he wanted to kiss his career goodbye, the decision was out of their hands.

When Gus had returned from his assignment to Leeds a year ago, the relief that he still loved her had demolished the last of the barriers she'd erected against her feelings for him. He was worth the risk—every shred of it—but it was too much to hope that it would be plain sailing.

"I need to tell you something," he'd said that very first night. "I've been a DI for too long, and if I'm ever going to climb at least one rung higher up the ladder, now's the time. But if it's going to cause a problem between us, it's better we deal with it straight away."

Gus was ambitious, and if she denied him the opportunity of promotion, some part of him would always resent it, however much he denied it. But she also knew what it meant. If Gus applied for promotion and was accepted, he would have to go wherever he was sent, possibly a hundred miles away or more, given the area covered by the Devon and Cornwall force. In most jobs that might not be the end of the world—traveling home on a Friday night, leaving early on a Monday morning—but not in their job. It just didn't work like that.

Stephanie had managed to push the threat of their separation to the back of her mind for months, but now it was happening. The moment of truth was coming—the time when she would have to decide if she was prepared to follow him wherever he was sent, maybe at the expense of her own career. And it was so much more than that. Stephanie had lived in this part of Cornwall her whole life; it was her home. She loved every inch of the beautiful countryside, the beaches, the cliffs. Her friends and family were here too. She would have to give up so much to be with him, and what if their relationship stumbled again, as it had before?

"Are you okay, darling?" Gus asked gently as she fidgeted next to him. "I know telling you not to worry is pointless, but stop dreaming up the worst possible scenario. I could be offered a job even closer to here."

She had to stop this, or she was going to ruin the day.

"It's not that, Gus. I'm thinking about Polskirrin." She rolled onto her back. That wasn't entirely true, although the events of the previous evening had been troubling her and they provided a useful diversion. "I know I shouldn't be so hung up on it, but the behavior of those people last night was weird. I just keep seeing images of strange rituals—ones in which women get killed."

"Bloody hell, that's a wild theory even for you! You don't even know that your Romanian girl was there."

Stephanie knew he was right, but she could often pick up feelings from a room full of people. The air felt different when they were upset, worried, angry, or—worst of all—evil. She hadn't been able to tell exactly *what* they were feeling last night, but it wasn't as simple as sadness—she was certain of that.

"You're right, but I want to find out more about Lidia Dalca. You had to be there, Gus. No one was looking at anyone else: husband and wife, brother and sister, friends—they all seemed remote from each other. The combination of the atmosphere, 'The Murder Game' on that notepad, Alex's place card—it gave me goosebumps. If Lidia went there last year, what was she walking into?"

"What—if anything—do you know about her?"

"I know she wasn't considered to be at risk, but some basic inquiries will have been made so I'll take a look tomorrow to see if there's anything there—friends, people she'd met who might have expected her to keep in touch. The usual."

"Tomorrow?" Gus said, lifting himself onto one elbow to look down on her. He knew her too well.

"Yes," Stephanie said, her tone determined. "She's been missing a year; another day won't hurt. Let's not spoil today."

Gus had the good grace to laugh. "Let's just get it done, shall we? If you're fixated on this, you won't be fully with me anyway."

"I was earlier," she said indignantly.

"You were indeed." He kissed her gently. "But don't forget, Polskirrin is important to me too. Come on, let's have breakfast and then we'll go."

He was right. And the more she focused on Lidia, the less space she would have in her head to worry about their unknown future.

*

If anyone was surprised to see Stephanie walk into the station with Gus, no one commented, and apart from a few friendly nods they were left to get on with their research.

The case file was ready and waiting for her, and Stephanie started to read. Gus opted not to look over her shoulder because it irritated her. Instead he pulled out his phone to read the news until she had something to tell him.

After half an hour, she was finished.

"Well?" Gus said.

"Pretty much what I was told. Lidia stayed in a hostel, paid a couple of days in advance. There's twenty-four-hour access to the place, so no one knows if she came back or not. She left a few clothes but she didn't have much, and had told another girl that if she got a job she was going to buy herself some new jeans—hers were falling apart. So the assumption was she'd moved on. No obvious links to any of the guests at Polskirrin."

"What now?"

"I'll try to get an interpreter—maybe the cousin—so we can talk to Lidia's mother. Find out everything the daughter said, check it was the right night. It's more than possible it was a different date, a different wedding. Let's see if we can get some better photos too. Perhaps we can jog someone's memory up at Polskirrin, if it's the right place."

"Do you want to contact the cousin now?" Gus asked, his face neutral.

"No, I don't. I'll get someone to set up a call for tomorrow." She pasted a bright smile on her face. "Come on, let's go and enjoy the rest of the day."

"You sure about that?"

"I am."

Gus was watching her as if he expected her to say something else. As usual, he was right.

"I'll just phone Nina Jarrett to check all their guests will still be there tomorrow in case I need to talk to them again. Then I'll get someone to ask for the photos."

"Is there anything I can do?"

She gave him a sheepish smile. "No, you're fine, thanks." But as she headed to the door, she stopped and turned. "Actually, there is. I made notes about my impressions of the original Alexandra Lawrence kidnap case after she died. They're in my personal file. Do you mind printing them out? I'll take them home to refresh my memory. I'll be back in a minute when I've got things moving."

Twenty minutes later they were in the car, Gus driving as Stephanie read through the papers he had printed for her. Gus hadn't had any further involvement in Alex's death once it was established that there was no crime, but Stephanie had taken a keen interest in the girl and what might have driven her to suicide.

"Oh, Gus, I'd forgotten what an awful time that poor girl had. It's heartbreaking."

"Go on," he said, without taking his eyes off the road.

"Imagine falling asleep and the next thing you know a sack's being forced over your head. It's too horrible to contemplate. She felt two pairs of hands holding her down as she kicked and screamed, and then someone else stuck something like a ball into her mouth, pushing the cloth in with it and making her gag."

"I remember she was raped more than once," Gus said, his mouth a straight line.

"She was—by several different men, she thought, although they never removed the sack so she didn't see them. One thing she told the police but begged them never to use—not even in court, if it ever came to that—was that after the first man raped her, he demanded a refund."

"He *what*?" Gus swiveled his head towards her before quickly turning back to the road.

"He wanted some of his money back because he said—although of course there was no way he could know this for sure—that she wasn't what he'd been promised."

"Which was?"

"A virgin."

CHAPTER 52

When I reach our room my first instinct is to throw myself on the bed and cry. The tension is building in me, hour upon hour, and I feel as if my chest is fizzing with it. I sit down and take a few deep breaths, following some of the strategies I give my patients when they're trying to control their speech. Nothing works. Maybe they're not designed for people who might be sharing a house with a killer.

I pull my phone from my pocket, but there's still no signal.

"Shit!" I step out onto the balcony, where it's a little better, and call directory inquiries.

The line keeps breaking up, and because I'm trying to speak quietly the operator keeps asking me to repeat myself.

"Penzance police station," I say as softly as I can, turning my back to the terrace in the hope that my voice won't carry. Finally, he understands me, and I hear a ping as the text arrives with the number.

I don't want to call from here. There is too much risk of being overheard, and I'm certain there are people here who won't appreciate what I'm about to do, so I grab a towel from the bedroom as if I'm going for a swim and head for the beach. If there's no signal there, I'll walk up to the top of the cliff and keep walking along the coastal path until I get one.

I sling the towel over my shoulder and push the phone into the pocket of my shorts, then run down the outside staircase and onto the terrace.

"Going somewhere, Jemma?"

The voice makes me nearly jump out of my skin. Isabel is standing in the doorway directly below our balcony. Could she have heard me ask for the number for the police?

"Just to the beach," I say with a nonchalant shrug. "Only to paddle. I'm not brave enough for this cold water."

"There are wetsuits, you know. They keep them in the boathouse."

She must see the look of shock on my face.

"Not in the apartment," she says, a sneer in her voice. "Underneath, where they keep the boat, although it probably won't be there. Andrew was talking about putting it in the water this morning so he can go sailing after lunch. If you run, you might catch him. You could sail away together." She laughs without a trace of humor and turns to go back into the house. I just catch her parting shot. "I can't wait to see what new revelations lunch is going to bring, can you?"

I stare after her for a second. She knows I want to get away from here, but maybe she's right about a swim. No one else seems uncomfortable with the idea of swimming in the spot where Alex died, so perhaps when I've called the police I should find a wetsuit—the cold water might be exactly what I need.

Matt has gone from the bench and no one else seems to be around, so, head down, I set off along the narrow track. Since I was last here the bushes seem to have grown denser, closer together, almost as if they're trying to block my way. Tendrils of ivy caress my flesh as I step beneath them, their touch feather-light, bringing goosebumps to my skin. The high banks cut out all sound, and I feel isolated, vulnerable. The rough steps seem more treacherous, their damp surface glowing in what little light penetrates the canopy, and I'm relieved to emerge onto an empty beach.

Isabel was right about Andrew taking the boat out. It's in the bay, pointing out to sea, but it's not moving. The small tender that I presume goes with it is on the shore, and I wonder if he has come back for something. I gaze around, but I can't see him anywhere. The cove is deserted.

I head for the flat black rocks past the boathouse—the ones Andrew dived from last year—and shiver as I remember how terrified I was that he would hurt himself. I get as far from the beach as I can and turn so I can see if anyone is coming. The signal is still not great, but I think it's good enough.

"Good morning. Would it be possible to speak to Detective Sergeant Stephanie King, please?"

"I'm sorry, but DS King isn't on duty today. Can anyone else help?"

I feel my shoulders sag. I was so pumped up with the thought of what I had to tell her, and now I don't know what to say. She's the only person I feel I can talk to—the only one who might understand. I want to tell her that I think the Romanian girl did come that night, and if I'm right someone must have seen her, spoken to her, and for some reason I don't understand they're refusing to admit it. But it's more than that. I have to tell her about Lucas and his murder game. If Alex's murder isn't just a figment of his imagination, how far will the killer go to cover his tracks?

But she's not there.

"Could you please tell DS King as soon as you can that Jemma Hudson called from Polskirrin? Could you tell her that I may have some information on the Romanian girl?" I pause for a moment, not knowing whether to say the rest or not, but in the end I think I have no choice. I give the policeman a message that I hope will make sense to Sergeant King.

"Right. Thank you, Ms. Hudson. Do you want me to get someone else to come out to you? You sound very concerned."

"No, it's fine. I'm probably getting things out of proportion. I'd just like to talk things through with DS King, to see what she thinks."

"Okay, I'll make sure she gets the message."

I end the call. There's nothing more I can do, but I'm restless, my legs twitching. I can see that Andrew—or someone—has left the doors to the boathouse open. I haven't brought a swimsuit with me, but maybe I could pull a wetsuit on over my underwear.

I stand up, grabbing my towel and shoving my phone in the back pocket of my shorts as I wander across the pebbly beach. Inside, the boathouse is much bigger than I expected, and extends back into the cliff, its full length invisible from outside. The space is illuminated to about halfway back by daylight spilling through the open doorway, but beyond that deep shadows hide whatever is there. As my eyes adjust from the bright sunlight to the dim interior I feel a jolt of shock and stop dead. In the far corner, somebody is hanging from a rope, two legs swinging backwards and forwards, two arms limp at the sides of the body.

A cry escapes my lips. I look behind me to see if anyone is there to help, but the doorway is empty.

What should I do?

I step cautiously forward and feel a breeze tickle the back of my neck. The body swings, its head hidden in the deep shadow cast by the roof. I move closer. I need to check if whoever it is is still alive. My mind flashes to Andrew—the tender on the beach—and I forget my fear and rush towards the body.

I'm about ten meters away when I let out a sob of relief. It's not a person at all; it's a wetsuit, hanging up to dry. Behind it I can see a rack with more black neoprene suits in all sizes, each on its own hanger. Slowly I head towards them, not yet free of the sinister sense of menace they have aroused.

As I move, I peer around the boathouse. There appears to be a vast range of equipment: an overhead hoist; racks on the walls with a couple of kayaks; all kinds of wet-weather gear; life jackets;

a small inflatable launch seated on a frame. I notice steps heading up in the far corner behind the wetsuits, and I presume these provide another route into the apartment.

It is absolutely silent inside the boathouse, and a crunch on the pebbles outside causes my heart to skip a beat. I swivel towards the sound. A man is silhouetted in the doorway, the sun behind him. I can't see who it is.

I'm about to take a step towards him when I sense a whisper of movement behind me. Before I can turn, my body freezes. Tiny pinpricks of fear shiver across my flesh as something is whipped over my head and pulled down, and I feel a scream building in my lungs. It bursts from my mouth, but the sound is muffled as the fabric is pulled tighter. I can barely breathe. *This can't be happening.* I thrash backwards with my arms, my elbows, my heart pounding in time with the feet I hear rushing towards me. For a moment, I think I'm saved.

But I'm wrong. My arm is grabbed and twisted so the soft skin is exposed. I fight, kick, try again to scream, but then I feel a sharp prick in my flesh. Strong fingers hold my arm in a vise-like grip and my mind becomes crystal clear.

I am going to die.

I'm gasping for breath now, the hood over my face sticking to my lips and nostrils as I fight to inhale. Sweat trickles down my back as I kick out at the person in front of me.

Then everything changes. My body starts to tingle—my arms, back, neck, feet. I feel heavy. My legs no longer respond to my demands to kick. The world seems to have slowed down, and all I want to do is fold slowly to the floor and sink into sleep. Somewhere deep inside I'm aware that I am being half dragged, half carried, up some stairs. But I no longer care.

CHAPTER 53

Nina thought they looked a sorry bunch at the lunch table. She'd hung around in the kitchen all morning trying to be useful but in truth had little to do with preparing the food. Her mind wouldn't settle on anything other than Lucas and everything he still hadn't told her. And what had he meant when he said he was going to bring her nothing but unhappiness? It had to be another woman— someone he visited when he was on one of his increasingly long journeys for the foundation.

Her thoughts were interrupted by Matt.

"Has anyone seen Jemma?" he asked, his brow wrinkled with concern.

"Have you tried your room?" Nina asked.

"No, I thought she'd be out here reading. Sorry to disturb lunch, Lucas. I'll go and see if she's there."

"No need. I'll ask Adrianna to go. She can tell her that lunch is ready."

As the housekeeper laid two platters of food on the table, Lucas turned to speak quietly to her in Italian.

Matt had risen in his seat and looked reluctant to sit down again. But Lucas nodded at him, and he lowered himself slowly back into his chair.

"Lucas, I'm sure we're all wondering what's best to do now," Nick said, his tone conciliatory. "It's been a difficult twenty-four hours, which I'm sure we all expected in view of the circumstances. But there have been accusations and threats, and I think it's time for us to make our way home and leave you to it. You and Nina need to try to get your lives back to normal, and you don't want us here muddying the water."

Nina wanted to cheer and say, "Yes, please—as soon as you can," but Lucas had been watching Nick as he spoke, his jaw set.

"No one is going anywhere, Nick. We will continue with the game. I have collected your notebooks from the dining room, so now we'll review every piece of evidence and carry on until I discover which of you killed my sister."

"Come on, mate," Nick began.

Lucas's expression didn't change, but Nina could sense the anger burning brightly, barely controlled.

"Nick, if you call me *mate* once more, I swear I'll throttle you. I know you think you've done me many favors in the last few years, but I've never asked you to, and I've never once taken you up on any of your kind offers. Be careful, *mate*, or you'll find yourself in a lot of trouble."

"Jesus, this is getting out of hand," Andrew said. He appeared to be about to say more when they heard the sound of the intercom at the gate.

"I'll go," Nina said, her voice little more than a whisper. She didn't look at Lucas as she rose from the table and made her way out to the hall.

Bloody hell, Stephanie thought as Nina took her and Gus round to the terrace where her guests were—in theory—enjoying lunch. If anything, they looked even more shell-shocked than they had the evening before, and when each of them turned to look her way, their eyes were glassy, unfocused. What else had happened?

"I apologize for disturbing your lunch," she said. "Some of you may remember my colleague Detective Inspector Brodie from last year."

Any surprise that Lucas might have felt at their appearance was hidden under a mask of politeness.

"What can we do for you, Officers?" he asked.

"We're here to speak to Jemma Hudson."

"As you can see, Sergeant, Jemma isn't here. Can I help?"

"No, I'm afraid not, Mr. Jarrett. Jemma called and left a message for me. She wanted to speak to me in person. I've tried her mobile repeatedly, but I can't get a response." She fixed her gaze on Jemma's husband. "Mr. Hudson—I'm presuming you're a mister, as you're a surgeon?"

"That's right. Matt Hudson." He seemed to be attempting a smile, but it was a weak effort.

"Where's your wife, sir?" Stephanie asked.

Gus still hadn't spoken. Stephanie had told him in no uncertain terms that he could come with her, but he was there to observe and mustn't interfere unless it was absolutely necessary. This was her investigation, not his.

"Jemma hasn't come down for lunch yet," Matt said. He was shifting around in his chair, clutching a fork in his hand as if his life depended on it. "Lucas, you asked Adrianna to tell her lunch is ready, didn't you?"

Lucas pushed some tomatoes around on his plate as if thinking.

"I didn't want to say anything yet, because Jemma asked me to delay telling you for as long as possible. I'm sorry, Matt; she's gone."

Matt sat forward on the edge of his chair. "What do you mean? When? How? The car's still here."

"I know. I organized a taxi to take her to the station. She didn't want you to know until after the train had left in case you decided to go after her. I think something upset her this morning— something she'd heard. Do you know what it was?"

Lucas raised his eyes to look at Matt with apparent innocence, but Stephanie could feel the threat in his words. Matt looked away.

"Why didn't she say goodbye?" he asked.

"I have no idea. It was her choice. No doubt you'll find out when you eventually catch up with her."

Stephanie said nothing. It seemed very odd that Jemma would call her with information and then leave.

"Mr. Hudson, can you please go and check if you wife's things have gone—if not her clothes, then at least her bag, her purse, her phone."

"I'll come with you," Gus said as Matt pushed back his chair. Stephanie knew Gus wanted to make sure Matt Hudson was telling the truth. She could feel how much he distrusted these people.

She waited until the two men had walked round the side of the house before she spoke again. "If it turns out Jemma *has* left, as you say, Mr. Jarrett, I'll need to talk to each of you. Although I didn't speak to Mrs. Hudson myself, she told my colleague that she believes Lidia Dalca *did* come here on the eve of the wedding last year, so I'll need to check with each of you whether you might have seen her."

Again, Stephanie had that strange sensation that no one looked at anyone else. They each found something of interest on their plate, in their glass, or on the roses hanging magnificently from the pergola above them. She hadn't planned to say any more until Gus was back, but she wanted to provoke some reaction from at least one person.

"Her message also said that you, Mr. Jarrett, believe your sister didn't commit suicide. You believe someone killed her."

There was no gasp of surprise from any of the guests. Not a flicker. And only Lucas Jarrett looked at her, his eyes filled with animosity.

CHAPTER 54

Stephanie didn't attempt to make polite conversation while they waited for the two men to return. The group at the table had said nothing since her pronouncement. They didn't speak to each other, nor did they eat any of the delicious-looking food, although most of them were gulping down the wine.

A few minutes later a forlorn-looking Matt Hudson walked back onto the terrace, followed by Gus, who gave Stephanie an almost imperceptible nod.

"Do you mind if DI Brodie and I sit down, Mrs. Jarrett?" Stephanie asked.

Nina glanced at her husband as if for permission before indicating the vacant seats with her hand.

"Can you confirm that your wife's things have gone, Mr. Hudson?" she asked as she took a seat facing Lucas.

Matt hung his head. "Her handbag's gone, and her toiletries. Some of her clothes are still here, but I expect she thought I would pack them in with mine, in the bigger suitcase. She's taken the smaller one."

"And where do you think she'll have gone?"

"Home!" he said as if it were impossible that she could have gone anywhere else.

"If you speak to her before I do, ask her to give me a call. Here's my number." Stephanie passed him a card, wondering for a moment what had happened to the one she had left the night before.

"Now, let's talk about the concerns voiced by Mrs. Hudson, shall we? In her message, she said she believed Lidia—the Romanian girl I asked you all about last night—may very well have been here. She didn't give any details of why she believed that, but when I speak to her later I'll ask. In the meantime, have any of you got anything to add?"

Her question was met with silence.

"Mr. and Mrs. Jarrett, if someone came to the gate, I presume they would have had to press the intercom button, and someone would have had to let them in. Am I right?"

"Not necessarily," Lucas said. "People were coming and going all night. She could have slipped through the gates as someone left. The gates open automatically when anyone approaches from inside the property to get out."

"A car could slip in undetected?"

"No, but a pedestrian could."

"I don't remember saying she was on foot. It's quite a walk from town, so that's a bit of an assumption."

Lucas just stared at her.

"Oh, for God's sake!" The outburst came from the man in the loud shirt with short, spiky hair, who Stephanie knew to be Nick Wallace. "Look, she was here—the girl. I saw her. Okay? I didn't see anyone speak to her though, and I didn't speak to her myself."

There was a muttered "Jesus, Nick" from his sister.

"Why didn't you mention this when I was here last night, Mr. Wallace?" Stephanie asked, her voice tight with anger.

He pushed long fingers through his hair, which made it stand up even more. "Because she was alive and well and heading away from the house."

Stephanie glared at him and, sensing her irritation, Gus took up the questioning.

"Where did you see her, and what was she doing, Mr. Wallace?"

"She was heading along the path away from the house. It leads to the coastal walk, or you can turn left down to the cove."

"You told us you were on the terrace, drinking my brandy?" Lucas said, his voice clipped.

"Yes, I did say that, Lucas. Because I knew what you'd think if I told you where I'd really been."

Lucas stared at his friend and seemed about to speak when Stephanie intervened.

"Mr. Wallace, please tell us more about when and where you saw Lidia."

"I was coming up from the beach. I'd just reached the main path when I heard footsteps. I thought it was Alex, so I dodged into the bushes."

"Why would you do that?" Lucas asked. Stephanie was tempted to say that they would ask the questions, but she waited to hear the answer.

"I didn't want her to know I was there. Okay?"

Lucas's stare was intense, and it seemed as if he wanted to ask more. But after a few seconds he looked away.

"Is the path not lit at night?" Gus asked. "I remember noticing some lights in the ground when we came here last year."

"The lights were on when I went down, but they went out when I was about halfway back. Anyway, I realized it wasn't Alex. It was a girl, but her hair was up in one of those donut things, as you said. I thought she would be frightened if she saw me, so I stayed behind the shrubs."

"Didn't you wonder why some strange girl was wandering around the grounds in the dead of night?" Gus asked.

"Not really. The coastal path runs for miles, or I thought maybe she was going down to the cove to meet someone."

"Someone from here? Another guest?"

"No idea. It wasn't me, but I can't speak for anyone else." He glanced from Lucas to Matt, raising his eyebrows as his gaze rested on Andrew. "Maybe it was Andrew, up to his old tricks."

Andrew just gave a dismissive shake of the head, clearly feeling this wasn't worthy of a response.

"You still haven't yet told us why you went to the boathouse," Matt said, speaking up for the first time since he'd realized his wife had gone.

"None of your bloody business."

"No, but it's mine." Lucas leaned forward.

Nick sighed. "For God's sake, I just wanted a quiet word with Alex, but she wasn't there."

"How do you know?"

"Lucas, can we drop this? Maybe we could talk about it privately?"

"No, we can't. Did you go into the apartment? And if you wanted to talk to her, why did you hide when you thought it was her?"

Nick's face was covered in a fine sheen of sweat. Without the smile, his mouth sagged and the dark circles under his eyes were more pronounced.

"You know why I wanted to talk to her!" he hissed. "And then I thought better of it. Leave it, Lucas, please!"

With that, he pushed his chair back abruptly and marched off round the front of the house.

CHAPTER 55

"Jesus, can you believe that idiot Nick Wallace?" Stephanie said as they walked into the study. Lucas had offered them the use of the room, so she closed the door and leaned against it as if barring all intruders. "He's not getting away with this. I'm going to track him down and find out what on earth he was up to, dodging into the bloody bushes. I *ask* you!"

"More to the point, Steph, we now know that Lidia was here, and I'm not sure that's good news. One girl dead, one missing. What the hell have we walked into?"

Stephanie felt a pulse of apprehension. "No one else admitted to seeing Lidia, but maybe they're all hiding something. And where's Jemma? Why leave a message like that and then just bugger off?" She paused. "I'm going to have to call this in—update the team."

"I know, and we also need to understand where Lucas Jarrett's theory about his sister's death has suddenly sprung from."

"No one's saying anything about that either. While you were off with Matt Hudson, I told them about Jemma's message to see how they would react. There wasn't a blink from any of them. Not a flicker."

"Well, whether or not Jarrett is right about what happened to Alex, there's a huge red flag waving madly in front of my eyes. If he's right, we have to wonder if Lidia was involved. Is she running? Did she see something? Or are the two incidents unrelated?"

Stephanie was suddenly glad that Gus was with her. She'd asked him to keep quiet, to stay out of her investigation, but this seemed so much bigger than a missing-person inquiry now. There was a restless, uneasy atmosphere, and Lucas Jarrett—the man who had seemed so broken this time last year—was like a caged tiger, prowling, searching for prey.

"I guess you're going to have to speak to Prescott about this, aren't you?"

Gus gave her a rueful smile. DCI Prescott was his boss in the Major Crimes team. "Sorry, Steph. I know I said I wouldn't interfere, but we can't ignore what we've heard about Alex. I just need his go-ahead to start asking questions."

"While you do that, I'll go and take my frustration out on Nick bloody Wallace then." She grinned at Gus and walked out of the study.

She got the distinct impression that Nick was hiding but finally found him on the far side of the house.

"Mr. Wallace, I appreciate you finally admitting that you saw Lidia, although it would have saved me a lot of trouble if you'd told me that last night." It probably wouldn't, given that no one else had acknowledged seeing her, but she wasn't about to tell him that. She wanted him on the back foot.

"I need you to think hard, and don't miss out a thing. Okay?" He gave a wary nod. "Is there anything else that you can think of? Did you hear any other voices? Was she alone? Was she talking on her phone? Did you see anyone on the beach?"

He seemed relieved at her line of questioning and was much more garrulous than he had been when Lucas had been grilling him.

"I didn't see another soul, I promise you. It was very quiet—the only thing I could hear was the sea. And she was using the light on her phone, pointing it down to see her feet because the lights had gone out. I told you that, didn't I? I really *was* keen not to frighten her, you know."

"I'm sure you were. Do you remember what time it was?"

"I can't be certain. I'd been at the beach for a while, like I said, but I would guess it was around 10:30, maybe a bit later."

"What can you tell me about the rest of Jemma Hudson's message—that Mr. Jarrett believes his sister was murdered?"

Nick's expression closed down, as if he had shrunk into himself.

"It's nonsense. Lucas really loved that girl, you know, and I can only imagine that when someone chooses to do what Alex did, it must make those close to them feel some guilt, however irrational that is."

"So why did you want to see her that night?"

Nick Wallace hung his head and Stephanie could no longer see his eyes. She waited, aware that he was trying hard to work out what to say.

"I sent some emails to Lucas. They were private, for his eyes only, but he told me Alex would have dealt with them. I went to check that she'd deleted them."

"And the content of these emails?"

"Unimportant."

"Clearly not."

He lifted his head to look at her. "Private—that's all." Nick's eyes told her that right now he wasn't going to admit to anything else. "If we're finished, I'd like to go and find Lucas to apologize for my outburst."

"We're done for now, Mr. Wallace, but I suspect this is not the end of it."

He stared at her for a second, then nodded and walked away. There was nothing she could do to force him to tell her the truth now, but if DCI Prescott decided to reopen the case into Alex's death, then Nick Wallace's obduracy would be a different matter.

Stephanie looked at her phone. No signal.

"Damn it," she muttered.

"Sorry I've been so long," Stephanie said as she walked back into Lucas's study. "It took me ages to find a spot with a half-decent mobile signal."

"Jarrett said we could use the landline," Gus said.

"Good." Stephanie reached for the phone. "I'm going to try Jemma again. I'm worried about her." Her call went straight to voicemail. "Bugger."

Stephanie threw herself into an armchair and sat back heavily, trying to convince herself that Jemma was simply unreliable. A soft knock on the door interrupted her thoughts and Nina popped her head in.

"Would you like some coffee?"

Nina looked tired. Whatever was going on here, she was suffering.

"That would be lovely, thank you, Mrs. Jarrett."

"Nina, please."

Stephanie nodded. "Would you mind asking your husband if he knows which train Jemma was going for, and could we have the name of the taxi firm that came for her?"

"Of course. I won't be a moment." Nina went out, closing the door behind her.

Stephanie turned to Gus. "While she does that, tell me what you're thinking. Because I'm bewildered by the whole set-up."

"I'm thinking, among other things, what a splendid day off this has turned out to be."

Stephanie felt a prickle of guilt and looked at his stern face. Then a corner of his mouth lifted. He was teasing her—at least, she hoped he was.

"Seriously though, DCI Prescott wants the inquiry into Lidia to continue with your team, but he's setting another investigation in motion to review the facts around Alex's death. He asked if we could liaise, and I said I thought we could manage that." He raised one eyebrow and Stephanie grinned.

It was the right decision, but it wasn't going to be popular with Lucas and his guests.

There was another knock at the door. This time a girl in black leggings, a long-sleeved T-shirt, and a white apron came in with two cups of coffee, closely followed by Nina.

"Lucas says that Jemma was aiming to get the 12:05 to Exeter. She would have had to change there. But he says he gave her a list of taxi companies and she made the call herself."

The girl put the coffee down, together with a plate of home-made biscuits, and left. For a moment Stephanie wondered how it must feel to have a housekeeper and other staff. She wasn't sure she would like it—too many people knowing her business—but it reminded her of an idea she'd had the evening before.

"Before you go, Nina, your housekeeper this year is new, I believe. Do you have contact details for the one who was here last year?"

"I don't, but Lucas might have. I could ask him."

"That's okay. I'll do that, thank you. What about the girl who just served us—was she here last year? I'm just wondering if there are any people on your staff who might have seen Lidia."

"No. Essi's temporary and she's only been with us for a couple of days. Sorry."

Another dead end.

But as Nina left the room, Stephanie remembered something. Lucas said *he* had organized the taxi, but now he was saying he just gave Jemma a list. Which was it?

CHAPTER 56

"You ready?" Gus asked.

"Yep," Stephanie responded, straightening her back. Their questions would no doubt be met with a stubborn determination to conceal or at least mask the truth—why else had Lucas Jarrett failed to tell them of his suspicions about his sister's death? But she wasn't about to give up.

Together they walked round to the terrace where the Jarretts and their guests were finishing lunch. A large dish holding a delicious-looking but untouched pear tarte tatin sat in the center of the table, and Stephanie's mouth watered as she wondered when she and Gus would next have a chance to eat.

Andrew Marshall was standing as if about to leave.

"Mr. Marshall, if you could hang on for a few moments it would be appreciated," Stephanie said.

He gave a small shrug and sat back down.

Stephanie turned to Lucas. "Mr. Jarrett, you told us earlier that you organized a taxi for Jemma Hudson. Your wife tells us that you gave Jemma a list of taxis to call. Which was it?"

"I gave her a list. Sorry, I should have been clearer. I offered to call one for her, but she said she'd do it from her mobile."

"Did you see her leave?"

Lucas looked as if he was trying to concentrate, to remember. But they were talking about earlier that same day. He couldn't have forgotten.

"No, I didn't."

"Where were you all morning?"

"In the study mostly, but I probably popped out a few times."

The study was at the front of the house. If a taxi had come he was bound to have seen it, unless it arrived when he was away from his desk.

"Did anyone else see her leave? Or see a taxi arrive?"

Stephanie looked around at the faces, all of them blank, and other than Matt Hudson, who looked uneasy, no one avoided her eyes.

Gus stepped forward. "As you know, the initial reason for this visit was to investigate what happened to Lidia Dalca, but there was more to Mrs. Hudson's message." Gus angled his broad body to face Lucas. "As I believe DS King has already mentioned, Jemma also said that you believe your sister was murdered, Mr. Jarrett. Is that correct?"

No one moved. Glasses raised to lips stayed in mid-air, but each pair of eyes slid away from Gus. Stephanie's gaze finally landed on Lucas, whose face was white, his eyes glittering.

"I've no idea why Jemma told you that."

For a moment, no one spoke. Then Andrew Marshall leaned back in his chair and stared at his host.

"Christ, Lucas, tell them the truth. You brought us all here solely *because* you think one of us killed Alex. If you believe that, let the police do their job." Andrew turned to Gus. "He's had us all playing a pointless game—who was where, who spoke to whom, who's not telling the truth about their alibi—and it's been totally meaningless. No one has been found to be lying—except maybe Lucas himself."

Lucas lunged forward in his chair, thumped his palms on the table, and looked first at Stephanie and then at Gus.

"This really has nothing to do with you. It's a private matter."

"I think you'll find that if someone was murdered, it *does* have something to do with us," Gus said.

"No, it doesn't. You concluded it was suicide. There were no signs of violence on my sister other than the minor injuries caused by the rocks. There is no evidence that she was murdered, so there's nothing you can do, and I would rather you didn't pursue this."

"But *you're* pursuing it, Lucas. Why don't you let the police help?" Nina's voice was soft, persuasive, almost pleading.

His glance darted to his wife and then away again, as if he found it too painful to look at her.

"And if we don't get involved but it turns out you were right, what's your plan then?" Gus asked.

"I'll deal with it. Now, if we're done here, can I show you out?"

"*You'll deal with it?* What the hell does that mean? You're worrying me, Mr. Jarrett. If you're thinking of taking the law into your own hands, I would strongly advise you to think again. We don't approve of vigilantism, you know."

Lucas said nothing and returned Gus's glare, undaunted.

"Tell us why you think she was murdered," Stephanie said. Lucas sighed, and Stephanie could see the strain around his eyes.

"Let's just say I find it impossible to believe that my sister would have killed herself on the eve of my wedding."

Stephanie spoke softly to Lucas, aware how sensitive a subject this was. "I'm sure you know that suicide is rarely a rational decision, although it might seem so to the person concerned. Your sister is unlikely to have sat down and planned to ruin your big day; she must have been totally overcome with all kinds of feelings that we don't understand."

"And what about the video?" Gus asked.

"Ah, the video. I'm not convinced it was a suicide message. Watch it again, if you don't believe me."

Gus wasn't to be silenced. "People kill out of anger, jealousy, for money—any number of reasons. But there generally *is* a reason. Why would anyone want her dead?"

"You'd have to ask her murderer that question. But people also kill to prevent a truth from emerging, a truth so dreadful that it would be life altering."

"Do you have a theory about what that might be?" Gus asked.

"That's why I invited everyone here. To find out what each of them is hiding, above and beyond what I already know." His gaze skimmed over each person at the table. "But I'm not looking for, nor do I want, your involvement. I repeat, this is a private matter."

Stephanie could feel the man's carefully controlled rage. If he was right and one of his friends had killed his sister, she couldn't imagine what he might do.

"Can I ask why each of you has chosen to stay knowing that one of you is suspected of murder?" Stephanie asked.

Once again, it was Andrew Marshall who chose to speak.

"Lucas has been a good friend for many years. I deplore what he's doing, but he's been part of my life for a long time, and if this whole thing with Alex has made him ill, which is the only explanation that makes any sense to me, then I'd prefer to do what I can to help him get over it. As for the others"—he lifted an arm to include his fellow guests—"some may be of the same mind as me. Others, I suspect, are terrified that Lucas—as the holder of all of our secrets—might punish them by revealing truths that are better left hidden."

No one seemed shocked or even surprised by Andrew's comments.

"Do you think we can have a word with you in private, please, Mr. Jarrett?" Stephanie asked. "Shall we go to your study?"

Lucas looked up and glanced around the table at his friends. Without another word, they stood up one by one, getting the message that Lucas preferred to stay where he was.

Nina took a little longer, giving her husband a concerned glance, but he shook his head just once, and she turned and walked towards the house.

Before either Stephanie or Gus could speak, Lucas rested his clenched fists on the table and leaned towards them.

"You have no idea what you've done. The very fact that you're here has made everyone defensive. They'll reveal nothing now, and all my meticulous planning is ruined. Without clear evidence that my sister was killed, all I'm able to rely on is the honesty of some—if not all—of my friends. I'm asking you once again to leave it with me, and if there's a case for you to pursue, I'll let you know."

"I'm afraid that's not how it works," Gus said, undaunted by Lucas's anger. "But you're right that there's no physical evidence, so tell me how you believe she was killed."

Lucas didn't answer Gus's question for a few moments. It seemed as if he was trying to decide whether he could fob them off in some way, but one look at Gus's eyes should have told him that here was a man who didn't give up.

"Alex used to swim when it was dark, and everyone knew that was her routine. Had I wanted to kill my sister—which I can assure you I didn't—I would have made her death look like an accidental drowning so it wouldn't be investigated too closely." His eyes became unfocused, as if he was seeing the scene he was describing and the thoughts were hurting him. "I would have waited on the rocks above the bay. As Alex swam out, I'd have dived in and held her under the water. She was slim, not strong, so it would be easy for someone to have wrapped their legs around her upper body, pinning her arms to her sides, holding her down until she drowned. There wouldn't necessarily have been any marks. You wouldn't have to squeeze tightly, just enough to stop her from moving."

Stephanie shook her head. "I've seen those rocks. They're very high, and not many people would be capable of a dive like that."

Lucas gave a dry laugh. "When we were kids we used to dare each other to dive from the wall above the swimming pool at my house, until Alex told my dad and he banned us from doing it because the pool wasn't deep enough. Nick was furious with her for spoiling our fun—called her a little snitch. But we'd got a taste for it, so in the summer we went to the coast and started cliff-jumping, or tombstoning as I think it's now called. But we dived too—from far greater heights than those rocks. We all dared each other to go higher. Any one of my friends would be more than capable, I can assure you."

Stephanie was watching Lucas. There was no doubting his anger, but it seemed off balance somehow. Had someone made that dive, or was his grief making him delusional?

They had reached an impasse. Lucas had no evidence, only suppositions, and Stephanie was keen to steer the conversation back to her investigation.

"Let's leave your suspicions there for the moment, although I have no doubt we'll be coming back to them. I need to ask you again about Lidia. Did you, or did you not, see her that night? And please tell me the truth, Mr. Jarrett."

Lucas raised his eyes to hers. She had never seen eyes like them, so rich and golden. She had to look away to concentrate on his words.

"Look. Since Nick told you that he'd seen her I've realized that she did come here that night. Honestly, with everything that was going on, with the wedding, and then Alex's death, it hadn't registered with me until just now. There was someone. She arrived ridiculously late, but I only spoke to her for a minute or two. Then I went in search of Nina to see if she wanted us to find the girl a job."

"And did she?"

"She wasn't in the bedroom, so I went back out and asked Lidia for her mobile number so I could call her when I'd spoken to Nina. Of course, that never happened. I did, however, offer to pay for a taxi to take her back to town, but she said she'd walk home along the coastal path. I told her I didn't think that was a very smart idea, but she said it would be okay. She was fine when she left me and headed towards the path."

"And were the lights on then?"

"Yes."

"And did you turn them off when she was halfway down to the beach?"

"Absolutely not."

"Well, it seems someone did, Mr. Jarrett."

CHAPTER 57

Underneath the drug-induced veil of lethargy I can feel the panic striving to push its way to the surface and my heart is thudding. I don't think I lost consciousness as I was dragged up the stairs, but for a while I lost the ability to control my movements. Everything seemed unreal, distant, as if it was happening to someone else. But gradually reality is forcing its way through and I'm trying to break out of this stupor.

I don't know where I am or how I got here. I don't remember anything after the boathouse. But now I'm lying on something soft. Is it a bed?

Why did they take me? What are they going to do with me?

Breathe, I tell myself. Slowly, in and out, I strive to calm myself and I feel my heart rate slow to a manageable race. Then from nowhere comes a new stab of terror.

Are they still here, in the room with me?

I listen intently, holding my breath to try to hear better, lying perfectly still so that not even a rustle of clothes disturbs the silence. If someone is here, surely I would know? I would feel them, hear their breath, smell their skin.

Nothing. All I can hear is the sea—and it's close. The waves are thundering onto the shore, and if I were to reach out, I'm sure I could almost touch them.

I twist my head from side to side, trying to rid myself of whatever is covering it. I tug on my arms, hoping to free them from the bindings holding them above where my head rests on something that feels like a pillow. I want to shout, to scream, but there is a gag in my mouth, and my throat is sore. I lie still for a moment, refusing to allow the terror to take hold. Someone will come. I know they will.

I think of the tender on the beach and wonder about Andrew. He must have been around somewhere. Will he find me here, wherever here is? But then I remember that he, more than anyone, knew I was jumpy, suspicious—I told him so. I believed the truth would be revealed if we were all honest with Lucas and with each other. Maybe he thought that would put him at risk.

Could he have done this to me? Am I in the boat, moored in the bay?

My shoulders ache, the gag has soaked up every bit of my saliva, and I can't stop myself from believing I'm going to die. The only thing that gives me hope is that they haven't hurt me. They could have killed me, dumped me in the sea.

But at the thought of what might happen next, I feel my breath getting shorter, and tears leak from my eyes, running down the sides of my face and into my hair. Of course they can't do that now. It's still daylight; I can see light through the fabric but no detail. They will have to wait until it's dark to take me out to sea and throw me over the side.

I think back to when they took me. I know there were two of them—the man in the doorway and the person behind me who slipped something over my head—a hood of some sort. I don't know who they were; they didn't speak. But now I remember that the hand holding my arm seemed soft. Was it a woman?

Whoever they are, they must think I'm dangerous. And I don't know why. I don't know what they think I know, but someone wants me silenced.

CHAPTER 58

"Gus, we can both see that Lucas Jarrett is more than willing to manipulate the facts to suit himself. He hadn't forgotten about Lidia at all—I could see that in his eyes. But what I'm increasingly worried about is what's happened to Jemma. He lied about the taxi, then tried to make out it was a misunderstanding."

"Misunderstanding my arse! Maybe that was for her husband's benefit, rather than ours, but I can't see why."

They were back in Lucas's study, but Stephanie couldn't rid herself of the suspicion that Jemma wouldn't have left without telling her husband or saying goodbye to anyone else.

"We should check who she called today—see if we can find the taxi company. I just want to make sure it all adds up."

"Or might I be right in thinking you want to be sure nothing worse has happened to her?"

Stephanie raised her chin and folded her arms tightly across her chest. "Maybe I'm overreacting, but why leave a message like that, then disappear and turn your phone off? Personally, I'd rather be safe than sorry."

"You're not overreacting. I don't trust any of this bunch an inch. Give me her mobile number and I'll see what I can do."

While he placed a call to ask one of his colleagues to check Jemma's recent mobile history, Stephanie opened the door into the hall. Nina was hurrying up the stairs. Had she been listening?

Stephanie's eyes followed her, admiring the way the staircase rose, turning not once but twice onto a landing that ran round the other three sides of the hall. Original artwork adorned the walls with bright splashes of color against the pale gray plaster, and it felt almost obscene that disaster could have struck in such a lovely home.

"Steph," Gus called, and she turned back into the study. "Someone will call as soon as they have any intel on Jemma's phone. It shouldn't take too long. And DCI Prescott's set up a full review of Alex's suicide, so we now have the dubious pleasure of interviewing the lot of them."

Stephanie grunted. "Let's hope they're a bit more forthcoming than they were earlier. I'd like to go back to the beach too. I want to remind myself of the layout, the path, think about where Lidia might have gone. And I want to see where the lights are turned on and off. If they're usually on, we have to ask if someone turned them off to cover something. It might have been a throwaway comment from Nick Wallace, but *had* someone arranged to meet Lidia at the beach? Or was he lying? Did he turn round and follow her? Had he already turned the lights off? And if so, why?"

"I'm not sure how seeing the place will help, but you're usually right."

"Thank you, sir. You're too kind," Stephanie said, her face deadpan.

Gus laughed. "I'll go and find Jarrett and let him know where we're going. It might be useful if he comes with us—give us a chance to find out what makes him tick."

It was a rare event for Gus and Stephanie to work a case together. Gus dealt with force-wide major crimes and Stephanie was a local CID detective, so it was only when the two coincided that a chance like this came along—and strictly speaking Lidia Dalca was her case. As she kept reminding him.

Gus held strong opinions that could sometimes be difficult to shift, but then so did she. Stephanie knew she could be bristly and defensive, just as Gus formed quick judgments of people that she rarely concurred with. But when he walked back into Lucas's study—as he would any minute now—she would feel a little jump in her heart at the very sight of him. She always did.

How would she cope if she couldn't see him, sometimes for weeks on end if he was on a big case? Today had certainly helped to push that gnawing anxiety to the back of her mind, but now as she waited for him, all her fears came rushing back.

Stop it, she thought.

Gus chose that moment to push open the door.

"You okay?" he asked, as always alert to her moods.

"I'm fine, just puzzling about Lidia and Jemma. Not to mention Alex."

His face said he didn't believe her, but he let it lie. "Jarrett says he'll be about fifteen minutes, so I said we'd wait. Let's talk to Chandra Tran. She's a quiet one, but I bet she's observant."

Opting to go in search of Chandra, Stephanie returned to the hall. The gentle splash of the fountain drew her eyes to the open front doorway, framing a view of the formal pond and the undulating lawns beyond. Chandra was sitting gazing into the water, apparently mesmerized by the fish swimming lazily to and fro.

"Do you have a moment, Miss Tran?"

Chandra lifted her solemn brown eyes to Stephanie's. "Of course."

She walked barefoot towards Stephanie, the only sound the gentle swish of her long mint-green silk skirt as it swung around her legs. There was something unnerving about her stillness.

"Is it okay if I call you Chandra?" Stephanie asked as they went into the study. Chandra smiled her assent as she sat down.

"We are now certain that Lidia Dalca came here on the eve of what was to be Lucas and Nina's wedding. Do you remember seeing anyone that night? She arrived quite late, and on foot, we understand."

Chandra's brow furrowed. "I think I might have seen her, although I didn't know until today that's who she was. After dinner, we moved out onto the terrace, but when Andrew left I went to sit by the fountain. After a while I saw what appeared to be a young woman walking down the drive. I thought it was Alex at first but later realized it couldn't have been. Someone went to meet her, but I left to try a little meditation before going to bed."

"Do you know who met her?" Stephanie asked.

"I don't know. I'm sorry. I don't think it was Andrew though."

"What made you realize it wasn't Alex?"

"Because I saw Alex—or rather heard her—shortly afterwards. I was taking the path round the north side of the house towards the yoga studio when I heard people speaking. I stayed out of sight, not wanting to interrupt. It sounded quite intense."

"Were you able to recognize their voices?" Gus asked.

"Oh yes. Matt Hudson's voice is very distinct. It's a little higher than the others'."

"Who was he talking to?" Gus asked.

"Alex. Her voice was raised, and she was crying."

"*Crying?*" Stephanie said.

"Yes. Matt was trying to calm her."

"And did you by any chance hear what they were talking about?"

Chandra put her head to one side. "Maybe, but it's nothing that would concern you. You're investigating the disappearance of the Romanian girl, and I'm sure it was nothing to do with that."

Gus leaned forward. "Chandra, we're police officers. If someone believes that a crime has been committed, as it appears Mr. Jarrett does, then whether they're right or not it's our duty to learn as much as we can. Please tell us what you heard."

Chandra sat silently in the chair, as if trying to find the right words.

"If Alex was crying," Stephanie said, "maybe she was far more unhappy than her brother realizes. He might find it easier to accept her death if we understand what was causing her so much pain."

"Lucas is angry," Chandra said. "He's not hurt or sad, which I find strange. He wasn't like this last year. I thought he was a good man—kind, even-tempered, generous. The best of all of them in so many ways. But now when he enters a room, waves of fury explode around him and bounce off the walls."

This vivid image of Lucas's emotions seemed startlingly accurate from everything Stephanie had seen. And she felt sure this woman had more to tell.

"If Matt Hudson's voice was clear, it could be useful to know what he said."

Chandra looked down at her clasped hands before she spoke.

"I don't make a habit of listening to people's conversations, but Alex sounded so upset that I wanted to stay close in case she needed me. Matt kept saying, 'Did you tell anyone, Alex?' He said it a couple of times, and I was worried that he was putting her under pressure. Then something like: 'It could be the end for me.' That's when Alex started to cry, and I heard her say, 'Why didn't you answer my text, Matt? If you'd come for me, none of it would have happened.' He said he didn't know what she was talking about, but I was beginning to feel uncomfortable about being there. I hadn't known they were there, you see, hiding in the gloom like that, and I had never intended to eavesdrop."

CHAPTER 59

A gentle breeze was blowing through the open window of Lucas's study, and Stephanie was glad of it. Since Chandra mentioned the text that Alex had sent to Matt, her mind had been spinning. What text? When did she send it? She remembered interviewing all the guests—Matt included—the previous year. She was certain Matt said he hadn't had any contact with Alex since her kidnap.

She tried to focus on what Chandra was saying, but there was a sharp knock on the door, and Lucas strode into the room.

"Are you ready to go down to the boathouse?" he asked, nodding politely to Chandra.

Stephanie looked at the other woman, who started to rise from her chair.

"Chandra, we might want to chat with you again later, if that's okay?"

She nodded, gave Stephanie a sweet smile, and made her way slowly out of the door.

Lucas cast her a sideways glance as she left. "What did Chandra have to tell you?"

"She had nothing significant to add about Lidia," Stephanie answered, neatly avoiding the question. "Shall we go?"

"Of course. I apologize for the delay. If you follow me, we'll go through the back door."

It was only possible to walk two abreast on the path to the cove, and Gus walked ahead with Lucas. Stephanie could hear them talking but wasn't party to their conversation.

As she emerged onto the beach, Gus was waiting. "Don't glare at me. I thought if I chatted rather than interrogated him, he might say more about his suspicions, but I was wrong. He didn't."

Stephanie wasn't listening. She was staring at the spot where Alex's body had lain a year ago, feeling again a wave of sadness that such a young life had been lost. The sound of the waves breaking softly onto the shore was soothing, and she breathed in the tangy fresh smell of the sea as she slowly followed Lucas and Gus across the pebbles to the boathouse.

Its double doors stood open.

"Do you have a boat?" Gus asked.

"Yes, a thirty-five-footer. We winter her in here, but to be honest I've barely taken her out for the last year. Nina's not a good sailor—it was something I used to do with Alex."

"So where's the boat now?" Stephanie asked.

"I imagine Andrew's taken her out. He put her in the water before lunch. He doesn't need crew—he can sail a boat with one hand tied behind his back, and it's fairly calm today. There's enough breeze to get up a bit of speed though."

"It doesn't worry you that the boat isn't here?"

"No. I'm sure it will be Andrew. He likes his own company."

Stephanie and Gus followed Lucas into the cavernous space, which was bigger than the whole of Stephanie's house, and looked around.

I hold my breath. Is that a voice? Yes! And it's more than one. They're close; I know they are.

My heart leaps. Is someone looking for me? Do they know I'm here?

There's no urgency in the voices—it sounds like an ordinary conversation, and I think it's coming from below me. I must be upstairs in the house or in one of the outhouses. But no, that's not right. The sea is close.

I must be in Alex's apartment. And someone is downstairs.

I don't recognize the voices, but I don't care. Maybe it's my captors, but I'm sure I can detect three—one a woman's, and two deeper. Men, their voices little more than a rumble.

This is my chance.

I can't focus. My mind is a blank.

The ache in my shoulders is unbearable and I try to shuffle up to reduce the strain. My face is hot inside the bag, my skin prickling, and I know my racing heart is making me sweat even more.

Breathe, I tell myself, trying to calm down. I feel the panic building. I have to control it. *Breathe! Think!*

There must be something I can do to attract their attention, but what?

I try moaning as loudly as I can, but over the thundering of the sea I'm sure the sound won't be distinct enough. I try to rattle whatever I'm strapped to, but it makes no noise.

I'm on a wide, soft surface that feels like a mattress, and with my fingers I can tell I'm tied to something with metal uprights. A bedhead?

I try to slow my thoughts down, to think rationally. There could well be a bedside table, and there might be something on it—a lamp, a book, a framed photograph.

I twist and turn, but I can't reach. And I'm breathing so heavily I'm sucking the fabric farther into my mouth, cutting off the air, so I hold my breath and twist my body to one side. The fierce pain in my shoulders nearly makes me give up. But I can't. I have to let them know I'm here.

I turn as far onto my side as my bound arms will let me and pull my knees up tight to my chest, then kick out as hard as I can. My feet make contact with something, and I feel a moment of elation as something crashes to the floor.

They must have heard.

I lie groaning, praying. *Will they come?*

"The lights for the path," Gus said to Lucas. "You mentioned they could be switched on and off from down here. Can you show us where, please?"

Lucas headed back out of the boathouse, followed by Gus. Stephanie was about to join them when she heard a heavy thump from overhead. She stopped and looked up. The men clearly hadn't heard it, but she was sure it had come from the apartment.

Lucas was opening a box on the wall just outside the door. It didn't appear to be locked, and as Stephanie approached he was showing Gus how the lights switched on and off.

"They light the path, but also the area around the boathouse so Alex could find her way back easily when there was no moon."

"Is someone upstairs in the apartment?" Stephanie asked.

Lucas looked startled. "No. Why do you ask?"

"I heard a bump as if something had been dropped on the floor. Perhaps we should go and take a look."

Lucas shut the door to the switches with slightly more force than seemed necessary and turned towards Stephanie.

"Oh, I know what it is. I asked one of the staff to come down each week for an hour to air the place and keep the dust down. That'll be it. I don't want anyone else going in there. I'm not ready for that."

"Shall we just check it out?" Stephanie asked again.

"No, it's fine. Look—why don't you make your way back up to the house and I'll pop in and make sure the cleaner's not fallen or dropped anything important."

"We could come with you," Stephanie persisted.

"No, but thank you. As I've said, no one goes in there except me—and the cleaner. I'll see you back at the house."

Lucas was blocking their way to the path that ran alongside the boathouse and up a slope to the apartment, and without a search warrant they had no right to go barging in, so Gus raised his eyebrows at Stephanie and turned to walk across the beach.

CHAPTER 60

"Did that little jaunt to the beach help?" Gus asked with a sideways glance at Stephanie as they approached the house.

"Probably not, but there's no need to take the piss. Seeing things again brought that morning back to me."

He nudged her lightly with his shoulder. "I know, and it gave us a chance to get a better handle on Jarrett. I was going to suggest that you interview the sexy guy, Andrew Marshall, but if he's out on the boat you're out of luck. Maybe you could hunt Matt Hudson down. I'll take Isabel, because at a guess she would wind you up."

Gus was right. Isabel was the kind of woman who seemed perfectly pleasant on the surface but who had a hardness to her that revealed itself in subtle bitchiness. Stephanie wouldn't trust a word she said, but hoped Gus could work his charm on her.

"If you see Nina, check if Lucas is telling the truth—that she knew nothing about Lidia. Oh, and ask her if she saw Jemma leave too, will you?"

Stephanie nodded and set off to look for Matt, but seeing Nick lazing on a sunlounger in his shorts as if he hadn't a care in the world, she decided to have a word with him about Andrew.

"Lucas tells us that Andrew Marshall has taken the boat out. Do you know what time he's expected back?"

"Not a clue. But if you want to ask him about that night, we all know where he was." There was a slightly sneering quality to his words which Stephanie didn't understand.

"You suggested earlier that he might have arranged to see Lidia Dalca. Was that a serious comment?"

"Not really, sorry. I was just winding him up. Andrew always had a reputation with the girls, but that night he was down in the orchard on his phone. I'm sure if you needed to you could check the duration and time of the call, but I can't imagine he had time to meet Lidia whatever-her-name-was down at the beach."

Just what she needed—some joker not taking the investigation seriously. Maybe she should remind him that he was the last person known to have seen Lidia. She decided to park that thought for now.

She was about to go in search of Nina when Matt Hudson stepped out of the back door of the house and hurried towards her.

"Sergeant King, have you managed to make contact with my wife yet?"

She shook her head. "I keep trying, but her phone seems to be switched off. We're trying to discover which taxi firm she called."

The lines between his eyes deepened. "It's not like Jemma."

Matt's skin looked waxy and, despite his tan, his bloodless face resembled that of a slightly jaundiced plastic doll.

"Mr. Hudson, can we have a chat about the eve of the wedding a year ago, please?"

"Of course, but I didn't see this girl you're asking about, so I'm not sure I can help."

"Let's go and find somewhere to sit, shall we?"

Stephanie didn't need to think twice about where to go. The north terrace was absolutely the right choice—the spot where Chandra had overheard Matt talking to Alex.

It felt good to be out of the hot sun, although she noticed Matt shiver as he sat down on one of the metal garden chairs.

"Can you tell me, in your own words, what happened that night after dinner."

"Not much, really. It had been a good evening—great food; we were all getting along well."

"You say that as if you didn't always. Had there been an argument?"

"No. Nothing like that. Nick was being his usual witty self—generally at everyone else's expense—but it was nothing more than a minor irritation. And anyway, it was Lucas's big day, not a time for petty grievances to be aired. We listened to some music for a while, but then people started to drift off."

"What about Alex? When had you last seen her before then?"

Matt focused on the hand he was running up and down the leg of his trousers. "A long time ago."

"Look, Mr. Hudson, we wouldn't be doing our jobs if we ignored what Lucas has been saying, so I need to ask about Alex too. We understand you were talking to her that night. What was that about?"

Matt sat back in his chair and cleared his throat.

"I guess you've been speaking to Chandra?"

Stephanie didn't acknowledge the question and Matt licked his lips. "During dinner Alex said she'd like to have a chat with me. To catch up, you know. Jemma said she was going to bed, so when Alex left and didn't head straight towards the cove, I knew she'd be waiting for me."

"What did she want to talk to you about?"

"Nothing much; we were just reminiscing about the past."

He wouldn't meet her eyes, and for a moment Stephanie wished she had waited for Gus.

"Did she give you the impression she was unhappy? Depressed?"

"No, definitely not. If she had I would have done something, said something, *helped* her." There was an edge of desperation in his voice, as if he felt he should have done better.

"But she was crying, wasn't she?"

Matt shook his head quickly, and Stephanie wasn't sure if he was trying to convince her or himself.

"She was upset for a while, but she thought someone might be listening and she clammed up. Then she left. But I thought she was okay by then. I'm sure she was."

Stephanie sat forward and rested her arms on the table.

"Someone was listening, Matt. They heard you say something about how it could be the end for you—or something like that. Do you want to explain that?"

"They must have misheard. I don't know what that could be about."

"Not good enough. Try again."

Two bright spots of color appeared on Matt's washed-out cheeks.

"There's only one thing I can think of—one way in which I thought I might get into serious trouble." He gave Stephanie a fierce gaze as if not sure he could trust her. "Alex told me something that I genuinely knew nothing about. On the night she was abducted, she said she sent me a text. She'd got her mum's phone and knew my number, so she told me that I would know where to find her and asked me to come and get her."

Stephanie felt a pulse of excitement. "And why didn't you?"

"Because I never saw the text." Matt's voice had an insistence, and Stephanie was sure he was telling the truth.

"I've read the report into Alex's abduction, and I don't think she ever mentioned sending a text, and there was no phone on her when she was found, and none registered to her name."

"No, that's right. Like I told you, it was her mother's phone. Well, that's not strictly accurate. Her mum had stolen it, and then it was lost when Alex was taken. So there was no way of tracing any calls."

"So why didn't she tell the police that she'd sent you a text? Why only now?"

Matt swallowed hard, and Stephanie was certain that his next statement was only going to be a partial truth.

"She didn't want to get me into trouble. She said they would have investigated me, and she knew it wasn't me who took her."

"Why was she concerned about you being investigated?"

Matt pressed his lips together and shrugged.

"Where were you when she was abducted?"

He took a deep breath. "I only know it was sometime during the night, so I guess I would have been in bed, alone. I was nineteen, it was nearly Christmas, and I'd had a few too many beers. I was at home—my parents' house—but they wouldn't have known what time I got in."

"And where had you been drinking?"

"In the pub in the village. It had been a bit of a tradition since we were all sixteen pretending to be eighteen. In the early days Lucas used to arrange it, but that year he was away so we decided to meet up anyway. But it was a dull affair. I played darts with Andrew and Nick. Isabel sat at the table sulking because we weren't all making a fuss of her. Then some guy came in and she left with him. We stayed another hour or so."

"And where was your phone?"

"On the table. It's not the kind of village where things get stolen."

"So who might have read the text, if you didn't?"

"Anyone, I suppose. Anyone in the pub that night."

"But you didn't see anyone with your phone."

Matt shook his head. "No."

His eyes darted away again. She believed him, but there was something more. She could feel it.

CHAPTER 61

It seems a long time since I heard the voices. I thought they would come, that I'd be saved, but I was wrong.

Hot tears of despair run down the sides of my face and into my ears, making my skin itch. *Why is this happening?* Maybe they're just waiting for it to get dark so they can slip me into the water, unheard, unseen. I imagine being weighed down so that I will sink, trying and failing to fight my way back to the surface, the instinct not to breathe so strong that it blocks the agony as I exhaust the last of my air.

I don't want to die.

The crying has blocked my nose, and I have no way to clear it. I feel as if I'm drowning in my own tears, and my bladder is getting fuller by the minute.

My body tenses as I hear a sound.

What was that?

I hold my breath, my limbs rigid. Another sound, and this time it's close by. A scratching noise, then a creak. I know those sounds. Someone is coming.

I hear a tentative footstep, then another. Coming towards me. *Is this it?*

I don't know whether I should make a sound or lie still. The steps are quiet, slow, as if someone is trying to prevent floorboards from creaking. I have to make a sound. What if they don't know I'm here?

I moan as loudly as I can, straining my neck, expecting any moment to hear a shout saying that I'm found. Matt must be missing me by now; maybe it's him. I moan again, and the footsteps stop. But they're close. Very close. And suddenly I know that whoever it is, they're watching me.

I can hear breathing, the whisper of sound going in and out of someone's lungs. But they're not speaking, and I lie still, suddenly conscious that I'm lying on what must be a bed, dressed in shorts, my top riding up and my arms stretched over my head.

I feel exposed, naked, every inch of my bare flesh vulnerable as his eyes run up and down my body.

What is he going to do to me?

I want to make myself smaller so he can't see so much of me and I try to pull my legs together and up towards my body. And still the only sound I hear is breathing.

The air shifts, just a fraction, but I know he's moving. Is he coming towards me or going away? An involuntary squeak of fear comes from my throat, and I tense every muscle in my body, ready to kick out with my legs if I feel the slightest touch on my skin.

But nothing happens. There is a creak as a floorboard is stepped on, and then a gentle click as a door closes.

He's gone.

For a moment my body sags with relief, then I start to tremble. Beyond my own fear I catch flashes of how Alex must have felt all those years ago—just a kid, tied like I am but stripped naked and raped. I take my terror and multiply it many, many times, and I no longer wonder why she was so disturbed, so damaged.

Instead, I wonder how she survived for as long as she did.

CHAPTER 62

"What a day!" Stephanie pushed her head back against the headrest as Gus drove out through the gates of Polskirrin.

They had decided there was little point hanging around for Andrew Marshall to return. It was already late afternoon and, according to Lucas, Andrew worked to his own timetable. It could be midnight before he showed his face. Stephanie was in no doubt that they would be back at Polskirrin the following day, so they would talk to him then and perhaps have another word with Chandra, who had gone to her room feeling unwell.

"I want to know what else Chandra was going to say about Jemma and what she might know. Or better still, I need to speak to bloody Jemma!"

"She'll turn up. Be patient. What did her husband have to say for himself?"

Stephanie filled Gus in on her conversation with Matt.

"You sound skeptical."

Stephanie sighed. "I just don't know what to believe. When Alex died I became a bit obsessed—I wanted to know what had happened to make her so unhappy, so I read the original kidnap reports, and I'm certain that there was no mention of a text message or a mobile phone."

"Were there no suspects?"

"Yes, one. An organized crime boss called Mirac Bozkurt, commonly known as the Quiet Man. He was into everything—prostitution, pornography, trafficking, drugs—you name it. But they had nothing on him, couldn't find a single link between him and Alex, and up until now it seems no one knew she was in Blair Jarrett's summerhouse. If she really did send that message to Matt though, it changes things—big time."

"We'll put in a call to the people on the original investigation as soon as we get back. They concluded that Alex's abduction was opportunistic, but what if someone in the pub that night read the message and knew where she was?"

Stephanie groaned. "I'm not sure that makes sense either. Matt said that, according to Alex, she wasn't specific about her location in the text. She apparently said something like 'you know where to find me.'"

Gus nodded, not taking his eyes from the narrow road ahead of them.

They were quiet for a few moments.

"What did you get out of Isabel Wallace?" Stephanie asked eventually.

"Not a lot. She says she went to her room for a while, and as she wasn't sharing with anyone that's hard to either confirm or deny. But she supposedly couldn't sleep because it was hot, so she had a shower and came back downstairs. She found Matt sitting on the north terrace on his own, which ties in with what he told you. He'd been there for about two hours, just thinking, he told her. They went for a walk but in the opposite direction to the cove. Originally they told Lucas they went for a walk straight after dinner. But that wasn't true."

"So why the hell did she say it was then? What a bizarre thing to do!"

"Her excuse was that she knew Matt had been talking to Alex and he didn't want Lucas to know."

Stephanie grabbed her bag from the floor and hunted around for some mints. "Those people have left me with a bad taste in my mouth—literally. Why can't they just be straightforward?"

Gus laughed. "They're protecting themselves. Jarrett is a bit of a loose cannon, and I get the feeling that if he suspected someone strongly enough, he could take the law into his own hands. The whole thing is unnerving. Nina seemed jumpy—even more so as the day went on—but I believed her when she said she didn't see Lidia."

Stephanie handed a mint to Gus and popped one into her own mouth.

"What now?"

"Let's see what the inquiries turn up. We know one of the strongest motives for murder is money, so the team will be looking into the finances of this bunch. Lucas's dad seems to have left Alex well off in her own right, from what we were told. So did anyone have anything to gain by her death? Was anyone taking money from her—or she from them?"

Gus's phone chose that moment to ring, and he put it on speaker.

"Angus Brodie."

"Gus, it's Ronnie. You wanted details of calls made by Jemima Hudson, but only for the last twenty-four hours—is that right?"

"For now, yes. What have you found?"

"She made two calls—one to directory inquiries and the other to Penzance police station. Both this morning. There's nothing after that."

"You sure about that? Any texts?"

"Nothing. Sorry if that's not the answer you wanted."

"Well, it tells us something. Look, Ronnie, I need to know whether the phone is still switched on, and if so where it is. If not, its last position. Can you get back to me ASAP, please?"

Gus pulled the car over onto the grass at the side of the road and turned to Stephanie.

"So Jemma didn't call a taxi company," Stephanie said, the weight of anxiety she'd been feeling all day suddenly heavier.

"She could have booked one online."

"I don't think so. Didn't someone say they can't get an Internet signal at Polskirrin at the moment? And there doesn't appear to be even 3G out there, let alone 4G. Anyway, Lucas said he'd given her a list of phone numbers."

"She's not taken their car—I checked. If Lucas had lent her a car, surely he would have said? The only other possibility is that one of the others drove her to the station." His voice dropped. "Or maybe she's still there."

"She could have been at the beach earlier, keeping out of her husband's way and waiting for Andrew Marshall to whisk her away on the boat. There might be no mystery at all about this." Even as she spoke, Stephanie didn't believe that.

"What do you want to do? Do we go back? We're only fifteen minutes away. Just remember some of her clothes have gone too, and a small suitcase. If she hasn't left, why have her clothes been moved, and by whom?"

"I know what you're thinking. You're wondering if she'd worked out too much about Lidia—or Alex? And had to be silenced."

"Jesus. Let's hope not. We can go back now and ask Lucas if he'll let us have a good look round, or we can wait and get a search warrant."

"He's not going to let us in without one, I don't think. Sorry, Gus, this hasn't turned out to be the anniversary celebration we had in mind, has it?"

"Celebrations anywhere near Polskirrin are doomed, it seems." He drummed his fingers on the steering wheel. Stephanie said nothing, hoping he would come to the same conclusion she had.

Finally, he turned his head. "You want to go back, don't you? You're worried about her."

"Yes, I am. We still don't know much about this Andrew Marshall guy. While you were speaking to Isabel, I pushed Nick a bit more about who Andrew was talking to on the phone that night last year. According to him, Marshall is marrying Chandra Tran so he gets his hands on his own boat—as her dowry. *Dowry!* In this day and age! It doesn't fill me with trust in the man, and he didn't hang around when we started to ask questions, did he? He just buggered off on the boat."

"Okay, let's go back. I'll organize the search warrant, and someone can bring it out to us."

Stephanie leaned over and rested her head on Gus's wide shoulder, and he bent down to kiss her softly on the lips. "Today may not have been the day we planned, Steph, but we've got lots more anniversaries to look forward to."

She certainly hoped so, and she reached out a hand to cover his, hoping he couldn't see the doubt in her eyes.

Her thoughts were interrupted by the sound of a siren heading towards them at speed. Stephanie swiveled her head to look as an ambulance came tearing along the lane.

"Shit! Do you think it's going to Polskirrin?"

"There's nowhere else along this road as far as I know. What the hell's happened now? It's only fifteen minutes since we left." With that, Gus slammed the car into gear, spun it round, and set off after the ambulance.

Stephanie leaned back and closed her eyes. She had the dreadful feeling that their visit had stirred things up, and that whatever had happened, it was somehow her fault for pushing too hard.

CHAPTER 63

Gus raced along the road keeping the ambulance in sight, leaning forward to concentrate on his driving. Stephanie sat silently by his side, clenching and unclenching her fists where they rested on her thighs as she considered and rejected multiple theories about what might have happened at Polskirrin. None of them were good.

The gates stood open for the speeding ambulance, and Gus followed it down the drive, then pulled over to one side so as not to impede its eventual exit. The paramedics rushed into the house with a distraught-looking Nina; Lucas stood by the front door, running his fingers through his dark hair. Stephanie and Gus jumped out of the car as he strode towards them, his expression bleak.

"It's Chandra. She's been taken ill. Nina tells me she's in a bad way. Nausea, vomiting, the works. Most worrying is the fact that her pupils are dilated and it's proving difficult to keep her awake. We can't find Matt. We'd hoped he could help, but in the end we decided to call an ambulance."

"Is everyone else okay?" Stephanie asked.

"Up to now, yes. If it's a bug there's still a possibility that some of us will come down with it, but if it's food poisoning we'll be safe. Chandra doesn't eat the same food as us. She brings her own—kimchi."

One of the paramedics came running out of the front door and headed for the ambulance.

"Excuse me," Lucas said. "I'd better get back in case I'm needed."

As he ran back towards the door, Gus turned to Stephanie. "I don't like the sound of the sleepiness and dilated pupils. That doesn't sound like a stomach bug to me."

Stephanie shook her head. "It doesn't, but I don't want to leap to conclusions just because of the circumstances that brought us here."

"Steph, we've got one woman dead, another missing—possibly two, if we include Jemma—and the owner of the house believes one of his friends killed his sister. I think you've been right all along that we should assume the worst."

Gus now had that intense look he always got when he thought he was getting close to understanding a crime, and Stephanie felt a shiver of apprehension.

"I think Chandra knew more about what was going on with Alex than anyone," she said. "She overheard the conversation with Matt, and she moves so silently I bet she's picked up all the pieces and worked out how they fit together. If I was up to something, I wouldn't want her around."

"You? Up to something? Never let it be said."

Stephanie gave him a dirty look and he changed the subject. "What does this kimchi stuff taste like?"

Stephanie smiled. "It's pretty strong. Good, if you like that sort of thing—which I'm fairly sure you wouldn't."

"Strong enough to disguise some kind of poison?"

"I think so, depending what poison it is. But it might be as simple as a virus and we're being overly suspicious. And it's not that easy to get your hands on poison, although if this was premeditated..."

"Let's not forget that one of the guests is a doctor."

"That's true. But do you think Matt Hudson would do something so obvious?"

Gus scratched his head. "Who knows? Chandra seems to have heard a lot of his conversation with Alex, so he might have wanted her out of the way until this game of Lucas's is over and they can all go home."

They couldn't ignore the fact that Matt's wife was missing either. If anything had happened to Jemma, Matt had to be their number-one suspect—the spouse always was.

"If Jemma's here, alive, we need to make sure nobody can sneak her off the property."

"And if she's dead?"

"Then I suspect she's at the bottom of the sea, Steph. And I'm increasingly inclined to believe that's where Lidia Dalca ended up too. Maybe she saw something she shouldn't have."

Gus leaned back against the car, eyes closed, deep in thought. Stephanie waited, unwilling to disturb his deliberations.

"I'm going to call the boss again—tell him what's going on and see how the intelligence gathering is—"

Gus's words were cut short by a flurry of activity. Andrew Marshall came tearing round the side of the house, his usual casual saunter gone, his eyes fixed on the ambulance.

"What's happened?" he shouted as he hurried towards the police officers. "I was just coming back up from the cove and heard the ambulance. Who's hurt?"

"I'm afraid it's Chandra," Stephanie said. "She's been taken ill, and we've been told she's quite weak. They'll probably want to take her in as a precaution."

Andrew started to run towards the house, but the front door was suddenly thrust open, and the two paramedics came out bearing Chandra on a stretcher.

Gus and Stephanie stood to one side as Andrew leaned over the stretcher to talk to his fiancée. All they heard was, "I'm coming with you," as he climbed into the ambulance.

Lucas stood at the door, arms folded, watching them go. There was no doubting the fact that he was worried.

Gus took a step towards him. "Mr. Jarrett, I'm sorry about this, but given everything that's happened and your suspicions about one of your guests, we need to check a few things as a precaution."

"You mean she might have been poisoned, I suppose. The thought had occurred to me, although I find it hard to believe." Lucas wasn't looking at them. He was watching the ambulance as it headed down the drive.

"Do you think we could have a word with your staff, please?" Gus asked. "It would be good to know what Miss Tran ate this morning."

"Chandra always ate her own food. It's in the fridge. I'll show you."

Stephanie and Gus followed Lucas along a corridor and into a bright and airy kitchen with a huge central island. A large fridge with two wide doors over a deep freezer drawer stood against a wall. Lucas pulled it open. One shelf contained a number of jars, one half full of what Stephanie assumed was kimchi; a couple of others looked untouched. The rest of the shelf was packed with fresh produce, including daikon, pak choi, and sprouting beans.

Stephanie pulled a forensic glove from her pocket and slipped it on.

"We'd like to take this jar and have it tested. I'm sure Chandra has just contracted a bug, but I don't think we can be too careful, do you?"

Lucas stared at the jar and then back up at Stephanie's face.

"Don't you need a search warrant?"

"You invited us in, Mr. Jarrett. We didn't search for this; you showed us. And if it is potential evidence of a crime, we need to take it now before it's destroyed or removed."

Stephanie watched Lucas's face carefully. He looked perplexed but not scared. If there was something wrong with the kimchi, he wasn't the perpetrator. She could be wrong, of course; he was a hard man to read.

Gus was watching him too, and Stephanie knew what he was going to say.

"I should also tell you, Mr. Jarrett, that we are in the process of applying for a search warrant for your home. It will include the boathouse, and we'll get a warrant for the boat too. Until the documentation arrives, we'll wait here."

They hadn't yet set the wheels in motion, but Lucas didn't need to know that. Stephanie could see he was uncomfortable.

"Why? What are you searching for? If it's evidence that something happened to that Romanian girl, you're not going to find anything. She never came into the house—I told you that. And if there'd been anything to prove that Alex was murdered, I would have given it to you long ago."

Stephanie shook her head. "This is not related to your sister. We're concerned about the fact that you told us Jemma Hudson had called for a taxi. But she didn't. It's Jemma we're trying to find."

Before Lucas could respond, Matt burst into the kitchen.

"Have you heard anything from Jemma yet? I tried her mobile, but there's nothing. I called her sister in case she'd heard from her, but she hasn't. Her sister's the first person she would call if she was upset."

"Does she have some reason to be upset, Mr. Hudson?" Gus asked.

Matt bit the corner of his lip. "We had words. Nothing serious, but it's not like her to go off like that. It was just something Chandra said."

Stephanie could sense Matt's confusion. It was as if he had found himself in a foreign country and couldn't work out how to get home.

"You should know that Miss Tran's been taken to the hospital by ambulance."

Matt's eyes opened wide. "Why? What's up with her?"

"Some kind of food poisoning, we think. Are you feeling okay? No nausea?"

He shook his head. "No, I'm fine. I'm sorry I wasn't here—I might have been able to help."

"Can I ask where you were?" Stephanie thought it a little strange that he had disappeared when his wife was missing, but she kept her thoughts to herself.

"I walked along the coastal path to get a decent signal." He waved his phone at them. "Is anyone else ill, Lucas? I've got some anti-emetics in my bag and some rehydration salts. I'll stick around and not go off again, just in case."

"What else do you carry in your bag?" Gus asked. "Anything which could have poisoned Miss Tran?"

Matt's lips parted, and he stared at Gus with what appeared to be genuine surprise. "Are you suggesting that I poisoned her?"

"Not at all. Someone else could have had access."

"Unless they knew a fair bit about drugs, I seriously doubt it. I'll check though." His gaze drifted towards Stephanie. "I thought you'd finished here."

"We have a few more things to consider, which we're discussing with Mr. Jarrett."

Matt looked at Lucas, his head to one side. "Lucas?"

"They've requested a search warrant."

"Why?" Matt seemed genuinely puzzled, but then his eyes opened wide. "Is this something to do with Jemma?"

Stephanie glanced at Lucas. It would be interesting to see what he would say.

"I was about to tell them that they don't need to wait for a warrant." He turned to Gus. "Inspector, please feel free to do whatever you think necessary."

"What are you looking for?" Matt asked, his gaze flicking between Lucas, Stephanie, and Gus as if he didn't really know who was in charge. Gus decided to leave him in no doubt.

"Jemma didn't call a taxi, Mr. Hudson—at least, not on her mobile. No one here has admitted to giving her a lift into town, and it's a very long walk, especially with a suitcase. There are no buses, so we need to check that she's not still here. We'll conduct a preliminary search and bring in colleagues if we need to."

Matt looked stunned.

"Lucas?" he said, as if his friend should know the answer.

But Lucas shrugged and turned to Gus. "Please feel free to do whatever you think necessary."

"Thank you. Can you call all the people in the house and grounds—guests and staff—onto the terrace, please? We'd like to know where everyone is before we start our search."

Stephanie knew Gus meant that he didn't want anyone destroying any evidence.

CHAPTER 64

"What did you make of their reactions?" Stephanie asked Gus after Matt left to round up the guests and Lucas went in search of Nina and the staff.

"Hudson is lost. He strikes me as a man teetering on the edge of a meltdown, and I'm not sure it's wholly related to his missing wife, although she's clearly a significant factor. As for Jarrett, he's a mystery."

"I thought he'd flip at the thought of a search warrant, but he almost seemed relieved. And I don't get that at all."

"Are you okay to check the house, Steph? I really need to speak to the boss again, and if we get everyone outside where I can see them, I can keep an eye on them while I make the call."

"No problem," Stephanie answered as Lucas came back into the kitchen.

"Nina is on her way and she's going to find Adrianna. I'd forgotten that I gave Essi the afternoon off; I imagine she's gone into town."

Lucas started pacing, hands stuck in the pockets of his shorts. He finally stopped and spun round to face them.

"You think something's happened to Jemma, don't you? I should have taken her to the station myself. I knew she wanted to get away, and I can hardly blame her."

There was no need for Stephanie to ask him what he meant; who would want to stay in a house where the host believed one of the guests was a murderer?

"We don't know, Mr. Jarrett. I'm sure she's fine, but we want to be certain. Let's join everyone on the terrace, shall we?"

Gus held out an arm to indicate that Lucas should precede them out of the house.

Nick and Isabel Wallace, Matt Hudson, Nina Jarrett, and the housekeeper Adrianna were assembled on the south terrace in the shade of the pergola. Without Andrew Marshall, Chandra Tran, and Jemma Hudson, they were a depleted group.

"Please sit, if you'd like to," Gus said. "As far as we can tell, Jemma Hudson didn't phone a taxi company to take her to the station, so we are forced to wonder if she's still here, although it seems some of her belongings have gone too."

Stephanie risked a glance at Matt, whose skin had leached of all color, other than the dark gray circles under his eyes.

"Sergeant King will do a preliminary search of the rooms in the house, and then we'll check the outbuildings, the boathouse, and if necessary the boat itself—which I assume is back, as Andrew Marshall was here earlier."

Stephanie took that as her cue to leave, and headed for the door to the dining room—a lovely room with a long, polished table bearing a wide pewter bowl overflowing with yellow roses. From there she made her way into the hall and then into a large sitting room with two huge cream sofas facing each other. The space was dominated by a stone fireplace, and Stephanie instantly imagined it on a cold winter's night, a log fire crackling, lamps lit.

A door led into another, smaller room—a snug, she supposed you might call it, with a TV and a couple of comfy-looking chairs. She climbed a second staircase to two spacious bedrooms, each with its own bathroom. Once again, there was no sign of Jemma or her suitcase.

Running back down the stairs, she made her way to the hall and up the main staircase to the guest bedrooms. It was easy to tell whose was whose. Chandra and Andrew's room had been stripped, and there was a strong smell of disinfectant but little in the way of signs of female occupation—no make-up or perfume bottles.

Nick Wallace's room said more about him. He always appeared ultra-casual in his loud shirts and flip-flops, but his bathroom told a different story, with a host of men's cosmetics and hair treatments. But no suitcase and no Jemma.

Isabel's room was a tip—clothes selected and discarded on chairs and the floor, and when Stephanie looked in the wardrobe she could see enough clothes to last the average woman a month. Many bore designer labels, and she had to wonder where this woman got her money. Maybe Gus's intelligence gathering would answer that question.

Finally, Stephanie made her way into Jemma and Matt's room. She pulled open a drawer in which each item was perfectly folded. In the wardrobe men's T-shirts were organized in color order, lightest to darkest, and she knew that if Gus did this she wouldn't be able to resist the temptation to jumble them all up.

If it hadn't been for the sparse assortment of women's clothes pushed to one end of the wardrobe, there would be no indication that Jemma had ever been here.

CHAPTER 65

Confident that Jemma was nowhere in the house, Stephanie went in search of Gus. She was feeling a flutter of eagerness at the thought of returning to the boathouse and hadn't forgotten the sounds she'd heard that morning. Despite Gus's suggestion that they might search the cottages closest to the house first, she resisted.

"I never thought she'd be in the house. If she's anywhere, it's the boathouse or the boat; I'm sure of it."

"And that's based on...?" Gus asked, his head to one side.

"Oh, shut up, Gus. I know the noise from the apartment earlier could have been the cleaner, as Lucas suggested, but I just have a feeling."

"Of course you do. And don't look at me like that—I trust your instincts. The only trouble is that if we both go to the cove and she's been stashed somewhere closer to the house, they have a chance to get her away."

"So put the two most trusted in charge of making sure no one moves from the terrace."

"Excellent! If only I could think which two that might be." He had a point. But they both needed to go to the cove, so Stephanie phoned for back-up from the local station while Gus spoke to the assembled group.

"I'm working on the assumption that most, if not all of you, want Jemma Hudson to be found, and on that basis you'll do as

I ask and stay here. All of you, until we're back. Mr. Jarrett will need to come with us, but more officers will be arriving at any moment and they will expect to find you all here. We would wait for them, but I think you'll agree that finding Jemma is a priority, and we don't want to waste any more time."

Gus was right. Stephanie felt a sense of urgency and was anxious to head to the cove. At first when she couldn't contact Jemma she had felt nothing more than a vague suspicion that something wasn't right, but now there was an atmosphere of unease, fear, even desperation. She had no idea who it was coming from; she only knew that the air was humming with it.

Even though the sun was sinking in the sky, it was still hot and Stephanie ran the back of her hand across her sticky forehead as she hurried down the path behind Gus, stumbling slightly over loose stones, only slowing a little when she came to the steps, slimy with sap from the overhanging bushes.

A welcome cool breeze met them as they reached the beach, and Lucas stretched out his long legs to catch up with Stephanie. "Apart from me and one member of the staff, no one has been in Alex's apartment since she died. I know you need to search, but please do bear in mind how important the place is to me."

"Of course," Stephanie responded without slowing down. "We're just looking for Jemma, or evidence that she's been there. We'll respect your sister's things. Did you go in earlier, after I heard the noise?"

She turned towards him and he gave her an apologetic look. "I didn't. I couldn't face it after all the talk about Alex. I rarely go in unless I absolutely have to, so I thought I'd ask the cleaner if she'd dropped something, but I haven't had the chance."

Stephanie felt a flash of irritation as she let him go ahead up the steep slope at the side of the boathouse. He should have done as he'd promised!

At the top, Lucas bent and moved the third stone to the right of the door. The key was underneath.

"Is the key always left there?" Gus asked.

"Yes. Alex never used to lock the door unless she was going to bed. But we've kept it locked ever since. It's easier to keep the key here."

It seemed rather an obvious place, should anyone want to get in, but Stephanie kept her thoughts to herself as Lucas unlocked the door and they stepped into a small vestibule. She breathed in. This didn't smell like a house that was uninhabited. There wasn't a hint of stale air, but neither was there any smell of food, coffee, or any of the other scents that spoke of habitation. It just smelled as if the air had been moved. Maybe when the cleaner came she opened the windows.

From the vestibule, they made their way into the sitting room. Nothing. It was as orderly as Stephanie remembered from their previous visit. There was an indentation on the sofa, as if someone had sat there recently—Lucas, probably.

All three of them stood silently. Jemma wasn't here, and Stephanie felt a stab of disappointment. *Where was she?*

Lucas's hands were pushed deep into his pockets, and he was clearly not happy that they were invading his sister's space, but Stephanie ignored him and stared around the open-plan layout. There were two closed doors, and she remembered the one on the right led down to the boathouse.

"That door is locked, Sergeant," Lucas said.

"Key, please." Gus held out his hand, clearly not prepared to take no for an answer.

Lucas peered at the open hand, and for just a moment Stephanie thought he was going to refuse. But finally he picked up a key from the top of the bookcase and walked to the door.

"It's a bit stiff. I'll do it."

He fiddled with the key, seemingly unable to get a proper grip on it, but finally he pulled the door open. "As I said, it leads to the boathouse."

Gus ignored him and stepped into the doorway. From where she stood, Stephanie could see a flight of stairs, and Gus started to descend, Lucas right behind him, into the boathouse below.

He's back. I can hear movement in the next room. There's a woman's voice too. For a moment I think it means I'm saved, but then I remember that I thought one of my captors might have been a woman. Is it both of them?

Half of me wants to be silent in the hope they'll go away. What if they're back to finish what they started? But the other half doesn't want to lose any chance, however slim. If it's them, they know I'm here. If it's not them, this might be my only opportunity.

I drag every possible morsel of air into my lungs and moan as long and loud as I can through the bag, the gag, through my dry throat, my running nose, and my chest aches for a clean breath of fresh air.

Stephanie was about to step through the door to the boathouse when she heard a sound and stopped dead. What was it? It sounded like a groan, and it wasn't coming from either of the men on the stairs. Her skin prickled and she spun round. There was no one else there.

"Gus!" she yelled through the open doorway. "Gus, I heard something—I think it was coming from the bedroom!"

Stephanie didn't want to wait for Gus. For a brief moment she wondered if there might be someone else in there with Jemma. Would it put her in greater danger if Stephanie charged in?

But everyone else was up at the house and she didn't want to delay a second longer.

She heard a thundering on the stairs, and Lucas and Gus burst into the apartment just as she thrust open the door to the bedroom.

CHAPTER 66

I hear a voice raspy with shock: "Oh my God, Jemma, are you okay?"

It's Lucas, and I squeal with fear as I try to twist away from him, instinctively drawing my knees up to my chest. *Lucas. Nick. Andrew.* I don't know which of them it was, but I'm terrified of them all. The squeals keep coming as I try to curl my body in on itself. I feel a hand touch me, and my flesh erupts in tiny prickles as the sweat runs down my back and I scream through the gag.

"It's okay, Jemma. It's the police. Stephanie King. You're safe now. I'm going to untie you, but no one else will touch you without your agreement. Just me. Okay?"

The gag around my mouth slackens. Then the hood is pulled gently off my head. I blink away the tears and see the blurred outlines of three people standing over me. As my eyes clear, I recognize the sergeant, her dark auburn hair falling forward as she leans over me, attempting a comforting smile.

To one side of her is a man with a close-cut beard. There's something familiar about him, but my eyes are drawn to Lucas, standing behind them, looming above them, watching me. He is making all the right noises of concern, but I don't trust him. I don't trust anyone. The tears are flowing freely now—part relief that I'm saved, part horror at what's happened, and then there's the pain.

"This is Gus. He's another detective, and he's going to untie your arms now. Is it okay if he touches you? He's going to try not to hurt you, and I'm here, Jemma; I'm not going anywhere."

I blink, and she must take that as a yes.

The man starts to untie my arms, slowly, carefully, and as they are released he gently holds them and gradually draws them back from above my head to my sides, clearly aware that any rapid movement will be agony after so long in one position. I try not to cry out, but piercing shocks shoot through my shoulders.

I can see Lucas watching me, wincing at my suffering.

My eyes drift from right to left, but I'm not yet ready to move my neck. I can see I'm in a bedroom, and at the edge of my vision is a window. I was right: I'm in the boathouse. They must have just dragged me upstairs, but I still don't know who they were, and the thought brings a new wave of fear.

"We're going to take care of you now, Jemma. I know you're sore, but are you hurt?" Stephanie asks.

I want to shake my head, but my neck is too stiff, so I mumble, "No. But I need the bathroom."

Four hands reach out to me, two on each side, and carefully help me to sit up. "Can you stand?" Stephanie asks.

"I don't know."

"Gus, get her a glass of water, would you?"

The man hurries from the room, and I sit, head bowed, wondering if I will make it to the bathroom in time but still without the strength to get there.

Fresh tears spring to my eyes. "Who did this?"

"We don't know, Jemma, but we're going to find out," Stephanie says as she hands me the glass of water.

I gulp down a few mouthfuls, brush the tears from my cheeks with the back of my hand, and shuffle to the edge of the bed, resting there for a moment, rolling my neck. Finally, I try to push myself to my feet.

"Let me help you." Stephanie reaches out and holds me until I've made it off the bed, but I feel unsteady and she supports me to the door of a bathroom that leads off the bedroom.

Lucas is just watching. Since his first shocked outburst at finding me, he's said nothing.

"I can manage from here," I say.

"Don't lock the door. We'll be outside," Stephanie says. "I promise you, I'm not going to leave you."

As soon as the door closed, Gus turned to Lucas.

"Could you wait outside the apartment, Mr. Jarrett? Please don't go back to the house and don't inform anyone yet that we've found Jemma."

"What about Matt?"

"Mr. Hudson will be told as soon as possible, but we want to talk to his wife first. If you wait outside, one of us will walk back to the house with you while the other helps Mrs. Hudson. But this is now a crime scene, and you must not come back inside."

Stephanie watched as Lucas's expression changed from shock to despair. She wondered if it was the idea of a horde of CSIs crawling all over his sister's apartment, or perhaps he was devastated by the fact that one of his guests had been attacked and held captive. He left the room, his shoulders hunched. A few seconds later they heard the outside door open and close.

As soon as he'd left, Gus went into the living room. Stephanie listened as he asked for immediate further back-up to secure the premises and organized the forensic team. She thought for a moment of the guests at Polskirrin. Who could have done this to Jemma, and why? Her thoughts were interrupted as Gus returned to the bedroom.

Stephanie nodded towards the bathroom door. "She's still in there, but she must feel like crap. Looks like she was drugged too—

she's very woozy. Why did someone lock her in here, Gus? It's not exactly a clever place to put her, is it?"

He shrugged. "It depends what the intention was. They didn't know we were coming today, so if they just wanted to keep her out of the way for a while, it would probably have worked. If you hadn't been like a dog with a bloody bone, we probably wouldn't be here at all."

Gus was right. Whoever had hidden Jemma here wouldn't have known she had already phoned the police. What better place than an apartment to which no one ever came?

I wash my hands and splash my face. I can still feel the fabric of the hood as if it's imprinted on my skin. I want to wash myself inside and out, to rid myself of the smell of fear on my skin and the taste of terror in my mouth. There's a searing pain across my back, shoulder to shoulder, and I open the mirrored cabinet over the sink, not caring that this used to be Alex's home. I need painkillers and I grab a bottle from among the toothpaste, contact-lens cleaner, and antiseptic cream. It's as if Alex still lives here.

Suddenly I start to shake, as the shock of it all hits me. I lower myself onto the toilet seat and drop my head between my knees, waiting for the dizziness to pass. A tentative voice outside makes me realize I've been in here a long time.

"Are you okay, Jemma?"

I push myself up slowly, open the door, and stumble out, still not sure I can hold my head up. I'm relieved that Lucas is no longer there, although surely he can't be involved if he brought the police to me?

Stephanie seems to notice my confusion.

"Come on, let's get you out of here and into the fresh air," she says. "That'll make you feel better. We're going to get some officers down here to check for evidence, but we'll take you back to the house, if you think you can walk. We'll help of course." She nods towards the man with her. "This is DI Brodie, by the way—Gus."

He gives me a somber smile as if he can feel my pain and confusion, and Stephanie guides me towards the door.

As she does I take a moment to look at the room. This is where Alex slept. Its color scheme doesn't speak to me of depression. The walls are painted a soft green, and the furniture is off-white, distressed at the edges. Bright green and white patterned cushions lie on the floor, where I presume they were thrown when I was tied to the bed. A table lamp is broken in the corner, but otherwise the room is neat and orderly, and cheerful paintings adorn the walls. I glance again at the dresser as something flashes in the sunlight pouring through the window.

It's a square-cut diamond earring. And there's only one of them.

CHAPTER 67

"Are you okay to come back to the house with us now?" Stephanie asks as I swallow the last of the water. "Your husband's there and he's worried about you. We need to get you to the hospital to be checked over so we can find out what they drugged you with."

I don't want to go to hospital, and I'm sure Matt will know if there's anything to worry about. All I want is to get away from here—from this house, from these people.

Gus holds the door open for us, and I see Lucas waiting outside. For a moment, I freeze. I wish he wasn't here, but I'm not alone so I force myself to put one foot in front of the other. Gus closes and locks the door, pocketing the key.

Stephanie speaks to me quietly: "We're going to need your clothes, I'm afraid, and then Gus will want to talk to you, so come on, let's get you to your room."

I don't know whether I can face them all, knowing that someone there is responsible for what happened to me. But I have no choice.

It's a strange feeling, trudging uphill towards the back of the house. Stephanie is holding my arm lightly and Gus hovers, ready to catch me if I fall. Lucas has his head lowered, looking at his feet as if he's unsure of his footing on the rough ground of a path that he's trodden many times. I feel like I'm about to walk back into a nightmare that I'd thought was over. There are people on the terrace: Matt, Nick, Isabel, Nina. Which of them wanted me out of the way, attacked me, maybe planned to kill me?

There's no sign of either Chandra or Andrew, and the detective tells me quietly that Chandra has been taken to the hospital. I stare at her with horror, but she doesn't tell me any more.

Nick is the first to spot us, and although I can't read his expression from here, I wonder if the detectives are watching to see if anyone is surprised at my return.

Matt follows Nick's gaze and puts the mug that's in his hand on the table and comes rushing towards us.

"Jemma! Thank God you're okay. What happened? Where have you been?"

"Don't touch your wife, please, Mr. Hudson. We need to take her clothes."

Matt flashes an astonished look at Stephanie King, but he says nothing.

"I'll talk to you later," I say to Matt. I can't help feeling that if we'd left when I wanted to, none of this would have happened.

Sergeant King nods at the inspector and leads me into the house, up the stairs, and into our bedroom. She waits while I remove my clothes, turning her back to give me some privacy.

"Do you have a dressing gown you could put on for now?" she asks. "We're going to have to swab the parts of your skin that were exposed."

I reach for the cotton robe that's lying on the end of the bed and go over to the chest of drawers to get some clothes to change into when they've finished taking their samples. The drawers are practically empty and I give a grunt of surprise.

Stephanie turns towards me.

"Ah," she says. "I should have told you that we believed you'd left of your own volition—mainly because quite a few of your clothes and all your toiletries have gone, together with the smaller of your suitcases."

I stare at her. "Where are my things now?"

"I'm sorry, Jemma, we don't know. But we'll be searching the outbuildings thoroughly. I'm sure they'll turn up."

I hate the thought that someone has been in here, rummaging through my drawers, packing my underwear, my toiletries, and I sit down abruptly on the bed. Stephanie takes a chair, clearly respecting my need to gather some strength for the inevitable questioning.

Through the open window I can hear the sound of people talking quietly on the terrace. After a few minutes, the voice of DI Brodie cuts through the subdued mumblings.

"Earlier today Jemma Hudson was attacked and held against her will in the apartment above the boathouse. We are treating the attack on her as abduction and false imprisonment, and Polskirrin—in particular the boathouse—is now a major crime scene. A full forensic team will be here shortly, and I would ask you to comply with their every request. Your rooms will be searched, and we may request the clothes you were wearing this morning. None of you are free to leave the premises without my express permission."

"You can't do that! I had nothing to do with it! I need to leave in the morning." It's Nick's voice, outrage ringing through his words.

"Mr. Wallace, I'm quite within my rights to arrest the lot of you on suspicion of conspiracy to abduct and falsely imprison Mrs. Hudson, and unless you agree to do as I ask that's exactly what I will do. Someone attacked Mrs. Hudson, and we *will* find out who. Within the next half hour more officers will arrive. For now, I would like you all to sit down and wait until I'm ready to speak to you."

I raise my eyes to Stephanie King's and see nothing but sympathy there.

CHAPTER 68

"Mrs. Hudson, please take a seat," DI Brodie says as I join him in the study. I'm nervous, as if I'm the one who's done something wrong.

He sits down opposite and asks how I'm feeling. Am I okay to talk? Is it okay to call me Jemma? I just say yes to everything.

The interview begins in earnest, but in truth there isn't much I can tell him. It could have been any one of the men at Polskirrin in the doorway—or maybe a stranger. I only saw him for a couple of seconds, backlit by the sun, and I've no idea who was behind me. At the time I thought it was a woman, but the impression is fading and I'm not sure now.

"Can I ask you, Jemma, if you told Lucas Jarrett that you were planning to leave Polskirrin this morning?"

I try to think back through the fog. I remember my little outburst about him telling the truth, but did I tell him I was planning to leave?

"I'm not sure. I'm sorry."

"Did you ask him for the name of a taxi company to call to take you to the station?"

"I don't think so. I remember shouting at Matt that I was leaving and I might have mentioned a taxi, but why are you asking me that?"

"We're checking everything, just so we can understand properly what happened."

It's not an answer really, and Stephanie starts talking about getting me to the hospital to be checked over. I don't want to go.

"We don't know what they drugged you with, Jemma. It might be dangerous, so we'll have to take a sample of your blood. It may help us to identify your attacker."

I shake my head, my neck finally free from the stiffness. "I don't feel ill any longer. Just tired and sleepy. Matt will know what to do."

It's as if mention of his name has conjured my husband up. There's a quiet knock on the door and his head appears.

"Can I just check that Jemma's okay? Nina says you think she was drugged."

"Mr. Hudson," Gus says, "your wife was injected with something which made her drowsy. We'll have to get the police surgeon here to take a blood sample as she doesn't seem keen to go to the hospital. Jemma doesn't remember passing out, but she also can't remember much of what happened after the needle went into her arm. Do you have any idea what she might have been given?"

Matt groans. "Oh no. Please don't tell me they used it on Jemma. For God's sake, that could have been dangerous."

"What are you talking about?"

Matt bites his lip and can't meet Gus's eyes. "After you told me what had happened to Chandra, I went to check my bag, to see what I had if anyone else fell sick."

"Where was your bag?"

"In the wardrobe in our room. But I keep it locked. The key was in my bedside drawer, so it seemed safe enough. The thing is, I had some midazolam, but it's gone." Matt's cheeks are flushed; I know he thinks this is his fault.

"And you've only just thought to tell us this?" Gus asks, a trace of impatience in his voice. "What is midazolam, and why do you have it? You're a plastic surgeon, not a GP."

"I know that," he says with a hint of irritation. "But I *am* a doctor, and if I'm needed I like to be able to help. Anyway, midazolam is a sedative. What Jemma has described—not losing consciousness but having a hazy memory of events—pretty much matches its effects."

"Is it normal to carry sedatives of that nature, just on the off chance?" Stephanie asks.

Matt casts an uneasy glance at me. "Midazolam is good for treating anxiety, and...well, I haven't been sleeping too well, so it's good to know I have something that will help if I need it."

I hadn't known that. Maybe I should have.

"Would you expect the average person to know what it is, or indeed how to inject it into a vein, which it appears they did?" Gus asks.

Matt gives a dismissive shrug. "It's not uncommon, especially for anyone who's had any medical interventions. As for the injection, drug addicts seem to manage okay without any training. But if you're looking at me, I can promise you I had nothing to do with this. I wouldn't hurt Jemma."

I know he's telling the truth. But there's something in his words that makes me want to concentrate. I think back to the night before—to the fact that someone had known on which side of the bed to place the book and the photograph. Had they looked through our bedside tables and found Matt's key?

Gus moves on from quizzing Matt, and I go over everything I can remember once more until finally Stephanie suggests that Matt takes me to our room.

"I'm not staying at Polskirrin tonight," I say to no one in particular. "I don't feel safe. I don't think anyone's safe."

"I completely understand," Stephanie says. "But we'd like you to remain in the area. If you decide to stay here, we can put an officer outside your door. You'll be safe. Or we can arrange transport, if you'd rather stay somewhere else."

I notice Matt glance at the detectives.

"I'd be happy to take you to a hotel if that's what you want, Jemma, but the police have said that, like everyone else, I have to stay here until they know who did this to you. And what if Lucas is right about Alex? I need to see this through until he has the answers he wants—for Alex's sake. I owe her that."

I stare at him. I don't know what he means or why he owes Alex anything. But I'm sure he's not going to tell me.

CHAPTER 69

The crime scene team had arrived and were down at the boathouse, although Stephanie had little hope they would find anything of use. The key to the apartment was kept in an obvious place, and any one of the suspects could come up with a plausible reason for being in there. Even fibers found on Jemma's clothes would be inconclusive. She could have brushed against anyone going into or out of a doorway. And as yet they had found no sign of the syringe.

There was a brisk knock on the study door, and it was pushed open.

"You wanted to see me?" Lucas said, a polite smile failing to hide the haunted look in his eyes.

"We did, yes." Gus indicated a chair and Lucas sat down.

"We've spoken to Jemma about her plans to leave Polskirrin this morning, and she tells us that she didn't ask you about a taxi."

Lucas nodded. "Well, I suppose that's true." Stephanie could sense Gus's mounting frustration at the lies and obfuscation. He didn't say a word, simply waiting for Lucas to continue.

"I heard her tell Matt that she wanted to leave, and so I offered her a list of taxis. It amounts to the same thing."

"It doesn't, but even that version doesn't tally with Jemma's."

Lucas gave a slow shrug. "I can't account for that. Maybe with everything that's happened to her she's forgotten. I printed the list from my computer. You can probably check that—or your tech guys can."

Gus gave him a long look, but it was clear Lucas wasn't going to change his story.

"Who else would know where the key to the apartment was, Mr. Jarrett?" Stephanie asked.

"Just about anyone. It's where we've always kept keys—third stone from the right."

"But if you didn't want anyone going in there, why not hide it somewhere more secure?"

Lucas let out a long breath. "In retrospect that would have been smart. But I thought my friends would respect my wishes and stay out of the apartment."

"What," Gus said, "even though you think one of them is a killer? You would still expect them to respect your sister's personal space?"

The note of incredulity in Gus's voice couldn't be missed, and Lucas's lips tightened.

"Hindsight is a marvelous thing, isn't it, Inspector?"

That was a statement they couldn't argue with, and for now they had nothing else to ask Lucas so they told him he was free to go.

As soon as the door closed behind him, Gus picked up the phone to update DCI Prescott while Stephanie paced the room, keen to know what their next steps would be.

As he hung up, he looked at her with raised eyebrows.

"That's three inquiries running now—Jemma, Lidia, Alex. And we'll have to see if it's soon to be four. Chandra is out of danger, but they're still running tests, so we won't know for a while if she was intentionally poisoned. Andrew Marshall asked for a message from Chandra to be passed back to us via the police at the hospital. She said she wanted to finish what she was going to tell us earlier."

"Which was?" Stephanie asked.

"That Alex told Chandra the morning before she died that she'd heard something at dinner the night before. She was convinced that someone at that table knew what had happened to her all those years ago. She told Chandra she needed to ask one more question before she would know for certain."

"And do we know what that was, or who she was going to ask?"

"No, or at least not yet. But I've said I want Marshall back here—he is, after all, a suspect in Jemma's abduction. There's an officer waiting to drive him. We still have to treat Chandra's illness as suspicious in view of everything else, but Jemma's false imprisonment is our number-one priority."

"She's convinced she was attacked because she'd threatened to call the police."

Gus gave her a grim look. "I suspect she's right. Someone doesn't want us here. The intelligence on all of them should start to come through soon, so let's see what that tells us." He glanced at his phone. "And why doesn't the sodding Internet work here? That's not going to help. I can't believe Lucas runs his foundation from a place with a flaky Wi-Fi signal."

He picked up the router sitting on the desk in front of him, and for a moment Stephanie thought he was going to bang it on the desk in frustration.

"Let me have a look," she said, taking the offending device out of his hands and carefully checking that all the leads were pushed fully in.

She crouched down to look under the desk and saw a cable dangling uselessly.

"Bloody hell! The line isn't even attached." Stretching forward she connected the cable and sat back on her haunches, raising her eyebrows at Gus, who looked ready to explode.

"Christ, that man's a control freak! I would put money on him disconnecting it while he played his little game so his friends were out of touch with their real lives. We've thoroughly buggered up his plans though. I guess the game is well and truly over."

Stephanie said nothing, instead grabbing her bag to pull out her laptop. She waited until he'd calmed down a little before asking if he would please read her the password from the bottom of the router. Within moments she was up and running.

"Let's go through everything again, starting with Jemma. Did you speak to the assembled guests about where they were this morning?" Gus asked.

"I did. Lucas says he was here, in his study. But no one can either confirm or refute that. Nick says he was lying on a sunbed next to Isabel. She concurs, so they both have alibis. But they're twins so who knows? Matt was walking—on his own. And we believe Andrew was out on the boat, getting it ready. We only have his word for that. Nina was in the kitchen."

"So not helpful at all then. Until we have something more concrete, let's look at motive—who had something to gain or something to hide? You'd been asking about Lidia's disappearance, and that was Jemma's main reason for the call. So let's run through what happened to Lidia that night, see if we've missed anything."

"I'll create a timeline," Stephanie said, typing into her laptop.

"Lidia arrived here in the late evening—her mother said she spoke to her sometime before ten. Shortly after that Chandra saw her coming down the drive, and someone—Lucas, it seems—went to meet her."

"He must have brought her round the back because Jemma heard her speaking to a man. Again Lucas, I assume."

Stephanie added a line to her spreadsheet. "Okay, he then goes to talk to his wife, who isn't there, and returns to Lidia to ask for her number and offers to get her a taxi, which she refuses."

"Correct, although the offer of the taxi might be an embellishment of the facts, given today's events. But, either way, Lidia sets off towards the coastal path let's assume sometime between 10:15 and 10:45." Gus leaned back in his chair. "Now, according to Nick

Wallace, the lights went off when he was on his way back up, and that's where he passed Lidia. He thought that was 10:30 or maybe a little later. We know Lucas didn't turn the lights off—or at least he says not—and it seems unlikely that it was Nick because why would he mention it?"

"I think we can be more precise than that," Stephanie said. "When I took Jemma up to her room I asked if she thought she had been attacked because she knew something about the night Lidia disappeared. She said she'd seen someone go down the beach path just after she went up to her room—we can assume that was Nick Wallace—but then she saw someone else quite a while later, and a few minutes after that the lights went out. The thing is, she could see the switch—it's on a wooden plinth at the top of the path—and there was no one near it. She's fairly sure that was at 10:40."

Gus pursed his lips. "Okay, that tallies with our timeline, but it means the lights were definitely turned off at the boathouse. There must have been someone else down there. We know it wasn't Alex, because she was talking to Matt. And if we're to believe Nick, it wasn't him either."

Stephanie was typing furiously, keen that they didn't forget a word of this.

"Did Jemma tell anyone else what she saw?" Gus asked.

Stephanie stopped typing and looked up. "Yes, she did. She told Andrew Marshall."

CHAPTER 70

Nina made her way up the outside staircase, balancing a tray on one hand as she knocked on the French windows.

"Jemma? It's Nina. I've brought you something to eat."

She heard a noise from inside the room, and Jemma opened the door a crack.

"Why did you come up the outside staircase?" she asked, her voice taut with suspicion.

"Because it was the quickest way with the fewest doors. Look, I know you're frightened, but why would I want to harm you?"

Jemma laughed without amusement. "Why would anyone? But they did."

"Perhaps they didn't mean it to turn out that way, and whoever did it might have had a very good reason." Nina kept her voice low, hoping a soothing tone would convince Jemma, but she saw a flash of anger in her eyes.

"There is no good reason on this earth for taking someone captive and drugging them, Nina."

Nina took a breath. "Can I come in? This is just tea and a sandwich. It's still a couple of hours till dinner, and you missed lunch so you must be starving. If you don't trust me, I'll eat some of it and have a cup of tea with you."

"I'm sorry. I'm sure the food and tea are fine, but I'm not hungry."

"Maybe I could come in for a moment, even if you don't want to eat? I'd just like to make sure you're okay."

With a reluctant sigh Jemma pulled the door open wide. Nina stepped inside, placing the tray on the chest of drawers. With her back to the room, she closed her eyes for a moment. She had to get this right. She had been practicing what to say, but now the words had flown from her mind. She turned to face Jemma, her hands gripping the edge of the chest behind her.

"I'm sorry you've been treated so badly in our home, Jemma. It's not what I would have wanted for anybody. It's been a distressing year, and I think maybe people have behaved in a way that isn't true to their character."

"Are you making *excuses*, Nina?"

"No, no, of course not. But the police say this is a serious crime, and that someone could serve a prison sentence—a long sentence—for this." Nina heard her voice falter. "False imprisonment carries a potential life sentence—did you know that? I looked it up. But if someone made a mistake, acted rashly, would you really want them to suffer that much?"

Jemma sat down on the bed, head bowed, her hands clasped between her knees. She seemed defeated, and Nina felt a flash of guilt about what she was trying to do.

"I don't know. For the terror I suffered, the answer would be a resounding yes. So until we know who did this and why"—Jemma raised her eyes to Nina's—"I can't know whether it's something I can forgive or not."

Nina had to look away from the challenge she saw there. She had said enough.

"I'll leave the tray here in case you change your mind and decide you'd like something to eat. Let me know if you need anything—anything at all."

Nina walked towards the French windows, and as she pulled them open, Jemma called to her: "Nina, the earring I gave you the other day—it was Alex's, wasn't it?"

She spoke without turning round. "I think it might have been, yes."

"It's lovely. She never struck me as the kind of girl to wear diamonds though."

"They were a present from Lucas. She wore them every evening, even if she was eating at home, on her own."

Nina held on to the edge of the door, wishing Jemma would stop asking her questions.

"Do you know if she was wearing them when she died? And if so, did the police return them to Lucas?"

Nina looked back over her shoulder. "No. Alex always took them off when she was swimming—she was scared she might lose one. The only thing the police returned to Lucas was a black bracelet she was wearing when she drowned."

Jemma lifted her eyes. "Are you sure?"

Nina gave her a puzzled frown. "Yes. Why?"

"It doesn't matter," Jemma said. But clearly it did.

CHAPTER 71

Since Nina left I've been puzzling over what she said, but Matt has come back to the room to tell me that Lucas is demanding that we all go to the dining room. He has something to tell us.

I don't want to go. I don't want to do anything he tells me to. I don't even want to be here. But if I go to a hotel I'll feel exposed, vulnerable. At least here I have a policeman keeping guard and the French windows are locked and bolted.

Matt has said that he's going to do as Lucas asks—of course he is—but I'm staying here in the room.

"Are you sure you're okay?" he asks, more attentive than he has been for a long time. But he's not really with me. He's twitchy, nervous, and now that I'm safe, I don't understand what's scaring him.

"Go, Matt," I tell him, and with a last look under lowered brows, he turns and walks out.

As soon as he leaves I push a chest of drawers behind the door. I've seen too many movies where the police officer keeping guard is distracted while someone sneaks into a so-called protected area.

I climb back onto the bed and feel myself drifting, the drugs not yet fully out of my system. Suddenly I'm back in the boathouse, looking at the wetsuits. Someone is standing in the doorway. I feel a rush of air behind me, and I'm falling, falling. Now I'm in Alex's bathroom, looking through her cabinet. There's something that isn't right. I don't know what it is. The door to the bathroom bursts open and in strides a woman. There's a man behind her, taller, looking over her shoulder, grinning at me. At first it's Lucas, then Nick, then Andrew. Their features merge and distort. The man's hands are reaching out towards my neck. I'm trying to back away, but I can't. I can see him, feel him, taste his breath—but my body won't respond. My heart is pounding, and I try to cry out, but I don't make a sound. He's getting closer, and finally, as his fingers reach for me, I manage to scream.

"Jemma! Are you okay? Let me in."

I wake from the dream and someone is banging on the French windows. My pillow is wet where I've been crying and my T-shirt is sticky with sweat.

"Jemma, open the door, for God's sake. Let me know you're okay."

Now I recognize the voice: it's Andrew.

"I'm fine," I shout. "Just a dream."

I don't want to let him in. I don't know if I can trust him. Why would he be sneaking up the outside staircase to our room?

"I want to talk to you about Chandra," he says in a hoarse whisper.

I take a deep breath. This is Andrew. He's always been kind to me. Can I trust him? I don't know, but I want to.

I struggle to sit upright and swing my legs over the side of the bed to stand up. I unlock the doors and pull them open. Andrew strides in and wraps me in his arms.

"Thank God you're okay."

I cling to him for a moment and then push him away. "How's Chandra?"

"She's going to be fine. The doctors are running tests, but now that she's out of danger they're non-urgent so they'll take some time. She thinks she might have inadvertently made herself ill. She was feeling nauseous—probably the stress of the last couple of days—so she took one of her herbal remedies. It turns out it contains atropine—belladonna to you and me. That would account for the dilated pupils. We don't know, and I don't think we should make any assumptions. They're monitoring her, but she wanted me to talk to you. I saw everyone was in the dining room, so I thought I'd give them a wide berth."

A thought hits me. How did Andrew know I was back if he hasn't spoken to anyone? How did he even know I'd been taken, and not left, as everyone had said? I look at him suspiciously, and his eyes open wide.

"I can see what you're thinking, but I've been speaking to the police. I'm so sorry it happened to you. What a mess."

"Where were you this morning?"

"Bloody hell, Jemma!" He reaches out his arms again and rests his hands on my shoulders. He takes a deep breath as if to calm himself. "I was out on the boat getting it ready because I wanted to go sailing this afternoon—I had to get away from this madhouse."

"You weren't on the boat. The tender was on the shore."

He shakes his head, his eyes never leaving mine. "Of course it was. I always swim out and back. Why would I take a boat when it's only a few hundred meters?"

I want to believe him, I really do.

"Listen," he says, squeezing my shoulders gently. "I like you, Jemma. And so does Chandra. She wanted me to talk to you, to tell you to be very careful. She says the problem is that you know too much. You know more than you think, but you mustn't do anything about it. Not until she's back and you can do what needs to be done together."

"What does all that mean?" I say, frustrated by the lack of clarity in the message.

"She wouldn't tell me anything else. She gave me a message for the police though and I've passed it on. I'm sorry, but it concerns Matt."

I feel a wave of weakness wash over me, and Andrew reaches out to hold me. I look over his shoulder to where a shadow looms in the open doorway to the balcony.

CHAPTER 72

Stephanie was trying to keep up with the information that was flooding in from various sources. Background checks had been under way for some time now, and they were getting a much more detailed picture of Lucas Jarrett and his guests, but putting it all together, linking it to the cases they were investigating, was proving more difficult.

Gus had concluded that he should focus on the major crime that had occurred at Polskirrin that day—Jemma's abduction. Stephanie was keeping Lidia's disappearance in mind while assessing whether anything might suggest Alex's death wasn't suicide.

"Don't restrict your thinking to the last twelve months, Steph," Gus said. "There's a possibility that her death might be related to the kidnapping thirteen years ago."

The investigations were so tightly intertwined it was almost impossible to put any degree of separation between them, and now that their mobiles as well as Stephanie's laptop were connected to Wi-Fi, emails were coming in thick and fast.

"There's a new piece of information about Lidia," Stephanie said. "She'd been working part-time at the local sailing club, in the bar. That's apparently where she heard about the wedding." Stephanie looked up from her laptop. "Does that suggest anything to you?"

"It suggests that we put a flag against both Andrew Marshall and Lucas Jarrett, both of whom are sailors and could easily have visited the club in the days before the wedding. Perhaps Marshall had agreed to meet her here, as Nick Wallace suggested?"

"Or Lucas," Stephanie suggested.

"The night before his wedding? Nice."

"But hardly unheard of," Stephanie said with a hint of disdain.

"Isabel Wallace has quite a checkered past," Gus said, reading from his phone. "She was arrested in her teens for possession of Class A drugs, and on another occasion held on suspicion of dealing. No charges, ultimately."

Gus slouched in his chair and carried on studying his screen.

"Result!" he growled, leaning forward to grin at Stephanie. "I think I have a good idea what Nick Wallace's emails were about. They were obviously sensitive, but unlikely to be pornographic if Lucas gave his sister access to his inbox. But look at this. If I'm right about the content of the emails, it gives Wallace a motive to want to silence Alex."

Gus passed his phone to Stephanie. There was a picture of a smart, smiling Nick Wallace standing next to one of the UK's most famous entrepreneurs. It appeared from the text that Nick had been working on the takeover of a company for this man, and its shares had soared, making existing shareholders a fortune.

"Shall I get him in here?" she asked.

"No, I think we'll see what Jarrett has to say on the subject first."

Five minutes later a despondent Lucas was sitting in front of them. There was an air of resignation about him, as if his plans had been completely thwarted and all his anger was spent. Gus wasn't showing any sympathy though.

"Mr. Jarrett, would I be right in saying that Nick Wallace is in corporate finance, helping clients to manage takeovers, mergers, etc.?"

"That's correct," Lucas said, his face expressionless.

"Then I need to ask you, has he ever offered you inside information about any of the companies he works with?"

Lucas leaned back with a sigh. "That's an easy question to answer. Yes. Frequently."

Stephanie sat up straight. She hadn't been expecting that.

"And what did you do with the information?"

"I tossed it. Or rather, Alex did. Nick had the bizarre notion that he was doing me a favor. As a *mate*." He spat out the last word. "I thought his behavior completely reprehensible, but he's an old friend, and I know it's his way of showing me how important he is. I told him he was being a jerk and ignored his emails."

"You realize it's against the law?" Gus said.

"As I understand it—but do correct me if I'm wrong—it's only illegal if someone acts on the information. As I didn't, I guess he's not guilty of anything other than being an idiot."

"You mentioned Alex?"

"Yes. She helped with the foundation, and all emails went to her. She forwarded anything that I needed to deal with to me, but I told her I didn't want to see anything from Nick unless it was friendly chat. So she ignored his not-so-subtle attempts to tell me which shares to buy."

"And do you think Alex might have been tempted?"

"Not for a moment. She wasn't a fool. Stupidly, I told Nick that Alex had all his emails on her computer. I can only think he went down to the boathouse that night to either delete them himself or persuade her to."

Gus leaned his elbows on the desk. "He said she wasn't there. Do you think he's telling the truth?"

Lucas returned his gaze without blinking. "Yes, strangely I do. Nick likes to show off, but he's a bad actor—always has been. He admitted to seeing the Romanian girl, and I genuinely believe he was on his way back up to the house. And anyway, Alex was killed much later than that."

There was a heavy silence.

"And how would you know that?" Gus asked quietly.

Lucas's body stiffened. "The coroner's report."

"I think you'll find that, due to the time spent in the water, the report only ever gave an estimate. So I'll ask you again: how do you know your sister was killed later?"

"My apologies. I assumed the time given was definitive. I must have misunderstood."

Lucas Jarrett knew something about his sister's death. As the door closed behind him, Stephanie could feel it and so could Gus; she could tell from his face. But before they could discuss their suspicions, Stephanie's email pinged. She glanced at the subject line: Lucas Jarrett.

"I've got the financial report for Lucas. Maybe this will join some dots." She read for a moment. "God, that man has some money! The foundation has its own accounts, but apart from a joint account with Nina, which seems to cover household expenditure, he has a number of personal accounts. There's nothing particular that stands out, other than payments to a private clinic every month for the past year."

"Where's the clinic?"

"Finland. Hang on, I'll look it up."

Stephanie opened a search engine and typed in the name of the clinic.

"It seems to be a holistic health clinic suitable for long-term rehabilitation, weight loss, injury recuperation, and so on."

"Relevant?" Gus asked.

"I don't know, but until we have more, he's bound to dismiss it as a charitable donation or something similar."

She was more certain than ever that Lucas was hiding something from them, but the statements told her nothing other than that Jarrett had a jaw-dropping amount of money.

"What did you make of his comment about the time of death?" Gus asked.

"It was never established precisely—there was quite a big window because of the temperature of the water—yet he seems to think he knows more than we do. We checked the time stamp on the video of course, but anyone with a basic technical knowledge can falsify that, and there was nothing to stop Wallace from going back to the beach, so I don't buy it that it proves his innocence. But I definitely got the impression that Lucas regretted mentioning the time of death as soon as he'd said it."

Gus had been half listening, half reading from his phone, but as she looked at him, waiting for his response, she saw his body stiffen.

"Oh boy," he said, his eyes opening wide. "We need to speak to Matt Hudson again."

"Why? What have you found?"

"Not only do we now have Andrew Marshall's message from Chandra suggesting that Alex believed Matt held the key to what happened thirteen years ago, but it also seems there's something going on between Matt and Isabel Wallace." Gus looked at Stephanie, and she could see his excitement. "He's been paying her ten thousand pounds a month for the last year, starting the month Alex died."

CHAPTER 73

My eyes haven't left the figure standing in the doorway to our balcony.

"What are you doing with my wife?" Matt says, anger clear in his voice.

"I'm doing what you should be doing. Looking out for her."

Andrew drops his arms and Matt slumps against the door jamb, his momentary bravado capsizing.

"Jem, I really don't blame you if you want to be with Andrew; I know I'm not much use to anyone right now. Lucas has gone to talk to the police, and he says they're examining every aspect of our lives. And there's something I need to talk to you about before you...do whatever it is you've decided to do."

Matt looks defeated, his eyes bloodshot and confused, so I turn to Andrew.

"I'll come and talk to you later. Is that okay?"

"Of course." He gives me a sympathetic smile, and without looking at Matt makes his way past him and out through the French windows. I hear his feet running down the staircase.

Matt is still leaning against the door jamb. "You'd better sit down, Jemma."

My heart is hammering in my chest as I perch on the edge of the bed. What can he possibly be going to tell me? Andrew told me that Chandra had said something about Matt, and I need to know what. But at the same time, I don't know if I *want* to know.

Matt drags a chair from against the wall, the scrape of its legs on the wooden floor making me shudder, and pulls it round to face me. A thin sheen of sweat coats his skin.

"What I'm about to say is going to upset you, and I can't tell you how sorry and deeply ashamed I am." He swallows hard as if he can't get enough saliva. "I sometimes wonder if before getting married everyone should have a duty to reveal the very worst of themselves, so there's never anything that can come back to bite them. But if we did that I suspect there would be considerably fewer marriages."

"Matt, you're talking in riddles. Just tell me—whatever it is."

When he looks at me I can see the conflict in his eyes. He still doesn't want to tell me, but he knows he must.

"The police will be looking at our financial records. And they'll discover that for the last twelve months I've been making payments to Isabel. She's the reason I've been working all hours."

I should feel something—a dull thud in my chest, dizzy, cold, anything—but I don't. I'm just numb.

"The truth is, she's been blackmailing me since we were here last year. And it's to do with Alex." He takes a huge gulp of air.

"There's something I never told anyone, and Alex swore she never did either, but Isabel found out. You see, when we were teenagers, Alex always liked me. Nick ignored her unless Lucas was watching, and Andrew treated her like a kid, which, to be fair, she was. She said I was the only one who showed her any respect. I had always been close to Lucas, but then the other two started to come along at the weekends too, and I never felt I was one of them—I'm sure you've realized that by now. They were like gods: so tall, good-looking, and girls were drawn to them like magnets, especially Andrew. It took me until I was to my twenties to grow into my face."

He gives me a lopsided attempt at a smile, and I know what he means. I've seen pictures of Matt as a boy. His features were unusually large and grown-up for a boy so small and young—the high forehead, the perfect straight nose, the symmetry. He didn't stop growing until he was eighteen, and by then he had a complex about his looks that it took years to rid himself of.

"Alex liked me though. *Really* liked me. I started to meet her when the others weren't there. And even when they were, we used to hide in the summerhouse together. We thought no one knew, but they did. Lucas took me to one side and had a word—said Alex had a crush on me, but she was only thirteen and he didn't want me to hurt her. He asked me to look out for her and understand the boundaries. He trusted me with her." Matt pauses and takes a deep breath. "And I let him down. But she was mad keen, and one thing led to another, and... You know how it goes."

He looks at me, hoping I will understand, and I stare at him. "She was *thirteen*, Matt. *Thirteen*!"

"Do you think I don't know that?" I hear the anguish in his voice, and he drops his head to gaze at the floor. "It only happened once, and I was so ashamed that I avoided her like the plague afterwards, which makes what I did even worse. She was so hurt, but she never told anyone. I would have deserved it if she had told Lucas what a bastard I was, but it wasn't long afterwards that he left on his world trip. Once he was gone I avoided all contact with her. I just hoped and prayed she would never tell anyone what I'd done. A few months later, just after her fourteenth birthday, she was kidnapped. I tried really hard to see her after she was found, but she refused to let me near her."

My mind is spinning. Clearly with Alex dead and no longer able to tell a soul, Matt would have believed he was home clear.

"Last year—before Alex died—Isabel followed me to the beach and told me what she knew. I denied it, and we had a terrible row. I spoke to Alex, and she swore she hadn't told anyone, not even

Lucas. When she died, I thought my secret had died with her. It was only after she was gone that Isabel told me she had proof—a diary she'd found in Alex's room. She'd been in and out of their house for most of that summer, so I'd no reason to disbelieve her. I wanted to kill her."

I know he means Isabel, not Alex. Once again, I see the child in the photos Lucas put up on the screen. I hate the thought that Matt, who was five years older than Alex, hadn't been able to resist what he knew was wrong. And then to reject the poor kid. How she must have suffered.

"Did you ask Isabel for proof?"

"Of course. She told me the only person she would show the diary to was Lucas, but she'd send a copy to you. I was too much of a coward to risk it."

"Why had Isabel waited all these years?"

"Had Alex been alive I'm certain she would have claimed everything she wrote was nothing but a childish fantasy. She wouldn't have let Isabel get away with it."

I don't know what to say. I have a strange feeling he wants me to feel sorry for him, but I don't. I'm angry that he didn't have the strength to resist Alex, disgusted at how he must have hurt her, and furious that he allowed Isabel to blackmail him.

"What are you going to tell Sergeant King and the inspector?"

"The truth, I suppose. If Isabel turns over the evidence to them, they might charge me, but I honestly don't think that a thirteen-year-old's diary is going to carry much weight."

"So why let her blackmail you then?"

He raises his eyes to mine for the first time and his voice shakes with his words. "Because I'm so ashamed. I wouldn't have been able to lie to you if she'd presented the evidence. And God knows what Lucas will do to me. His respect means so much to me. It's hard to explain, but he rescued me from a difficult time, and this is how I repaid him! I couldn't bear the thought of either of you knowing. I would lose both my best friend and my wife—although I suspect that ship has already sailed."

He gives a bitter laugh and I feel sorry but wonder if he's right. Not just because of this, but because of how he's behaved—building barriers between us to protect himself should I, in the end, choose to reject him. I understand it now, but I'm not sure it matters.

Before I can respond there's a knock on the door and a voice calls through: "Are you there, Mr. Hudson? It's Sergeant King. We'd like to talk to you, please."

I see nothing but resignation in my husband's eyes.

"I'd better go," he says, leaning towards me and grasping my hand. "I'm sorry, Jemma. I can't tell you how sorry I am."

He stands up and pushes the chest of drawers away from the door, turning at the last minute to give me a weak smile. Then he's gone.

CHAPTER 74

Stephanie thought Matt Hudson looked as if the events of the last couple of days had drained the lifeblood out of him. He started to talk even before he'd been asked a question, and it seemed that with each sentence he uttered, his voice grew quieter. She leaned forward in her chair to hear him better.

"So there you have it," he said finally. "That's why I've been paying Isabel. She's been blackmailing me, but I can't prove that. She, however, claims she can prove I had sexual intercourse with an underage girl, so I don't know where you'll take it from here."

"It's an interesting question," Gus said. "Alex isn't here to ask, unfortunately, so we'll have to consider our next move carefully. The news is full of allegations of historical sexual misconduct right now, so it could be said that you had a motive to kill Alex, if her brother is right about her death."

Matt's face was a picture of horror. "I wouldn't have killed Alex! You have no idea how fond I was of her. She was such a brave kid before everything that happened to her."

"Do you think Lucas Jarrett really believes his sister was murdered?" Gus asked.

Matt didn't hesitate. "Absolutely. I've never seen him like this—anger is burning in him so brightly that it's distorting the person he's always been. I thought it was madness when he first told us, but I'm wondering now if he might be right. I was talking to

Alex that night. She was upset about something, and I know it's difficult to understand the mindset of a suicide victim, but I'm a doctor and I promise you there was no hint of depression in her manner. I was stunned when we heard she was dead, and appalled that I might have missed the signs."

"According to Andrew Marshall, Chandra had spoken to Alex that day. Apparently, Alex thought you held the key to who had abducted her and planned to ask you that night. Do you know who it was? Were you involved? You say you didn't see Alex's text message, but how do we know that's true? Is that why you killed her?"

Matt's eyes filled with tears. "Please don't say that. Don't even *think* it. If I'd seen her message I'd have known exactly where to find her, and I'd have been there like a shot. I never saw it, but I don't know how to prove it."

"Alex had the power to destroy you. It was a golden opportunity for you."

"Yes, I was a bastard; I treated Alex shamefully. But I would never have let her stay there on her own all night. *Never*."

"But who else would have understood her words, Mr. Hudson? Who else would have known what 'you know where to find me' might mean?"

"*Anyone!* Or at least anyone who had spent time at Lucas's dad's house. Alex used to hide in the summerhouse whenever her brother had his friends over, until she got a bit older and a bit bolder. Everyone knew it was her favorite place. They didn't know what had happened there—between me and Alex, I mean—but Lucas, Nick, Andrew, even Isabel would have understood. It wasn't me. You have to believe me."

Gus had pushed him hard, but they had finally let a distraught Matt go. Stephanie believed in his innocence, and he seemed devastated by what he'd done and by how he had let Alex down, but he was wrong to think he should have recognized the signs of depression in someone who was bound to have shrouded herself in layer upon layer of emotional self-defense.

Stephanie picked up the phone to call the senior investigating officer in Alex's original abduction case.

"There was definitely no mention of any text message," he said, a note of urgency in his voice. "But this changes things. Alex hadn't planned to leave home that night. It was a spur-of-the-moment decision, so we believed no one knew where she was going. That's why we had to conclude it was opportunistic, although we were never happy about it."

"The files said that you suspected Mirac Bozkurt. What was the reasoning?"

"Alex told us that the man who seemed to be in charge had a strong accent and a very quiet voice, and when he spoke, everyone else shut up—hung on his every word. Bozkurt's known as the Quiet Man and is head of an organized crime gang, but as usual there was nothing to pin on him. Never bloody well is. Anyway, we checked the records of all his known phones, although there were no doubt others. I've got the records here. I'll send you the details, but there are no calls to Bozkurt from anyone close to Alex."

Stephanie ended the call, promising to get back to the officer when they knew more.

"Tell you what, Gus: if any one of Lucas's friends had anything to do with Alex's abduction and rape, it gives him a substantial motive to murder her, if he thought she was on to him."

"Yep. Conspiracy to kidnap could mean life imprisonment, same as murder. Perhaps he thought he had nothing to lose."

A ping from Stephanie's email interrupted them. It was the promised list of calls. Each number had a name attached, but none of them meant anything to her.

She sighed with frustration. "I know this all happened thirteen years ago, Gus, but I just think the text message might be really important. Why on earth Alex didn't tell the police, I don't know." She paused. "Well, that's not true—I do know. She thought it might get Matt into trouble, and she probably didn't think it was important as only he would have seen it. Poor kid. Anyway, I'd like to get everyone together who was in the pub that night—see if they can jog each other's memories. Between them they might remember who could have looked at Matt's phone. Maybe Alex remembered incorrectly—perhaps she said exactly where she was going."

"Much as it pains me to say this, your instincts do have a strange and irritating habit of being better than mine when it comes to reading people. Let's do it."

CHAPTER 75

Since Matt left I've been unable to focus. I need to get outside into the open air, away from every little reminder of my life with him—his reading glasses next to his side of the bed, the Sleepbuds in their case, the neatly ordered clothes hanging inside the wardrobe that I carelessly left open. I stand up and walk out onto the balcony. Nowhere feels safe to me, but fear seems the least important of the emotions that are battling for supremacy, and the house and grounds are crawling with police so I'm sure no one is going to hurt me now.

Slowly, I make my way down the steps, my bare feet making no sound on the stone. There is no one around, and the silence feels ominous. I walk across the grass—cool on my feet as the afternoon fades to evening—towards the Japanese garden. I'm halfway down the path when I hear voices, the first high-pitched, fast, urgent.

"Don't, Lucas. Please, I'm begging you—don't say anything. Not yet."

"I'm sorry. I shouldn't have brought you here. It was cruel, and it's so unfair to Nina. She needs to know. It's going to hurt her so much, but the only thing I can do now is tell the truth. Put an end to the lies."

There's a sense of despair in his voice, as if it's all too much. I can just make out two figures on the other side of a clump of black bamboo. It's Lucas, and he's grasping the shoulders of a young woman with strawberry-blond hair. It's the girl who helps around the house—Essi. He pulls her close and wraps his arms around her, resting his cheek on the top of her head. Her arms go tightly round his waist.

Poor Nina. This is going to tear her apart. I take a step back before they can see me.

I still don't want to go to my room, so I head round to the front of the house, hoping I won't see anyone. I catch a glimpse of a police officer placing a few bags—evidence I presume—in the back of a van, and spot another two heading towards the path to the beach.

As I turn the corner of the house, I see that I'm not going to get the solitude I crave: Andrew is sitting on the edge of the formal pond. I'm about to turn away when he spots me.

"Are you okay?" he calls.

I make my way across to him and sit down. He looks slightly lost.

"I'm fine, but what about you? You're worried about Chandra, aren't you?" This has always been one of her spots.

"More than I would have believed possible. I've always been so independent, a bit of a loner, never wanting to settle down. But whatever my shameful reasons for agreeing to marry Chandra, she soothes me somehow."

I smile at him. "That's good to hear, Andrew."

We're quiet for a few moments, watching the fish glide slowly, lazily, through the water.

"What about you?" he asks. "How are you feeling about things between you and Matt?"

"I don't know right now. There's just been a lot to deal with, and—"

A strange and unlikely sound interrupts me. Through the open door of the house I hear the deep, sonorous beat of the gong that usually summons us to dinner. I give Andrew a puzzled look.

"We can ignore it, if you like," he says. "It's clearly Lucas assembling us all for some reason."

I think about what I heard in the Japanese garden. Surely he's not going to tell his friends before he speaks to Nina? Whatever it is, I don't want to be there.

And yet I do.

Something has to break through the cloud of dead air that is suffocating every one of us.

"Let's go," I say.

Andrew gets up from the low wall and follows me as we head towards the dining room. Isabel and Nick are already there, and Nina comes in from the kitchen just as Matt enters from the hall. He shoots me a nervous glance, as if he's worried that I'm going to share everything he's told me.

Finally, Lucas walks in accompanied by the two detectives.

"The police have asked me to gather you all here," he begins, looking at each of us in turn, and I feel a momentary relief that this isn't about Lucas and Essi.

DI Brodie steps forward. "I don't believe it's necessary for Mrs. Hudson or Mrs. Jarrett to stay, if you would prefer not to. Or in fact you, Mr. Jarrett."

We all stare at him, bemused, but no one moves.

"It concerns the night that Alexandra Lawrence was abducted shortly before Christmas nearly thirteen years ago. We know you were in New Zealand, Mr. Jarrett, so it's really a question for those of you who knew Alex and were in the country at the time."

Still no one moves.

DI Brodie nods towards Stephanie, and I see his eyes soften. I realize for the first time that they're a couple; either that or he would like them to be. Stephanie steps forward.

"It has recently come to light that on the night Alex was kidnapped she sent a text to Matt Hudson."

She pauses, and it seems as if the air in the room has thickened. I feel Andrew's body tense with surprise, but no one comments. I look at Matt, but he has his head bowed, unwilling to meet my eyes or those of his friends.

"Although we've been unable to check the content of the message, we've managed to get archived records of Mr. Hudson's phone. He did receive a text that night from an unknown number, but Mr. Hudson claims he never saw it and didn't delete it from his phone. If we believe him, that means someone else did."

Again, there is a sense of breaths being held.

Matt's head jerks up, and he looks fiercely at Lucas. "I promise you, the first I heard of it was when Alex told me last year. If I'd known she'd sent me a text, I'd have told the police immediately."

Lucas doesn't respond, but I watch his expression and he doesn't look surprised. He already knew.

Stephanie carries on: "I understand that Andrew Marshall, Nick Wallace, and Isabel Wallace were all in the pub that night with Matt Hudson. Did any of you see anyone touch or look at Matt's phone that night?"

Andrew is standing next to me, so I can't see his expression, but Nick looks worried.

Before he can say anything, Isabel speaks: "I wasn't there for the whole night. I left—the boys were all playing darts."

"Did you leave alone, Miss Wallace?"

"Probably. It's a long time ago; I can't remember."

"Well, I can," Andrew says, "and you didn't. A guy came in looking for you. I remember because Nick was a bit stressed about you leaving with him. He looked like trouble, but you came over to reassure Nick that he was fine beneath all that brooding hostility."

Matt stands straighter. Andrew has clearly reminded him of something.

"Who was the man, Miss Wallace?" Stephanie asks.

"God, I don't know! Some bloke I'd met who looked more interesting than any of these three." She laughs, the sound resembling stone scratched on glass.

"You *do* know," Matt says, his mouth tight. "I remember him. He looked Eastern European. High forehead, large eyes. Armenian or Turkish, at a guess."

Isabel sneers at Matt. "You've got a better memory than I have."

Matt gives her a look of pure hatred that no one misses. "For faces, yes. But in this case I can also remember his name! My dad was an avid Arsenal fan, and back then Arsène Wenger was their manager. That's why this guy's name stuck. You told Nick you knew him. 'It's only Arsène,' you said, although there was nothing French about your guy."

Isabel's attempt at nonchalance is starting to wear thin, and I can see the corner of her mouth twitch as she attempts an indifferent smile. It seems the detectives don't miss it either. Stephanie gives Gus a wide-eyed look, as if Matt's words mean something to her. Gus nods and turns back to the room.

"Miss Wallace, we'd like to talk to you in private, please," DI Brodie says.

There is a horrified silence. What are they saying? That Isabel's boyfriend, if that's what he was, read what was on Matt's phone?

I glance at my husband and see he's gone white. His head juts forward, towards Isabel. "It was you, wasn't it? You saw it, the text. You, more than anyone, would know exactly what the message meant, where Alex would be, and you hated her enough to think she deserved it."

"Come on, Matt," Nick says. "That's a bit of a leap. Just because some guy came into the pub to meet Isabel doesn't mean a thing." He turns to the police. "Aren't you making a bit much of this?"

"Mr. Wallace, leave this to us, please."

There's an expression on Stephanie King's face that tells me she knows something we don't, and it's exciting her.

I glance at Lucas. His eyes are black with emotion, but I can't read him.

The police are about to usher a pale-looking Isabel from the room when Matt starts again, as if he can't stop himself. "And to think I let you blackmail me! God, I'm so stupid!"

Isabel turns towards the door, but Lucas steps into her path. Before the police can intervene, he speaks. There's a quiet intensity to his voice. "Blackmail you about what, Matt?" Clearly this is one thing that Lucas didn't know.

Matt looks as if he wishes he hadn't started this, but then he sighs. "She read Alex's diary. She knew what had happened between Alex and me."

The police have stopped trying to hustle Isabel from the room. They're watching, listening, as the secrets are revealed.

"What bloody diary?" Lucas spits out the words. "Alex never kept a diary in her life. What in God's name is this all about?"

Matt lifts his head to stare at Isabel and for a minute is silent. Then it's as if something explodes inside him, and he lunges across the room towards her, hands outstretched as if going for her neck.

"You fucking bitch! You made it all up." Before he reaches her, the inspector grabs him. He's bigger and broader than Matt, but my husband's fury almost wins him the battle. "Alex told me she hadn't told a soul about us, not even Lucas. So how did you know, Isabel? How could you possibly have known?"

I hear Andrew mutter under his breath, "You stupid bugger, Matt. She was just a kid." But strangely Lucas is unmoved, and I realize that he might not have known about the blackmail, but he knew about Matt and Alex.

"*Enough!*" DI Brodie shouts. He releases his hold as the fight drains out of Matt. "DS King, please take Miss Wallace to the study. The rest of you, calm down. You're all still suspects in the false imprisonment of Jemma Hudson, so unless you want me to carry out my threat to arrest the lot of you, you need to cool it."

With that and a hard stare at each of us in turn, the detectives escort Isabel from the room. Without another word, Matt stalks towards the door to the terrace.

"Matt, I need to speak to you," Lucas says, his voice raw, his words clipped.

For once it appears Matt is about to ignore his friend, but another voice stops him dead.

"I should have done something when I saw the bullets." Nick's eyes are fixed as if he's looking inward, remembering. No one speaks, certain there's more. "She got bullets in the mail. It's a classic gangland threat, but she said they were a joke and begged me not to tell anyone. I knew she was scared. Then she came home one day bleeding, with her clothes torn. She said she'd fallen over. I knew what it was—knew she had to owe money for drugs, big money. But I didn't do anything." Nick's voice drops to a whisper. "I didn't fucking do anything."

Before anyone can speak, he charges out of the room, slamming the door behind him.

Time stands still for a moment, as if no one knows what to say or do. I'm struggling to make sense of it, but a quick look at Lucas tells me that he isn't. He grasps the back of a chair and slumps forward as if the air has been punched out of him.

Matt again turns towards the door.

"Stay a moment, Matt," Lucas says, and Nina mutters something about delaying a dinner that I'm sure no one will eat and scurries from the room.

Andrew pushes himself off the wall. "I'll leave you to it."

Lucas turns the chair he's holding and sits down heavily, indicating with his hand that we should do the same. Matt shoots me a glance that tells me he doesn't want me here, but I'm going nowhere.

"I knew about you and Alex," Lucas says quietly. "She didn't tell me until the night she died. She was adamant that it was her fault, you know, although I don't accept that. But she never blamed you. I guessed at the time because one day you were laughing, joking, teasing, and then suddenly you wouldn't even speak to her. I find that much harder to forgive, although Alex made all sorts of excuses for you—said she'd done something inexcusable, and she'd hurt you. But I knew what she meant. She believed she was the instigator and so bore the guilt. She was used to that, with our mother making her the scapegoat for everything in her miserable life."

Matt can't look at either Lucas or me.

"I need to ask you a question, Matt, and you need to tell me the truth. Did you ever tell a soul about what happened between the two of you?"

Matt's head jerks up. "No! I swear I wouldn't ever do that. I was stunned that Isabel knew."

"Me too. And I know Alex didn't tell her. Nor did she keep a diary. She did tell one person though, and one person only. This was never made public, but the first guy who raped her paid over the odds." Lucas takes a deep, shuddering breath. "He was promised a virgin, you see, and plucky kid that she was back then, she told him when he'd finished that he'd been cheated. He wasn't her first. He hit her and accused her of lying, but she yelled that she wasn't and mentioned you by name, Matt, thinking it made what she was saying more credible. She never told the police about you though."

I feel sick, and the words burst from me before I can stop them. "I know what you're suggesting, Lucas. Isabel could only have known about Matt from the men who took Alex, so she had to be involved. We all heard what Nick said, but however much trouble she was in, surely Isabel wouldn't have told someone where to find Alex? Why would she do such a dreadful thing?"

Lucas looks at me, and I see nothing but sadness in his eyes. "She hated Alex and blamed her for splitting us up, but Isabel was never in love with me. The main attraction was always my money because she never had enough of it for the lifestyle she wanted. She'll stop at nothing for cash—as Matt has found out—and if she was in trouble, she would have thought only of how best to get out of it unscathed."

I think he's wrong about Isabel's feelings for him, but it no longer matters.

Matt has a look of intense concentration on his face, and he starts to talk, as if to himself. "The night Alex died I was sitting on the terrace when Isabel came to find me. It was at least half an hour after Alex had left me there, but Isabel had wet hair. She said she'd just had a shower." He looks at Lucas. "Do you think…?"

Lucas throws his head back and groans. Matt reaches out and grasps his friend's shoulder, and I cover his hand where it lies on the table. Whatever has happened here, whatever Lucas has done, he is a man whose sister was brutally attacked and then years later killed, and it seems that every last bit of Alex's pain was caused by someone he knew. We give him a moment, and finally he lowers his head.

"I hope in time you'll understand why I put you all through this hell to get answers. I needed to know which of the people I'd brought into our lives was a killer. Alex told Chandra that she'd never suspected her abduction was connected to anyone she knew until the first night you were all here last year. Even then she had no idea who it was. Maybe they'll never prove that Isabel's a killer, but conspiracy to kidnap is a serious charge. They'll put her away for years."

Lucas looks at me as he says the words, and I recognize the message in his eyes as he gives me a regretful smile.

Finally, the last piece slots into place. Now I understand it all.

CHAPTER 76

The moment Matt said the name Arsène, Stephanie had felt a jolt of excitement. She'd seen that name—she remembered it on the list of calls made to the crime boss known as the Quiet Man on the night of Alex's abduction—so as Gus recited the police caution to Isabel, Stephanie quickly scrolled through the phone log.

There it was—a call between Arsan Manukyan and Mirac Bozkurt about fifty minutes before Alex was taken from Blair Jarrett's summerhouse. Isabel had told Arsan, and he'd passed the information on. They'd found the connection that had eluded them for all these years, and Stephanie felt a moment of elation, although whether they had enough to charge Isabel, let alone convict her, remained to be seen. Without the text message, it was going to be hard to prove. All they could hope was that they would find the evidence to convict Bozkurt and Arsan, and that one of them would admit that the information had come from Isabel.

As soon as Stephanie had closed the door behind the policeman tasked with escorting Isabel to the station for questioning, she flung herself into a leather wingback chair and stretched out her legs.

"I'm exhausted."

"Me too, and hungry! But well done, Hawkeye. How the hell you remembered that name from the list, I don't know."

"It's a gift," she said with a grin. "Good news is, Hampshire police know where to find Arsan. He's been on their radar for years. Do you think this means that Isabel killed Alex?" Stephanie asked.

Gus shrugged. "It's certainly a strong possibility. If she knew Alex had worked it out, Isabel had one hell of a motive if she was to avoid a long stint at Her Majesty's pleasure. But we still have no evidence that she *was* killed, although we obviously need to keep digging. How clever are we, solving a case we weren't even investigating?"

He pulled a rueful face, and Stephanie had to admit he was right. They had three inquiries on the go, all unsolved. They still didn't know if Alex was murdered, or what happened to Lidia, and crucially they were struggling to find evidence of who attacked Jemma.

At that moment, there was a knock on the door.

Stephanie stood up to open it. "Jemma! Are you okay? What can we do for you?"

There was a hint of determination in the woman's expression, and Stephanie stood back to let her into the room.

"I'm sorry to disturb you, but I saw Isabel leaving and thought this might be a good time to talk to you."

"Of course. Have you remembered something?"

Jemma shook her head. "Look, I've been thinking about what happened to me earlier. It really was terrible, and I'm so grateful to you for finding me..."

There was a "but" coming, and Stephanie knew it. She glanced at Gus's stony expression. He was watching Jemma carefully, as if he knew what she was thinking and didn't like it.

Jemma took a deep breath and her words came out in a rush. "I've looked up the possible sentence for false imprisonment, and I don't hate anyone enough to put them through that. So I'm here to tell you that I don't want to press charges against the person— people—who attacked me."

Gus leaned forward in his chair, his brow creased. "What they did to you was brutal, Jemma. There's no excuse, even if they *are* friends."

"I think I know why it happened though, and I don't think there was any real intention to hurt me."

"So tell me—why *did* they think it necessary to attack you, to drug you, to drag you upstairs with a bag over your head, to gag you, to tie you up, to leave you for several hours to wonder if they were going to kill you?" Gus asked.

Stephanie winced at his words, obviously designed to shock Jemma and remind her of what she had suffered.

It worked. Her eyes filled with tears, and Stephanie gave Gus a fierce look, which he ignored.

"It was the worst experience of my life, and I don't condone what they did, but in a way I don't blame them either."

Gus leaned back and folded his arms. "Well, I'm sorry to disappoint you, Jemma, but this is a serious crime. I think it's highly unlikely that a prosecution will be dropped if we succeed in identifying the perpetrator. If that happens, you will be required to testify."

Jemma nodded. "Fine. But you know where I stand now, so I'll leave it with you. And I really do appreciate what you did for me. Thank you both."

With that, Jemma gave them an apologetic smile and left the room.

Gus threw his pen on the desk. "Bloody women. I'll never understand them."

Stephanie decided not to take him to task on that comment. They had spent the best part of the day trying to discover what had happened to Jemma Hudson, and she understood his exasperation.

"Why would she decide that?" he ranted. "Do you think she's being coerced?"

"Maybe she believes it was Matt who imprisoned her, desperate to keep the police out of things because he wanted to hide the blackmail."

She stood up and walked over to where Gus was seated. With a quick glance outside to check no one was around, she bent and kissed the top of his head. "You have been a complete star today, DI Brodie. How about I take you home and show you some love and appreciation. I don't think there's much more we can do here this evening, do you?"

Gus raised his head and gave her a slow smile. "Sounds good to me."

At that moment she didn't care who saw them, and she lowered her lips to his. She wasn't going to let this man of hers go, and she vowed to stop panicking about the future, to make the most of the time they had together in the knowledge that somehow they would work it out together.

The shadows outside were lengthening, and it was time to leave Polskirrin under the control of uniformed officers, who would remain while the forensic team completed their job. Stephanie would be back tomorrow; she wasn't prepared to give up until she knew what had happened to Lidia.

She reached out and was about to unplug her laptop when it pinged with an incoming message from the inquiry team in Penzance. It seemed they had finally come up trumps with the most recent photos of Lidia Dalca. Stephanie clicked to open the pictures but groaned when she saw them. It was hard to get a clear impression of what Lidia really looked like as she posed and pouted in true selfie style.

The best one was of a smiling Lidia in a skimpy vest top. She was half turned away from the camera, looking back over her shoulder. Her happy grin brought a momentary smile to Stephanie's face, until she remembered that no one had seen or heard from this girl for a year. *Where was she now? What had happened to her?*

With a flicker of regret that they had failed to find her, Stephanie went to close the image when something caught her eye. She stared at her screen, enlarged the photo, and quickly opened another file on her computer.

"Oh crap! Gus, come and look at this."

CHAPTER 77

The detectives don't think much of my decision, and who can blame them? Without my testimony, I think they're going to find it difficult to pin my abduction on anyone, but of course I know who it was now. I know who both of them were.

And I know why.

It's hard to forgive the fear or the pain, and the inspector's words ring in my ears. I can't help thinking there must have been another way for them to silence me. They wanted to prevent me from phoning the police, not realizing they were already too late, and I know that by making that call I started a ball rolling downhill, gathering momentum, and the result is likely to be devastation for at least three people.

It's Nina I feel for most. I know she'll suffer and I don't want to make things any worse than I know they're going to be. She too has guessed some of it; I knew when she brought me a sandwich that she'd worked out who had imprisoned me. But I don't think she knows it all.

Matt is in the room, packing. If I go up there he'll find it difficult to look at me. He'll be waiting for me to open the discussion that we need to have. But I'm not ready yet, so I make my way out onto the back terrace.

I don't want to see anyone, so I head to the Japanese garden to hide in peace. I'm halfway down the steps before I see Lucas. My heart thuds. He's inside the pagoda, speaking to someone who is out of sight. My head is telling me to run, my limbs charged for flight. But my heart tells me that I have to face him—to tell him what I know. It makes me an even bigger threat than I was before, but my feet keep on moving, almost of their own volition.

How will he take it? Is his secret worth killing for?

It might be.

As I reach the bottom of the steps, he hears me and his head swivels round in alarm. He moves quickly out of the pagoda and walks towards me, keeping me away from whoever is in there.

But he doesn't need to hide her. I know who it is.

"Jemma, are you okay?" Lucas asks, his tone concerned.

"Just about, but it's no thanks to you, is it?"

His eyes search mine and then he closes them for a moment. When he opens them I see nothing but sadness. "I'm so dreadfully sorry, Jemma. I can't excuse what I did."

At least he's not denying it, and any lingering fear seeps from my body as I sit down heavily on the stone bench.

"No, you can't. I was absolutely bloody terrified, Lucas. I thought I was going to die." I hear my voice crack, and I'm cross with myself. I need to be strong, even though right now I don't know what I'm going to do with the knowledge I have.

He sits down next to me but doesn't touch me. He must know that I would flinch from the feel of his flesh on mine.

"I can't justify my actions and I won't try, but it was never supposed to be for so long. And I drugged you because I thought it would be easier on you. Midazolam reduces anxiety, and it's supposed to make you forget what happened."

"Well, it didn't bloody work. I was petrified, and I remember every moment."

Lucas drops his head. "I can't tell you how ashamed I am of what I've done, but I needed time to work out who killed Alex. I had to stop you calling the police—I thought they would confuse things.

I didn't know it was too late. I came back to check you were okay, and I nearly let you go then, but you were bound to report it, and then they'd have been all over us. As they were anyway, in the end."

I laugh at that. "You were scared they might just work it all out, weren't you?"

He looks at me then, trying to judge how much I know. But he's not sure, so the best he can do is try to make amends.

"I'll come with you to the police. I'll tell them—admit to what I did. I've been so angry and I know I've made some bad decisions. You were one of them, although possibly not the worst."

"And Chandra?" I ask.

He looks at me with what appears to be genuine surprise. "I didn't do anything to Chandra, I promise. No one did, I'm sure. Andrew's told me the stress upset her stomach, and she thinks her own remedies made things worse."

"And what about your partner in crime? Is she going to come forward and face the police too? She's just as guilty as you for what happened to me."

Now he looks scared, but not for himself.

"Don't blame her, Jemma. She just did as I asked." He still hasn't grasped it.

"I won't tell them who it was, Lucas, so you can tell her to come out from where she's hiding."

He leans towards me. I think he's going to plead with me. I know he wants to protect the status quo, and I can't decide yet whether to let him. But the decision is taken out of my hands when I hear a voice behind me.

"Mr. Jarrett!" It's Stephanie, her voice urgent and slightly out of breath. "I'm sorry, sir, but we need to talk to you. Can you come back to the study?"

"Will it wait, Sergeant? I'm just making sure Jemma's okay."

That's a bit of a stretch, but I don't comment.

"We do need to talk to you, sir, and it really can't wait."

I notice that DI Brodie is behind her, at the top of the steps.

"Can we talk down here?" Lucas says. "I don't mind what you say in front of Jemma."

I look at Stephanie, and she seems uncertain.

"It's quite a delicate matter, sir. I think it would be better if we spoke in private."

Lucas is getting irritated. He thinks the worst is over and everyone will go home. He gets to his feet and I stand next to him.

"Please, Sergeant, after today's revelations, just tell me—whatever it is."

Stephanie turns to look at her boss, who gives a slight shrug and walks down to join us.

"Actually, I think it's a good thing that Mrs. Hudson is here, as she was the only other person to see the body on the beach last year," DI Brodie says. "When you confirmed your identification, Mr. Jarrett, you said you'd looked at the deceased's face. Is that correct?"

I glance at Lucas, and his lips are white. "Yes. I lifted her head when she was still in the water, to check if she was breathing. But she wasn't. Her hair was wrapped around her face and her neck, but I knew it was Alex. She swam there every night. Her skin had been scratched a little by the rocks, and was puckered from the water, so when the tide lowered her onto the shore, I left her facedown. I didn't want anyone to see her like that."

"Mrs. Hudson?"

"No. I didn't get close. But I recognized her hair."

"Why do you want to know this now?" Lucas asks.

"Did your sister have a tattoo on her left shoulder?" Stephanie asks.

I know what's coming, and I can feel the tension in Lucas's body, close to mine.

"I don't know. She always wore long-sleeved tops, and she preferred to swim alone—I told you that. What sort of a tattoo?"

"A small butterfly."

"Why do you want to know this?"

DI Brodie was watching Lucas's face as he spoke. "Because we've just received photographs of Lidia Dalca. She had a butterfly tattoo on her left shoulder. And Sergeant King, who has a startlingly accurate memory, remembered the body from that morning. We've checked the photos, and the person found dead in Polskirrin Cove had a similar tattoo. I'm sorry, Mr. Jarrett, but we believe the body was not that of Alexandra Lawrence; it was Lidia Dalca who died that night. You saw what you were expecting to see, I'm afraid. Your sister."

Lucas collapses back onto the bench and drops his head. I can see he's shaking. He wasn't expecting this. No one speaks, and the police give him time to adjust to their revelation. Eventually he lifts his head, and when he speaks his voice cracks with emotion.

"I told you she wouldn't have committed suicide the night before my wedding."

Gus Brodie speaks gently: "I know this must be a hell of a shock, sir, but we need to talk to you. We'll be asking for blood samples from Lidia's mother so we can check against the stored DNA of the victim, but in the meantime, we need to ask ourselves where your sister is."

Lucas stares at them. "I think the video says it all. She didn't mean she was going to kill herself; she meant she was going to leave. She's out there somewhere, and if she wants to be found, she will be."

Brodie looks at him through narrowed eyes. I can see he's trying to decide what to believe.

"You thought someone had killed your sister. Do you now think they planned to kill Lidia?"

"Of course not," Lucas says. "Isabel obviously mistook Lidia for Alex. Oh—I don't know. Can you please just give me some space to think about this, to take it all in?"

Stephanie looks at her boss. "Of course. We'll be in the study when you're ready."

They turn and leave us.

The police have been gone for five minutes now, and neither Lucas nor I have said a word. I sit down next to him, not knowing whether to speak or not.

"You knew, didn't you?" he says finally.

"Yes." In spite of everything he has done, I feel sympathy for him. "It took me a while to put it all together. When you showed us the photo of Alex that you said you'd taken a month before she died, there was something that bugged me. Chandra noticed too and was planning to talk to me about it. Then I remembered. It was the bracelet—Chandra only gave that to Alex the day she was killed, and yet she was wearing it in the photo. The contact-lens cleaner in the bathroom of the apartment, which you said you'd left just as it was. Why would someone with twenty-twelve vision need contact lenses, unless it was to change the color of her eyes? The earrings that you bought her, one of which she lost in the wood. Who else would have been wearing them? I guess she likes to spend time in the apartment, pretending none of this has happened. Oh, and I think I heard your car leaving the night before her body was found." I pause for a moment and look towards the pagoda. "You can come out now, Alex."

The girl we have come to know as Essi walks slowly from her shelter, those gray eyes terrified, unsure of what I'm going to do. I don't know myself.

"Wasn't it a risk, being here?" I ask.

Alex's voice is quiet, husky with strain and no trace of an accent. "Lucas didn't want me to come, but I thought it was safe. I don't look anything like the old Alex, and I kept out of Nina's way.

On the odd occasion I had to speak to her, I gave her a beaming smile—something she'd rarely seen from me in the past. But I wanted to be here—to listen, to see what I could learn."

I can see why no one recognized her with her straightened nose, short strawberry-blond hair, red lipstick, gray eyes, and so much more flesh on her body, plus a smile on her face.

"We didn't think it mattered because the original plan was for me to appear at the end of the game—to take my place at the table and face the person who tried to kill me. If someone had recognized me earlier, we would simply have adjusted the plan. But we knew no one would. People don't look closely at the girl clearing their plates or making their bed."

I'm sure she's right and I turn back to Lucas. "At the inquest, you were scared. I thought you were distressed at listening to the details of Alex's death, but you were terrified, weren't you?"

He nods slowly. "I knew that identification by a close relative was standard practice and it was all the police needed, but I kept thinking they might show a photo. You barely knew her, but when Andrew arrived I was horrified. It was only when it was over and the verdict of suicide was given that I was able to start planning this—to try to find out who had wanted Alex dead. I became obsessed because their actions had forced me to make decisions that are indefensible."

I know what he means, but I still have to say the words. "I find it hard to forgive the pain you've caused Lidia's family."

"I know," Lucas says. "I'm deeply ashamed of that—it wasn't supposed to happen the way it did. It was a spur-of-the-moment decision and one I've regretted ever since. But I had sworn to keep Alex safe after everything she'd suffered, and I'd failed. I didn't plan any of it, and as soon as it was done I knew it was unforgivable, but I couldn't find a way back. I was so *angry* that I'd been put in this position, disgusted with myself for not finding a better solution." He looks up at Alex. "But I was never angry with Alex.

I understood how she felt." He gives her a gentle smile and turns to me. "You must do whatever you believe to be right, Jemma. I won't blame you, and neither will Alex."

My chest and limbs are heavy with sadness as I walk away from them, back up the steps. The sun is low in the sky now and will set soon, which is good because I just want this day to be over.

Matt is standing on our balcony, looking for me. Another decision I have to make. But for now all I want to do is get as far from here—from all of them—as I can.

EPILOGUE

I watch as Jemma walks away from us. I want to run after her, tell her it's not Lucas's fault. It's mine. I made him do it because I was terrified. I didn't want to die, but someone tried to kill me. I saw it with my own eyes.

I'd spent twelve years believing Matt had ignored my text—failed to come to my rescue when I needed him. And yet I never told anyone. I thought the police would question him about us, maybe even suspect him, so I said nothing. I didn't think it mattered.

Then, when everyone was talking at dinner, Isabel mentioned how Matt always used to leave his phone lying on the table for show and I realized in that moment that someone else might have read the text. But who?

Everyone believed I'd gone to bed the night before Lucas's wedding— everyone except Matt. But when I finally left him and went down the path in the dark, I reached the beach and saw there was someone else there. A girl. I didn't know who she was, but I didn't want to frighten her, so I stood in the shadows at the bottom of the path and watched as she stripped to her underwear, let her black hair down from its bun, and ran into the sea.

She seemed so happy, turning onto her back, laughing up at the stars—much as I did every night. Then she turned over and swam out into the bay.

I suddenly sensed movement on my left, coming from the boathouse. The lights were out, but I could just make out a figure in a black wetsuit, running up the rocks to the very far end. The girl had reached the mouth of the bay where it opens into the ocean, and the figure dived into the water almost without a sound, as I've seen Lucas and his friends do so many times.

There wasn't much of a struggle. She was a slight girl, and strong legs wrapped around her would have held her arms tight to her sides while her head was pushed under the water. Then I saw long, slow strokes coming towards the beach, and I turned and ran back to the house, to Lucas.

He was out on the terrace, looking for Nina. He ran towards me as I came out through the end of the path.

I was hysterical. "Lucas, someone just tried to kill me! God, Lucas, someone wants me dead! They think I am dead. I don't want to die, Lucas. I thought I did, but I don't." I was crying, wailing, and Lucas gave me a shake to calm me down and said we had to go back down to the beach to see what had happened. We met no one on the path—the killer must have gone up to the house through the wood.

I couldn't stop sobbing, and I knew Lucas didn't believe me. Nevertheless, we both dived into the sea and searched, swimming in circles, trying to find the body. We failed, and Lucas said I must have been wrong. I knew I wasn't. And anyway, her clothes were on the beach.

He wanted to call the police, said he would keep me safe. But no one knows how it feels to be taken captive, held against your will, thinking every minute that you are going to die. Until it happens to you.

I remember every second of what happened to me years ago as I lay naked, exposed, shivering, while the men came, one after another. I live with it daily, but Polskirrin had always been my safe place, and suddenly it wasn't. I couldn't stay another second.

Lucas begged me—I would ruin Nina's day. But I was terrified.

"The killer needs to believe I'm dead," I cried. "If I'm at the wedding, they'll try again!"

"But if you disappear there'll be a full-scale investigation. You're worth a lot of money, Alex—Dad saw to that—and no one will expect me to just let it go."

In the end, we decided we had to cover all our bases. We had to have an explanation for my disappearance should we need one—maybe for Nina's sake—so we made a video. Dear Nina. She's suffered so much because of me. Everyone else would be told that Lucas couldn't find me. I wasn't in the boathouse so I must have decided to go away for a while. They might think it a strange decision but would probably put it down to me just being Alex. The killer, of course, would believe Lucas was wrong—that I was dead, washed out to sea. We never thought the video would be seen as a suicide message. Isabel must have wondered about that—about whether she hadn't needed to do what she did if I had been planning to kill myself all along.

We thought the body would turn up farther down the coast long after everyone had left, and no one would think it had anything to do with Polskirrin. We had taken the girl's clothes in case the killer came back and realized it wasn't me they'd killed, so there was nothing to tie her to the cove, and we replaced her clothes with mine just in case. And I'd ripped off the bracelet that Chandra had given me, flinging it onto the pebbles in disgust. It clearly hadn't given me either strength or determination. I was in pieces.

At 3 a.m. Lucas whisked me away to the empty house of a friend until he could get me out of the country. For months I couldn't stop going over and over what had happened, trying to decide who it could be. Had Matt had time to get down to the beach? Yes, through the wood, and in many ways he had the best motive. Or so we thought. But what about Andrew? Nick? Never for a moment did I suspect Isabel.

Lucas went to the cove early the next morning so he could "discover" my message. Instead, he found the girl's body floating in the water, and he didn't know what to do. The killer would realize I was alive—that they had killed the wrong person—and I would be in danger all over again. Then Ivana started screaming my name, and Lucas couldn't think fast enough. In a moment of madness, he saw the bracelet where I had thrown it and slipped it onto the girl's wrist. He told the police

Ivana had found the body. It just seemed better that way, but then of course she had to be sent away.

Lucas was trying to protect me, although afterwards he was horrified by what he'd done. But he did it for me. He thinks he let me down all those years ago. He thinks my kidnap, all the rapes, are his fault and he should never have left me alone with my mother.

He's wrong of course.

Finally, he persuaded me to go to a clinic in Finland for treatment to make me strong, to make sure I'm never afraid again. I didn't think I ever would be, but I am now.

I look at my brother, who has broken every one of his own rules of decency and honesty for me, and I'm terrified. He and I are guilty of conspiracy to pervert the course of justice. We know that. And we could both go to prison.

I know Lucas will have three big concerns driving his next decision—the impact on me, on Nina, and on the foundation. He won't even think about himself. But he's struggled with this for long enough.

I watch as he gets to his feet and holds out his hand. I know what he wants to do—he can't bear to lie for another moment.

I take his hand and we walk together, brother and sister, towards the house, the study, and the police.

A LETTER FROM RACHEL

Dear Reader,

I would like to say a huge thanks to you for taking the time to read *The Invitation*. If you enjoyed it and would like to keep up to date with all my news, offers, competitions, and latest releases, just sign up at the following link. Your email address will never be shared and you can unsubscribe at any time.

www.rachel-abbott.com/contact

Like all my books, *The Invitation* started with a single idea: what would you do if someone had tried to kill you and believed they had succeeded—especially if you were already traumatized by events in your youth? How would a family member react if he believed the killer to be one of his friends? I loved dreaming up the creepiness of the identical clothes, the table setting, the same food, and the drama of everyone suspecting everyone else, and hope you enjoyed it too.

It's a pleasure to be able to keep in touch with readers, and one of the places where this can happen is in my special Facebook group—Rachel Abbott's Partners in Crime. It's a place where readers can chat about everything thriller related and discuss books they have enjoyed from a wide range of authors. I know that many of my readers already base their reading choices on recommendations from other group members, and I'm delighted that it's such a success. If you haven't joined in yet, you can find it at facebook.com/groups/PartnersInCrimeRA/.

I also send regular newsletters, so that I can share some of my own favorite reads and let you know when I'm going to be out and about. It's always great to meet people who have read my books and to have an opportunity to answer any questions. I also use the newsletter to let people know when any of my books are on special offer, so if you've not already signed up and would like to do so, here's where to go: www.rachel-abbott.com/contact.

And of course there is always social media—currently I'm on Facebook and Twitter. I still haven't quite got into Instagram, but I do keep trying!

Of course, I always love to hear from readers, and I would be delighted to hear if you enjoyed *The Invitation*, so feel free to tweet me or leave me a message on Facebook. And one very special plea—if you have enjoyed this book, I would be thrilled if you would leave a review on Amazon. Every author loves getting reviews, and I'm no exception. And of course, it helps other readers to find my books.

Thanks again for taking the time to read *The Invitation*.
Best wishes

Rachel

f RachelAbbott1Writer
🐦 RachelAbbott
🖥 www.rachel-abbott.com

ACKNOWLEDGMENTS

Research is one of the stages of writing a book that I enjoy the most, and none more so than with this novel. I remain overwhelmed by the time that people so generously give in helping me to get the facts right. Any mistakes are mine, and mine alone.

As always, I have to begin by thanking Mark Gray, my police advisor and a former Detective Chief Inspector, whose input was crucial and so enlightening. His detailed explanation of the process of identification of a body by their next of kin—in particular at the scene of a death—helped shape the story, and he tirelessly responded to my requests for the most minute details about the investigation process.

A special mention goes to the Penlee Lifeboat crew, who didn't blink when I approached them in Newlyn Harbour to ask where bodies might get washed up, given a particular point of entry into the sea. In the end, I didn't use this information, but it was kind of them to give me their time and expertise.

Thanks also to Amelia Coffen, one of my lovely readers, who won a competition to come up with the name *Polskirrin* for the cove and the house. I love it!

I would also like to extend my thanks to all at Bookouture, in particular Kathryn Taussig, Kim Nash, Noelle Holten, and Alexandra Holmes, together with the wider Bookouture team.

It's a pleasure to work with such a professional and committed group of people.

There are some individuals who are invaluable to my writing life and top of that list is my agent, Lizzy Kremer. She and her colleagues at David Higham Associates—in particular Maddalena Cavaciuti, Harriet Moore, and the foreign rights department—are a dream team.

Tish McPhilemy keeps me sane in the office and adds sparkle to everything she does, brightening those days when the administrative tasks can't be ignored any longer with her relentless good humor.

The life of an author can sometimes be a little insular, so special thanks must go to all the writers, bloggers, and readers with whom I chat—either at events or online—and who are so kind and generous with their feedback and support.

And finally, my love and thanks to John for his understanding and encouragement. I couldn't do it without you.